APPLE BLOSSOM TIME

An unforgettable novel of love and war

Everyone told Laura Ansty that her father had died a hero's death in France in 1918. However, Edwin Ansty's name did not appear on the Ansty Parva war memorial and the villagers were strangely reluctant to talk about him. Was there some terrible secret Laura was not allowed to know. Laura was twenty when the Second World War broke out and she was posted to Egypt in the ATS. She found love – or thought she had – but realized, almost too late, that her heart belonged much nearer home. And always, haunting her, was the mystery of her father, whom she had never seen...

APPLE BLOSSOM TIME

APPLE BLOSSOM TIME

by

Kathryn Haig

Magna Large Print Books
Long Preston, North Yorkshire,
BD23 4ND, England.

British Library Cataloguing in Publication Data.

Haig, Kathryn
Apple Blossom time.

A catalogue record of this book is
available from the British Library

ISBN   0-7505-1773-5

First published in Great Britain by Corgi 1997

Cover illustration © Jean Paul Tibbes by arrangement with
Transworld Publishers Ltd.
WW1 Soldier by The Imperial War Museum

Published in Large Print 2002 by arrangement with
Transworld Publishers

Magna Large Print is an imprint of Library Magna Books Ltd.

Printed and bound in Great Britain by
T.J. (International) Ltd., Cornwall, PL28 8RW

For Hugh and Rachel

It all began and ended in a garden.

I have dug the holes, good and deep, deep enough for a couple of spadesful of manure, wide enough to spread out the fan of roots without cramping. I have had a good teacher. Shrouded in sacking, the saplings are propped against a growing tree, waiting for me to make up my mind. No hurry. There's another hour of daylight yet. And I've waited for such a long time.

It's good planting weather – Tom would have looked out of the window and rubbed his hands together with anticipation – soft drizzle, no frost, no gales. Drifts of fallen leaves have banked in corners, deep and soggy, blown down before they could change colour. The earth is still sufficiently warm to encourage a little tree to establish itself before winter.

Little, bare, twiggy things. They look nothing now. You wouldn't guess that in a few months' time they will burst into a pink and white froth of blossom. Well, not quite, not yet. That's an exaggeration. There will be only a few blossoms, but each one will be perfect, rosy-tipped. Then there will be apples, one or two only, perhaps, to start with, but the next year there will be more and then more.

My feet are cold, though, and my hair is wet, misted finely at first, but now beginning to drip down my collar. Silly to sit here much longer. It'll be a long, cold journey home, even though the blackout has been lifted and there are lights again, headlights and streetlights and station name plates and road signs at last. It's been so long. Suddenly the night world looks naked, exposed under an unfamiliar glare, shameless. It's harder to see the stars.

Time to go home, then. Soon. Not quite yet. Please. I'm not quite ready yet to begin. There are ghosts. The air is buzzing with them and I have to sit and listen while they whisper to me.

I sit here in the rain and the silence and think back to that other garden and to that other Laura. Not so very long ago, a lifetime. I feel as though I'm watching her from a great distance. She is a stranger to me.

I can remember the smell of smoke, bitter and blue, and the pungent ripeness of the manure heap, turned and watered, Tom's pride. I can remember the creaking shift of the glasshouse as the wind leaned against its warped frame, dislodging sodden wads of rag that Tom had hoped might plug the cracked panes. I can feel the way the splintered bench seat snagged my khaki lisle stockings. Everything past its prime, rotten, broken, worn out past mending.

I can remember reading my mother's letter over and over, not understanding a word of it, a foreign language I had never learned, yet recognizing the unmistakable sound of truth. I watch a younger Laura spread the pages covered in bold, loopy writing across her knee and I can still feel the prickle of the serge skirt and the ferocity of her pain.

My darling Laura

*We've always been such good friends, you and I.
We've always been able to talk, haven't we, about
anything. Not many mothers and daughters can say
that...*

*This time, I can't talk to you. I don't have the
courage to face you...*

*We didn't mean to keep secrets from you. We just
thought, your grandparents and I, that you didn't
need to know... I wish I didn't have to tell you now.
Please, please, please... don't try to ask me about it. I
don't know any more. Maybe I don't want to...*

*Don't let this change your thoughts of your father.
He was quiet and kind and strong and he would have
adored you. Let that be enough.*

Forgive me.

And at last I understood. Those annual silences.
My grandmother's frozen stare during the two
minutes on Armistice Day. The fact that my
father's name was missing from the village war
memorial and from the brass plaque above the
lectern in St Michael and All Angels, although all
the dead boys of Ansty Parva were remembered
there. I used to think they were Michael's angels,
khaki angels for a soldier saint. There were
Ruggles and Blackdown, Colebeck and Kimber,
a brace of Shellards, three Attwoods – all the
families of the village, people I knew. I knew their
mothers and fathers, their brothers and sisters.
But Ansty was not there.

I hadn't understood then and, as I grew older,
it still didn't make sense. Nothing was straight-

15

forward. Nothing was the way I wanted it to be.

My grandmother was Lady Ansty of Ansty House, who lived all alone among endless corridors and shrouded rooms and ugly portraits of men in uniform and framed sets of medals and crossed swords that hung on the walls, their outlines drawn in dust, while Mother and Tom and Kate and I all crammed into the old gardener's cottage with the piano from Ansty House. She was doubly an Ansty, for she had been some sort of cousin, convolutedly removed, of her husband.

Sometimes, she'd take me for a walk along the portrait-lined corridors. I'd dawdle along behind her, lumpish and resentful, grudging every moment not spent kicking fat old Barney over makeshift jumps in the home paddock.

She'd point out the great-uncle who'd died at Sebastopol and the great-great-uncle who'd been mutilated in an unmentionable manner by Pathans during the retreat to Jellalabad (if they were really such distinguished soldiers, why hadn't they managed to die of old age?). My great-grandfather was there, portrayed wearing the star and medals that were kept in a little glass-topped table in the library: Knight Commander of the Most Eminent Order of the Indian Empire; the Punjab Medal, with bars inscribed Mooltan and Goojerat; the Indian Mutiny Medal with its bars, Defence of Lucknow and Central India. Framed above a display of his collar and star of the Knight Grand Cross of the Most Honourable Order of the Bath was my grandfather, looking far more ferocious than the mild-mannered old man I vaguely remembered, a generation older than Grandmother, shuffling around on gouty feet, not recognizing me when we passed on the stairs.

My father was not there.

My father was nowhere, not watching me from the walls, not enshrined in dusty display cases, not even tucked into the maroon leather photograph album that was so heavy I could only comfortably look at it when sitting on the floor. I didn't know what my father had looked like.

'Like you,' Mother said, vaguely, and quickly: 'or rather, you are like him, because he was there first.'

I'd look in the glass, wondering, but only myself looked back. Did he have that thin, straight nose? That stubborn chin? Did he look cross all the time, so that people called him cross-patch, when really he was just thinking?

Mother must have been fibbing. Her answer had been ridiculous. How could a little girl look like a grown man?

What was he like? I still didn't know.

Who was he?

Grandmother Ansty would click along the polished floors, pointing out the portraits of people who didn't matter any longer, in her little, high-heeled shoes, not looking in the least like anyone else's grandmother, not at all cosy and cottage-loafy. Other people's grandmothers had bosoms, solid, stately, encased shelves, all of one piece, that never moved, no matter what. My grandmother had – I realized with surprise when I grew old enough to notice – breasts. There was no getting away from it. Two of them, small and quite separate, they moved of their own accord.

She was my father's mother, but not Kate's grandmother. I'd queried that once.

'You are an Ansty. Kate is not an Ansty. She is no relation to me,' Grandmother had explained, quickly and briefly, as though she found the subject embarrassing. Children are very quick to recognize an adult's embarrassment. She answered the way she had done, long before, when I had asked her why her pug, Buller, was trying to cuddle the leg of the table.

'But why isn't she?' I'd persisted.

'Tom is her father and your mother's second husband. It's quite simple.'

'And why isn't my own father on the stone cross with all the other dead soldiers?'

'A mistake,' Grandmother had said, in her usual, brisk fashion. She turned her back on me to fiddle with a flower arrangement, so I couldn't see her snapping, bright eyes, only her tiny, trim figure in its fashionable short frock and the corrugated waves of marcelled grey hair. 'Your father was a hero and died for his country. Never forget that. I'll see that it's put right.'

Then she had changed the subject. No-one – certainly not I – had the nerve to persist once Grandmother decided that enough had been said. But the name of Edwin Ansty had never been added to the base of the granite cross in the churchyard.

And now I knew that it never would be.

1931

When I was twelve, a fortune teller told me I would find myself behind bars one day.

'Laura! You're going to go to prison!' gasped Kate.

None of her business. I hadn't wanted her to follow me, anyway, tagging along, grumbling and whining. She had no right to be listening to my fate. It was private, like going to the doctor and discussing your waterworks. If she wanted to find out the future, it should be her own future, not mine. I didn't mind Pansy coming in. No-one ever minded Pansy. But Kate was Kate and she was there too.

'Don't be silly,' I snapped, trying not to show that I was shaken. Behind bars? ... murder? ... blackmail? ... fornication? That was really bad, it was in the Bible. 'Don't tell me you believe in all that fortune-telling nonsense.'

'Well, if you don't, why did you waste sixpence on it, eh?'

'Because – well...'

'...because the fête's supposed to be raising money for little black babies,' Pansy lectured, in her vicar's-daughter voice, that she only used when she really meant it. Her thin, fair-skinned face was flushed and earnest, all red and white, no normal coloured bits at all. 'And if no-one spent any money, there wouldn't be any to send

19

to Africa, so there wouldn't he any point in having a fête in the first place, so we might as well all pack up and go home. Besides, Daddy's been working frightfully hard persuading everyone to come – Mummy always used to do that, when ... when she was able.' Pansy stopped, looked down, looked up and began again. 'So it's our duty to spend as much as we can.'

'And that includes you, meanie. You're such a miser, Kate. I know you've still got at least ninepence left, even after pigging out at the sweet stall.'

'Didn't, didn't, so there ... anyway, I'm saving it for something special... Laura – what do you think you're going to do – murder someone?'

'Probably you ... but they wouldn't send me to prison for that. I'd get a medal from the King! Anyway, that wasn't a real gypsy. Everyone knows it's only Mrs Pagett being mysterious.'

'She looked really gypsyish to me. You never know...'

I thought of the dim tent lit by a red lamp with chewed-looking fringes, of the velvet curtain sprinkled with faded stars, of the veiled woman with the husky voice, the sweet-and-sickly scent that seeped from her robes when she held out her hand to take mine. I didn't know anyone who smelt like that, like a vase of chrysanthemums when the water hasn't been changed.

'Of course it was Mrs Pagett. Didn't you see her shoes – no-one else has bunions like that!'

But I shivered as I spoke. You never know...

'"Thou shalt not suffer a witch to live." It says so in the Bible. And my father definitely wouldn't allow any witches at the church fête. So it was Mrs Pagett. So there.'

'Did you know that all the soldiers who died in the Great War had crosses on the centre of their palms?'

'How d'you know?' I scoffed.

'Abbie told me.'

'And how does Abbie know – did she look at them all?'

'She read it. It was in that black book of hers – you know the one with the red hand on the cover, the fortune-telling one, so it must be true.'

'Just run along and play, won't you,' I said, in a pretty good imitation of a superior big sister, 'like a good little girl.'

Kate whisked her fat little hand from mine and spiralled off, her plaits spinning out like a chair-o-plane, chanting 'Laura's going to prison ... Laura's going to prison...'

'Shut up!' I hissed, as though anyone could possibly hear her above the racketing of the steam organ.

But she was gone, irritating as a gnat, stinging and flying. The faded pink and blue flowers of her frock blurred and blended with all the other flowery cotton frocks. As acutely as though I could hear them chinking, I knew that there were three silver threepenny bits in the pocket of Kate's matching pink-and-blue-flowered knickers. And I knew how she was going to spend them. The knowledge gave me a fierce little pain round about the place where Abbie said her indigestion always bothered her something cruel.

I didn't have to see her. I knew. Kate would

21

giggle and wheedle and flirt with big blue eyes and Mr Doughty on White Elephants would mark down the leather camera case (Nearly New) from a shilling to the sticky ninepence that Kate would fish out of her knicker pocket – without even turning her back on him to do it.

It would be Kate who would give the case to Martin, Kate who would say, 'I'm sorry there isn't a camera in it, but I didn't have enough money for that, of course. Still, one day you'll have a camera of your own and you'll be famous and take pictures of film stars and it'll fit into this case.'

And Martin would go red and look pleased and say 'Gosh, thanks, Kate' instead of 'Gosh, thanks, Laura.'

It was all my fault, of course. I hadn't seen the case until I'd already spent threepence on a scented hanky for Mummy and another sixpence on a little mat embroidered in lazy daisy stitch to sit under the china hairpin box on Grandmother Ansty's dressing table (only her hair was short, so she didn't use hairpins, so perhaps I'd wasted my money – I wonder what she kept in the box). Then there were some aniseed balls for Pansy and pink coconut ice for me and a geranium cutting for Tom and some scent for Abbie to put on when she went to the pictures with her Frank, who ran the shop and who was courting Abbie with delicacies – 'a little bit of something nice for you,' he'd say. I was feeling really pleased with myself by the time I got to White Elephants.

When I saw the camera case, I only had sixpence left. There it was – just right – smooth, tan leather with all its straps and only one or two little scratches that would polish out with some Cherry Blossom and a bit of spit – the way Tom always cleaned his shoes and they were amazingly bright, even if his jersey was often frayed at the cuff, because Mummy couldn't thread a needle to save her life. Just right for Martin.

But Mr Doughty wouldn't sell it for sixpence. 'I really couldn't go down that far, Laura, not so early in the day, not such a nice case as this.' I could tell that he wanted to let me have it, but with Miss Casemore's gimlet eyes on him, he wouldn't dare.

'But there's no camera in it. What use is a camera case with no camera?' I had whined. Kate wouldn't whine. She already knew that grown-ups didn't give in to children who whined.

'No end of use, dear. You could keep ... well, anything in it, really ... bibs and bobs, you know, buttons or keys and so on. Lovely leather. It must be worth a shilling of anybody's money.'

'But I haven't got a shilling.'

Mr Doughty sighed. 'Come back at the end of the afternoon, Laura, and if it hasn't gone by then, maybe ... I can't promise, mind, but we'll see.'

But it wouldn't be there by then, I knew that. It was too nice. So I blued the last of my money on Mrs Pagett's palmistry and all I got for that was the threat of growing up into a convict.

I wandered around the stalls with Pansy, penniless, my hands filled with the treasures I'd bought for all the people I loved. No, not all the people. I had nothing for Martin – Martin who was going away and might never come back and wouldn't even remember me if I couldn't give him something precious that he could use every day.

'Shall we have a turn on the Hoop-la?' suggested Pansy eagerly.

I shook my head.

'Teas, then? They'll be selling the scones off cheap by now.'

Irritatingly neat still, after a long, hot afternoon, Pansy's fresh face and starched frock contrasted so obviously with my own grubby mouth and limp cotton, that just being with her made me feel more out of sorts than ever. And that made me feel guilty, because Pansy was so nice. She never minded what people said to her and that made me more irritable, and so on and so on...

'No – you go if you want to. I say, Pansy, I don't suppose you could...' No good. I wouldn't be able to pay her back until the new term's pocket money. She'd certainly lend me ninepence – she was my best friend, after all – but she'd probably hand it over with one of Mr Millport's many boring proverbs. 'Neither a borrower nor a lender be,' she'd say, though very likely she wouldn't mean it. She couldn't help it, any more than she could help always having a clean hankie tucked in her sleeve. It was just the way she was brought up. 'You go if you like,' I said, sulkily. 'I think I'll go home now. I've got a lot to carry.'

The field was growing quieter now. The WI cake stall had sold out long ago, before Pansy's father had even properly opened the fête – you

24

had to be quick or ruthless or have a friend on the stall who'd put something nice under the counter for you. The bran tub was just about empty with a mess of bran on the grass where frantic little hands had scooped it. The steam organ still whirred and rattled its jaunty, old-fashioned tunes, the cymbals still clashed and the gilded figure on the front still waved his baton, but Mr Gilbert was carefully folding away the concertinas of punched cards that magically became music. This would be the last tune.

The tea ladies were trying to wash up with the last of the hot water from the urn. Damp tea towels – every tea towel in the village, you'd think – were hanging like soggy flags, pegged to the guy ropes of the tea tent. Fay and Mary Cranham were untacking their horrid, hairy little ponies that were supposed to give rides, but spent most of the afternoon with their hooves dug firmly into the grass, no matter how much Fay whooped or Mary whacked.

Trestle tables threw long, wobbly shadows across the grass. There was only a sprinkle of visitors still left. The stall holders packing up all looked happily dishevelled, hats askew, cheeks reddened by the sun, pocketed aprons bulging with money still to be counted into satisfying piles. They called jolly remarks across to each other – hadn't it all been marvellous, hadn't the weather been kind, hadn't people been generous, didn't feet or backs, or both ache but hadn't it all been worth it?

Mr Millport went slowly round all the stalls saying his thank-yous. He lifted his hat at each one, showing the pale, bony scalp and fringe of white hair that made people who didn't know better think he was Pansy's grandfather.

The air was golden and dusty, thick as honey. On Garden Produce, Mother was packing overgrown marrows into cardboard boxes. So many marrows. Everyone had given one – how generous – so, of course, not one had been sold. They'd all be on Tom's compost heap by the morning, along with the box of maggoty little windfalls from Miss Casemore's unpruned tree – small, but delicious, very choice variety, she'd assured Mother. Mother's hair was sliding out of the heavy knot she wore on the nape of her neck. Her thin, bare arms were red on the upper surfaces, white as milk below.

Tom was balanced on one end of the trestle, his long, thin body bent like a half-shut penknife, his legs swinging. Helping Mother, he'd call it – that meant watching her, laughing with her, just being with her. I looked at him carefully, trying not to look as though I was looking. He seemed to be all right. It was important that Tom was all right. It had been a hot day and there had been a beer tent as well as teas. After a night of what were (diplomatically) called Tom's Dreams, the beer tent would have been a strong attraction.

His Panama was pulled well down over his eyes, but suddenly he saw me and gave me a wave that said all sorts of things. Oh, there you are. Nice to see you. Had a good afternoon? Come and give us a hand. But I pretended I hadn't noticed him after all.

The White Elephant stall was empty except for

a basket with no handle (donor unknown), a china cruet set shaped like pecking chickens with holes in their beaks for the salt and pepper (one of young Mrs Gibson's wedding presents) and a set of cork table mats with pokerwork views of the Isle of Wight (from Miss Ridley whose sister lived in Shanklin so everyone knew who'd given the mats).

The pink coconut ice stirred uneasily in my stomach and expanded into a sweet, glutinous mass – stickier and far more, surely, than I had eaten in the first place. I had nothing for Martin and tomorrow he would be gone.

Tomorrow he would be gone.

In the tack room, the air was still and cold, dry enough to make me cough, somehow thin, compared with the sunlit richness in the yard. Empty pegs, like ghosts, hung round the walls, each one named – Hercules and Ajax, Talleyrand and Columbus, Sirius and Orion – as though the pegs themselves had identities. All gone. Of all the horses who had answered to those names, only one was left, old and fat and beloved.

No-one ever came here except me. I dipped the chamois leather into the bucket, then squeezed it almost dry and turned the saddle over to wipe the sweat off the quilted linen lining. The saddle was older than me, older than Mummy, perhaps as old as Grandmother. Once it had been as bright brown as a chestnut in its husk, but now it was dark old-conker brown, supple with years of Kho-Co-Line, worn thin as a glove in places, but good for a few more years yet. It smelt of all the

27

horses on whose backs it had sat, but most of all, of Barney.

It wouldn't be for ever. Of course, I'd see Martin again. Of course, he'd come back to see his family and then Mother would invite him to tea or something, but it wouldn't be the same.

He'd always been there, you see. Not a play-mate – our ages were too far apart – but just there, far above me, taller, faster, stronger, remotely kind. He'd been a listening ear when I was troubled, a friend when I thought I had none, yet young enough to tease about the down that sprouted on his upper lip. We rode together, sometimes swam together, shared silly jokes, dreamed dreams.

He was going to be a photographer, one day.

'Will you take all the pictures in *Tatler*,' I'd asked, 'or photograph famous people coming off the liners at Southampton?'

'Not that sort of photographer,' he'd replied with scorn, 'not pretty pictures. I want to show people what the world is really like. I want to show them streets and factories and parents working and children playing. I want to show them laughing and crying, waking and sleeping. I want people to touch and feel and smell when they look at my pictures.'

'I'm not sure people want to do that.'

Martin shrugged. 'Probably not.'

And I was going to be – well, what? *Not* just get married and have children. *Not* just sit around waiting for some man to come and get me. Then what?

'I'm going to breed cats...'

28

'They seem to manage that very well without any help from you!'

'Shut up! You know what I mean. And I'm going to puppy-walk hounds, lots and lots of them. And I'm going to ride to hounds three times a week and be terribly dashing.'

'That's not being something,' Martin had objected, 'that's just doing something. What're you going to *be*, Laura? Something or nothing?'

'Anything I like – I just can't think of anything at the moment.'

But that had been a long time ago, when dreams were still there for the dreaming, before I discovered that one day I'd find myself behind bars.

Now Martin would he a man, a working man, and wear a stiff collar and a shiny, blue suit and maybe grow a moustache like his father and laugh with that horrible, squashed-plum laugh. I knew that photographers used dreadful chemicals and that his hands would be stained. Maybe he'd get spots where his collar rubbed his neck, or grow his nails too long to be decent for a man, as Tom would say. It was too awful to bear.

Could that happen to Martin? I hated the thoughts and I hated myself for thinking them. Horrid little prig. I knew I was a snob – Pansy would never have thought stuck-up thoughts like that, even her most secret feelings were good – but I couldn't help it. Martin was nearly grown up and everything would be changed and change was ... change was scary.

You didn't know where you were when things changed.

29

Look at Tom. Most of the time he was perfectly ordinary and perfectly nice and even just a bit funny. The right sort of grown-up. Then sometimes – not often, but more often than once in a blue moon – he'd be a different person. Sweaty and shiny and smelling of decayed fruit, laughing too loudly or crying. Anything could make him cry. A sunset. Seeing my mother washing up. A song. Most often a song. He had a brittle, dead leaves sort of voice. I'd lie in bed and listen to him sing.

'I want to go home, I want to go home,
I don't want to go to the trenches no more,
Where the whizzbangs and shrapnel they whistle
    and roar.
Take me over the sea, where the Alleyman can't
    get at me.
Oh, my! I don't want to die, I want to go home.'

Look at me. Well, I'd rather people didn't look at me, really. I didn't know what I was. One minute, it seemed, a child no older than Kate. The next – certainly not grown-up, Grandmother made it perfectly clear that I wasn't old enough to stay up for dinner with her, whatever Mother might allow, but far too old to come home with grazed knees and torn pockets like Kate.

Then what? A hybrid. A changeling. Lumps and bumps and curves where I should have been flat. Too old to do this and too young to do that. Change made me feel unsafe, as though the world had started spinning in the opposite direction. If I didn't hold on tight to everyone I loved, we might just go flying off into the outer darkness.

He would be different when he came back, if ever he came back. He wouldn't be the Martin whose nose would always tilt to one side because he had defended me against bullying I had barely understood.

I had stood at bay in the playground one day in November. We were all wearing poppies. A monitor had brought a tray of them around the school and we'd each given a penny, even the Pocknells, when everyone knew they hadn't a penny to bless themselves with. Everything was drab – the sky and the asphalt and the grim, sensible, no-point-in-doing-more-washing-than-you-have-to colour of school clothes. The only brightness was the little dot of scarlet on each child's chest.

They crowded me against the railings. I could feel each iron rod pressed into my back and the gap between each. It was my first term at school and I didn't know the rules. Perhaps this is what you had to do – incomprehensible, but so was everything else, every day.

I wasn't crying. I didn't know enough to cry. I could sense the threat, but couldn't understand it. I didn't know why this heavy-breathing, jostling crowd should have chosen me.

'You didn't ought t' be wearin' thick.' Josie Pocknell pointed at the poppy wired around a button on my cardigan.

'You go' no righ'.'

'They'm not for the likes a' you.'

A hand came out to grab it, but I jerked back. I

31

didn't know what the poppy was for, but snatching it was as personal as pulling my pigtails. It was pretty and it was *mine*. Tom had given me a penny to buy it.

'Gi' 's it yere, you.'

'No, it's mine.' I clasped both hands over the flower. 'You've all got one, anyway.'

'Don't an' we'll bash you and git it off'n you anyhow.'

They shoved and poked, not quite daring – not quite yet – to knock down a five-year-old. Everything seemed huge to me, their hands, their boots, their voices. Great open mouths. Great bushes of hair topped by nodding bows. I clung irrationally to my poppy and looked for a gap to escape through, like a rabbit for a hole.

'Lookin' for somewhere to run – like your ol' man?'

My old man? What old man? I didn't know any old men except Dr Gatehouse and he didn't belong to me.

'I haven't got an old man,' I said.

And they all laughed. I didn't know I'd said something funny. I joined in. It must be a joke, then, and they weren't really going to hurt me.

But then the poking got rougher, from fingers that seemed to be all bone with no childish softness. It began to hurt.

'Le's see 'er run, then. See 'ow fast 'er do run.'

The hand that grabbed my poppy this time got it and the button the poppy was wired to and the wool that the button thread was stitched through. All that was left was a frayed hole in my cardigan.

And then I started to howl – more with anger than fear, I like to think now, but maybe that's just wishful thinking. Maybe I was scared. And at the awful sound, my tormentors began, to look uncomfortable. One or two drifted away, then others. All except one great lad, Dennis Rudge, a gurt bwoy they'd have called him, who grabbed me and shook me. I howled louder, great, gulping, tearless sobs that frightened me with their power, so that I began to cry the first real tears. Maybe he was trying to hurt me. Maybe he was just trying to shut me up. I don't know. It's all so long ago.

But I remember what happened next. Dennis was grabbed from behind by another boy and, they fell in a thrashing, kicking, biting heap. The ring of children forgot me and circled the fighters, cheering on their favourite, so that I couldn't see what was happening. I could hear grunts and thuds. That was all.

No-one noticed me sneak away to hide in the outside lavatory, safe until the bell rang for lessons. I shut the door and perched on the seat with my legs drawn up, so that no-one should see my little black boots through the gap below the door. I kept my handkerchief over my mouth to block out the stink from the open drain that flowed through.

And when it was over, when Mr Casemore had separated the fighters and told them to stand outside his study until he was ready to deal with them, my poppy and everything it had seemed to represent to the children had been forgotten, replaced by a more exciting event.

Dennis Rudge was thrashed for fighting. Martin Buckland was sent home to have his broken nose set by his mother in a casing of stiff flour and water paste. And when he came back to school, his face disfigured by two black eyes above a great wedge of homemade plaster, he had been thrashed too.

By then, Armistice Day had gone and everyone had forgotten what the fight was about in the first place. But I hadn't forgotten. And now Martin was leaving.

I turned my face aside, in case the first tears should fall on the leather and ruin my good work. And then he was there – Martin, thin and brown, crooked-nosed and smiling – as though I'd conjured him up, leaning across the half-door, watching me. He might have been there for ages. And I knew that, shiny blue suit and stiff collar or not, to me he'd always be Martin.

'You'll have that polished away to a greasy spot if you go on like that,' he observed. 'I thought I'd find you here.'

'Yes,' I answered stupidly.

'I wanted to thank you for the present.'

'The present?'

'It was such a kind idea. I know I haven't got a camera for it yet, but one day I will. So – thank you.'

He dangled the leather case by its strap and the evening sun glossed over the scratches and made it look even smarter than I had remembered.

'That's all right. What did Kate tell you?'

'She said you'd clubbed together to buy it. She

said you'd beaten Mr Doughty down from a fantastic price.'

'Yes, we ... we...' I wanted to join in the fiction, to make Martin believe how much Kate and I cared for him, that we'd spent an afternoon together bargaining away our last pennies, but somehow the words wouldn't come out right. And again the taste of the coconut ice came back to reproach me. If I hadn't spent my money on that... And Kate had wrongfooted me, as somehow she always managed to do. All those accusations, no less bitter for being silent, that jealousy, when all the time she'd been planning to share with me the pleasure of giving. Didn't she understand? I didn't *want* to share it. It was to have been my idea, my present to Martin. I'd rather he didn't have it at all than share with Kate. I didn't *want* her to be kind.

I rubbed away at an imaginary dull spot on the leather. My voice was gruff and churlish. 'That's nearly right. Only it was Kate's money, not mine. I'd spent all mine.'

'Well, anyway – I like it very much. It's the best present I've had for ages. I'll take it with me everywhere.'

And I wasn't experienced enough to wonder how much was true and how much was a kind-hearted boy trying to cheer up someone much – well, three and a bit years – younger.

'Shall you be very famous?' I asked.

The evening sun was so bright behind him that I couldn't see if he laughed. His head and shoulders were like a dark portrait in a frame, an end-of-the-pier silhouette cutout. But his voice told me that he was smiling, so I could imagine his face for myself.

'Don't wait up for it! I don't suppose anyone'll trust me to do more than scrub the darkroom floor for years. One day they might let me out to cover something really exciting, like a fête or a produce show. Look out for pictures of the winning giant marrow – you just might see my name in tiny print underneath!'

'All those marrows! D'you know – every single one of them was still left at the end of the day. Tom's compost heap will be submerged in marrows!'

'It'll look like a torpedo dump.'

I started to laugh at last. 'And people will be so offended.'

'They'll peer over the wall secretly, to try to identify their own.'

'They'll creep in tonight and make off with them in the darkness and in the morning they'll be able to swank and say that their own isn't there.'

'Mr Ruggles climbing out'll meet Mr Treadwell climbing in...'

'...and he'll stuff his marrow up his jumper and talk about the weather...'

Sillier and sillier, our voices rose higher and higher, children again, with tomorrow's parting forgotten for a while.

'...and the whole village'll have stuffed marrow for supper tomorrow night.'

'And next year the produce stall will be swamped by marrow and ginger jam.'

I giggled so much that my nose started to run,

until I knew that I was crying, but nothing would make me admit that to Martin. I was weak with laughing. Oh Martin, don't go, don't grow up and leave me here still a child.

At last we couldn't laugh any more. I could hear Kate's voice calling me in to supper and, by the exasperation in her tone, I guessed she'd been calling for a while. Martin heard her too.

'Well...'

'Yes...'

'I'm not going far, you know.'

'No...'

'We'll keep in touch.'

'Yes.'

'Goodbye, Laura.'

If I'd been older, would he have kissed me? Perhaps. Would he have leaned over the door and pecked me on the cheek? The lips, maybe? No, on second thoughts, he probably wouldn't. He was much too sensible to do anything soppy like that. And we were both too well brought up. People like us didn't do that.

But I wondered suddenly what it might be like. I was chilly and tired and miserable and the thought of Martin's kiss started a little, hot glow where I'd never had one before. It was like the kitchen fire in the early morning, greyed over with ash until Abbie got down on her knees and blew a tiny spark into life.

I tried to say, 'Goodbye, Martin,' but the sound wouldn't come out right. It was just a squeak.

He held out his hand over the door and I put mine in his for a farewell, grown-up handshake. When we had done that, our hands stayed together for a few more moments.

In the tiny cottage living room, filled to discomfort by the piano from Ansty House, Mother was playing, comforting, meandering, evening music that I didn't recognize. Her hair was turned to untidy, sunlit cobwebs, silver and gold. Her thin, bare arms were striped with dying light. The notes seemed to drop from her fingers like crystal beads. Tom leaned against the piano and tried to catch the remains of the day for his crossword. Their heads were quite close together. The rest of the room was dark, always dark, never brightened by the small square of window. If she had needed music, Mother wouldn't have been able to see it anyway.

I leaned against the door frame, suddenly tired, and wondered what it would be like to have someone belong to you as completely as Tom belonged to Mother.

Mother didn't lift her head, but said, 'Kate's out looking for you, darling. Didn't you see her?'

'No.' True – I hadn't seen her, just heard her.

'Oh, well – it's cold supper.'

'But I warn you,' said Tom, looking up and grinning, 'get yourself an invitation somewhere else tomorrow – it's stuffed marrow.'

Hearts don't break, particularly young, healthy ones; they just feel like it. He waited for me to laugh and looked surprised when I didn't.

'I'm not very hungry. Do you mind if I go up to bed?'

'Too much sun and excitement, I expect. Well, if you must, you must.'

'Honestly, Tom! You sound just like some old, Scottish nanny!' Mother always scolded him like that – loving and laughing and warm. 'Off you go, Laura love. Have an early night.'

I kissed them both goodnight and the vague, tinkling music followed me upstairs to the room I shared with Kate. I dabbed feebly with a flannel and cold water, cleaned my teeth, got into my pyjamas and climbed into the bed that was tucked under the sloping eaves. Kate must have arrived home probably hot and annoyed because she'd failed to find me.

I hadn't wished him good luck. I'd let him go without once saying 'Good luck, Martin'. I wished it – of course – but did he know that? Did he know what his going really meant to me? How could he, if I didn't tell him?

The music had stopped and I could hear Abbie with the supper dishes, slopping along the passage in her too-big shoes, singing.

'Teach me how to kiss, dear, teach me how to
  squeeze
Teach me how to sit upon your sympathetic
  knees.'

There was the scraping of chairs and the clink of cutlery. Once Tom laughed his telling-a-joke laugh and Mother protested feebly, 'Darling...'

It all sounded so far away, much farther than just downstairs. Far, far away and not in the least important. I drew my knees up to my chest and hugged them. Too much coconut ice and Martin was leaving and I had discovered that I was going to grow up to be a convict.

Martin never came back. Five weeks later, his father had a heart attack and his mother moved to Winchester to be near her son's work. The chances were that I might never see Martin again.

1941

The gypsy, or Mrs Pagett, or whoever she was, had been right. I was behind bars, but not in the way she had meant – or I had thought she had meant, at any rate.

Through barred windows, I looked out on to the side windows of another hut, with its own bars. If I twisted my neck very hard, I could squint along the side of our hut and see a dusty, camel-coloured parade square, almost the same colour as our starched tropical drill, beyond that, a fence of tall, dried rushes that rustled in the breeze off the river. Everything was the same. Even the sky seemed to be the colour of Nile dust, the sun dull and metallic.

'Well, if this is the Mysterious East, you know what you can do with it,' muttered Grace, tightening her belt around an already minute waist. Grace was the only one amongst us who'd dared to have her uniform tailored to fit. The rest of us wore khaki sacks, stiff drill skirts and Aertex shirts, that fitted where they touched. She

40

smoothed down the skirt with the palms of her hands. 'I've got sand in my teeth, sand up my nose, sand up my ... knickers.'

'You didn't say that yesterday.'

'Yesterday was yesterday and it still had novelty value. Today I feel as though I've been stripped and rubbed down ready for a gloss finish.'

Crammed with our kitbags into the back of an open Bedford lorry, we'd been assaulted by Egypt, by its heat, its noise, its smells. Our truck had inched away from Maadi station, threading between laden donkeys and flocks of fat-tailed sheep, taking its turn behind battered Thorney-croft buses decorated with blue beads against the evil eye, creaking carts, staff cars carrying red-tabbed officers, signal-bearing Don Rs on motor bikes.

Delicacies that we'd forgotten even existed spilled on to the streets outside shops no bigger than wardrobes: oranges and dates piled high in crates; vegetables bigger than we'd ever seen before; cans of paraffin; sacks of sugar; bales of silk; bundles of charcoal; baskets of eggs – enough eggs to whip up a mountain of meringues.

'And not a powdered egg in sight,' sighed Vee in ecstasy.

Pansy took a deep breath. 'Smell that? That's coffee, that is, real coffee!'

'Smell that?' Grace giggled. 'That's donkey manure, real donkey manure!'

'I'm not so sure it's only donkey, actually,' I remarked, watching a little boy lift up his jellaba

41

and squat down at a corner.

Coffee, dung, Turkish tobacco, paraffin, spices, foul water, all mingled into a sort of nasal cacophony, rivalled only by the noise. Donkeys brayed. Hucksters shouted. Engines backfired. Sheep bleated. Shoe-shine boys drummed up custom. Only the black-robed women with firewood or water on their heads were silent, swaying along with the flop-flop walk of a camel through sand.

Little boys ran alongside the truck, banging the side with sticks or the flats of their pale-palmed hands. One, more daring, clung on to the tail-board and peered over the side at the uniformed English women, holding out one hand to us. 'Father dead, mother dead,' he chanted in a sing-song voice. It was hard to resist the appeal in his long-lashed brown eyes, but we'd all been warned about beggars, so we turned our faces away. Just as well Pansy wasn't sitting at the back of the truck, or she'd have emptied her purse for him! He hopped off, yelling something. I was glad none of us could understand, although his gestures were quite plain enough.

Then we were out of the little town and being driven along a wide avenue lined by flame-flowered casuarina trees, where large houses – Home Counties under a blazing sun, equatorial Esher – sat back amongst parched lawns swept by gardeners with stiff brooms. There were swimming pools and shady verandas that made us gasp for long, cool drinks and garden chairs.

None of those for us at Maadi Camp. The ATS quarters were guarded by grinning, armed soldiers, fresh from India. They didn't say anything as our truck rolled through the gates, but their expressions told us that this was a real cushy billet for a regular soldier!

A genteel, distracted second subaltern with a millboard met us and introduced herself as Miss Carstairs. Her gingery-fair skin was red and blistered and I wondered how she could still burn, considering how long we'd been on voyage round the Cape. We stood in the sun while she briefed us quickly on life in Cairo, which seemed to be a succession of things we weren't allowed to do: no sunbathing – sunburn would be treated as a self-inflicted wound and punished accordingly (one law for us and another law for them); no travelling through the City of the Dead except on duty and in military transport (as if we would!); no going out in the evening, even off duty, except in uniform; no going to the men's quarters, even in the day, in any circumstances – or vice versa (from what I'd seen so far, that wouldn't be a hardship!); no crossing boundaries marked by a round white sign with a black X, which meant Out of Bounds to All Ranks; and no – absolutely no – going to the Berka.

'It's not a desirable area,' she explained and, if anything, turned even redder. We ought to have taken pity on her. She couldn't have been much more than nineteen, but we were young too and the young are pitiless. We stared as blankly as though we had no idea what she was talking about (and I'm not sure that Pansy was pretending). 'It seems to be a traditional haunt of ... of members of the oldest profession, if you take my meaning. Yes, well...' She looked down at the notes on her millboard. 'Well, anyway ... Corporal Gibson will show you to the stores, where you can collect your bedding. Tea is at 1800 hours. Now – are there any questions?'

Beside me, Vee took a deep breath and I knew what she was going to ask. 'Don't you dare!' I hissed and gave her a nudge with my foot.

'No? Jolly good. Well, off you go, then,' said Miss Carstairs, sounding more like a nursery school teacher than a soldier. 'Duty begins tomorrow morning and there will be a tour of the Museum of Hygiene at 1400.'

Dismissed, we tossed down our packs in one of the huts and took stock of our new home.

'Well, what on earth did we come all this way for? We might as well be in Aldershot!' Vee said in amazement. 'Same old row of iron beds, same old pile of mattress biscuits...'

'Same old blankets, grey, woollen. Same old cupboards, green, metal, c/w shelves...'

'Same old view of the Pyramids? Look out here, girls,' called Grace. 'Perhaps it's a little bit different from Aldershot, after all.'

In one direction we could see the minarets of Cairo citadel, needle sharp, and there, to the west and across the Nile, were the tops of the tallest Pyramids. We trooped out onto the veranda. Beyond the water towers, beyond the NAAFI hut, the ablution blocks and the latrines, two triangles stood black against a huge sun that dropped out of sight, sudden as a theatrical lighting effect, while we watched. None of us spoke for a while.

'Well...' said Vee at last. 'That certainly knocks Piccadilly Circus into a cocked hat.'

The last thing that I saw before lights out was Pansy in her blue-and-white striped regulation pyjamas, buttoned carefully up to the neck, kneeling by her bed to say her prayers. Ansty Parva or Maadi, she would never miss them. It was oddly comforting.

For a while that first night I'd lain awake, listening to the noises around me. I'd grown used to the small sounds of sleeping women, particularly these women. For eleven weeks the four of us had been crammed into a cabin designed for two. The captain's diversionary tactics had taken us from Liverpool, north-west towards Greenland – were we really going to Egypt or was it just another SNAFU – Situation Normal All Fucked Up? We heaved around on the Atlantic and pretty soon none of us cared where we were going, so long as we actually arrived. If two hundred women, shoehorned into cabins, felt ill, God knows how the two thousand soldiers felt, swinging in their hammocks in the airless, fume-filled hold. By the time the ship swung southwards, we were all several pounds lighter.

By now I could distinguish Pansy's little, whiffling breaths, polite even in her sleep, across the room. Thank goodness for Pansy. She kept me sane when military bureaucracy might have driven me mad. We'd been so lucky to be able to stick together. Vee's dry cough, which had been so irritating at the beginning of the long voyage around Africa, no longer bothered me. Grace was usually quiet, except now and again, when she'd mumble to herself. That didn't bother me any longer, either. The other four beds in the hut would soon be filled by the next draft.

A vicar's daughter, a débutante, a shop girl and me. What an odd collection. Saintly Pansy, motherless daughter of a saintly father. Grace, with her wicked grin and her extra long stride that always clipped the heels of the girl in front when our squad was drilling. Fluffy-haired Vee, whose cap wouldn't sit straight and whose magnificent bosoms were never meant to be covered by pleated, button-down pockets. And me – skinny, stubborn and far too bolshie to make a good soldier.

We'd been through basic training together, scrubbed ablutions together, polished lino, heaved coal, plastered each other's blisters, battered each other's caps into more becoming shapes. We'd stood in line, shivering and half-naked, on FFI, Freedom From Infection parade, to put up with the indignity of a medical officer pulling out our knickers to the furthest limit of the elastic (none of us had a clue to what he was looking for). We'd all had stiff arms at the same time from inoculations against every disease known to man, given by an orderly with a blunt needle and a sense of humour that would have done him credit in the Gestapo. We'd been homesick together, seasick together, put up with the attentions of hundreds of men together, all the way round the Cape, eaten, marched, slept, slapped mosquitoes, laughed and cried together. No wonder we were friends.

I shifted around on the joins of the three-piece

biscuit mattress, strange tonight, but soon these lumps would be as familiar as my own bed in Ansty Parva. My tummy was full of mince with a funny little square of pastry that tasted like a mortarboard, carrots, mashed potato, stewed plums and custard – the ideal diet for a soldier in the Nile valley.

It was our first night in a bed that didn't rock for – oh, ages. How odd it felt, not to be moving, like a mild case of seasickness. No danger of torpedoes here, no need for warship escorts. No air raids either. Cairo wasn't like a war zone at all. Well, not yet, anyway. Nor could I see that it ever would be, even though the Italians had bombed Maadi before we had arrived. They never got as close as that again. Rommel and his Panzers may have been on their way, with almost legendary verve and dash, but there was still an awful lot of sand between them and Cairo.

I wondered sleepily how Mother and Tom were managing, whether they were safe, whether Grandmother would ever be reconciled to her evacuees from Bermondsey, whether Kate was settling down in the WRNS. She'd been so envious of my posting. I don't know what she'd imagined – a sort of 1940s *Arabian Nights*, I suppose – a cross between *The Thief of Baghdad* and *The Garden of Allah!*

'I'd give anything for a posting like that,' she'd said. 'Almost anywhere sounds exciting compared to Somewhere On The Clyde.'

From what I'd seen so far, we were going to be as closely guarded as a harem. No romantic stranger would be likely to get a chance to gallop off with me to the Casbah – more's the pity!

Now that I'd stopped travelling, there'd be a chance at last for letters to catch up. The last letter I'd had from Mother had been weeks ago and the news in it already stale by the time I'd received it.

And, in the end, I wondered how many more names would be added to the list on the granite cross in the churchyard of St Michael and All Angels. Would mine be there – or Pansy's or Kate's? I wondered if there'd ever even be an end.

And then I had fallen into an uneasy sleep in which I had walked down row after row of village memorials – granite crosses bleak on the sweet green grass of England. I was counting the names, but the numbers wouldn't add up, no matter how hard I tried. I knew I was looking for one, particular name, but I couldn't remember what it was. I couldn't remember, but it seemed to matter so much. Someone. Somewhere. Someone was missing. A sense of urgency pushed me on. There was so little time. The grass around the crosses was powdered with scarlet petals. I reached Z and then went back to A again – it had to be somewhere, I would recognize it when I saw it – until woken by Pansy's stealthy movements, as she rose and dressed to begin early shift at the cookhouse. Very softly, she was humming *Onward Christian Soldiers!*

Combined Services Detailed Interrogation Centre (CSDIC) was supposed to be a secret, one of those military secrets that everyone has something to say about. Everyone knew there was something behind the high fence and the armed guards, but nobody knew for certain what (although you could make a jolly good guess just from the name) and very few people went freely in and out of the gate.

There was a PoW – mostly, though not all, Italian – camp at Helwan, guarded by New Zealanders, rows of tents behind barbed wire and guard towers. Any prisoner who looked interesting would be brought to CSDIC before being shut up in Helwan. In my impeccable shorthand I took notes of the interviews. When I'd slaved over unruly grammalogues in Bournemouth, I couldn't possibly have imagined the use to which my country would demand I put them.

Brown, dusty and humiliated, the prisoners trooped in and out, to have questions that seemed to me random and extraordinary tossed at them by a long-haired Field Security Corps major, a fluent linguist who had been an Oxford don before the war. He wore his uniform like a woolly cardigan and was supposed not to have a single matching button anywhere on his clothes. Whether or not the questions made more sense after interpretation, I don't know, but the answers when they came – if they came and often they did not – sounded very disjointed. I think he was too clever for them and, like many clever people, he didn't have the common sense to realize this.

Major Prosser had been very exercised over whether the Italians ought to be allowed to say prayers for Mussolini during mass. He was so worried that he'd referred the question to a higher authority. Back came the answer, 'Yes – he needs it!'

The questioning was not physical – we left that to the Nazis. It was more in their line. The Geneva Convention prevented interrogation of prisoners, so we simply asked them questions. They didn't have to answer. Some did. Some didn't. Sometimes it only lasted a minute or so. Sometimes, if Major Prosser was convinced there was something to be discovered, he'd bash on.

He never seemed to need to stop to eat or go to the lavatory. The trouble was that he imagined that his staff also had elastic bladders. I cut myself down to one cup of tea at breakfast, just in case. I'd arrive with a fistful of pencils sharpened at each end and scribble on until my hand seized up. Once I didn't last out and had to make up interesting answers when I came to transcribing my notes the following day. No-one noticed.

It was very hard to look at these men as they shuffled around in trousers without braces and boots without laces and not feel pity. These were the men of Rommel's terrible Afrika Korps, who'd rolled our advancing army right back to the borders of Egypt, cancelling out all the gains we'd made against the Italians. These were Mussolini's mobsters, the men who'd gassed whole Ethiopian villages. Weren't they? At least, that's what we'd been taught.

But though Greece and Crete had fallen, Tobruk still held out and Rommel hadn't got around to reserving his room at Shepheard's – not yet, anyway.

Sometimes I'd glance up from my squiggles and find I was looking at a man dumb with misery. A few were still cocky, quite a few more obviously relieved at being out of the war, but most were stunned by what had happened and was happening to them. Seeing your enemy when he's trying to hold up his trousers makes hating him very difficult.

I tried very hard not to stare. I didn't want to be forced to see them as real people. I didn't have the courage. I was there to take notes. That was what I was good at and that was what I'd do. What made it harder was that I wasn't supposed to talk about my work, even to the rest of the girls back in the hut. They knew I was a shorthand writer and that was all. They didn't even envy me my clean hands. Vee thought it was frightfully dull compared with being a driver.

'At least we get to see the world. All you see is a stuffy office with bars on the window, poor old girl.'

But it was the girls of the Mechanized Transport Corps (MTC) – pistol-packing Mary Newall's private army, débutantes to a woman in Savile Row tailored uniforms – who got all the plum driving jobs, according to Grace.

'It's those rather natty blue chiffon scarves they wear round their necks,' she complained. 'Frightfully flattering compared to a khaki collar and tie. And silk stockings – why can't we wear silk stockings? So they get the ambulances and the staff cars. We get the ration trucks!'

'Important things, rations,' said Pansy, solemnly. 'More important than generals in staff

51

cars. An army marches on its stomach.'

'Who said that?' teased Vee. 'Your dad again? He's a card, your dad!'

Pansy came in, took off her shoes, fell backwards on her bed, still in her cook's whites, and groaned, 'What a so-and-so of a day!' (the worst language she ever allowed herself).

'What's up, love?' Vee asked, looking up from polishing her buttons. She slotted the brass button stick around the next one and began again. 'Been made to whitewash the potatoes this time?'

'I don't think I can stand this country much longer.'

We all looked up then. The tremor in Pansy's voice was real and so unlike her that it caught our attention. Cheerful, willing Pansy, always ready to take on someone's work or to make someone's life easier. Complaining is part of army life – where would we have been without a good moan? – but if she sounded like that, we knew she must be pretty miserable.

'They say it's the hottest summer here for fifty years. It's a beast of a country,' Grace agreed in a cheerful tone. Stripped to her khaki undies – hilariously military – she was squinting into a scrap of mirror, trying to put her long, blond hair in pin curls. 'Has it taken all of one week for you to discover that?'

'I can't stand the flies ... I can't stand them. Really. The kitchen is full of them. The flypapers are black with them. There are flies licking the sugar, flies drowning in the milk if you leave it out for just a moment – and the milk is watered down, anyway, before we get it. All the milk is boiled. All the water is boiled. It's so hot in the kitchen, they might as well boil me – I wouldn't notice! The cockroaches are as big as mice...' UGH

'I hope you don't dangle your feet out of bed like that at night,' warned Vee solemnly. 'The cockroaches'll eat the hard skin off your toes – quick as you like.'

Pansy screamed and pulled her feet on to the bed as though she'd been bitten.

'Saves you having to bend down to cut your toenails, though,' laughed Grace. 'Pansy – love – we're only teasing. We didn't mean it.'

We all sat down on her bed. The springs creaked.

'Come on, Pansy, cheer up.'

'It's not that bad.'

'Worse things happen at sea.'

Pansy gave a sniff that turned into a weak giggle. 'My father says that.'

'Sensible man, the Rev,' declared Grace. 'The trouble with us is that we don't get about enough. How long have we been here – a week? All we've had is a trip to the Museum of Hygiene and that's given me nightmares every night – I never knew men's bits and pieces could look like that! We haven't so much as toured a Pyramid yet. Honestly, you'd think we were in a nunnery. It's time we made up for lost time. So get your glad rags on, girls...'

She opened her cupboard and whisked out the kind of evening dress I'd always longed for and would never have been allowed at home – slinky, bias cut, slithery – of the four of us, only Grace could possibly have worn it (or afforded it).

'I don't believe it,' gasped Vee. 'Are you telling us you brought that all the way from England in your kitbag?'

'Why not? I hear one of the MTC girls has arrived with a wedding dress, veil and all. Now all she needs is a man!' Grace held the dress against herself and twirled round. 'I haven't been dancing in ages. We deserve some fun.'

Pansy had sat up and was beginning to look interested. 'But we're only allowed out in uniform,' she protested weakly.

'Good heavens! What difference does that make?' exclaimed Grace, foxtrotting down the length of the hut, oyster-coloured satin swirling around khaki cotton stockings. 'We owe it to the boys to look our best. Don't you know there's a war on?'

Giggling, suspiciously bulky, with uniform tunics and skirts dragged over our frocks and caps perched on freshly washed hair, we went off to catch a tram into Cairo. Two stopped for us, but we waved them on. The inside of each was packed and passengers hung on to every possible outside projection, as it lurched and clanged along. The conductor swung along the outside to collect his fares. Then we were lucky enough to hitch a lift into town with a cheerful New Zealander who was only too pleased to give us a leg up into the back of the Bedford.

The road to Cairo led through the mausoleums and tombs of the City of the Dead. Here whole communities, caretakers and their children and their children's children, lived in tombs like miniature houses, the spare rooms of the dead, without water, without sanitation. Families took up residence for forty days to ease their loved one into the spirit world with food and drink and worldly goods. ●Naked children played in the dust. Disturbed by the draught of our passing, flies rose in a hideous swarm, a black, crawling blanket, from the carcass of a dog. Vee was looking over the other side of the truck. She didn't see the bloated horror underneath.

Pansy saw and didn't look away. Her shoulders heaved. "'And the houses of the Egyptians shall be full of swarms of flies and also the ground whereon they are,'" she whispered.

'What's that?' shouted our driver.

We'd picked up a bit of speed when Vee, sitting up in front, screamed and grabbed the driver's arm. 'Stop! Stop! There's a child...'

The emergency stop threw us into a huddle of arms and legs. Suddenly, there were children everywhere, swarming up over the sides of the vehicle, grabbing everything they could lay their hands on. Spare wheel, tool kit, two jerry cans of fuel and one of water, tow rope – all gone in less than the time it took to sort ourselves out. The body in the road disappeared, too.

'Shit,' the Kiwi shouted, banging his hands on the steering wheel. 'I should've known. They'll cut off my balls and use them for conkers! Begging your pardon, ladies. Next time I'll run over the little bugger, no questions asked.'

The truck was going to Kasr-el-Nil Barracks,

55

source, they said, of all the bedbugs in Egypt, and to avoid questions we were dropped off around the corner, on the far side of the Semiramis Hotel, which was HQ British Troops in Egypt, the peacetime garrison.

'First things first,' said Grace, who seemed to have put herself in charge of our outing. 'Let's drop off these frightful togs. We can whip into the Victory Club and leave them there. And then ... well, let's see, shall we?'

Having dropped off our uniforms, Grace hailed a gharry and told the driver to take us to Groppi's Garden. The driver flourished his whip and the skeletal horse took off in the extraordinary two-legs-on-the-same-side trot that covers the ground so fast.

'You seem to know where you're going, all right,' remarked Vee.

'Oh, I have a cousin here, with HQ BTE. He's been here for years. In fact, he said he'd meet us at Groppi's tonight.'

'He what?' I started to laugh. 'Oh, you're a cool customer, Grace. No wonder our spontaneous outing is so well organized. You had it all planned.'

'Of course. You can't leave these things to chance, you know. I may be a new woman, but the thought of four girls wandering on their own in Cairo looking for company is a bit too dicey, even for me. We'd find plenty of company all right, but whether we'd want it is another matter. Now George has promised to dig out another three chums and we can have some fun.'

'Oh, I'm not sure...' Pansy hesitated. 'We don't

really know them...'

'Oh, Pansy, just enjoy yourself. It'll help you forget about the flies!'

By the time we reached Groppi's Garden in Sharia Adly Pasha, the sudden Egyptian sunset was over and the garden was lit by tiny, twinkling lights. Greedily I sucked in the colours of flowers and of dresses, so exotic after our monochrome life in camp. The air was heavy with the scent of stephanotis and jasmine, overlaid, even more enticingly, by coffee and chocolate. It was hard to believe we were even in the same world as dust-coloured Maadi Camp.

We walked into the garden in a shy triangle, with Grace striding at its apex. Little tables and chairs were set out on a sandy floor, far enough apart to ensure that whispered intimacies were not overheard. From one table, a tall man in uniform came forward.

'Georgie, darling.' Grace turned her cheeks one after the other to receive his kisses.

'Beautiful as ever, Grace,' her cousin replied. 'Changing tyres seems to suit you. Now – allow me to introduce...'

Andrew. Bob. James. It was difficult to tell them apart at first. All young. All tanned. All dressed in freshly starched uniform, with self-consciously new single pips on each shoulder, distinguished only by their cap badges – two hussars and a gunner. All with the slightly gawky, endearing mannerisms of the well-brought-up young Englishman. Nineteen? Twenty? Boys only and – thank God – far away from any real fighting, so far. Only Grace's cousin George was different: older, more confident.

The two cousins seemed to have an enormous number of relatives to catch up on. They kept up a lively chatter that disguised the fact that the rest of us were sitting in shy silence. I sipped from a glass of chilled lemonade made from real lemons – when did we last see a lemon at home? – and looked round the garden.

Expensive-looking women in silks and veiled hats, with fur capes draped across the backs of chairs, broke apart cream cakes with miniature, pearl-handled forks, but never seemed to eat any. So how had they grown so plump? Stout men with slicked-back hair and too much jewellery sipped mint tea from tiny glasses and watched the women over the rims. The air was full of whispers and intrigue.

Vee saw me looking. 'See that one over there,' she whispered, nodding her head towards a far corner, where a ravishing Levantine woman was nibbling the ear of a British colonel, 'the one with that dinky blue cocktail hat with the feather? She's really a man! She's a German spy sent by Goebbels to undermine British morals! Her bosoms are really a secret wireless transmitter. Only the colonel's a German spy, too, and they don't know each other!'

I spluttered into my lemonade and had to make an embarrassed apology.

Only Grace, in her oyster satin, looked as though she might possibly belong in this artificial place, that is, if you didn't look too closely at her carefully painted nails and see that they were broken short and that she hadn't been able to cream the oil stains from her hands, no matter how she tried. As for Vee, Pansy and me, we stood out in our cotton afternoon frocks and sensible, low-heeled sandals. We looked as though we'd got lost on the way to a tea party at the vicarage.

'Well, now, where are you boys taking us?' asked Grace coyly.

'Where d'you fancy? Fleurent's? The Deck Club? The Continental? It's only just round the corner and you get a better dinner there than on the boats.'

'There's a bit of a problem – well, two, really,' I said, the first time I'd spoken since acknowledging the introductions. 'Grace looks wonderful, but we're not properly dressed for evening...'

'Good enough to eat,' declared Andrew or Bob or James. 'And...?'

'...and the Continental's out of bounds to ORs.'

George coughed slightly. 'So's just about everywhere else a chap can take a lady. Anyway, I'll bet a fair sprinkling of the officers you see around, aren't officers at all.'

'Told you so,' hissed Vee.

'Whyever not?' I queried.

'Because the lads arrive on leave, with all the back pay they can't spend in the desert burning a hole in their pockets, determined to have a good time. Their first visit is the barber and a bath. The second is a good tailor, who can run up an officer's uniform overnight. Then – look out, Cairo! Sun, sand, sin and syphilis!' yuk

'Oh, dear,' whispered Pansy.

'Sorry, my dear, but that's the way it is. D'you

59

know, I actually found myself chatting with my own signaller on the terrace at Shepheard's the other evening. Decent sort of chap. Very bright.'

'Are you telling me that I've been wasting cracking good salutes on other ORs?' Vee burst out indignantly.

'Not all of them, no – some, probably. Anyway a good salute is never wasted, my dear. Keeps you in practice! So, there's no problem,' George went on. 'I take it you're not actually going to advertise your rank?'

'Well, we're not going to put our uniforms back on, if that's what you mean, Georgie,' teased Grace. 'The Continental it is, then. Let's go. I'm starving.'

We breezed into the Continental's roof garden restaurant. The tables were packed with men in uniform and glamorous women – you'd hardly believe there was a war on, the lights blazed up into the sky, blanking out the stars – so we were quite lucky to be shown to a table by the dance floor, with only Pansy hanging back. 'Come on, Pansy,' Vee encouraged her. 'You haven't got your army number tattooed on your forehead!'

We'd forgotten what real food tasted like: fresh meat and butter and cream and cheese and vegetables not boiled away to a mush. I made an awful pig of myself and, with relief, I saw the others were too. George ordered champagne to begin with, then a claret like purple velvet.

'Let's have some more champagne – nothing like champagne with a sorbet to finish,' George suggested.

'Perfect. I once made a vow never to drink

anything but champagne.' Grace's careful pin curls were relaxing and her hair curled round her face in a wicked sort of way. 'But the vicar said I'd have to have wine at communion, like it or lump it!'

'I say,' giggled Vee, 'are you trying to get us tiddly?'

'Never!'

'Just as well, because I could drink you chaps under the table any day!'

But Pansy couldn't. Her thin face was flushed and she was smiling to herself as she watched the rather bad floor show of belly dancers and acrobats. When it was over and the blonde American hostess called Betty had left the stage, a band struck up a quickstep and the dance floor was quickly filled.

I was beginning to be able to tell the young men apart now. This one was Andrew – at least I was fairly certain he was. He held me very close, closer than I'd ever danced with a man before. It was comforting and exciting at the same time, to be held in strong arms under a tropical sky.

We made a fancy turn and I found myself staring straight at Miss Carstairs, who was dancing with a tiny man in a kilt. She looked at me as one looks at someone whose face is familiar but won't quite fit into place. I gave her a dazzling smile – a smile of equals. She'd never, never know me once I was back in khaki again. For some reason, that gave me such a silly sense of freedom. For the first time, I returned Andrew's rather vacuous smile. We were young and the moon was full – or if it wasn't it ought to be – and the band was playing a sentimental tune.

'"Here we are, out of cigarettes,"' Andrew half-sang, half-whispered.

'Pom, pom, pom, pom, pom-pom,
"Look how late it gets.
Two sleepy people, by dawn's early light,
And too much in love to say 'Good Night'."'

I relaxed and rested my head on his chest. His top button pressed into my cheek. His warm breath stirred my hair. It felt so nice.

'It's awfully noisy up here, isn't it?' he murmured in my ear. 'Shall we take a breather outside?'

I didn't say anything, but I may have nodded. Andrew took my hand and led me from the dance floor. We avoided the lift and began to walk downstairs.

The corridors were very quiet, and dimly lit.

'This way,' said Andrew, leading me by the hand.

'Are you sure?'

'Of course.'

At the end of a corridor, he opened a door with one hand, keeping the other firmly round my wrist. I pulled back.

'Where are we going?'

'It's all right,' he said, but that wasn't really an answer.

It was dark, quite dark. With the door closed behind us, I could only hear and feel him. He pushed me back until I could go no further. I could smell starch and feel the line of a shelf pressing into my back. My hand touched a pile of towels. A linen cupboard, then, just one more door at the end of a silent corridor of doors.

Stupid. Stupid. How could I have let myself get into this situation? Above the wholesome scent of freshly ironed sheets, I could smell his sweat. He was breathing in short, shallow gasps.

He began to nuzzle round my neck. His breath smelt of all the things we had eaten and they weren't delicious any longer, they were disgusting. I slid away from him, along the shelf, until I was in a corner. But that was even worse. He wedged me firmly in with his weight. I'd never known what a man felt like before. He was nudging, nudging at the tops of my thighs, a pressure that demanded what I wouldn't give and I couldn't squirm away any longer.

'Be nice,' he whispered, 'be nice to me.'

My heart started to hammer. This was all he had wanted, all evening. The wine and the music and the laughter, all to lead to this. A cheap little ATS girl, that was all I meant to him, I wasn't a person at all. I was useful, necessary, expendable.

It was stifling in the cupboard. I was afraid that I might faint. Bright sparks flashed in front of my eyes. Would he hurt me? Would he hit me?

'Don't ... please don't...' I begged.

And suddenly I was angry. The sound of my own voice, pleading and submissive, a victim's voice, made me angry enough to fight back with any weapon I could lay my hands on. With the surge of fury, I felt strong again.

No, no, no. Not here. Not now. Not with him.

Stupid. Stupid. This wasn't what I meant by war effort. I hadn't come all this way to be treated like this. It wasn't going to end like this. Pathetic, sweaty little boy. How dare he? How *dare* he?

I stopped struggling – it only seemed to excite him further – and clenched my fists down by my sides. I summoned up from memory the frigid voice that Grandmother Ansty might have used to a parlourmaid caught sweeping dust under the carpet.

'*What* do you think you're doing?' I demanded.

'Just let me ... you'll like it...' His hand was on my breast, careless of how I felt, squeezing, hurting. 'I won't hurt you ... please ... please...'

His other hand was scrabbling at my skirt, trying to pull it up. His mouth was seeking mine. I turned my head, this way and that. His lips left wet prints on my cheeks.

'You'll like it,' he whispered hoarsely again. 'Please...'

I raised both hands and got hold of his hair. I tugged hard, harder, pulling his head backwards. Then – right, left, right, left, I slapped his face.

'Take your hands off me, you smutty little schoolboy,' I hissed. 'Or I promise you I'll see you court-martialled.'

'You don't mean that.' But his hands had gone smartly to his sides.

'Just try me! You're a disgrace to your uniform. You ought to be horse-whipped and sent home. Now open the door and get out of my way.'

No-one in sight, thank God. Andrew came out after me, his tie askew, his hair everywhere and my fingermarks on each cheek. I looked up and down the corridor and stupidly thought how furtive we seemed. We couldn't have looked more guilty if I'd actually surrendered to him.

'Take me back to my friends, please,' I commanded. I sounded terrifyingly formidable, even to my own ears. Just as well he'd never know I was scared enough to vomit.

We walked back up to the roof. Andrew tried to take my hand.

'I say, you won't ... you won't...'

'Won't what?'

'I mean to say – it was only a bit of fun. I wouldn't have hurt you. You won't *say* anything, will you?'

'What do you think?' I snapped.

As we climbed the stairs, I wondered what I'd do if my friends weren't there. Supposing they were in other, darkened rooms. Supposing...

But they were there, all of them. Vee was dancing with James (I think). Grace was catching up on the next generation of relatives and friends with her cousin. Pansy was sitting quietly by herself. She looked half-asleep and Bob was completely so. His cheek rested in an ashtray.

George hailed us before we were halfway to the table. 'So there you are, you two. Just in time. We're all off to the Deck Club. We'd given you up. Naughty, naughty!'

'Grace,' I said quietly, 'I think it's time we all went back to camp.'

'You don't mean it...' Grace looked up at me, looked at Andrew and knew. 'Whoops!' she said, tipsily. 'P'r'aps you're right. Georgie darling, it's been wonderful – we must do it again soon – but

65

be an angel and grab us a taxi. It's time for all good girls to go up the wooden hill to Bedfordshire.'

'You never used to be a spoilsport, Grace. I hope you're not getting a khaki mentality. Won't you just have *wahed* for the *sharia*, girls? Just a little one for the road, eh? To please old Georgie?' George asked, pompously, then he looked at me, too. 'Oh, well. Perhaps not.'

We were all pretty subdued next morning. Grace stood at the next basin, as we cleaned our teeth. 'All right?' she asked quietly.

I nodded, took a sip of boiled water and spat out.

When I came off duty later, the duty NCO told me there was someone called Mr Kenton waiting to see me. From a distance, the young man standing by the gate could have been any one of the three – young, smart, hat at a non-regulation angle, khaki drill well pressed – but I was certain it would be Andrew and I didn't want to see him. He had a nerve – more than I'd given him credit for. I didn't want to have to listen to his pleas and his justification. I hoped he'd sweated all day in case I'd report him. Maybe I still would. Maybe the fear of that would be punishment enough. I hadn't made up my mind. I felt vengeful enough for anything.

But it wasn't him.

'I ... er ... I came to say...' James Kenton looked down at his suede desert boots and up at the sky. 'I came to apologize.'

'Do you have something to apologize for?' I asked, acidly.

'No ... yes ... well, we all have, really.'

'And you drew the short straw? Bad luck.'

'No, I ... I just thought someone ought to say ... you know – sorry.'

Poor lad. It must have taken some courage to come and face me. No-one had made him do it (at least, I hoped not). Maybe he wasn't as bad as the others. Maybe they weren't all carbon copies of each other, after all.

'Thank you,' I said, still crisply, but not quite so much the *grande dame*.

'It's just that ... we're all off up the blue quite soon and it's hard... Well, you don't know quite what to expect out there, do you, and you don't know how you'll behave. You think about it quite a lot. You don't want to go until you've been everywhere and done everything ... oh, dear ... that's not what I meant to say. I'm sorry.'

'What you're trying to tell me is that you three hatched a plan to see who could roger an ATS girl last night. Did you have a bet on it? Was there a prize for the first one to prove he was a man? I hope you're proud of yourselves.'

He blushed painfully. 'It's not meant to be an excuse. I'm just trying to explain.'

'Well, you have, but I don't think you've made it any better.'

'I know. It's just getting worse the more I say. It was inexcusable and I'm sorry.'

He looked at me and smiled. Under the shade of his hat peak, I could see that his eyes were very blue, long-lashed and innocent. His smile was

67

heart-stoppingly sweet, without guile, open as a child's. It took away all the arrogance that his uniform gave him. It turned him into an awkward young man who was trying to apologize for something someone else had done. I had to admire him for that. I could just see him at school – not that long ago, head of house, I guessed, but never dynamic enough to be head of school – stepping forward, owning up, playing the game. We weren't officer and other rank any longer, simply two people who were trying to get back into step with each other.

'Would you please allow me to make amends? I'd like to prove that we aren't all animals. Would you let me take you somewhere when you're next off duty?'

'Certainly not,' I snapped.

'Of course you'll go,' said Vee. 'You'd be mad not to. Stay in this dump for an evening, when you don't have to? You want your bumps read, you do! What's your excuse, then? Washing your hair – again?'

'I must say, I did think he was rather sweet,' said Grace. 'Best of the bunch. The teeniest bit young, maybe – I'm not wild about bum fluff, myself – but beggars can't be choosers.'

'That's a bit below the belt,' I complained.

'You know perfectly well what I mean, darling. This place is like a nunnery – and I should know. Six years in a Belgian convent school was quite long enough for me.'

'And he was a perfect gentleman when we were dancing,' Vee added, 'which is more than I can say for your cousin, Grace.'

'I expect you encouraged him.' Grace gave a smile that robbed her remark of its bitchiness – almost. 'He's never been able to resist well-endowed women.'

'Cheek!' Vee flung a hairbrush that fell well short of its target.

'What do you say, Pansy?' I asked.

Pansy looked at me as though she'd just come back from a very long journey and was rather surprised to find that she'd come back at all. 'Vee's not that big – just ... just a bit round.'

'No, silly, I mean about tonight. Should I go or not?'

'If you fly with the crows you'll get shot with them.'

'What on earth is she on about now?' Vee demanded.

We took a gharry over the English Bridge, away from the teeming city, away from European Cairo. We left behind the stately buildings of Garden City, with their echoes of an imperial past, the stucco fronts, the balconies. We left the crumbling streets without names, without existence on the fine linen Ordnance Survey map of the city. And if they weren't on the plan, they couldn't possibly exist and couldn't therefore be homes for thousands upon thousands of name-less people.

I saw James look out from the carriage upon the unmapped streets and recognized my own thoughts reflected on his smooth, troubled face.

Then we were passing through fields of

potatoes, of beans, of onions, through mud-brick villages where dogs chased our carriage and women sat in the shade of their doorways, making fuel cakes of buffalo dung and straw, where children either ran after us with hands outstretched or threw stones. So many – beautiful children, children with goitre, children with milky, sightless eyes. *Oh oh oh*

The worst heat of the day had passed, but the flies hadn't gone to sleep. They clustered around our heads, buzzing about our lips but never quite alighting, trying to drink from the corners of our eyes. James seemed terribly troubled by them. He flicked his head in a constant, nervous twitch, but they came back every time. I wondered how he'd manage in the desert. I wondered how soon he'd find out.

There was already a crowd when we reached Giza – when was there not? The arrival of more than 100,000 servicemen, all of them keen to see a Pyramid at first hand and send a picture home to prove it, had been a gift to the hucksters and donkey men. As we got down from the gharry, we were jostled by sellers of beads and scarabs, of bits of pottery – very old, very genuine – and of scraps of papyrus – very rare, see, Pharaoh's own writing. There were sellers of postcards and maps and fly whisks. We were offered camel rides and donkey rides on patient, fly-plagued animals. No-one seemed to mind when we waved them aside. Why not? There were plenty more where we had come from.

We walked out to the Sphinx, marvellously serene, in spite of the newly built blast wall between its paws and the sandbags propping up its chin. Its noseless face, scarred and abraded by desert winds, was horribly leprous, like the beggars who sit outside the mosques, stumpy hands held out. It seemed right that it should look that way. Two soldiers were walking along its spine, arms held out in a mock tightrope act, challenging history. I had the feeling that the creature only had to shrug its shoulders to send them tumbling down.

We went back to the Great Pyramid and the pedlars were still there.

The entrance was a grave-robbers' tunnel, a crouch-high pathway into blackness, hot and moist near the entrance, then suddenly graveyard chill. Trustingly, we shuffled behind an embassy secretary, who was following a spinster of uncertain years, who was following two New Zealanders, who were following the guide's pinprick candle. The air was still, solid, weighty. I could touch it, part it in front of me and feel it close again behind. Ahead, always just ahead of the candle, I could hear the leathery flutter of bats' wings.

Directly in front of me, the secretary stubbed her toe and tripped. She gave a giggly squeal that – unfairly – made me really dislike her. After a few more yards, James balked.

'Sorry – I'm not awfully good at being shut in,' he whispered. The age-old darkness swallowed his voice and gave it back again, drained of life. 'Sorry to be a bore. You go on and I'll meet you outside later.'

But I followed him back out, not too sorry

71

myself to escape, but not likely to admit it either. As we turned to go, the candle went out. The secretary squealed again. I heard the guide's sing-song voice demanding, 'Ten piastres, sirs and madams. Ten piastres for more light.'

Outside again, James looked very embarrassed. 'I feel such a fool. Have I spoiled your visit?'

'Not at all,' I answered politely. 'It was very stuffy in there. What would you like to do instead?'

Heavens, what was I doing there with a claustrophobic young man whom I scarcely even knew, who'd only asked me to be with him to apologize for a companion who'd tried to rape me and who was so bored and so boring that he hadn't said a word on the journey? I'd have been better off staying behind to iron my kit for next day's inspection. It might have been more fun.

'Feeling fit?' asked James, looking up. 'Schindler's Guide says it only takes about fifteen minutes.'

'That sounds a bit optimistic. Anyway, why go up at all?'

'Oh, because it's there, I suppose. That's as good a reason as any. Because everyone does it. Coming?'

James bounded up the sides of Cheops's great tomb, like a Labrador puppy going upstairs. His hat fell off and tittupped down the Pyramid face, over and over, getting dustier and dustier. James's hair was toffee brown, sun-streaked, baby soft. There was a sudden division, marked by a red pressure line, between brown face and the pale skin where his hat had been.

'Never mind,' he laughed and puffed at the same time. 'I'll get it on the way down. Gosh – fifteen minutes not up yet? It's further than I thought. Are you all right?'

But I didn't have breath to answer. He held out his hand and grasped mine. His was surprisingly strong, hard, golden brown and dusted with gold hairs.

In the end, we didn't reach the top. There was a noisy party of South Africans up there doing a clumsy conga on the plateau where the Pyramid's point had been removed. They were carving their initials next to the ones left by Napoleon's Army of the Nile. We were content to squat a little lower down, knees and hamstrings aching, watching evening creep over the sand, gold and silver, blue and violet, spreading silkily in one direction to the green fields by the Nile and in the other, all the way to the war and forever after. It didn't look like the same gritty, dun-coloured dust that got into our hair, our teeth, our tea.

The pedlars, tiny below us, were packing up, heading back to their villages. The South Africans came down from the top, slipping and sliding and ricking their ankles, on their way back to the cinemas and the bars. The evening breeze off the desert chilled my sweating skin. I shivered.

James was quiet. He sat forward, his arms wrapped around his knees, staring towards the desert. He was silent for so long that I thought he'd forgotten I was there.

'We don't have anything heavy enough to stop them, you know,' he said at last. 'A 2-pounder won't stop German armour. We've got nothing that will hit hard enough, move fast enough. They're blasting the hell out of us.'

His face was so naked, I couldn't look at it. This lonely place had stripped away his youth and beauty.

'What will it be like, d'you think?' he asked.

'I don't know,' I answered honestly. 'I'll never know.'

'Will it really be like – you know – the swimmer into cleanness leaping?'

'Rupert Brooke – yes, I know it.

"Naught broken save this body, lost but breath;
Nothing to shake the laughing heart's long
  peace there
But only agony, and that has ending..."'

'"And the worst friend and enemy is but Death,"' he finished.

'Tom – my stepfather – used to quote it, sometimes, and then he'd laugh.'

'Why laugh?'

'He drinks. Not often, but often enough.'

'We had to learn it at school. If it's really like that, I don't think I'd mind too much if ... if my turn comes ... but if it's not ... if it's not clean...'

That was my time to tell a lie, my time to console him with platitudes. He would have believed them. He wanted so badly to believe. He was young.

I wished I could. I wished I could help him with brave words and kind lies. But I couldn't think of any. I said nothing.

With thin, brown fingers he picked off a flake of

74

stone and let it bounce down the sides of the Pyramid, faster and faster, taking a little avalanche of dust with it.

'It's the new boys catch it, they say. If you survive six months, you'll probably make it. Only I don't want to let everyone down – the lads, you know. I'm afraid I'll scream and shout for help and put people in danger to come and save me. That wouldn't be right. But maybe I won't be able to help it.'

'You'll be all right,' I said softly, not knowing whether I believed it or not.

'Will I?'

But I couldn't make a promise.

We woke our snoozing driver, who drove us back to Cairo faster than he brought us out. It was too dark to see the egrets roosting in the driftwood along the river banks, but we could smell the eucalyptus – winter in England, drops on a handkerchief to clear a stuffy nose, Vick spread on flannel and bound round a skinny chest – and hear the leaves rustle drily in the evening river breeze. The bridge was decked with coloured lights. There were houseboats, light-spangled, with music that blared and jangled. It was wartime, but the war had not touched us then.

'I'm sorry. I've talked too much. Boring for you.'

'That's all right.'

'No, really. It was very rude. I don't usually. It must have been the tunnel and the dark. All that careful preparation for death. It made me feel funny. What an awkward time to choose to bare

75

my soul. Not very entertaining for you. Sorry.'

'I didn't mind. Really.'

'When I come back, may I see you again, please?'

'Yes. That would be nice.'

I wouldn't have let him kiss me. It hadn't been that kind of day. But anyway, he didn't try.

The war crept closer and still we went to ENSA concert parties, *Hello Happiness* and *Spotlights*, to the open air cinema, Shafto's Shuftis, to see *Gone with the Wind*. At the end of the performance, as the Egyptian national anthem was played, the British soldiers leaped to their feet and began to sing to Verdi's music:

  'King Farouk, King Farouk, you're a dirty old
     crook
  As you walk down the street in your fifty-shilling
     suit
  Queen Farida's very gay, 'cos she's in the family
     way—'

and it got a lot worse than that. It was the sort of happening when you don't know whether to join in and snigger or walk out in indignation. Heaven knows how the Egyptians bore it. Pansy was scandalized.

Vee was utterly captivated by Scarlett O'Hara. She went round for a week after that, tossing her head and flicking her skirts and trying to lift one quizzical eyebrow (but, no matter how she screwed up her face, the other one kept following it).

76

'She had the right idea, that one. Always leave them wanting more. Oh, if only some man would carry me upstairs like Clark Gable and have his wicked way with me – but most of the blokes round here couldn't even lift me, let alone carry me.'

We went swimming at the Maadi club, where kind volunteer ladies served tea and sandwiches. We danced and danced, with no shortage of willing escorts. A girl could he out every night of the week with a different man and no-one would call her fast and loose, the way they might in England. Besides, there was safety in numbers. How could you get too serious about a man if you only saw him once? as Vee remarked.

In the early morning, before the heat became too much, we drilled on the dusty square. With Grace now as right marker, so she couldn't trip anyone up, we formed fours and went off at a cracking pace, convinced that our little platoon was the equal of the Brigade of Guards any day. Sergeant Gulliver bawled at us to slow down.

'Westonbirt – bring that squad back here! What do you think you are – the Rifle Brigade? If the drill book says a 27-inch pace, ladies, then a 27-inch pace I shall have, and not an inch more nor less.'

Grace and Vee struggled daily to keep their vehicles roadworthy. They constantly had to strip down and clean sand out of carburettors and filters or adjust plugs. We'd been reinforced by a new draft from home by then, clerks and storewomen, and all the beds in our hut were occupied, but we four, the originals, stuck together in rather a clannish way. We weren't surprised that more than one of the new girls arrived pregnant – there weren't many ways to while away the time on a troopship!

We had fire drills and air-raid drills. We scrubbed latrines. We had kit inspections, when a diffident Miss Carstairs tried not to enquire too closely as to the state of our clothing.

'You seem to be short of all your collars, Westonbirt.'

'At the laundry, ma'am.'

'And a suspender belt.'

'Laundry, ma'am.'

'And your spare shoelaces.'

'Laundry, ma'am.'

Sergeant Gulliver had no such scruples. She was only too keen to point out if we were diffy a hook on a khaki brassière or our knicker elastic was frayed. She poked and meddled amongst our belongings in a way that really put my back up. I hated even more when, before a parade, she'd jerk our hats straight or tweak our ties.

'If she touches me just once more, I swear I'll swing for her!'

'Can't you see, she enjoys it more when you're angry,' said Vee, wisely. 'She looks into your face and she knows you're fizzing and she loves it. Don't get mad – there's no future in it. Just keep your face straight, say "Yes, sergeant!" like a good little girl and think to yourself *Ma'alish!*'.

Pansy put her first tape up. We'd always known she'd be the one. We toasted her in cocoa, as she stitched the single chevron into place.

'It could have been any of us, really,' she said,

modestly. 'I was just lucky they were short of a shift NCO in the cookhouse.'

'Absolute rot,' Grace retorted. 'You deserve it.'

We wrote letters home and had airgraphs, miniaturized on to film to save cargo space and enlarged at their destination, back. When they came, we read them to each other, sharing families. We heard about Grace's grandfather, who was a Scottish earl, complaining that his shoot had gone to blue blazes because his keepers had all enlisted. We heard about Vee's grandmother, whose shopfront had been blown in by a land mine, but who'd opened a stall in the street outside the very next morning rather than close down for 'that bloody little Herr Schicklgrueber'. We all felt as proud of her as though she were our own joint grandmother.

We wrote a round robin to the crew of a ship on Atlantic convoy who'd appealed for penpals and sent them a snap of the four of us and a camel. With hats at every angle but the correct one and arms linked, we grinned out from the picture, tanned, laughing, confident. We hoped it would give the sailors a few smiles. God knows they deserved one, out there on the freezing Atlantic run. On the back, Vee scribbled, 'Guess which one's me (and it's not the one with a hump)!'

Busy, busy girls. Don't you know there's a war on?

The lights still blazed and the music still played. Cold, dark England, rationing and air raids seemed a lifetime away. The sun still shone, blinding, pitiless, a white light that lanced

79

through your eyes and into your brain.

After a month, James came back out of the blue for two days. We dined at Le P'tit Coin de France and danced at the Deck Club. How extraordinary – I was really pleased to see him. We seemed to laugh a lot – I don't know why, everything seemed funny – but James didn't say very much.

I never knew where he'd been, what he'd done, what he'd seen. And I couldn't tell him what I had been doing, either. We had no friends in common, no shared background; none of the shorthand that passes for conversation made much sense. We had nothing to talk about. So we didn't talk.

'Do you have a snap of yourself?' he asked as he dropped me back at camp on his last evening. 'I'd rather like one, if you don't mind. It would remind me that there's something in my life apart from sand and flies.'

So I gave him one that Vee had taken outside our hut. I was squinting into the sun, shielding my eyes with one hand. Not very flattering, but it was the only one I could lay hands on.

I watched James put it in the top pocket of his battledress and button down the flap. Then he was gone. I'd have watched the tail lights of his car disappear down the road, but a raucous carload arrived at the gate, so I turned and went in.

And when he'd gone, up the blue, not knowing when he'd be back, I couldn't get the last dance we'd danced to out of my mind.

"'I'll be with you in apple blossom time...'" I sang in the voice that had got me thrown out of the church choir, until even Pansy said she'd scream if I didn't choose something else.

'Chucking up again, love?' Vee said to Pansy. 'That's the third day in a row.'

'Touch of gyppy tummy, I expect,' answered Pansy, wiping the sweat from her face. 'Everyone in the kitchen's got it.'

'Boiled eggs, that's what you should eat. Nothing but boiled eggs. Never fails. They bind you, you see.'

'If the cooks have got it,' said Grace, looking up from painting her nails, 'God help the rest of us.'

My dear Laura

Thank you so much for the snaps. Your friends all look very jolly – apart from the camel. I'm so glad that you're happy and that Pansy and you have not been separated.

We are all well here. Kate had a few days' leave last week and looks as though life in the WRNS really suits her. She is a dispatch rider now and delivers urgent messages on her motor-cycle round – here Mother had scratched out the name of the naval base – *the town where she is based. I worry about the raids, which are very heavy there, as they are all round the coast. Do you think the censor will leave that bit in? I'm sure everyone knows that if Kate is in the WRNS she must be based by the sea somewhere. Letter writing is so difficult nowadays. One never knows what will be officially disapproved.*

She brought a charming young Pole home with her.

At least, I think he was charming, but as he spoke no English, I'm not completely certain. He smiled a lot, at any rate, and showed rather too many gold teeth for Tom's liking. He clicked his heels and kissed Grandmother's hand, which, of course, reduced her to eating out of his hand! He seemed totally besotted with Kate, but she was rather offhand towards him, so I think that particular spark is cooling. Just as well, perhaps.

Tom still refuses to join the Home Guard. He says that he had quite enough of all that sort of thing in the last lot. When Mr Treadwell asked him what he'd do if he found a German paratrooper in the garden, Tom said he knew perfectly well how to defend his family and that marching round the village with a hoe over his shoulder proved nothing. Mr Treadwell isn't talking to us any more. He says we're closet collaborators! 'Come the day' and we'll probably be first on his list for elimination.

Poor Tom – he works very, very hard in the market garden, especially now that Grandmother's rose garden has been completely dug up – she insisted on it – and planted with potatoes, with only that stupid Ruggles boy to help. Tom finds all this sniping and backbiting very depressing. And you know what happens when he is depressed. Surprisingly, Grandmother is completely on his side.

I have told Tom that he must see if he is allowed a Land Girl to help. I'm sure there's enough work for at least one. Tom says 'yes' and does nothing about it. He's dreaming a lot at the moment – more than usual – and wakes shouting out, in an awful sweat, and won't be comforted. He turns his back on me and lies awake afterwards, fighting sleep, as though he's afraid

82

to lose control of his mind again. I feel so helpless.

Abbie has (at last) consented to become Mrs Frank Horrell and runs the shop with the same vigour that she used to run us. Dear Frank, he may have got more than he bargained for! But Abbie is wonderful to us and Frank still slips round to the kitchen with 'a little bit of something nice'. I don't know what we'd do without them.

Poor Mr Millport is looking rather frail. He misses Pansy dreadfully, of course, and, at his age, is finding getting round the parish rather a trial. I'm certain that he'd be allotted a petrol allowance if only be asked for one, but be won't. His old Austin has been mothballed and put up on blocks for the duration. He calls it part of his war effort and has taken out something – I can't remember what, something vital – so that the Germans won't be able to get it started when they commandeer it (he says they definitely won't have spares for English cars, so that's all right – how reassuring!). He cycled right out to Thurlow's farm last week to comfort Mrs Thurlow. Her second boy went down in the Atlantic and the poor woman is utterly distraught. It was a horrid day – absolute cats and dogs – so Mr Millport now has a nasty cough, but won't go to bed. Perhaps you'd better not tell Pansy. He wouldn't want her worried. On the other band, she ought to know, but by the time you get this letter be will probably be better again. I leave it to you to decide.

I think she really ought to come home. Her father can't manage on his own much longer. I'm sure he's not eating properly (but then, who would, with Mrs Attwood cooking?). Do you think she could get a discharge? Perhaps on compassionate grounds? He

83

would be so cross if he knew I was writing this to you. Oh dear ... what's for the best?

Grandmother has given up evacuees – much to her relief (the last bunch weren't even house-trained). She had a terrific row with the billeting officer (Mrs Treadwell in a smart felt hat instead of her usual headscarf) about the state of the mattresses and told her, very concisely, where she could put the next bunch. But someone has to take the poor little mites...

To be more exact, she has started taking in lodgers! I can't name the aerodrome in a letter, but many of the young men stationed there are married and have nowhere for their wives to stay, either on a visit or permanently, certainly nowhere they can have some privacy. It's all very sad and romantic. So Grandmother now has her beds almost constantly occupied by young wives (and sometimes girlfriends, but we won't talk about that – Tom called her a high-class procuress the other day – quite uncalled for and I really mustn't laugh!). I wonder how many of the next generation will have been begotten in Ansty House? But it's heartbreaking if a husband fails to come back from a mission. Those poor girls. They need someone...

Grandmother looks terribly chic in trousers and with her hair wrapped up in a turban – she looks younger than she has any right to be! She dashes around everywhere, chairwoman of this, secretary of that, on the committee of the other, putting me quite to shame. As if that wasn't enough, she's a dab hand at knocking elderly chickens on the head and skinning rabbits.

I've been feeling a bit dreary and sorry for myself recently – not for any reason that I can think of. My fingers are so stiff from weeding carrots, all I can do on the piano is make beastly, Bartok-like noises. Maybe I'm coming up to that awkward time of life. What a horrid thought. Mustn't grumble, grin and bear it, women always say, but I feel as though I've done quite enough grinning and bearing lately. A jolly good grumble would probably do me the world of good. Oh dear – how depressing ... I'm sure Mrs Miniver would just give a sweet smile every time she felt a hot flush coming on and offer it up as part of her war effort.

Both my girls are well and happy. There's no bombing here. We're eating well. The weather's good. Tom has been on the straight and narrow for months. You see – I'm counting my blessings – always a worthwhile treatment for a fit of the glums!

Plums – I feel I shall never be able to look a plum in the face again. Bottled. Jellied. Jammed. Pickled. Can one curry plums? Use the skins to sole shoes? Send the stones to the ack-ack battery for ammunition? And still they plop down from the trees for the wasps and blackbirds to guzzle. There just isn't enough sugar, so the jam will probably not keep anyway, though I boiled it good and hard. It seemed to set well enough, so fingers crossed. I exchanged some eggs for sugar with Mrs Gifford, who doesn't have a sweet tooth.

As Mr Millport says, the Lord is bounteous – but sometimes He gets in a muddle: the gooseberries got sawfly and powdery mildew (one or the other would have been quite sufficient) and apples this year are going to be very scarce here. Our trees only seem to bear fruit every other year, which is very inconsiderate of them.

Well, my darling, this must all sound very petty to

you. You are worlds away from worries about powdery mildew and sugar rationing. You are always in my thoughts and in my prayers. We are very proud of you and the fine work you are doing. Say hello to all of your chums from us. We all send heaps of love to you.
Mother.

The prisoners weren't rolling in the way they used to. Life in CSDIC was getting a bit stale for Major Prosser. So after training in the use of an encryption machine, I was moved on to coding and decoding signals. It was shift work, a painstaking and thankless task – one mistake, maybe no more than a single letter, could turn vital intelligence into gibberish – and I frequently ended my shift with a crashing headache.

I knew everything and nothing. If I'd been put up against a wall and threatened with instant execution, I couldn't have told the enemy anything interesting, unless you call knowing that Major Prosser liked three sugars in his tea vital information! It was like trying to work out what a 3,000-piece jigsaw represented by looking at a handful of pieces – all of them sky. A spy could have gleaned more useful information simply by watching the way different cap badges appeared and disappeared in Cairo.

British in berets and 'fore-and-afts' with a sprinkling of red caps, Australians and New Zealanders in wideawake Boy Scout hats, Indians in *pugrees*, Free French in *képis*, Poles in *czapkas*, South Africans in solar topis – and all topped by cockades, badges and flashes of every colour – it was a spy's delight. There was a story going

86

round that two intelligence men wandered around Cairo dressed in German uniform, just to see who would challenge them. After two days without even being noticed, let alone arrested, they gave up the project!

Any intelligent spy would simply prop up the Long Bar at Shepheard's. It was said that the whole Order of Battle for the desert war could be discovered quicker there than at HQ. Joe, the Swiss barman, was widely believed to be a spy, but that didn't stop men from being indiscreet in the chummy, all-jolly-chaps-together atmosphere.

But something was certainly brewing. Even I could tell that. The daily flurry of paper became a blizzard. Equipment, fuel and men flooded into Alexandria and Port Said. Soon the question was not if there was to be a westward offensive, but when...

James was back in Cairo. No letter or phone call. Just a car waiting outside the gate when I finished shift. His eager smile. His shy laugh. Browner. Thinner. Quieter. Daring now to kiss me when we met, gently, respectfully.

I'd run down to the gate and there he was. I'd surprised myself by running. I'd been caught by surprise again when I saw him. I'd read in books all about hearts dancing and leaping – silly things like that – but it was true. How unexpected. How odd. My insides gave a sudden lurch, a flip-flop of delight. James. I *wanted* to see him. It was so *good* to see him.

He hadn't stopped in Cairo on his way to

Maadi. He still wore scuffed desert boots and shabby shorts, topped by a fearful, grey jersey with holes in the elbows and a scarf tied round his neck to keep out the sand that rubbed and caused desert sores. Tossed into the back of the car were a smelly sheepskin waistcoat and his hat. He needed a haircut. He looked wonderful to me.

Right there, in front of the guards, he'd kissed me: just a quick peck of welcome on the cheek, but I'd heard a chuckle and an appreciative smacking of the lips from behind. Then, further down the road, he pulled in at a quiet spot and kissed me again, this time like a man, not a brother.

'I hope you don't mind,' he said, raising his head, and there, for a moment, was the ghost of the shy schoolboy looking out at me.

I smiled. I cupped my hands around his face and drew him to me again. His lips were firm and his mouth tasted sweet and cool, like water in the desert. I laced my fingers in his hair, feeling the scrunch of sand in its softness. His chin scratched mine.

'I've missed you so much,' he whispered hoarsely, 'so much.'

I sat on the terrace at Shepheard's Hotel until James came back. No-one would appear in filthy shorts here. Elegant women and parade-ground-spruce men lounged in basket chairs under the shade of a wrought-iron balcony, listening to the tinkling tunes played by the resident trio and watching passers-by on Sharia Ibrahim Pasha, the restless pantomime of Cairo's streets. In

Ezbekiah Gardens, sellers of magazines with names like *Saucy Snips* and *Laffs* were thrusting their booklets under the noses of bored soldiers who'd read too many already. The quack doctors of Ezbekiah were lifting their shutters from windows filled by jars of lurid, dubious elixirs.

Bathed, shaved and changed, James looked more like the young man I'd first met. He flopped into a chair beside me and ordered lemonade for us both from the waiting, white-robed *sufragi*.

'That's better. I don't know how you could bear to be in a confined place with me – I smelt like a ferret! Gosh, I've dreamed of this,' he said when the drinks arrived. He held up the glass. Beads of condensation trickled down the outside. James ran his finger down and licked off the moisture. 'Better even than a cold beer. I went to the lavatory upstairs–' James gave an apologetic grin. 'Sorry to mention it, but even I'm human – and as I pulled the chain, I thought, there goes three days' water ration! Have you ever tasted water filtered through an Italian gas mask? No, I don't suppose you have – I hope you never do. Foul and always hot. It even curdles the tinned milk in your mug of tea. Never anything cold to drink. You clean your teeth and save the spit. When you've got half a pint, you have a wash. Then you wash your socks in it.' I shuddered and he laughed. 'Oh, we're all terribly resourceful. I shan't tell you half the tricks we get up to. It'd only put you off your dinner. So, before that happens, tell me where you want to go. I've got eight hours and a lot to pack into it!'

'Eight hours? Is that all?'

I felt a stab of dismay that caught me unawares. Like the pleasure I'd felt on seeing him at the gate, all my emotions suddenly seemed more intense and more painful. Colours were brighter. The light was whiter. Everything was paler, darker, louder, quieter, sweeter, sharper, than I'd ever known before.

'Well, it was eight.' He looked at his watch. 'We've used up nearly three of them already, I'm afraid. I'm with a Jock column – mixed infantry, armour and artillery. I've only come back to pick up a convoy of reinforcements and guide them out to join the column. We have to be back in position before daybreak. Laura, I'm sorry. It's the best I could do.'

'Don't say it – yes, I know there's a war on! I just thought you must have some leave due, or something.' Was that really my voice: the thin one with the quaver at the end of the sentence?

'No. There won't be any leave just yet. Not for a while, probably,' he said quietly.

It was the nearest he could get to confirming what I'd suspected from all the signals activity. Something was brewing.

Eight hours. Less.

James leaned forward and covered my hand with his own. 'Let's go somewhere we can dance,' he whispered. 'I want to put my arms round you and it had better be somewhere public – for your sake!'

We went to all the smart places, but we didn't, after all, do much dancing. Everywhere was full of people having a good time. Young men, briefly

90

back from the desert, had brought with them a terrible thirst and more money than they knew what to do with. We drifted aimlessly in and out of the Scarabee, the Kit Kat Club, Madame Badia's, and everywhere we went the noise and the crowds drove us out again.

Those precious eight hours. Like water through sand, they were dwindling away and there was nothing we could do to bring them back. The knowledge of how few were left made James tense and irritable. A bolder man might have taken a room in a hotel for the little time remaining, and a bolder woman might have accompanied him there. But we were not bold. Not at all.

A car full of raucous young men and women was weaving in and out of the traffic. There were squeals of excitement and shouts of indignation as hands grabbed tarbooshes worn by passing Egyptians. James's arm moved me in from the edge of the pavement, with a protective, possessive gesture. His face was grim. There'd be more carloads around somewhere, playing the 'tarboosh game' – how many tarbooshes could be grabbed in twenty minutes. What fun; what a pointless insult to the population.

Exhausted by the exuberance of the streets, we found our way back to Shepheard's. In the Moorish Hall, under a coloured glass dome, we sat in plump, antimacassared chairs set by a little, octagonal table. It might have been Torquay.

The trio on the terrace was still hard at work and their music reached us faintly. They had been joined by a singer for the evening. A couple

91

of hussars were trying to hang their berets on the opulent breasts of the two ebony caryatids which flanked the staircase. They seemed to find their failure hilarious.

'Trouble is,' said one in a penetrating voice, 'the nipples aren't big enough. Need to stick out more to make a decent hat rack. We should speak to the manager about it.'

'I'm sorry,' said James quietly, leaning forward. 'This hasn't been a great success, has it?'

His hand lay palm upwards on the table, thin, brown and supplicating.

'It doesn't matter,' I answered. But it did matter and we both knew it.

'The time was so short and I wanted to do so much in it. Will you let me get you a taxi back to Maadi? I haven't time to go with you.'

I nodded, dumb with misery. We wasted the last few minutes left, sitting in silence. James was half asleep. Once or twice his head dipped forward and he jerked it back, trying not to show how tired he was. He'd come straight out of the desert and was leading a convoy back before daybreak. He'd used on me the time he ought to have been sleeping.

Had it been worth it? I could almost have snapped at him for disturbing my peace of mind, upsetting my balance, when time was so short. Better not to have come at all, than this rushed and inadequate meeting, that had promised so much and given so little. So little time. In every way, so little.

Then I saw his gentle and unhappy face and knew that I was wrong. He looked across at me as though I had spoken my thoughts aloud and he had heard every one of them. Don't listen to my thoughts. Don't listen. I didn't mean it, James, I didn't mean it. It's been worth every frustrating moment, if it's given something to you that you wanted. I had an urgent longing to cradle his head against my breast, to stroke his hair, to make it all better.

The voice of the singer, a plump Lebanese, came through clearly from the terrace, a little shrill, not quite in key, singing an old song that my mother would have recognized, now popular again, but giving it a plangent, oriental unfamiliarity that turned it into a lament.

Sweet and simple words. Apple blossom and sunshine. All the things we missed amongst the sand and flies and sweat and day-and-night hubbub, muezzins' calls and drill sergeants' shrieks, the things we didn't even notice we missed until suddenly their absence was too painful to bear.

Apple blossom, pink and white on grass that was too lush for the ponies to eat, and pale English spring sunshine, chased by showers across sky the colour of a thrush's egg, and church bells.

And wedding rings.

James suddenly smiled, heartbreakingly brilliant. 'That's it, an omen – a wonderful idea – I've wanted to say it and haven't dared...'

St Michael and All Angels in Whit Sunday white and gold. Hedgerows starred with tiny, scarcely-valued flowers. The comforting drip-drip of rain from a catslide roof. I was sick with longing.

'Will you marry me, Laura? Please?'

Then I was back and the hussars were still braying and the Lebanese was still singing and the street smells of patchouli and dung were more nauseous than before.

'James, I ... I can't'

'Why not? It's the answer to everything. Give me a good reason why you won't.'

'It's so sudden. We hardly know each other.' I'd have laughed to hear myself if he hadn't been so earnest. Heavens, weren't these the selfsame weak excuses I'd read in romances? Kate bought magazines that offered versions of these words almost every week. And the heroine always ended up marrying the hero in the end. But somehow, I didn't see James and me in those roles. I was too ordinary and he was too young for happy ever after.

'I said a *good* reason,' he teased. He was so confident. No-one had ever said 'No' to him before and meant it. He knew I'd agree in the end.

'Well, then...' I ticked them off on my fingers. 'Number one – I'm older than you...'

'Not much – a year, two years at the most. Can't be more. Don't treat me like a schoolboy. What difference does age make?' he broke in, impatiently.

'It just does, somehow. Number two – we really don't know each other...'

'Enough. How long do we need? I know all I need to know about you and I know that I love you.'

'Let me finish. You asked for my reasons, so

listen. Number three – there's a war on...'

'All the more reason. Listen, Laura...' He picked up my hands, both of them, and cradled them between his own, holding them against his chest. He bent his head and kissed my counting fingers as though he could kiss away my doubts. So young. So eager. So innocent. 'This is the answer. We're right for each other. I know it.'

I looked back on how I'd felt earlier in the evening. I remembered the sudden surge of joy at the sight of him, weary and dirty. I remembered the flare of passion at his kiss, the way a hollow within me had opened and been filled at his touch. Was this loving him? It must be. What else could there be? How would I recognize it? How else would I feel? How does anyone know?

And yet the doubts remained, no larger than a piece of grit, but as irritating, rubbing and rubbing until, one day, they might make a desert sore.

But if this wasn't love, what was it?

'Laura, I love you,' he pleaded. 'And we don't know how much time we'll have.'

I'd known he was going to say that, right from the beginning I'd known. If I'd been more experienced, I'd have recognized that plea for the emotional blackmail it was. The ultimate pressure. Turn me down now and if anything happens to me, you'll always regret it. If I die, it'll be your fault.

Not that James meant to force my feelings to match his own. He didn't mean it. He didn't know what he was saying. But once the words had been said, they couldn't be unsaid. We both knew.

In a day, a week, a month he could be dead.

So little time. So little time left. Our lives were running out, sand through the hourglass. Why shouldn't we take what we could, while we could? Hold out your hands and take what life gives. Don't fool yourself that you'll be allowed to keep it. In a little while, it will be snatched back again.

I looked at James, wondering at his youth, his beauty, his innocence. And he loved me. I was certain of that.

'You'll be something worth coming back for,' he said.

How could I say no?

It's odd the way you don't notice quite obvious things when you ought to.

I came back to the hut late that evening in a strange, lighthearted, exhilarated mood. I had put my fingers into the fire, snatched out a treasure and got away with it. For now. I wanted to hug my joy to myself and yet I wanted to jump up and tell everyone within earshot – the guard on the gate, the duty NCO, my friends, everyone.

James and I are going to he married.

Grace and Vee were sitting on Pansy's bed, one on each side of her. Vee had an arm around Pansy's shoulders.

Just for a moment, I thought she'd had bad news about her father. Poor Pansy. How would she cope? I wondered however we'd manage to comfort her. Then, I realized... And all the things I should have noticed before, but didn't – how often Pansy was sick, the way she'd sit some-

96

times, just staring, withdrawn – suddenly became blindingly clear.

And I was supposed to be her friend. I was supposed to look after her. Mr Millport would never have let her leave home to join the ATS if I hadn't been joining up, too. He hadn't exactly entrusted his daughter to me, but near enough. She was all he had and he'd let her go. She could have been safe at home in Ansty Parva, helping him to run the parish. She should have been. She'd have done it so well.

'Pansy – oh, no.'

Pansy had had more than her fair share of gyppy tummy, but none of the rest of us had. And now we all knew why.

She lifted her tear-stained face, greenish beneath her tan. 'Oh, Laura – what will Daddy say?'

Then she burst into fresh tears. Grace and Vee budged up on the bed to make space for me. We sat in a tight, miserable huddle, our arms around each other, and cried together for a while.

After a bit, Pansy struggled free and blew her nose. 'It's all right. I feel a bit better now.'

'That's the whole point, love, it isn't all right,' said Vee. 'So what're we going to do about it?'

'Pansy, you mustn't mind my asking – Miss Carstairs will ask you anyway – was it...' Grace seemed to have lost some of her confidence. If this could happen to Pansy, of all people, what might be lying in wait for her? '...is it someone you like very much? Could you get married?'

I knew the answer, even if Grace didn't. What a silly question. When had Pansy ever had the chance even to get to know someone? She'd scarcely been out of the sight of one or other of us, except to go to work. And Pansy wasn't the sort of girl to form an illicit liaison in the cookhouse store cupboard. Unbelievable though the alternative was, I was quite certain Pansy hadn't fallen in love. Then how?

'No,' answered Pansy, quite firmly. 'I'm not getting married.'

'But who?' Grace persisted.

'We don't need to know,' I said quickly. 'It's none of our business.'

'Yes, it is,' Pansy replied, 'because we're friends. And the answer is that I don't know.'

It was such a shock, more of a shock, even, than the fact of her pregnancy. Pansy pregnant was terrible. Pansy pregnant by some unknown man was even worse, somehow. Pansy raped was ... too awful to bear.

'Oh God, Pansy love,' cried Vee. 'Who was he – the bastard? You should have reported it. They might have got him for it. You should have told us.'

'I don't know,' Pansy went on in a thin, determined voice, 'because I was too drunk to know what was happening.'

And then I knew. I looked over at Grace and saw that she, too, had understood what Pansy was trying to tell us at the very same moment.

Grace said slowly, 'It was that night, wasn't it, that we all went out with George and the three others?'

Pansy nodded.

Grace went on. 'Pansy, was it George? Please

don't let it be George. He's married and has three children. No, it couldn't have been – we talked all evening. At least, I think we did. I can't remember... Perhaps... Pansy – who was it?'

'I don't know. It doesn't matter.'

It mattered to me. I knew it hadn't been Andrew, because he'd been too occupied trying to do the same thing to me, trying to win the bet. Who'd be first to get into the knickers of an ATS girl. Bob? He looked too drunk to manage a willing and cooperative woman, let alone one who didn't know what she was doing. James... Oh, God, please. Not James. Don't let it be James...

Impossible. He couldn't. He wouldn't. Hadn't he come to make a mass apology the next day? He hadn't had to do that. He could just have ignored an unsavoury little episode, written it down to experience and written us off as convenient sluts. But he didn't and I had respected him for his courage.

I wouldn't believe it. It wasn't James. I would shut the thought away, tight and secure, and never, never let it out again.

'Pansy, you weren't drunk,' I protested. 'Perhaps you were just a bit...'

'Tiddly? Squiffy? Is that what you were going to say? Nicer words than drunk? What's the difference? I'd had too much to drink to know what I was doing. Wine is a mocker, strong drink is raging.'

'It's my fault,' Grace said quietly. 'I shouldn't have let George order all that champagne. You're not used to it.'

'It's no-one's fault but my own,' replied Pansy in that soft, strong voice. 'I'm not a child. I'm a grown woman and responsible for my own actions. No-one *made* me drink anything. I just did. But, Laura...' Her protective shell cracked. 'Oh, Laura, what will Daddy say?'

It didn't seem the right time to tell them all that I was going to marry James.

Pansy and I had our interviews with Miss Carstairs and then with Junior Commander Cranfield on the same afternoon, one after the other. They were formal interviews, hats on, ushered in by the CSM, with more salutes and foot-stamping than usual and every other word seemed to be 'ma'am'.

'What are you going to say?' I asked Pansy.

'What do you think?'

'No, I mean – they'll ask all sorts of questions.'

'Well, I can't answer them. Anyway, I wouldn't if I could. It's my business. It's my baby. No-one else's. I'm the one who has to carry the can.'

Funny – all those years I'd known Pansy, nineteen, twenty, longer than we could both really remember, and I'd never known what a tough streak she had. I'd have thought she'd have turned to jelly. I would.

I went first and told them that I was going to get married, would like to continue to serve and requested permission to live out of barracks. I was told to put my request in writing and that was that. Oh yes – and I was congratulated, by way of an afterthought.

Major Prosser had been very straightforward.

100

'Jolly good,' he'd said, 'but don't get any silly ideas about babies, will you? Lots of time later for babies. I need you here. There's work to do.'

It's nice to be wanted!

Pansy went into her interview looking as though she were on her way to execution. In a way, she was. The CSM stood by the door, holding it open.

'Right, Millport, you next, *jeldi*. Put your hat straight. Lef'. Ri'. Lef'. Ri'. Lef'. Ri'. Halt. W/434004 Lance Corporal Millport, ma'am.'

I gave Pansy an encouraging smile as she quick-marched past me, then hung around the orderly room as nervous as though I were on the carpet, waiting for her to come out.

'Well?' I demanded when she reappeared, quick-marched back out again by the CSM and dismissed. 'Oh, Pansy, was it awful?'

'Not that bad, really. They're too used to girls like me to make a song and dance about it. There's a well-defined procedure, so no-one need feel embarrassed. Do it by the book – paragraph 11 – I swear she had the manual open on her lap!'

'But are they sending you back to England?'

'Oh yes – eventually, when there's a passage, but that might not be for ages – months, maybe. Miss Carstairs was quite clear about that. Exigencies of war, etcetera. Using up a berth that could be used by fighting men. Should have thought of that before I did what I did. Let down the side. Thought better of me. I don't deserve my stripe. Don't I know there's a war on, blah, blah, blah.'

'But it's not fair. Why don't you tell them what happened? Or will you let me tell them? Pansy, please?'

'No. No. It's my business. I got myself into this mess. I don't want a fuss. And they won't let me work after three months – can't have soldiers popping buttons on parade...'

Her passivity made me so angry. Her acceptance of blame, the mantle of martyr that was almost visible about her shoulders, that she had worn so cheerfully since she was a child ... if she hadn't been Pansy, I could have throttled her.

'Then what's going to happen?'

Then she gave a short laugh that startled me, that didn't sound at all like Pansy. 'They'll send me off to a house for naughty girls. Apparently, I'll have lots of company there!'

I wrote as soon as I could to tell everyone about my coming marriage. I wrote: 'James and I are going to be married.' Simply that. Then I stopped and looked at the words. There they were, in wishy-washy blue ink on rough paper. It must be true then. Somehow, it still didn't seem real. Perhaps because James had disappeared within minutes of his proposal, I felt that it must all have happened to someone else, that I was just a spectator. We hadn't had a chance to discuss the when and where and how. Or even the why. But someone must have believed it, because I was deluged with good wishes – from Mother, from Tom (who was scarcely ever known to write to anyone), from Grandmother and from Kate.

I didn't tell anyone about Pansy.

Well, you are a dark horse. Mother has just told me that you're engaged to be married to some gorgeous young man (and he must be gorgeous or why are you even thinking of marrying him?). It was a complete bombshell. We'd no idea you were even slightly serious about anyone, let alone thinking of tying the knot. You lucky thing! I always knew you'd beat me to the altar – wasn't your favourite story 'The Tortoise and the Hare'?

I'm simply bursting with questions. How old is he? How tall is he? What colour are his eyes? Tall, dark and distinguished, I'll bet. Do you have a snap you could spare? I'm longing to see my future brother-in-law! Doesn't that sound odd? I'll be a terrific auntie to all your littlies.

Has he given you a ring yet? Choose something romantic and oriental, something that will always remind you of your exotic meeting. Oh, and make sure it's expensive (very), while you're at it. Useful insurance. I would. Fat chance!

We're all so sorry that we won't be with you on the great day, but that's war. Grandmother feels quite done out of a marquee on the lawn – not that there's much of a lawn left any more and a marquee in the onion bed doesn't have the same style, somehow. (By the way, you don't say when it is? Soon? No point in waiting, these days.) Still, a wartime wedding is frightfully romantic (though there's rather too many of them these days to be really smart) and at least you'll have Pansy as a friendly face from home. She'll make a perfect bridesmaid and I shall be spared the agonies of having to wear frilly pink organza! Will you have time to have a honeymoon? Where will you

go and what will you do?????
Write soon and tell all!
Love and kisses from Kate.
P.S. There's no-one in my life at the moment. Laszlo turned out to be an absolute cad and a married cad at that. Still, a girl can hope, can't she?
P.P.S. Guess who turned up the other day? You never will, so I'll have to tell you. Martin! Isn't that amazing? He was on leave from some sort of army film set-up. Mrs Buckland has moved back to Ansty for the duration – says her nerves are shot to blazes. Well, they would be, wouldn't they – no-one ever had nerves quite like hers! He looks frightfully dashing in khaki and with three stripes up, too. He outranks both of us! We went for a quick drink together in the Green Dragon, for old times' sake, and ended up gossiping until closing time. Ted Colebeck threatened to throw us out! I must say, he's turned out better than you'd imagine. I do like older men. They really know how to treat a girl!

I read the letter over and over, but I read the P.P.S. more often than anything else. I tried to imagine Martin as he must be now. What would he be like? How would he have changed? A man, not a boy, married maybe – quite likely, and with children – Kate didn't say, but she probably didn't care, anyway. Yet the image that I conjured time and again was Martin as he had leaned over the stable door and said goodbye. I had waited and waited. But he had not come back.

And what possible difference did it make to me now? We were strangers. I didn't suppose he'd thought of me once in all those years. All the same, I wished that Kate had not scribbled down her afterthoughts.

After some months of inactivity or of sporadic activity, on 18 November, preceded by two disastrous raids that achieved nothing but lost lives, Operation Crusader was launched with the aim of relieving Tobruk. The tanks of XXX Corps roared into the desert to hook upwards and destroy the enemy armour. Mainly infantry, XIII Corps was to surge along the coastal strip, avoiding enemy strong points at Halfaya and Sollum, to meet XXX Corps at Tobruk.

That was the plan. One hundred thousand men, 600 tanks, 5,000 other vehicles advanced through icy winds and driving rain. Sand turned to slush, clogging engines and bogging down vehicles to their axles. Men had to endure cold, wet grit instead of hot, dry grit working its way into their clothes, but it still caused desert sores, creeping under ridges of skin, into the most sensitive places.

By 19 November the impetus of XXX Corps had been halted by the German airfield defences at Sidi Rezegh. XIII Corps was making progress towards Tobruk, but would have been in danger if Rommel had decided to concentrate his energies there. If he had known that the battle on 23 November – *Totensonntag* – would be the bloodiest and most costly to date, he could have driven the British forces right back into Cairo.

Instead, he made an impetuous miscalculation. Pulling his forces off the attack, he led them in a flat-out gallop for the wire of the Egyptian frontier, attempting to cut the British supply lines, stretching his own supply lines beyond their limits and cutting himself off from fuel and ammunition. Overextended, he was forced to retreat westwards again.

Rommel's 'dash to the wire' had given XXX Corps time to recover and, by the end of the first week in December, a week of heavy fighting around Tobruk, he was forced to begin withdrawal from Cyrenaica. The exhausted British, weakened by the diversion of reinforcements to the Far East following Japan's aggression at Pearl Harbor, were unable to pursue and confirm their advantage.

Tobruk was relieved. Operation Crusader was publicized as a resounding success.

But Rommel was only taking a breather. During the week following 21 January, he scattered the British 1st Armoured Division, roared through Cyrenaica again, burst through our defences at Sirte and retook Benghazi.

The legend of the ᐧDesert Fox was freshly embellished.

'It didn't feel much like a victory,' said James, 'but they told us it was, so it must have been. To read *Parade*, you'd think we'd chased the Afrika Korps all the way back to Berlin, with their tails between their legs.'

But you survived, I thought, and you're here. That makes it a victory.

We followed the *sufragi*, Ahmed, up dingy stairs, green below the dado, cream above, just like an English boarding-house, and waited while

106

he unlocked a door. He led us into a dimly lit room.

'Very nice room,' he said.

'Is it all right, darling?' James asked anxiously. 'Will you he able to stand it?'

I looked around the shadowy, over-furnished room. It had the mildewy, graveyard smell of space shut up for a long time. Louvred shutters painted stripes of light and dark across the floor. Dust motes whirled in the light and landed on huge, dark, polished pieces of furniture, ornately French – a mirrored wardrobe, a dressing table, a stuffed chair, a long cheval glass. An enormous bed, stripped and bare, took up the whole of one wall. I turned my face away from it – it was too naked, too obvious – but everywhere I looked it was reflected back. The room seemed to be full of beds.

The *sufragi* obligingly bounced the mattress up and down for us. A spring twanged. 'Very good bed,' Ahmed sniggered. 'Very good bed for jig-a-jig.'

James's face was scarlet. He busied himself with the shutter catches, making more noise than he needed to, catching his thumb in the latch. When he pushed the shutters outwards, they squealed. A flurry of dead leaves was pushed off the sill.

'There's a garden,' he remarked, trying to sound more cheerful. 'That's a jolly useful thing to have when the hot weather comes again.'

I looked out to a sandy square. A cracked fountain stood in the middle, its basin stuffed with leaves. Creepers grew up the walls, long, long, bare bines with a tuft of growth at the top, resting for the winter or dead. The garden was full of a papery rustle.

Our landlady, Madame Bouvier, was laying out a line of saucers along the wall. From behind a bush, ears back, belly-crawling, came half a dozen mangy cats, only two still carrying a complete tail. The little woman in black, desiccated as her garden, crooned to them in Lebanese French. When she stood up, she noticed us watching. She straightened her red wig and smiled, a perky little smile, then waved, and the sun sparked coloured fire from her jewelled fingers.

There was an answering flash from the ring on my left hand – soft, pure, very yellow Arab gold, cushioning an opal, a rainbow trapped in a bubble. We'd wandered through the maze that was the bazaar of Khan el Khalili, lanes scarcely an arm's stretch wide, dim as a cave, roofed by bright, white light. James was determined to find something worthy – as he put it – of me, if it meant he had to spend all he had. I was intent on finding something beautiful, but not outrageously expensive. In a cupboard-sized shop that smelt of mint tea and tobacco, we'd found what we were both looking for.

'A ring for a queen,' the seller had told us. 'Queen Elizabeth herself has nothing more fine.'

Vee had drawn in her breath when she'd seen it. 'Bad luck,' she'd whispered.

'Nonsense,' I'd snapped, covering the opal with my other hand.

I think I will like Madame Bouvier. I don't like her room, but I like her.

I turned to look at James. He seemed to be defeated by the awfulness of it all. But we'd looked at so many rooms already, rooms with bedbugs, elegant rooms we couldn't afford, rooms over a brothel.

'This'll do very well,' I said.

And so we were married, in the early spring of 1941, when the pleasant, English summer temperature of Cairo winter was rising and the sun had a sting to it again, a reminder of what was to come.

Grace borrowed a camera and snapped everyone and everything, but the film was accidentally exposed, so I have no pictures. I have to rely on memory. The camera never lies, but perhaps my memory does.

I see Vee and Grace in uniform, but with gardenias pinned to their tunics and silk stockings they had bartered for with the South African WAASes. Vee is crying and laughing and hugging and crying again, sometimes all at once. Pansy's cheap cotton frock is straining over a bulk that looks indecent on such a tiny girl. Most of the time, she stands with her arms crossed and her shoulders hunched, as though trying to hide.

I see the padre, with khaki trousers visible below his robes, standing outside the little wooden hut he called the garrison church. I see Grace's cousin George giving me a smacking, wet kiss on one cheek before he escorts me to the altar, and Major Prosser giving me a dry peck on the other cheek when I come back again, a married woman.

There is Madame Bouvier, still in black, but black velvet this time, stamped with gold. She is crying into a scrap of lace handkerchief and her rings still flash, though duller in the dim church.

I see me – how funny, how can I see myself? – thin and brown in a heavy, corded-silk dress copied by a Levantine dressmaker from an old copy of *Vogue*, how old I didn't know, but certainly pre-war. My strong, springy hair is veiled by the Brussels lace mantilla worn by Madame Bouvier to mass. It smells of her, of patchouli and tuberose and – surely not – cats? From sleeves that come to a point below the wrist protrude my rough, brown hands, but they are camouflaged beneath a bouquet of white lilac. I look unnaturally elegant, rather withdrawn, rather puzzled, as though I can't quite remember how I've got myself into this situation.

I see James standing before the altar, young and grave in perfectly pressed uniform, blond-brown hair caught in a halo of light, the boy warrior. I see the sudden blaze of joy that lights his face, brighter than Madame Bouvier's rings, brighter than I could ever deserve, as he turns to see me coming towards him.

He loves me.

I see the laughing, crying, kissing group outside Shepheard's, hurrying us into the taxi in case we miss the train to Alexandria, at the same time holding us back for more kisses and handshakes. I lean out of the window and throw my bouquet. Pansy catches it – just a reflex action – and for a moment everyone else is filled with embarrassment. Her face is very white, but she goes on

110

smiling the tight little smile she has worn all day. She looks as though she will go on smiling it in her sleep, just in case someone is still watching. Then James pulls me back into my seat and kisses me, very deliberately, to cheers from the onlookers.

We have three days – three days to pretend to be grown-up, married people.

He loves me.

I see all these things now, but did I really see them then?

James pulled down the blinds, blanking out the lush, damp greenness of the Delta. No sand here. The earth was black, seamed with ditches, quilted with straight, green, growing lines, patterned with patient, black buffalo, knee-deep in mud, with white egrets and scarlet ibis and bent-backed *fellahin*. James went round the carriage, shutting them from view.

He put his hand on my hair, left it there for a second, long enough for me to feel it fluttering, then ran his fingers down my cheek, my neck, down to my breast, where they trembled again, feather-light, scarcely daring to be there. I covered his hand with my own, holding it in place, showing him that he had a right to do this, so that he could feel the softness and the swell. Beneath his touch, the nipple contracted, soft no longer, and peaked, startling us both. I didn't know it could do that.

'Let me look,' he said, 'please let me look.'

I undid the top button of my blouse. 'You don't have to say please to me,' I whispered.

His hands felt hot and damp, even through the cotton, as he undid the remaining buttons with clumsy fingers. The air in the carriage was still and humid. It smelt of smoke and steam and cracked varnish. The seats were prickly. I felt a trickle of sweat run down my backbone. He pushed the blouse back off my shoulders and fumbled behind me to unfasten my brassière.

'Let me,' I offered, but he gave it a wrench and it parted. My breasts were cupped in his waiting hands.

James gave a long, shuddering sigh. 'How lovely.'

The carriage heeled slightly, as the train began a long curve. James laid his cheek on my breasts. 'How lovely,' he whispered again. The curve deepened, wedging us into a corner. There was a film of sweat between his skin and mine. With a grinding of wheels, the train slowed, juddering and jerking round the bend. His lips fastened round a nipple, sending a pang like a hot wire down through my belly. His mouth was voracious and I arched my back with the sweet, unexpected pain of it. James opened his mouth in a soundless cry as a shudder ran through him, then another and another. Then he was still.

'Oh, God ... I'm so sorry,' he said, as I gathered my clothes, and his voice was raw with shame. 'I didn't ... I couldn't...'

I touched his cheek. It was damp. 'It doesn't matter.'

'I'm so sorry.'

He didn't look at me as I dressed. There was an emptiness within me, a hollow where none had been before. A sense of expectation still hung round us, of promises unfulfilled. I felt as though I had been robbed, but I didn't know why.

When my last button had been fastened, James pulled up the blinds. The train drew into a station and we sat in opposite corner seats looking at the crowd, a blameless married couple.

If Cairo is Arab, then Alexandria is Mediterranean, a Greek city of peeling stucco built around a sweeping bay, cooled by sea breezes, a holiday town with beach huts and barrage balloons.

And just as one might expect in Sidmouth or Ilfracombe, there were genteel maiden ladies of uncertain age running boarding-houses with sheets of rules pinned up on the backs of bedroom doors. Where do they come from, these stiff-lipped ladies in corsets, pillars of the Church? Who has brought them to such unlikely places? Who has left them there, colonial driftwood, to support themselves as well as they are able? Miss Howell pointed out her rules to us, as she showed us to our room.

NO more than ONE bath per week.
Apply to management for bathroom KEY.
Front door will be locked at 11 p.m. SHARP.
NO noise after 10.30 p.m.
NO eating or drinking in rooms.
Use of CRUET – 6d per week.
NO sand in the bedrooms.

'Does she think we're going to make sand

castles on the floor?' asked James with a giggle as he flung himself backwards on to the bed. The springs twanged.

'Sssh. She'll hear you.'

'So what? We're respectable married people and we can twang the bedsprings as much as we like.'

'There'll probably be another rule handwritten at the bottom of the list tomorrow. NO bouncing on the beds! Did you see how suspiciously she glared at us when you registered us as Mr and Mrs Kenton?'

'Silly old spinster!'

James lay on his back with his arms behind his head, watching me unpack the few things we'd brought. I put my hairbrush on the lace mat on the dressing table and our two toothbrushes together in a mug on the washstand.

'There,' I said, pretending to arrange them like flowers, 'they look just right together.'

'Perfect. As though they've known each other all their lives.' Then, suddenly serious, he said, 'I wish I could take you somewhere smart instead of this dump. I wish I could take you somewhere where you could dress for dinner. I'd like to see other men admiring you across a restaurant. I'd like them to envy me.'

'Silly.' I made a little kissing motion towards him. 'Alexandria's packed to the rafters. I'm just surprised we found a room at all. Anyway, I don't care about dressing for dinner. I'm happy just as we are.'

'But we'll have three whole days to pretend there isn't a war. We can swim and lie in the sun and just do – whatever we want to do, whatever

114

makes you happy. Shall you like that?'

'It sounds wonderful.'

'I love you, Laura,' he said, quietly.

The answer came easily to my lips. 'I love you, too.'

Hand in hand, we walked through blacked-out streets – Alexandria was far more vulnerable to bombing raids than Cairo – to the Cecil for dinner. The air from the sea was salty-sweet and refreshing. I felt more energetic than I'd felt in Cairo, bubbling with a sense of expectation, like a child on a trip to the beach.

The Cecil was packed, like the rest of Alexandria, with men and women in uniform, mostly naval personnel in white duck, so much less oppressive than the acres of khaki I was used to. We had a drink in the bar while our table was being prepared. James had a whisky and then, because our table still wasn't ready, he had another, both doubles.

Noticeable, like ourselves, amongst the white duck, a group of soldiers came in, mixed officers and NCOs, an unusual combination in a social setting. I looked across at them, squinting as I tried to read their shoulder flashes at such a distance. I couldn't make them out.

I don't know what made me pause and look again. Some memory, some tightening of old cords that had loosened with time. There was just something...

On his way back from the bar with another whisky, James stopped to talk to the group in khaki. They were sloppier than one would expect

115

soldiers to be. In fact, now I looked at them closely, they were very scruffy indeed – hair too long, buttons missing, cuffs undone, boots that looked as though they didn't know what a polish tin was for. They all had their backs to me, but there was something about one of them... Brown hair, rough battledress with three chevrons on the sleeve, nothing special, giving the impression of being tall, although he was sitting, no different from a thousand and one soldiers. Yet I found myself staring, frowning, trying to recapture something almost forgotten, something I wasn't quite sure if I wanted to remember at all.

James made a gesture to me to come over and join in. When I reached him, he put his arm around my shoulder. He was swaying very slightly and there were beads of sweat on his top lip. The other men all politely stood up.

'Gentlemen,' James said, 'this is my wife.'

'Hello, Martin,' I said.

You came too late, Martin. Where have you been? I waited and waited. Since I was twelve years old, I've been waiting for you to come back. But you stayed away too long. I couldn't wait for you any longer. What did you expect? How was I to know? I had a life of my own to lead. And then – *then* – you decided to come back. Too late. It would have been better for both of us if you'd never come at all.

'Congratulations, Laura.' Taller, browner, thinner, older – when he smiled, he was just the same. And his crooked nose would never change.

116

That's my fault, I thought, he got that fighting for me. 'And congratulations to you, too, sir. I hope you'll both be very happy.'

Martin put out his hand. First he shook James's hand, formal and correct, then he shook mine – a copy of the day he went away. Only this time, we were both older. He leaned forward and kissed my cheek. Something shafted through me, fierce and jolting, pleasure and pain. His lips were cool and firm. I felt his dark stubble graze my skin. When he stepped back, I found that I was staring, wide-eyed and embarrassed.

'We've waited far too long for a table in this Godforsaken hole,' James declared. 'The place is crawling with wet-bobs. Why don't we all go out together and take pot luck in town?'

Chet's Circus, they called them, otherwise known as a part of the Army Film and Photographic Unit, a roving band of newspaper and film photographers loosely bound together in uniform, in case they were captured, but acknowledging no military authority. Spit and polish didn't seem very important to Fleet Street.

Have you seen any of those classic pictures of the Western Desert? There's the one of a bayonet charge across rubble-strewn sand, a tense and vibrant image of desert warfare. Actually, it's a picture of Australian cooks well behind the line, attacking the cookhouse, with a well-placed tame explosion creating the dust of battle. A fake, but a brilliant one and the newspaper proprietors loved it.

Then there's the one of infantrymen taking

117

cover behind a damaged tank, its tracks blown off, slewed across the sand. Another fake. It's a picture of an already disabled tank that had been brought into the workshops for repair. The explosion that gives the whole scene its credibility is again a dummy one.

'Well, what do they expect?' argued the newsreel photographer they called Terry. He shoved aside the plates with the fatty bits of meat that none of us could stomach and the skewers that had once held *souvlaki*. He leaned forward with his elbows on the greasy tablecloth of the harbour *taverna*. 'There's our lords and masters at home shouting out for bigger and better pictures of war and there's us in the desert – pointing our lenses at thousands of square miles of bloody sand. We might just turn up where the action is – but then again, we're just as likely to go pissing off in the wrong direction.'

'I'm not so sure,' said Martin slowly. 'I don't like deceiving the public. We're here to show them what's actually happening – not to make it happen. What do we think we are – gods or something?'

Bill passed round the retsina bottle again and all the glasses were refilled. The turpentine taste seemed to dry all the moisture from my mouth. The more we drank, the thirstier I became.

'But we are showing them,' argued Terry. 'We're not making things up. We're not deceiving anyone. War actually looks like that – only we're probably not around to snap it at the time. All we might see is a puff on the horizon. Is that going to hit the front page? The public needs to know, has a right to know. So we make it happen. But those pictures aren't lies.'

'I just don't like it. Christ, there are men up there in the blue getting killed, while we're down here remaking *War and Peace*,' Martin maintained. There was a stubborn set to his chin that I remembered well. I could have told the others that there was no point in arguing with him when he looked like that. 'We owe it to the men who are fighting and to their families at home to show things as they really are – warts and all. And if the propagandists don't like it, that's too bloody bad. Sidi Rezegh isn't Hollywood and there's not much glamour in a desert war.'

'If you don't like it, Martin, then maybe you should move on,' Bill suggested, with some pique. 'Bugger off up the sharp end. Salve your conscience. I bet your pictures won't be as good, though.'

'Maybe I will.'

'Well, I think they're all terrific,' put in James, 'and I think you're all terrific chaps, barnstorming around without weapons, making newsreels.' He turned to me with a sweet, fuzzy smile. 'Aren't they terrific chaps, darling?'

'Yes,' I said, quietly.

They sat, swapping stories of desert life – a life that I couldn't share. These strangers had more in common with my husband than I had. They talked about setting the hand throttle on a truck and sitting in the back playing cards while the driverless vehicle bowled along for mile after mile, along hard-packed sand. They talked about the difficulties of navigating, of tying a string

119

from the bonnet to a row of nails along the top of the cab and, every hour, shifting the string one notch along. They talked about the way a sandstorm swoops across the desert, drawing everything after it, sucking all the oxygen out of the air with a roar like an express train. They talked about catching flies in jam-smeared cans, dowsing them with petrol and tossing in a match. The smell was like burning flesh, a flavour, even, like the taste that lingers around a burnt-out tank for days afterwards.

The bare light bulb was making my head ache. It swung to and fro from a long wire speckled with grease and dead flies, throwing giant shadows on to a bare wall. The blackout curtains didn't allow any of the heat to escape. The bead curtain over the door clicked like knitting needles, but no air passed through. The puddle left on my plate looked more like engine oil than olive oil. The ugly, glass ashtray, with METAXA written in blue round its edge, spilled crushed butts on to the table. James put his arm around me and drew me in closer to his body.

'I am a lucky man,' he declared to anyone who would listen. 'No, really. I am a very lucky man.'

'Yes, you are,' said Martin.

Martin had pushed his chair back, balancing it on its two back legs. Through a blue smoke haze, I watched him. Nothing of the gentleness, the kindness of the boy I remembered seemed to be left in the man. Like a dead leaf stripped to its ribs, what was left was a dried replica of Martin. His body was all bone and muscle.

I would have loved to talk to him the way Kate

had done, but Kate was not me and I was not Kate. We could have gossiped about all the people we knew at home, caught up with each other's news, in the easy way we had been able to talk once, a long time ago, when we had been best friends. But I was looking at a lean, hard stranger. Too much sun and sand had scored his skin into a web of fine lines around the eyes. Two bold lines swept from his nose to the corners of his mouth. He looked very tired. I had loved the boy. I wasn't sure that I even liked the man.

And then he turned towards me, his hazel eyes intent, the pupils large and black, examining, assessing. He could read my thoughts. He could reach into my very soul. And I knew, as clearly as though he'd spoken, that he'd never forgotten me. Again I felt that rush of pleasure and pain, white-hot wire. It was like nothing I'd ever felt before, and when it was over I was left with a weight low down in my stomach.

I couldn't sit any longer and watch him across a table. I couldn't bear to sit any longer and let him watch me.

'James,' I said softly, but he didn't hear me. I tugged his sleeve to catch his attention. 'James, it's late. We'll be locked out at eleven.'

'Plenty of time,' James maintained.

'The door is locked at eleven SHARP – in capital letters – and if we don't get a move on Miss Howell will shut us out. I don't particularly want to spend the night in a beach hut on Sidi Bishr.'

'Oh, oh – playing the little wifie already, eh? I hope you're not going to turn out to be a shrew.'

121

James gave me a squeeze that almost unbalanced me. 'P'r'aps you're right. Well, gentlemen, time to go – newlyweds and all that!'

The others gave a conspiratorial laugh – all lads together – that made me sweat with embarrassment. I didn't look at Martin as we went through the bead curtain into the blacked-out street.

Miss Howell was waiting at the door as we went in.

'Ssshhh!' whispered James as we went upstairs and then he began to giggle. 'I think I'll have my allotted weekly bath now. D'you think she's got the bathroom key handy? Or do I have to apply in writing, in triplicate? Now, now, no laughing, darling. That's another rule. It's not funny. We could be bombed tonight and I don't want to go to heaven with dirty feet.'

'I will have silence, if you please,' Miss Howell hissed.

James sat on the bed and pulled off his shoes. 'Good chaps, tonight, weren't they? All good chaps.'

I nodded.

He swung his legs up on to the bed and, by the time I'd cleaned my teeth, he was asleep.

I lay in the dark and listened to my husband's breathing. I'd pulled the curtains back and a cool breeze from the sea came through the open window. James's body burned mine where it touched. My skin seemed to have trebled its usual number of nerve endings. Each time he moved, I felt the sensation jar through me, irritating and exciting at the same time.

He turned over and flung an arm across me.

His hand searched for and found my breast, cupping it contentedly. I could have screamed. There was a tight, angry knot in my belly, hot with longing, dark with shame. And I didn't know whether the ache was for my husband – or for Martin.

There were lights on the horizon, spasmodic flickers out at sea. From far, far away, so far that it was almost like the earth stirring in its sleep, there came the rumble of guns.

Early in the morning, before either of us had woken up, Miss Howell knocked on the bedroom door. She handed in a folded paper.

'There's a driver downstairs and he says he'll wait.'

Our honeymoon was over.

On 26 May, the Afrika Korps began an attack that was to roll the British right back into Egypt. Not all the *esprit de corps* and individual heroism of the Eighth Army could halt the inexorable push. Out-generalled and out-fought, we fell back from Gazala to Tobruk. In three days Tobruk fell, its loss a terrible blow to British morale. Pursued by Rommel, a defensive line was staked out at Mersa Matruh, where large numbers of British troops were trapped in Matruh fortress. Then, falling back again, harried all the way, we formed a new line at Alamein.

If this fell, there was nowhere to go. The road was clear all the way to Alexandria.

German radio broadcast a message to the women of Alexandria: 'Get out your party frocks, we're on our way!'

It was 1st July. They called it Ash Wednesday.

Major Prosser had hauled out the contents of the filing cabinets even before I reported for work. They lay in a tottering pile on the floor.

'Get these burned, Kenton,' he ordered, without looking up as I came in the door. 'Then come back for more. And make sure they really are burned. I don't want military secrets blown all over Maadi.'

In a perforated dustbin, I burned papers all morning, stirring them thoroughly to break up the ashes. The sand outside the hut was smutty with trodden-in embers. My uniform was smeared all down the front with ash, ink, smudged carbon. Even used carbon papers had to be burned, in case a newly arrived enemy should decipher their mirror-images. My skin was seared. There was smoke in my nostrils and ash in my hair. A dark plume rose straight up into the dry air, speckled with black, rising flakes of paper, matching other columns all over the camp, all over Cairo, as the British burned their secrets.

'What now, sir?' I asked when I had finished.

Major Prosser had the twitchy air of a man who hadn't expected to find himself issued with a revolver and who wasn't quite certain whether or not he'd have to use it, or, indeed, be able to use it.

'Now, Kenton? Well, now you can nip down to the NAAFI, like a good girl, and bring me back a cheese and onion wad. We'll all have a cup of tea and wait for Rommel – eh? Shouldn't be long, they say.'

'Is there anything else for me to do?'

'Probably not. Not at the moment. No, no – not at the moment. I don't think. Nothing I can actually ... think of.' He looked round the empty office and tried a little joke. 'Nothing left to do, is there?'

'May I have your permission to go into Cairo, please?'

'Good heavens – whatever for?'

'I have a friend there. She's – she's had a baby and I want to see if she's all right.'

'Better not. Better to stay put. Much safer here, you know ... a woman on the streets, alone ... some Egyptians are very pro-Jerry ... you can't really trust them ... never trust a Gyppo is the best advice I can give you.'

'Please, sir?'

'Go, then, if you must. Perhaps you ought to – yes, perhaps you ought to bring your friend back here.'

There seemed to be more military transport than usual on the road between Maadi and Cairo. I didn't have to stand for very long before being given a lift in a staff car that was going into the city to pick up its usual passengers. The driver was an ATS girl I vaguely knew.

'There's a terrific flap on,' she told me. 'My brigadier's been going backwards and forwards all night. They say there's going to be an all-out bombing raid on Cairo tonight and that the Afrika Korps'll just stroll in over the rubble tomorrow. They say they've been burning all the papers at the Embassy and GHQ.' She looked over at my smutty face and hands. 'So it's not just a rumour, then?'

'I really don't know what is and what isn't.'

'The WRNS were evacuated the day before yesterday, but it'll take more than Rommel to shift the Tatty-ATS, eh! But just in case, I've been swotting up on this.' Out of her pocket she pulled a thin, orange-covered book. *Kriegsdeutsch*, I read: *Easy Texts in Military German.* 'You never know.'

Some people certainly believed the rumours. In the poorer areas, nothing seemed very much different, apart from urchins who ran after the car shouting, 'Rommel come, you go. Heil Hittallar.' But in the centre of town the streets were jammed with cars heading east towards the canal zone. Some had strapped mattresses on to car roofs as protection against bullets and falling masonry. Outside every bank, jostling, panicky queues stretched for several blocks. The station was jammed with women and screaming children, all entrances blocked by luggage. The British flag was coming down and the most forward-thinking shop owners were already hanging red, white and black bunting.

The heavy Humber staff car was slowed to a crawl, its driver skilfully double-declutching through the low gears.

'Crikey,' she said, 'this is a flap and a half, all right.'

'Drop me off here,' I asked, after we'd inched down Sharia Khedive Ismail for twenty minutes. 'I'll walk the rest. And good luck.'

'Best of British, then. See you in PoW camp,' she laughed and crunched the gears, lurching the car forward.

Alone, without the small protection of a car and driver, I was far more conscious of the turmoil that had taken over the city. The street sounds were different. The new noise was shriller, more urgent. Crowds that a few days ago would have parted before me in my uniform, now obstructed me. Feet, elbows, hands were suddenly in my way. People dragging suitcases didn't care if they cracked me across the shins. No-one was vindictive, but I was yesterday's woman and tomorrow belonged to a different army.

The unmarried mothers' home was an oasis. Pansy was sitting in the garden, under the shade of a vine-covered trellis, in an armless nursing chair. She didn't hear me coming and I stood for a moment, watching her as she watched her son.

Her thin face, still only a child's, was painfully rapt. She looked at the baby with the same greed that he latched on to her nipple. His eyes were screwed tightly shut in an ecstasy of sucking. Both his fists were clenched and he beat the air with them, in time to the rhythm of suckling.

She had called him Jonathan – gift of God. 'How else did he come to me?' she asked. 'Sometimes we don't want what God offers us. He holds out His hand with a gift in it and we're so ungrateful, we ask Him to take it away. But He knows best, after all, and, if we have any sense, we accept His gift in the end.'

I watched her and was caught unaware by the beauty of her composure and the sharpness of my longing. I was a married virgin and I wanted ... I wanted so badly.

'Pansy,' I said softly, afraid to startle her out of

her intensity.

Even though I spoke so gently, she jumped and the baby's mouth fell away, a milky O. She guided him back on to a breast that was swollen, solidly blue-veined, unnatural as a deformity on her virginal body. She laughed and flinched at the same time as he took a fierce hold again.

'What a lovely surprise,' she said. 'I've missed you, Laura. No, I don't mean that. That sounds as though I'm reproaching you. I mean, it's always so good to see you.'

'Things have been rather hectic. There's a bit of a flap on.'

'Oh?'

'Major Prosser sent me to bring you back to camp.'

A lie – well, truth-stretching, anyway, but I'm certain that's what he meant.

'But why?'

'There might be fighting tomorrow. He thinks – we all think – you'd be safer back in uniform.'

'How silly. Who'd hurt us?'

I looked round the garden. Three or four girls in an advanced state of pregnancy were strolling around in a dreamy calm. From over the wall came hoots and yells, the sound of another traffic jam.

'Pansy, this is war and if the Germans come you'll be an enemy alien. God knows what'll happen to you and Jonathan if Cairo is overrun tomorrow.'

'The same thing that'll happen to you, I imagine.'

'No – I'm safe, I'm in uniform. They can't do

worse than put us all in PoW camps. But there's no Geneva Convention for you. You shouldn't be here. You should have been sent home months ago. Supposing the Egyptians decide to rise against us?'

'They won't,' she said, with infuriating calm. 'Better the devil they know than the devil they don't know.' Sated, Jonathan had fallen asleep. With her free hand, Pansy fastened the buttons of her blouse. 'Look,' she whispered. 'He's asleep. How can I possibly drag him all the way to Maadi?'

'Sometimes ... sometimes I wish I could shake some sense into you!'

But Pansy's calm was catching. By the time I left her, I felt far less anxious. Who said the Germans were coming? We still had an army and the Desert Rats didn't know how to give in.

Somewhere out there – I'd no idea where – was my husband. We'd been married for four months and spent one night together. Was he tired? Hungry? In pain? Afraid? I'd no way of knowing. I could only hope that he was safe. My thoughts went back to the frightened boy who'd confided his fears to me as we sat on top of a Pyramid. He knew now – the best of it and the worst of it. He'd never face the unknown again.

I thought of him so often. Pictures flicked through my mind as though someone were fanning through the pages of a photograph album. I saw him jammed with his driver and gunner into the sardine can of an armoured car. I felt the sizzling heat, smelt bodies and high octane fuel. I heard the groan and squeal of tracked vehicles, a factory full of pigs being made into sausages, felt the bone-shaking thrum of engines. My head buzzed with the crackle of the wireless network, hoarse voices, falsetto with excitement or fear, order and counter-order, the network-blocking buzz as someone forgets to take his finger off the send button. Over everything, making me break into a sweat, was the smell of burning.

I wished I'd asked Pansy to send up a prayer for James. Her line to the Almighty was such a clear one. Mine had so much static coming over it that He'd find it pretty difficult to hear me. I tried, anyway. I tried.

Madame Bouvier was packing. Her red wig had slipped over one eye and she made no attempt to straighten it.

'Oh, my God! Oh, my God!' she cried when she saw me. 'What are you doing here? Do you want to bring Germans to my house?'

'There're no Germans here, Madame.'

'But they are coming. Ahmed has gone and taken the cutlery with him. He knows the British are finished here. Tomorrow he will come back to dance on my grave and begin a new job with the German who will take my house. And who will take care of my poor cats?'

She crammed a crazy collection of things into a faded carpet bag: a candlestick; a tin of corned beef; a little black cocktail hat with feathers; a cake slice; a suede jewellery roll (not so crazy, that); an enamelled hand-mirror; a pound of coffee...

I put my hand gently on her arm. It was stick-insect thin and shaking.

'Really, Madame, I promise you... No Germans... Why don't you sit down. Let me make you a nice cup of tea.'

'Who can drink tea at a time like this? You are English. What do you understand? I go to mass every day, but they can always tell. Don't you know what it is for Jewish people when the Germans come?'

But Rommel never came. He threw his exhausted army again and again at the Alamein defences, but the line held.

Madame Bouvier unpacked. Ahmed came back again and said he'd been to his grandmother's funeral. Major Prosser mourned the documents he need never have destroyed. Pansy carried on feeding and bathing and changing Jonathan with monumental calm.

'I told you so,' she said.

And three days later, I was called into the company commander's office. She stood up when I was shown in.

'Sit down, Laura,' she said.

And I knew...

All the bells in Britain rang when the news of the recapture of Tobruk came through. On that Sunday in November, the air that had been silent for three years reverberated with a joyous clamour, peal after peal.

I stood in the garden and listened to the bells of St Michael and All Angels. Surely, they had never rung like that before. The bats in the belfry would never come back. It sounded as though the ringers were trying to shake the tower to its foundations. The pale lime mortar would crumble to powder. From every death-watch beetle hole in every beam would pour fragments of masticated wood. Mrs Attwood would be furious on Monday morning when she came in with her broom to give the place the once over and found it covered in centuries of dust.

There was a pain in my chest, like a cruel hand squeezing, wringing me out, but I was already dry. I was sand, I was dust, my heart was embalmed. Tobruk was ours again. Rommel was really on the run, this time for good. The war in the desert was as good as over. And James would never know how much he'd contributed to that victory.

I stood in the garden and listened to the bells. And after they had stopped, the sound went on in my head, as though the air still vibrated, as though my eardrums had taken on a life of their own.

Conscious that Mother and Tom stood in the doorway, anxiously watching, I pulled up my coat collar and walked down the lane to the vicarage to watch Pansy playing with Jonathan.

1944

A hero, they said, and they gave him a medal, so it must have been true.

It was a long time before James's commanding officer's letter reached me. He was a busy man – he had a war to fight; my posting back to England had been sudden – a few days of mad activity, followed by ten weeks of mind-numbing passivity, as the troopship steamed the long, safe Cape route home.

Pansy and Jonathan had kept me sane during the dreary voyage. If Pansy had not been lucky enough to get a berth back on the same ship, I might have lost any contact with reality. There are so many widows in wartime – young women with children, with no families, no friends, no support, no home – in far worse a situation than I. They have to make the best of things and get on with living. At the time, I thought that might be better. I had nothing to do for ten weeks but stare at the sea and think. But I had Pansy's love and support and Jonathan was a constant delight.

On the day we disembarked in England Pansy was back in uniform because she hadn't been officially discharged and because nothing else fitted. As she walked down the gangplank, Jonathan in her arms, a docker shouted, 'Crikey, look what the ATS are being issued with now!'

And I found I could laugh.

Major Prosser had recommended me for further intelligence work, with welcome promotion, and I wore the Intelligence Corps badge on the left side of my tunic with pride. A rose within a laurel wreath – soldiers described it as a pansy resting on its laurels. I had been at Bletchley for some time before the letter reached me.

Bletchley Park – even the name is classified. I hardly dare think it, let alone speak it. All I could tell them at home was that I was doing clerical work in the Home Counties. True enough, if not the whole truth. Mr Churchill called the Park and its operators 'my golden goose that never cackles'. I don't intend to change that.

We were a mixed crowd, mostly WRNS, but with a good sprinkling of civilians and a few soldiers and airmen. The boffins were a world apart – scientists from Oxford and Cambridge, the best mathematical brains in the country, linguists, musicians, crossword solvers, chess players, sometimes all of these, indicative of a particular type of brain – who mysteriously beavered away in all sorts of places: in the mansion, the apple store, in huts and concrete blockhouses all over the Park. And then there were the debs – girls of good family, but (so it was said – how cruel – it can't have been true) like Pooh, of very little brain, who worked in 'C' block, known as Deb's Delight, keeping the vast card indexes up to date. It was a vital task and they did it well.

Sometimes the Park, with its copper-domed

Victorian mansion and ornamental lake, reminded me of a girls' boarding-school. I almost expected to see a gaggle of girls with red knees and lacrosse sticks running across the grass, pursued by a games mistress shouting, 'Cradle, girls, cradle!' Sometimes it felt as though we were working in a university technical laboratory, sometimes it was very like being a factory hand. Scarcely ever did it feel like the army.

James's CO's letter finally found me, having chased me from Cairo via Gibraltar and Catterick, six months after James had died. It lay in my pocket all through a dank, January day when my breath seemed to have frozen even before it left my nostrils. Muffled in greatcoat, scarf, fur boots, I sat all day, with mittened fingers like blue sausages, operating a cipher machine rather like a typewriter designed by Heath Robinson. The air in the hut was stale and icy at the same time, still and heavy, cold as bone, cold enough to make your face ache with every breath. Even thirty bodies working at feverish speed didn't generate enough energy to warm my nose. Yet the rumour was that in other huts, where the mysterious code-breaking machines, the bombes, were operated, the heat was enough to make operators faint – Hut 11 A was known as the hell-hole. I'd have swapped gladly.

In my pocket, the letter was a focus of heat. I could feel it glowing, a little hot spot, a message from the desert. I never thought I'd have missed the sun. I never dreamed that I'd long for that fetid, noisy, harsh, utterly impossible country.

England seemed so drab, so austere and mono-chrome. It was like reaching the end of *The Wizard of Oz*, that moment when the glamour of the Emerald City is replaced by black and white Kansas. If I'd been Dorothy, I'd have kept a sharp eye open for another pair of ruby slippers! Had it always been that way? My eyes had been seared by the brilliance of Egypt and England would never look the same.

I could have read the letter during NAAFI break or during lunch, but I held back. All through the jolting bus ride back to digs in the village of Milton Keynes, as shift workers were dropped off and picked up, I was tempted to open it, but I wanted to be alone.

My landlady raised her head from *The People's Friend* as I walked in the door. 'Oh, it's you,' she said – as though anyone else would have dreamed of choosing to walk into that cheerless semi-detached, given a choice. So many people had been drafted to work at BP that local lodgings were scarce. 'Tea's in the pot,' she said, licking a finger to turn over a page.

I put my hand on the teapot. Tea was in the pot, all right, and had been for at least an hour by the feel of it.

'It doesn't matter,' I answered.

'Suit yourself.'

There was a fusty smell upstairs, blankets long unwashed, mattresses unturned, slut's wool under the beds, windows not opened from September to May. I looked in the handle-less cup where I kept shillings for the gas meter. Empty. I'd been certain ... but I could never

136

prove how many had been there. That was something else I'd need to hide away in future. Even after promotion, I was earning little over a pound a week. I couldn't afford to lose my gas money. There'd been something like three days' pay in that cup. How could I have been so stupid?

I kept my only pair of good stockings under the mattress along with a little paper bag of Lux soap flakes especially for washing the stockings. My one precious lipstick was in the toe of a spare pair of shoes. If that sounds dotty, well, you'll understand if I say it wasn't just Tangee. It was Revlon Cherry Coke, produced like a conjurer by Grandmother from who knows where. She was so clever like that.

Vee would have had such a laugh about it. 'You're getting so suspicious,' she'd have said, 'a real old maid.' Is there such a thing as a married old maid? 'You'll be hiding your kirby grips in the teapot next and accusing the postman of peeping at you through the letterbox – lucky chap – go on, give him an eyeful, Laura, do. Make it worth his while!'

Heavens, I missed them – I missed them all so badly. There was nothing to laugh about any more.

But it wasn't imagination that had rifled through the contents of my dressing table a few days ago and it wasn't imagination that had gone off with the shillings in the cup.

I raked through my bag and all my pockets, looking for some more gas money, but all I came up with was a few coppers. I pushed them into the meter slot, one by one, turning the knob after each. The popping, blue flame didn't do much to improve the temperature in my room. It wasn't even worth taking off my greatcoat.

I slit open the little packet, then sat a while with the letter in my hand, not unfolding it, not even certain, now, that I wanted to read it at all.

All ranks join with me, James's commanding officer wrote... *condolences ... well-liked and respected young officer ... tragic...*

How many letters like this had that poor man to write? How many were written daily, weekly, monthly? How many since the beginning of the war? When he died, would he wear them, like Marley's ghost, in a long tail that rustled after him wherever he went?

I would be less than honest with you, if I did not say that James made a shaky start with the regiment. He was rather shy and unsure of his capabilities. He matured very quickly, however, into a thoroughly professional soldier. He met his death fulfilling his duty in a manner far above that required of his age and rank.

There are three men still in the regiment now who owe their lives to your husband's courage. With no thought of his own safety and in full view of the enemy, whilst under heavy fire, James rescued them from a burning gun-towing vehicle and would not leave the scene until all three had been taken away for medical attention. It is a tragedy that he should, himself, have died of burns sustained in the rescue.

It may be some comfort to you to know that he was

well cared for and kept free from pain until his death. The unit padre was with him at the end.

I have recommended your husband for the highest honour this country can award for bravery. I have no doubt that my recommendation will be favourably viewed.

I have the honour to be, Madam,
Your obedient servant...

In the packet were a fountain pen with a crossed nib, a watch with a broken glass, a few Egyptian coins and a photograph of me. It was the picture that Vee had taken outside our hut, the one I'd given to James on one of his short leaves. So carelessly I'd handed it over, unloving, not bothered whether he kept it or threw it away, not ever expecting that I should be his wife or his widow. And now it had come back to me. It was a picture of a different girl, a smiling, suntanned, carefree girl. I didn't recognize her. One corner of the snap was missing, the edge black, crumbling and charred.

On the back, he'd scribbled in a childish hand, *My darling Laura, Maadi Camp, September 1941.*

And in the end, it hadn't been as he had wanted. I knew how much his CO's words about freedom from pain were worth. It was kind of him to try to comfort me, but I knew too much. It hadn't been clean, not like the swimmer into cleanness leaping. We had quoted poetry at each other, children mouthing adult words, not knowing what they meant.

I sat on the sagging bed in an icy room and felt again the chill evening wind from the desert, plastering my sweat-soaked blouse to my skin. I saw it ruffle James's sun-streaked hair, heard his voice...

'*...if it's really like that,*' he'd said, '*I don't think I'd mind too much ... I don't want to let everyone down – the lads, you know...*'

And I heard my own answer. '*You'll be all right...*'

What had we known?

I thought about the last time I'd seen him. His kitbag was packed at his feet, the driver waiting downstairs. I'd looked out the window and seen the soldier, lighting a cigarette in cupped hands, lounging against the side of the Austin 'Tilly'.

'I'm sorry, Laura,' James had said. 'It wasn't supposed to be like this.'

'Don't you know there's a war on?' I'd said, with an attempt at a smile. 'We're both soldiers. We know the form.'

'I know things haven't been ... the way they ought to have been between us.' Even through his tan, I could see his young skin darkening, an ugly, embarrassed colour. 'It wasn't ... I didn't mean...'

'Sssh. Never mind. Better luck next time,' I'd said and kissed him.

'I love you, Laura,' he'd said. He'd just touched my cheek and then he was gone. I heard his boots clattering down the stairs, heard the car door slam. I looked out of the window, but the driver had accelerated away too quickly for me.

I love you, Laura.

I lay down on the narrow bed and buried my

140

face in the pillow. My throat contracted, my chest hurt too much to cry. All I could do was make a hard, gasping noise that gave me no relief.

James, oh, James, I wish I could have loved you enough.

So many letters – from Major Prosser, from Miss Carstairs, from Grace's cousin George, even from DDATS – that string of initials that meant a very high-up Queen Bee – in Egypt. Some were from people I didn't even know – friends of James's family – some from complete strangers, but all of them saying, in their own way, the same thing: James had been a hero and I must be very proud of him. I wasn't certain where the scared boy had ended and the hero had taken over, but it had happened, some time.

At home, people would stop me in the churchyard, or as I walked down to Abbie's shop, and say the same thing. So it must have been true. Everyone was so kind. It was a sort of benevolent persecution. I felt that if just one more person said the word 'proud', I might be driven to serious violence. The kindest ones just patted my hand and smiled and walked on.

'You must be sure and remember every detail, Laura,' Mrs Buckland insisted. 'I shall want to know all about the red carpets and the flunkies and the throne. What the Queen was wearing – bless her – and if the little princesses – not so little now, of course – were there and whether all the windows in the Palace are taped for bomb blast. Wherever would they get enough material for blackout for all those windows? But I expect

141

they have shutters or maybe they don't use all the rooms at night. Such an honour, dear, to go to the Palace and such a shame it has to be ... well, you know ... such a shame you have to lose your husband before you get invited...'

She didn't mean it like that, I know.

'And the VC, too ... a hero ... you must be very proud. Such an honour for the family. A sort of justice, don't you think? Not that it could actually make up, of course, but maybe just a little bit...'

'I'm not sure that I quite follow you, Mrs Buckland. Make up for what, exactly?'

'Well, for what happened to your father, of course, Laura. All that unpleasantness, all that unfortunate talk, not that we ever really knew, no-one did, but there it is, you can't stop people talking. It's only human nature, after all.'

'What about my father?'

My voice was tight and strained. Mrs Buckland looked at my face and turned guiltily away, natural colour staining the skin around the neat little circles of rouge on her cheeks.

'Oh dear ... you didn't ... oh dear ... I must fly, Laura, I've left some chutney simmering and the pan will catch and be quite ruined...'

'Mother – did you love my father?'

'I ... why, Laura ... what an extraordinary question.'

'Did you?'

Her hands fluttered vaguely, hands that I remembered as being calm and lovely, as graceful as butterflies. Long-fingered still, now they were

142

red and chapped, swollen at the knuckles, a worker's hands.

'It's all so long ago, darling.'

'Not all that long ago,' I persisted, cruelly. It was like breaking the butterfly. 'You should be able to remember whether or not you loved your husband. Did you or didn't you? I have a right to know. He was my father.'

She looked straight at me. I was ashamed by the directness of her gaze. I couldn't look at her.

'Yes, yes, of course. You have a right. Well, then – yes, I loved him when we were married. Does that satisfy you?'

'And afterwards.'

'And afterwards, too, but for a different reason. That's all.'

'But...'

'Laura, that's all. I don't want to talk any more. What happens within a marriage is private. You should know that.'

Oh, yes, I, of all people, ought to know that.

'Tom, did you know my father very well?'

Tom was grafting fruit bushes, a fiddly job, so, of course, he couldn't look up.

'We were friends,' he said, his voice muffled by the twist of raffia held between his lips.

'Good friends?'

'Yes.'

'How long did you know him?'

Deftly, he wound the raffia around the splice: two varieties bound as one, because Tom had decided that they would be good for each other.

'Oh, donkey's years. School, OTC, joined up

together – you know – like you and Pansy.'

'So what was he like?'

'Look here,' Tom said, straightening. Frosted sunlight struck off the blade of the grafting knife. 'What's all this about?'

'I just want to know.'

'Cut along, there's a good girl. I haven't got time to chat just now. If you must stay, you can make yourself useful and pass me a few more lengths of this stuff. That's the ticket.' He concentrated on the splice for a moment longer, then raised his head and looked at me. 'I don't want you bothering your mother with all this nonsense, Laura.'

'Why?'

'Don't ask stupid questions. Because you'll just upset her, that's why, and I won't have Diana upset. So let that be an end of it.'

'Grandmother, do you have a picture of my father?'

'I'm sure I must have.'

'I've never seen one.'

'Really? That can't be true. I expect you've just forgotten.' She poked her elegant fingers into the chicken's vent and pulled out its guts, neat as you like. They spilled on to the sheet of newspaper. 'This poor old dear's so ancient,' she remarked, 'she'll have to be casseroled from now to next week before she's fit to eat. I wonder if it's really worth the fuel.'

'No. How could I possibly forget?' I queried. 'For all I know, he might have been a Hottentot.'

'Now, don't be so silly, Laura. Really, for a

144

woman of your age, you have the most absurd ideas.'

Grandmother picked over the guts, sorting them into a useful pile and a not-useful pile, carefully separating the liver from the greenish gall bladder. I watched fascinated, horrified. Yet the thought of chicken casserole, tough or not, made my mouth water. Neck, gizzard, heart and liver went into the stock pot. Lungs, intestines, crop and gall bladder were rolled into the paper, out of sight, out of mind, quick as a wink.

'Isn't it amazing,' she said, 'how much a chicken can pack into such a small space? You'd never think it'd all fit. Still, I suppose we're much the same.'

She washed and dried her hands, scooped up a big blob of Glymiel jelly from the jar on the windowsill, creamed her fingers meticulously and slipped her rings back on again. I wondered why Mother's hands looked so different.

I leaned against the door frame, preventing her from leaving the scullery.

'What was he like?' I demanded. 'I want to know.'

'Laura – dear – what is the matter with you? Are you feeling quite well? Now, don't hold me back. I have a WVS committee meeting. I have to change into uniform.'

'I want to know,' I said again, stubbornly. 'I have to know.'

'I'll look out some things for you,' she said, sidestepping me neatly. 'One day. When I have a spare moment. Remind me.'

There were so many letters that I didn't think anything when I opened another amongst a batch of three delivered that morning. It wasn't a letter, just a single word.

DISGRACE

I stared at it, baffled. The meaning was sinister, the intent was malevolent, yet I didn't understand it. Then I shivered, screwed the paper and its envelope into a ball and tossed them into the fire. I felt better once they were gone.

'Mr Millport, did you ever know my father?'
'Your father, Laura? Oh, bless you, yes. I knew Edwin very well.'
'How well?'
'I knew him all his life. Did I baptize him? Let me think. Perhaps. No, no. I don't think so. I think that was my predecessor. I certainly prepared him for confirmation, however. I do remember that. That must have been 1910, I think. Probably. Or 1911. Perhaps. No, no. I'm wrong. It was definitely coronation year. Which year did it rain so terribly? I remember it well.'
Pansy rearranged the few nuts of coal on the fire, as though, by catching them by surprise, she might coax a bit more heat out of them, but they were stubborn.
Jonathan was playing on the rug in front of the fire, building something unrecognizable from bricks. He wasn't a baby any longer, but a beautiful little boy just beginning to walk, with frank, blue eyes in a rosy face. A piece of coal

146

flared briefly. Before it died away, it highlighted Jonathan's hair as he bent in concentration over the bricks. It was a warm, toffee brown, fading to gold at the ends. Something I couldn't quite grasp, some memory, some echo, made me stare. And once I had started, I couldn't stop staring.

Pansy must have noticed. She twitched the rug closer around her father's knees in an over-busy gesture. She frowned and shook her head at me across him, as if to say, 'Don't tire him', but I was ruthless.

'Tell me about my father,' I demanded.

'What do you want to know?'

'Everything.'

He looked at me with milky eyes. Wisps of hair straggling below a woolly cap gave him a fey, pixie look. Puck might have looked like that if time had ever caught up with him. His unlined, innocent face was reproachful. 'What sort of everything is there to tell about a boy who died when he was twenty years old? He was a nice boy. They were all nice boys.'

'I don't want to go.'

'You don't have any option, my dear,' said Grandmother briskly.

I trundled after Grandmother with the wheelbarrow, patiently following as she moved around the gooseberries and redcurrants. In one corner, a sulky bonfire smouldered, sending up a column of smoke the same colour as the sky. The few vegetables left standing looked frost-bleached and sorry for themselves, even the brussels

147

sprouts, although everyone knows they're no good at all until they've stood through a couple of frosts. Pigeons had stripped the cabbages to purplish ribs.

'I used to love this time of year,' she said, straightening with a sigh. 'Curtains drawn early. A roaring fire. Crumpets for tea, butter and honey dripping through all those delicious holes. Then upstairs for a long, hot bath before dinner – gallons and gallons of hot water, I can scarcely believe how much. And now – now I spend more time taking coal off the fire than putting it on and I wouldn't recognize a crumpet if it jumped up and bit me on the nose! Come along, Laura. Pick up that pile there. You're slacking. This should have been done weeks ago. I certainly don't remember being so uncomfortable during the Great War. We seemed to manage things better then. Of course, I was younger. That probably makes a difference.'

She was trying to divert me, but I wouldn't he put off.

'I can't face it.'

'The women of this family have always "faced it", Laura, as you put it. You *shall* go to Buckingham Palace. You *shall* receive your husband's medal and you shall *not* whine. And no *can't* or *won't* from you, please.'

Snip, snip, snip went her secateurs among the gooseberries, trimming away weak or crossing shoots, shortening the fruiting branches to half their summer length. She enjoyed pruning. She never could abide anything superfluous. I picked up a twig and began peeling back the bark, dead

148

and brown on the outside, living green on the inside, revealing the pale wood beneath.

'But James's parents will be there and I've never met them.'

'That is to their shame, not yours. Just be perfectly polite. In the circumstances, I think, perhaps, a little kiss on the cheek may be due, but certainly nothing more. Nothing emotional, please. That would be too distasteful. They'll want the medal, you know,' Grandmother added, with a sharp, little tilt of her head that said, as clearly as words – just let them try.

'Surely not.'

'I shouldn't be at all surprised. It's yours by right and don't let them tell you otherwise.'

It was better and worse than I'd feared. So many widows, some with small children in tow. Parents with tears in their eyes. Servicemen on crutches or in wheelchairs. A Guards band playing solemn tunes before and jaunty tunes afterwards. Photographers' flashes. An atmosphere of emotion well tamped down, of pride, of love.

His Majesty looked ill. His eyes were shadowed and his cheeks too thin. His Sam Browne belt sagged very slightly over a hollow chest. Yet he spoke kindly to everyone in a careful voice, avoiding words that began with consonants that might cause him difficulty, thinking before he spoke and, because of that, making intelligent and thoughtful remarks.

The Queen was – just herself: round and rosy, smiling as always, in a squirrel-trimmed hat that matched the sleeve trimmings of her delphinium

149

blue edge-to-edge coat. She was so natural. No wonder people loved her. She helped to make an emotional occasion into a bearable one.

When my turn came, I went forward, saluted and the King put James's medal into my hands. I looked down at the bronze cross with its dark crimson ribbon. The lion standing on the crown looked pugnacious. The words FOR VALOUR blurred before my eyes.

I will not cry, I will not cry. I could almost hear Grandmother's voice. *Nothing emotional, please.*

'You must be very proud,' I heard His Majesty say, his voice inexplicably distant, as though I were hearing him down a telephone, 'of your husband's brave deed.'

I couldn't answer, just nodded, saluted again and it was over.

Outside, there were photographers, wanting to record the moment. 'Just hold the medal out – both hands – that's right, love. Look at it. Good. Good. Now look up. Again. Can you manage a little smile? Just a little one? No? Never mind. Good.'

And James's parents. I had expected not to like them. I don't know why. Perhaps because they had made no effort to get in touch with me. I was their only son's widow and we were strangers. But then, perhaps they'd thought the same about me. I was the outsider who'd become their son's next-of-kin. I was the one who'd been informed first of his death. The army's responsibility had been to me, the woman he'd known for only a few months, not to the parents who'd raised him. They'd had to hear of his death from me – the most difficult letter I'd ever written and I had done it badly.

As it was, I couldn't like them, but I couldn't dislike them, either.

They were like the figures on weather houses – you know, the sort you could buy at the seaside, the next stage in sophistication from hanging up a piece of seaweed. The little woman comes out with a sunshade when it's sunny, the little man with an umbrella when it's rainy. Mr Kenton wore a striped suit and a bowler hat, a stiff collar and carried an umbrella. Mrs Kenton wore a tailored costume, a hat with a spotted eye-veil, a little fox stole, with teeth and glassy eyes, and carried an umbrella. The veil wasn't thick enough to conceal that she'd been crying. I was taller than either of them.

We shook hands and, mindful of Grand-mother's advice, I gave Mrs Kenton a quick peck on the cheek. It was soft as a cushion, smelling of violet-scented powder, still damp from her tears. She's a mother who has lost her only son, I thought. I mustn't forget that.

'I'm so glad to meet you at last,' I said and wished I had had the sense to bite back the last two words. They sounded too like an accusation.

'Things are rather tricky these days. My business keeps me very busy and Mrs Kenton suffers from her nerves,' Mr Kenton answered stiffly, conscious of the reproach I had never intended.

'Did you stay in town overnight?'

'Yes,' came Mrs Kenton's reply. 'We stayed at Brown's.'

'Comfortable, I hope.'

'Oh, yes, yes. Very nice, thank you. An undisturbed night. No raids.'

'It's a good day for it,' Mr Kenton remarked, looking up at the sky.

I wish we'd known each other better, I thought. I wish we'd had time. We could have been such a comfort to each other, instead of standing like strangers in a bus queue, discussing the weather. But my husband and their son had run out of time.

'Would you like to see the medal?' I asked.

'Yes, yes, that would be very nice. Thank you.'

I put it into Mrs Kenton's hands.

'It's very handsome,' Mr Kenton said, in a tight, small voice, looking over his wife's shoulder. 'Most ... er ... most distinguished.'

She didn't say anything. She turned it over. On the reverse, the clasp was inscribed *Lt J S E Kenton, RA* and in the centre of the cross *30 June 1942*, the date of the deed which had won him this decoration. James had died three days later. Her hands were shaking so much that Mr Kenton took the medal in case it fell to the ground and put it back into its velvet-lined box.

'Would you like to keep it?' I asked. Grandmother would be furious, but it was none of her business. 'I think that's what James would have wanted.'

The longing in their eyes was naked, shocking. Well-bred, middle-class English people should never look so voracious.

'No, my dear,' he said at last. 'It's very good of you, but it's yours. You didn't have him very long.

152

We had him all his life.'

For the first time, Mrs Kenton looked straight at me and I couldn't mistake the bitterness in her voice. 'Of course,' she said, 'it would have been so different if you'd had children.'

We parted with promises to keep in touch and we all knew that we'd do nothing of the kind. There was nothing to keep us together.

All the way back to Bletchley, I stood in the corridor of a train packed with soldiers going on leave. There were sleeping soldiers in the luggage racks, kitbags everywhere, a card game going on with the cards laid out on knees. The air was blue with swear words and cigarette smoke, almost unbreathable, bluer still after dark, lit only by tiny, blued bulbs. I stood with my back jammed against a door handle and thought about Mrs Kenton's accusation.

She blamed me for the fact that they would have no grandchildren to console them for their loss. Perhaps she thought I'd been too busy with my own job, too selfish to give it up for a woman's proper role. Perhaps she thought I'd denied her son something he must have wanted. Thank God, she would never know.

A young woman, too thin, too pale, holding a small child by the hand, tried to get past on her way to the lavatory. The child had a green bubble blowing from one nostril. I flattened myself against the door as far as I could (supposing it opened?) and a couple of the card players stood on their kitbags to try to give her some room to pass. She looked so apologetic, but no-one seemed annoyed at being disturbed – it was just

153

the way things were. The soldiers were like patient beasts of burden: advance, retire, go home, come back, live, die – they just got on with it.

'No point in trying to get in there, love,' called one wag as the woman turned the lavatory door handle. 'They're standing on each other's heads in there.'

I thought about Pansy, about Jonathan and how much she loved him. Supposing, just supposing, James and I had ... I had to face up to the word, just to think it was painful ... supposing we had actually managed to consummate our marriage. I turned my face to the window, but there was nothing to see. Hurried along by the speed of the train, raindrops rolled diagonally across the pane, left to right, streaking the soot, making the weather seem even worse than it was. People would stare at my scarlet face and wonder. Guilty conscience. Impure thoughts.

Supposing...

And I realized that, whatever other regrets I may have had about my marriage – and there were many – my childlessness was no longer one of them.

Three days later, the second letter arrived.

I unfolded the single sheet of paper. There was a picture, cut from the *Daily Telegraph*, of myself after the ceremony at Buckingham Palace, holding James's Victoria Cross, looking awkward and bulgy in my ill-cut uniform.

Underneath was written, in huge, clumsy letters:

HERO'S WIDOW
COWARD'S DAUGHTER

I felt sick.

Same ill-formed capitals. Same cheap paper, blue-lined, torn from a pad. Same vindictive writer, doing his or her best to hurt and succeeding – oh, succeeding so very well.

Work at BP was arduous and off duty I was lonely. I missed the companionship of life in barracks more than I'd ever have thought possible. In particular, I missed Grace's rebellious sense of humour and Vee's bubbly personality. They both wrote regularly – they were splendid correspondents – but their warmth came only second hand. There was little to lighten life in digs with Mrs Granby in Brickfield Cottages.

We never talked about our work, we never gossiped, even over tea and buns in Hut 2, the NAAFI; we just got on with what we had to do. The Park and its staff were growing beyond recognition. Army and ATS, Royal Navy and WRNS, RAF and WAAF, Free French, Americans, Poles – an extraordinary conglomeration of talents – we just got on with our own business and never minded anyone else's. One hut didn't know what the next hut did and never asked. This may well have resulted in the wheel being reinvented on a daily basis, but that didn't matter. Security was paramount.

BP had no aerials, for fear of making it

conspicuous from the air, and couldn't receive wireless traffic, so dispatch riders on motorcycles roared in and out all day and night, carrying signals from outlying listening stations for decoding. Talk of a second front was guarded, but the sense of anticipation began to grow.

Released one morning for a quick cup of tea, I was amazed to find Kate sitting in the NAAFI hut.

'I don't believe it,' I cried. 'Kate, how wonderful!'

'Hello, Laura,' she said, as though we'd seen each other only that morning. 'I thought I'd bump into you.'

'What are you doing here?'

'Fetching mysterious bits of paper and taking them away again. I've been posted to Whaddon Hall as dispatch rider for this place, so you'll be seeing quite a lot of me.'

She wore clumsy, blue overalls, a leather jerkin and heavy, motorcyclist's boots. Her bubbly, blond hair looked incongruous on top of a smudged face, with the shape of her goggles outlined in mud round tired eyes, although she'd taken the trouble to reapply her lipstick – Kate couldn't survive without lipstick! On the table were her helmet and gauntlets. She looked nothing like the little sister in ankle socks that I remembered – illogical, I know, but my memory of Kate seemed to have become stuck some time in 1939 – but when she smiled, she was quite definitely Kate. How marvellous!

'I'm so glad to see you,' I said, giving her a hug and a kiss.

156

Half a dozen WRNS ran past the window clutching bulky, brown paper bags close to their chests.

'*What* was that?' Kate exclaimed, looking over my shoulder and through the window.

'Oh, that,' I answered, casually. 'No-one's allowed to look at secret equipment, so it's always moved in paper bags at high speed. And at even higher speed if it's too big for a bag. We just close our eyes and pretend nothing's happening. Welcome to the madhouse, Kate!'

When we could organize time off together – and that wasn't easy – we'd have high tea at a drab little tea room in Buckingham. Spam fritters or mashed potatoes with a scrap of cheese, done up to look like sausages (if only!), all with lashings of tea. Compared to Mrs Granby's sacrificial offerings, it was heaven. There were frequent concerts at the Park. So many talented musicians had been gathered there. There was a choir and several chamber music groups. Maybe we'd go to the pictures, managing to catch the last bus back, or perhaps just go for a walk if we were feeling poor or Mrs Granby had gone off with my gas money again.

'Honestly, what's that woman *doing* with your rations? Running a restaurant on the sly?'

'Just burning them, I think, by the smell in the kitchen. Blames it on having given her best pots and pans to salvage. Every time an aeroplane goes over, she looks up and says "There goes half my bleeding kitchen!" Still, look on the bright side. The local pig club must be doing

157

pretty well for swill.'

Kate dragged me, much against my will, to see *Desert Victory.*

'You were there, Laura. You helped to *make* that victory, for heaven's sake.'

'Hardly.'

'Don't be so modest. How many people in the audience will be able to say that, d'you think? You ought to stand on your chair at the end and tell everyone what it was really like.'

'And get thrown out on my ear, most likely.'

Everything about it was so familiar and yet as distant as though I'd come back from the moon. Flickering along the long, blue beam from the projection box, swirling with cigarette smoke, came pictures more real than any I had watched in Shafto's Shufties in Cairo. I hated it and yet was fascinated by it. I wanted to close my eyes and yet I couldn't tear my gaze from the screen. It was a triumph – of military daring or of propaganda, depending on how you viewed it.

There was a long, long silence, building up to the demonic artillery barrage that launched the battle of El Alamein. The audience roared to rival the guns. I had too much to think about to join them. I remembered the way Martin had condemned mockups. But this was real. Three photographers died taking the footage of battle that was greeted with a cheer in British cinemas.

'You ought to move in with me,' Kate suggested one evening, as we treated ourselves to a rare fish supper. We'd been to see *Now, Voyager* – a real weepie – I could have cheered when Bette Davis finally stood up to her frightful mother. 'I've got

158

a lovely landlady, a real sweetie, and I'm sure she could squeeze in an extra bed.'

It was very tempting. It would have been marvellous to move in with Kate and to enjoy her bright and breezy company. But I had to remind myself that Kate was young and free and that I was a widow. She'd want to go to dances, have boyfriends, have some fun. She deserved it, she worked so hard. I didn't want to get in the way of any social life she might have. Who wants an older sister hanging around like a wet blanket?

'I'd love to, but it's too far away for night shifts. I'm on nights every third week.' I sprinkled extra vinegar on my chips. 'Mmm. Gorgeous.'

The fish shop was blessedly warm. Even the smell was enough to satisfy hunger. I could've stayed there all night. I licked my fingers and smiled and tried not to show how much I longed to move in with Kate.

'You're not looking well, Laura.'

'Just tiredness, I expect. I'm not very good at shift work. We do one week of days, one week until midnight and one week from midnight to 8 a.m., so you never get enough time to get used to a working pattern. Still, we're all in it together. Mustn't grumble.'

'I'd've thought there's more to it than that. Mother said...'

'So you've been talking about me,' I snapped.

'Nothing we can't say to your face. Look, Laura darling–' She laid her hand on top of mine. 'You've had a rough time, but – now hit me if you feel like it, I shan't mind a bit, well, not much, anyway – James has been gone for nearly two

159

years and you only knew him for – what? – nine months? ten months? You only spent one night together, for heaven's sake. Oh, God, I shouldn't have said that. I'm sorry. I'm sorry. What a thing to say. Forgive me?'

She looked at me anxiously as though she expected me to behave like Bette Davis, to lean over and slap her or burst into hysterical laughter or generally show far too much emotion. As if I would. I had learned to keep my feelings as closely under wraps as the secret equipment at BP. I kept my heart in a brown paper bag.

'Nothing to forgive,' I said, quietly, and meant it.

'But don't you think James might have wanted you to pick up your life again? I'm sure he wouldn't want you to spend the rest of your days grieving for a marriage that ended almost as soon as it began. That wasn't his fault, but it wasn't yours, either, so why should you have to pay for it? It's terribly sad, but it's war. It's the way things happen. It's not normal for someone of your age to live the way you do.'

What platitudes! Any minute now she'd say that I had a duty to my dead husband, who'd died for my freedom, to live life to the full again. I'd read an answer like that to some poor little girl in an agony column. What sort of advice was that? What do these people know about loss? How do they know what a dead man might or might not want? All James ever wanted was not to die. And if Kate had told me to buck up like that, I think I might really have slapped her.

All the same, it was difficult not to smile. How

like her! I had a feeling that Kate's sex life was flourishing in a way that mine never had. She had that look about her – you know – complete, finished off properly. Well, good luck to her!

'Don't worry, Kate, I won't throw a fit of hysterics and I won't hit you, either. Just let me be. I'm quite all right the way I am.'

'Rubbish! You're turning into a fusty old hermit. Come dancing with me. There's an all-ranks do at RAF Cublington next Friday. They're running a bus. Come with me and we'll really show them how! Please, Laura,' she appealed. 'We'd have such fun together.'

'I'm sorry – no, really I am – but I'm on evenings that week.'

'And if you weren't, you'd swap with someone just to make sure that you were. OK, I'll let you off this time, but I'm not beaten yet!'

I wanted to share my secret with Kate. I needed to talk to somebody. I had destroyed the two anonymous letters, but that didn't mean that I'd forgotten them. I was becoming obsessed by them, by the secret at which they hinted, shameful and dark. The intense concentration demanded by my work kept my brain occupied throughout every moment I spent on shift, but even I couldn't work all the time. In the morning after night shift while I tried to sleep, in the evening polishing buttons and shoes, mending my stockings, washing my underwear, drying my hair, every moment, I thought about them.

I could close my eyes and reproduce the illiterate hand. I had searched through stationery counters until in Woolworth's I had discovered paper that matched the letter in every way: rough, wartime quality that made the ink leach, blurring the letters; sixpence a pad, frustratingly ordinary; hundreds, probably, sold every week. I had held the second letter up to the light – fingermarks, blotchy and indistinguishable. I had sniffed it – tobacco and ... and ... what? Something familiar. I just couldn't quite recall. It would come to me. The postmarks had told me nothing. I'd thrown the first envelope away too hastily and the second was blurred.

And then, as I'd done with the first, I had burned those hurtful pieces of paper, letter and envelope, holding them cautiously between finger and thumb, poking them into the gas flame, watching the paper catch, flare and die, neatly sweeping up the ashes from the hearth. Quite gone. Nothing left.

Only they hadn't gone. They were still with me. They never left me.

I needed someone to talk to. I had tried at home, but no-one was willing to talk to me. Mother? Tom? Grandmother? Edwin Ansty's wife, his best friend and his mother, a dumb triumvirate. Who could break their silence? Wherever I turned, I met resistance. They weren't going to give me any answers.

What did they think I was going to ask? What were they afraid of? Why shouldn't I know about my own father? Why was he never mentioned? Why had he vanished from my life as though he had never existed? I knew his name, but nothing else. No photograph, no letters, no memories, no name on the war memorial. I might have been the product of an immaculate conception.

Perhaps I could have talked to Kate. She, at least, would have listened. She wouldn't have fobbed me off, as though I were just an inquisitive child demanding to know where babies come from. But Kate and I did not share the same father. Why should she care? The man described as a coward was no relative of hers. How could I explain to her? Would I say 'Kate, I think our mother is hiding something from me?' Kate's loyalty would have to be to our shared mother, of course. If even *she* wouldn't answer my questions, why should anyone else? Kate would say 'Pay no attention. There are plenty of head cases about. The war brings them all out of the woodwork.'

That was a comforting, if convenient, thought. A disturbed person. Someone grieving, perhaps, or jealous, or lonely. All I had to do was keep that idea firmly in my mind. Yes, but who? And why? Why me?

Someone must know.

Suddenly summer had arrived and suddenly, too, aerials sprouted on the edge of the woods behind 'D' block. We speculated, though guardedly, that something very important must be happening to override the earlier decision that BP should not be too noticeable from the air. The speed with which coded messages were received, decrypted into plain German, translated, recrypted back into our own code of the day and passed on to commanders could already be down to as little as thirty minutes. If that time now had to be shortened still further, something was obviously up. There was a renewed feeling of urgency in the air that reminded me slightly of the flap in Cairo – everyone seemed to be on their toes, tense and excited – but this time we weren't waiting for the enemy to come to us. We were taking the war to him – all the way.

It was my turn for a 72-hour pass and I was cautiously warned that I ought to make the most of it. It would be the last for some time. No-one would be having leave that summer of 1944. Rumours of the opening of a second front were stronger than they'd ever been. No-one could be spared when the moment finally arrived. And who in their right mind would want to miss it? Certainly not I.

I travelled home almost reluctantly. There was too much going on and I didn't want to be left out. Yet, after a beast of a journey cross country, the train having been shunted into every siding between Waterloo and Salisbury, the prim cottages of Ansty Parva were a welcome sight. The sky was still bright, gold streaked with lilac, but the earth was dark as I trudged up the drive of Ansty House, noticing the unwelcome changes.

Everything looked very run down. The gravel of the drive was thick with weeds. The shrubbery was overgrown, laced with brambles, unkempt as an old man's beard. The chickens, already cooped up for the night, occupied a wire mesh run beside the dry fountain. Most of the lawns had been dug up and those that were left had pigs rooting on them. Pigs! Grandmother's latest obsession. Pigs meant bacon, sausages, hams, pork, crackling, sage and onion stuffing, apple sauce – my mouth watered. Not such a bad idea, after all.

I stood quietly in the open doorway of the gardener's cottage. Nothing seemed to have changed here. The same shabby-elegant furniture, too much for the room, was shoved all anyhow around the walls. A tiny fire of apple tree prunings, just enough to take the chill off the early summer evening, burned in the black chasm of the fireplace, its spicy smoke scenting the room. The blackout curtains had not been drawn and the light had not been lit. The window was open, so that the fragrance of stock and mignonette drifted in and mingled with the smoke.

Mother was playing the piano, one of Bach's complicated rhythmic patterns. It sounded as sunlight might sound, shining through tall trees, dappling the grass gold and green. It was a comforting sound. As a child, I'd lain in bed so often, listening to Mother play, failing asleep to sweet, barely recognized tunes. Some things never change. I hadn't wanted to come home, but it was wonderful to have arrived.

With a discordant jangle, fierce and shocking, Mother broke into the soothing rhythm. She pounded the keys three times with clenched fists. Her spine and shoulders were rigid with rage. The beauty, the peace of the scene were smashed. It was as though someone had taken a

165

hammer to a perfect statue.

I felt as though I were trespassing. I turned to tiptoe away, to enter the house again with more noise, more warning, but she was too quick for me.

'Laura?' When I turned to look at my mother, the remains of her fury still blazed from her eyes, but as I watched, she won the battle. 'Laura, darling. Where did you spring from? Are you on leave? How marvellous. You should have warned us. We'd have met you at the station.'

'It was all rather sudden. I scarcely knew myself. Mother – are you all right?'

'Never better.' She put her arms around me and kissed me. I could feel her bones, puny as a bird's. They poked me, even through the sturdy serge of my uniform. The hair that I remembered as soft as a kitten's was dragged back and wound under a woollen turban. She wore tweed slacks and an old shirt of Tom's. 'I'm afraid it'll be pot luck for supper tonight, but we'll see what Grandmother can produce tomorrow. It'll be so cosy, just the two of us.'

'Aren't we waiting for Tom?'

'Tom won't be home for supper, I don't think. Anyway, he wouldn't want to keep you waiting. You must be starving after your journey. Was it awful?'

We sat down together to the reheated remains of vegetable pudding – a mixture of vegetables barely moistened by gravy and encased in potato pastry. It was rather dull fare, even first time round. On its second appearance, it was not improved.

'Oh, dear.' Mother gave a resigned sigh. 'It's rather like trying to chew a hole in an army kitbag. Pastry has never been my strong point.'

'It's not that bad,' I lied, blatantly. 'If Mrs Granby gave me this, I'd be in seventh heaven.'

'Do you mind if I turn on the wireless while we eat? I always like to have the sound, even if I don't really listen.' She switched on the set. 'I always used to like J. B. Priestley at this time on a Sunday night. He has such a comfortable voice, I always think, rather like a Christmas pudding smoking a pipe. Such a pity Mr Churchill had him taken off.'

We chatted lightly about who was doing what in the village, but all the time I was aware that my mother was ill at ease. She seemed to be giving me only half her attention. Above the murmur of our voices, she was listening for something and I knew that it was for the sound of Tom's returning footsteps.

'Tom was fined last month for growing gooseberries instead of carrots. He's frightfully upset.'

'No wonder. Fined? For growing one thing instead of another?'

'Root vegetables give a better yield per square yard of cultivation, I'm told. So market gardeners are expected to produce a certain yield off their acreage. But Tom doesn't quite see things the same way.'

'But how does anyone know what he's growing?' I asked.

'Oh, that's easy. Tom blames the *Gauleiter* of Ansty Parva!' Mother giggled. 'Mr Treadwell. He knows everything. If there ever is an invasion, we all know which side he'll be on.'

'Good Lord! I thought we were fighting to keep that type out of Britain. We seem to have quite enough home-grown Nazis.' Yuk

'I'm so glad you've come today,' Mother said as we cleared away the few dishes. 'I've got a treat for pudding. Such good timing.' She took a single banana from a blue-and-white Chinese bowl and laid it on a wafer-thin Spode plate in front of me. 'There you are. I won it in a WI raffle. Isn't that tremendous luck?'

She stood by my chair, a little, triumphant grin on her face, her hands behind her back, like a child giving the apple to the teacher. I looked from Mother to the banana, freckled black on its yellow skin, and back to my mother again.

'I can't eat this,' I said. 'It's too precious.'

'But darling, you must. Someone has to. I can't stuff it and mount it on the wall like a trophy. It's for you.'

'The army feeds me so well,' I lied. Well, the army did, but Mrs Granby certainly didn't. I'd have loved that banana. My teeth ached for it. 'And you're getting...' No, I couldn't say it. 'You've lost a bit too much weight. You have it.'

'Oh, no. I couldn't. I'm absolutely full.'

'And what about Tom? He'd love it, I'm sure. Where is Tom?'

'He's busy,' she said, quickly. 'And the banana will be black by tomorrow. It'd be a sin to waste it.'

I took another plate, garlands of roses and forget-me-nots, and put it on the table in front of

Mother. Both plates were cracked, but they had been as long as I could remember. All our plates were cracked and our cups chipped. Then I sliced the banana and put an equal number of slices on each plate. I laid a pearl-handled fruit knife and fork beside each.

'There you are,' I said, laughing. 'You can't argue now. Pretend you've just reached the end of a four-course dinner. Pretend you're just toying with dessert.'

Mother laughed too, put a slice in her mouth and gagged. 'I'm awfully sorry. I just don't think I can manage it.'

'Mother, where *is* Tom?'

'I'm not sure,' she whispered.

'The Green Dragon?' I guessed.

'Probably. That's where he was last night. But the night before that he went over to Middle-hampton and... Laura, where are you going?'

'To the Green Dragon.'

'You can't'

'Watch me.'

'Laura, don't...' I heard her call as I went out the door, but I was in no mood to listen.

I marched out with my uniform cap set at an aggressive angle. The short cut to the village was through the walled garden, where a low green door led into the churchyard. It was just as well that the route was as familiar to me as the way to bed. My torch with its two enveloping layers of tissue paper barely lit up my shoelaces. My sensible, flat shoes crunched on the gravel as I strode through the garden.

God, I was angry. I was angry enough to pull

Tom out of the Green Dragon by the scruff of his neck. Did my mother really think I hadn't heard her pound the piano in rage and frustration? Did she think I hadn't seen how worn and thin she had become? Throughout my childhood, we had tiptoed around, warned by Mother – Tom's not feeling too bright, don't disturb Tom, don't upset Tom, he gets nervous, he had a bad time in the war. Well, this was another war and we were all damn well having a bad time. Why should he be especially protected against it? He said he loved my mother, he said he adored the ground she walked on. Couldn't he see how ill she looked? Couldn't he see what was right under his nose? It was a funny kind of love that never even noticed the loved one.

There was a light in the potting shed, a tiny, unblacked-out pinpoint of light. I wasn't going to have to walk as far as the Green Dragon, after all. A thread of sound reached me from the shed, wavering and uncertain, wandering around the tune and coming back to it again.

"'If you want to find the old battalion,
I know where they are, I know where they are,
I know where they are.
If you want to find the old battalion, I know
where they are
They're hanging on the old barbed wire...'"

I looked in the window. Tom was sitting on an old stool, with his back and head propped against the wall of the shed. A cigarette dangled from limp fingers, a curved tip of ash drooping from it, as though he'd forgotten it was there. His eyes were closed. His voice was a ghost, creaking, like the opening of a rusty gate.

'"I've seen them, I've seen them,
Hanging on the old barbed wire.
I've seen them, I've seen them,
Hanging on the old barbed wire."'

I pushed open the door, going quickly in and shutting it again so as not to release any more light, then I leaned across him to pull the old sack that did for a blackout curtain.

He opened his eyes and gave me a wobbly smile. 'Laura – my favourite girl...'

'What exactly are you doing here?' I asked, curtly.

'Just having, a little rest. Tired, you know. Long way home. "There's a long, long trail a-winding into the land of my dreams, Where the nightingale is singing and a white moon beams..."'

The atmosphere of the shed was so familiar – Jeyes fluid, compost, dust, cobwebs, stored apples and pears, the smell of childhood – but tonight it was overlaid by something sharper and sourer. Even Tom's sweat seemed to be alcohol-tainted.

'Have you come to take me home?' he asked. 'Dear girl – how kind of you.'

His smile was vague, unfocused, but piercingly sweet. He seemed simply to be fading away, like fine old linen worn to its threads. Mother had turned him sides-to-middle so many times for so many years that there was nothing left to mend.

I had the feeling that if he stood in front of the light, I'd be able to see right through him.

I had come to shout at him, to snap him out of it, to bring him to his senses, do all the sensible, practical things that would make him realize that his behaviour was unacceptable, but when he smiled at me – damn him, damn him – I couldn't do it.

'Come along,' I snapped, loving him, hating him. 'It's late.'

'And you've had a long journey. How thoughtless of me. If you would just...' He held out his hand, long bones bound together by parchment, and I hefted him up from the stool. 'Thank you so much. Most kind.'

Slowly, we walked together down the garden path, our feet crunching in unison. Tom hummed quietly for a bit, then began to sing again, in that thin, threadlike voice. It was like listening to a phantom.

"'There's a long, long night of waiting, until my
  dreams all come true,
Till the day when I'll be going down that long,
  long trail with you.'"

He put his arm around my shoulder. Tears like snail tracks glittered on his cheeks. 'I loved your father, you know, Laura. Edwin was my best friend. I really loved him.'

While I was away, Ansty Parva had been turned into a military collecting area. Along with every other village in southern England within striking distance of the coast, it had been stuffed to capacity with waiting troops and vehicles. The winding lanes were being crushed beneath the weight of heavy armour. No-one spoke about it, but we all knew that they were waiting for the signal to begin the greatest invasion ever planned. True

In the morning, I strolled into the village, feeling oddly naked in a cotton summer frock, utility length, skimming my knees, but the feeling of warm air on bare legs was delicious after heavy uniform stockings. My hair wasn't tucked into a tidy, military hairstyle, but floated in the breeze, tickling my neck. It felt so good. It made me feel younger, even carefree.

There was Josie Shellard – Josie Pocknell as I remembered her – holding a toddler by the hand and pushing a pram. She waved to me across the street and I went over to see the new arrival. It was a beautiful baby, tiny and perfect, with tight black curls and skin like milky coffee.

'What a little darling,' I said, picking up the baby's rattle and shaking it. The baby made a disconnected grab and missed.

'Just like a little mommet, in't 'e?'

'What's his name?'

'Arthur,' answered Josie, with a stubborn defensiveness, 'after his grandad.'

'That's nice. And do you like having a baby brother?' I asked the little blonde girl who held Josie's hand with the tenacity of an octopus. The child just stared back at me with her mouth open. I never was any good at talking to children.

Miss Casemore wasn't around any more to

twitch her lace curtains and shake her stick at boys who bounced balls against her garden wall, but her brother had come out of retirement to teach again when his younger replacement had joined up. Stan Doughty was a PoW, so far as anyone knew anything about him – poor boy, somewhere in Malaya. The two Thurlow boys and Dennis Rudge would never come home.

Everything was the same and yet subtly different. The canes that had supported Mr Kimber's prizewinning sweet peas carried runner beans now. There would be no Victoria sandwiches, with equal weights of butter, sugar, eggs and flour, at the produce show, only eggless, fatless, sugarless wonders. The women who won prizes now could really call themselves good cooks.

The traffic was much heavier. Before the war, there'd been a tractor or two, maybe a delivery van, Dr Gatehouse's car and that was all. Now military traffic roared along the narrow lanes, forcing cyclists into the hedges. The sky was riven by the white vapour trails of aircraft.

I called into the shop. Abbie was behind the counter, trying to serve two Americans, who lounged across the scarred mahogany. Somehow, they seemed to take up more room than British soldiers. Their voices were louder, their bottoms, for some reason that I couldn't fathom, seemed bigger and their trousers tighter. They all seemed to walk like Robert Mitchum. Fighting with the everyday shop smell of carbolic, boiling beetroot and mice, they had brought the smell of aftershave, chewing gum and Lucky Strikes, the

174

scent of luxury.

'Of course I haven't got any scented soap,' Abbie was saying, as patiently as though she spoke to a not-very-bright child, 'and I haven't got any handcream, neither. This is Ansty Parva, you know, not Hollywood. Nor the Post Exchange, neither. We don't have that much of a call for it – there's no beauty queens in this village!'

'You're surely right there, ma'am,' replied one of the GIs.

'Cheeky monkey!'

'Come on, now, ma'am, have a heart,' wheedled the shorter of the two. He leaned towards Abbie in a friendly manner. 'How'm I supposed to impress my lady friend? All you English ladies expect a Yank boyfriend to be a cross between John Wayne and Santa Claus. Now, if you look at me, you'll surely see that I'm no John Wayne.'

I couldn't help giving a little, snorting giggle. Gosh, he was right there. He looked more like Edward G. Robinson! His companion turned round and gave me a long, assessing stare that finished at my ankles. His jaws were slowly moving, like a contented cow. He should have had a buttercup between his lips, not a matchstick.

'Here I am,' went on the little GI, 'stuck out in the middle of nowhere – I mean a cute little village like this – livin' in a goddam Nissen hut, no Post Exchange for miles, not even a Clubmobile or a doughnut dugout. Now, ma'am...' His voice dropped to a confidential whisper.

'What have you got on your shelves that'll make a nice young English girl take pity on a lonely guy like me?'

'Well, if I was you...' Abbie looked carefully around the shop. 'I'd take them something to eat. Get the mother on your side first, before you do try to get your feet under the table, if'n you knows what I mean. That's half the battle, I always says. Now, it just so happens that I got a little spot of something nice...' She slapped a greaseproof paper package on the counter. 'Pork chops. Now if these don't have 'm eating out of your hand, I don't know what will, really I don't. That'll be 10/6 to you.'

I drew in my breath in horror. I'm surprised the soldiers didn't hear me. 10/6? More than five days' pay for a British private soldier.

The GI took a handful of change out of his pocket. 'I don't get the hang of your funny money yet. Take it out of that, will ya.'

Abbie whisked away most of the coins and put them, not in the till, I noticed, but in a side drawer.

'How about it then, Duchess?' The other American, silent until now, took the matchstick out of his mouth and winked at me. 'How about you an' me seeing the sights together?'

I put my hands on the counter, so that the sun highlighted my wedding ring and struck rainbows from the opal that James had given me. Unlucky, Vee had called it, and we had all laughed at her. James had said that he didn't need to believe in omens – he had me for his good luck charm.

176

'That's very kind of you,' I answered in my most frozen voice. 'I'm afraid that I'm not able to accept.'

'What hubbie don't know, hubbie can't grieve over,' he laughed.

'Now that's quite enough of that,' said Abbie, sharply. 'I'll have none of that dirty talk in my shop – and to a widow, too. Her husband died for his country when you two was still polishing your boots on the other side of the Atlantic.'

'I get it,' said the soldier who'd bought the chops. 'You don't like our company, but our money's good enough for you.'

Even Abbie looked embarrassed and I wished myself a million miles away from the shop.

'No offence, young man?'

'None taken, ma'am.'

When they'd gone, Abbie came round the counter and gave me a hug. 'You'm a breath of fresh air, you. How long you got this time?'

'Abbie – 10/6 for chops? Off the ration? You'll get into terrible trouble.'

'You got no cause to stick your nose in the air, miss,' she scolded, but I could see that she didn't hold it against me. 'Where d'you suppose they chops come from? If your gran chooses to kill a pig or two when the inspector's not looking, that's none of my business – and none of yourn, neither, if it comes to that. She'll tell him it was struck by lightning in that storm last week.'

'But that's ... that's black-marketeering.'

'Spirit of free enterprise, she calls it, says that Francis Drake was a pirate by any other name and Frank agrees and so do I. So make what you

177

like of that. I don't know. Such a fuss about a liddle bit of meat.'

Everything was the same and not the same. Tom's secret drinking had come out into the open. Mother was living on her nerves and wouldn't admit it. Grandmother seemed to have turned to racketeering, with Abbie as her eager acolyte.

Don't be so stupid, I told myself, how could you expect things to be unchanged? Are you the same girl who went away? Why should Ansty Parva be any different from any other place in Britain? Why should you imagine that time stands still here, just because you want it to? Can you put everyone to sleep for a hundred years, just by wishing? It was a sort of arrogance to believe that, of all others, only this one, deeply loved village would come through unscathed.

But, all the same, I had thought it and it was a shock to find that I'd been wrong.

Mrs Buckland popped up as though she'd been hiding behind her hedge all day, just waiting for me to pass.

'Laura – just the person,' she said in her breathless little voice. 'Come and have a cup of tea.'

'Well ... I...' I racked my brains. There must be *something* I ought to be doing.

'Now then, I won't take no for an answer. We haven't had a nice little chat for ages and the kettle's just on. Come along.' She swung open the gate for me. It sagged on its one hinge, scraping a groove along the path. 'Martin's home,' she added, dangling the words like a carrot in front of a donkey.

Inside, her cottage was as primly neat as I remembered. The same china figures stood on the same crocheted mats in precisely the same positions on the same highly polished tables as they had when I was a child. There was the giant cup and saucer, with *We'll tak' a cup o' kindness yet* written in loopy gold lustre letters round the rim. There was the little girl in nightgown and mob cap, climbing into bed. There on the mantelpiece was the spill vase, shaped like a tree trunk. Two curly china lambs crouched at its base.

Mrs Buckland might never have been away. She'd made the great journey to the city, to Winchester, hadn't liked it and had come back again, to resume life in Ansty Parva without a skipped heartbeat. Perhaps the net curtains weren't quite so stiffly starched – who could lay hands on starch these days? – but there were still scarlet geraniums in pots on the windowsills.

In fact, the kettle hadn't been on. It was just simmering on the edge of the stove, where it sat all day, every day, with just a thread of steam rising from the spout. Mrs Buckland quickly pulled it on to the hotplate. 'Martin'll be so pleased to see you, I know,' she confided. 'Martin ... Martin...' She rattled with just the tips of her nails on a closed door.

'Go away.'

'I can't so much as get into my own scullery when he's at home,' she said, with a half-apologetic, half-proud smile. 'Martin, Laura's here.'

'She'll have to wait. I can't come out now.'

His voice was exactly right – impatient, brisk, take-me-as-I-am-or-leave-me-alone. If he had rushed out at once and made a fuss of me, like everyone else seemed determined to do, I wouldn't have been able to cope with it. Being handled with kid gloves doesn't ease the pain, it simply makes the wound more sensitive. I felt like screaming whenever anyone asked, in that special, sympathetic voice reserved for the bereaved, how I was feeling now. But Martin treated me as an old friend should. I began, at last, to relax.

Behind the closed door, a tap was running. I couldn't hear anything else.

'I don't know – he used to be such a biddable little boy,' sighed Martin's mother, as though her son had only just been given his first pair of long trousers. 'Never gave a moment's trouble to his father and me. But when he's working on his pictures, he puts up the blackout and locks the door and I don't think Mr Churchill himself could get him out of there before he's ready.'

'I don't mind. Really.'

Mrs Buckland laid a tea tray with a lace-edged cloth and eggshell china, patterned with tiny violets. She pottered about, fetching a matching set of teaspoons and sugar tongs in a red leather box from the sideboard drawer. I'd have been happier with one of the blue-and-white striped mugs from the kitchen, but I'd never have dreamed of saying so. There were about a half dozen lumps of sugar at the bottom of the bowl. When she offered it to me, I shook my head.

'No, thank you. I don't seem to care much for

sugar any more.'

'So much better for the figure, dear, I always think. Mr Buckland always used to like me a bit on the plump side, if you know what I mean, but I'm not sure he was right. I feel much better for losing a pound or two. Girls nowadays all look so fit – such strapping young Amazons. Rationing is a blessing in disguise, in some ways.' There was a sound of a key turning in a lock. 'Oh, there you are at last, Martin. Not before time. Why don't you sit down and have a nice cup of tea with us.'

'Hello, Laura,' he said softly. His voice crept under my defences and touched me in a place that was still sore. Don't, Martin, don't let me start feeling sorry for myself. Please.

In that pretty room full of fripperies, he looked like an animal in a cage. He stood with his shoulders slightly stooped, his head bowed beneath sloping beams. He had lost his desert tan, but he was still as thin as he had been when I last saw him, that long ago evening in Alexandria, when I still had confetti in my shoes and a married lifetime ahead of me. Out of uniform – that bulky, scratchy, unflattering battledress – he ought to have reminded me of the Martin I used to know. He didn't. He was thin and tense and taut and utterly desirable. There were freckles of something purple across the front of his shirt – paint, perhaps, or dye or the chemicals he worked with. When I looked at him, I couldn't look away again.

'Well, if you won't sit down, why don't you show Laura your darkroom, or my scullery, I *should* say. Mind you, he takes a lovely photo,

181

though it's not for me to say it...'

'I'd like that,' I said, standing up quickly, to make it difficult for him to refuse.

The little room faced north, but with the blackout blinds carefully fixed and the windows closed it was stifling, with a smell that made my nostrils twitch, like the chemistry lab at school. There were trays full of liquid on an enamel kitchen table and one still in the sink. The tap dripped into it, slowly and irregularly. Martin had changed the single ceiling bulb for a red one. Clothes-pegged to a string around the walls hung half a dozen damp prints.

'There's not much to see,' he said apologetically. 'It's just a room.'

I nodded, not certain what to say. The pictures round the walls were a black-and-white blur. I stepped closer and saw that they were beautiful.

Here was Ansty Parva, preserved for ever. I saw the bold sweep, ridge and furrow, that followed Alfred Thurlow's plough, the squabbling gulls that trailed him across land his sons never now would farm. Enlarged and enlarged again, the chalky soil took on an enduring pattern that marched for miles across the downs of England, across land that had never been under the plough until now. I saw Dick Kimber splitting hazel rods, his clumsy fingers handling the cleaver with delicate sureness, for the half-finished sheep hurdle propped behind him. Stan Rudge, in ancient leather knee protectors like a horse's travelling boots, was halfway up a ladder with a bundle of long straw over his shoulder. There was Josie Shellard, transformed into a beauty because she smiled at her children, black and white, and Frank Horrell spreading a few tins and packets across the length of his empty shelves, making do.

It was as though Martin had been hurrying to capture all this while it was still there. I could sense the urgency that had pushed him on. The war had touched Ansty Parva. Tomorrow, next week, next year – the war would be over and we both knew that we would never go back to 1939 again.

There was the Green Dragon, the old men in collarless shirts and shapeless hats playing dominoes and paying no attention to the GIs clustering round the bar. There was Martin's mother, hanging washing in the garden and taking not a bit of notice of the convoy of tanks on the other side of the hedge. She was bracing herself to hoist the washing line into the wind with the clothes prop. A sheet was blowing back across her face and she was laughing.

I wanted to say how splendid they all were, the people I had known for as long as I could remember, but I didn't know any words that wouldn't sound patronizing.

Martin began to take down the blackout. His hands were brown and long-fingered, their backs dusted over with silky, black hairs. He pushed open the scullery window and the spicy scent of mignonette wafted in and clashed with the chemicals. There wasn't anywhere I wanted to be more than that drab little room.

Mrs Buckland popped her head round the door. 'I don't know what you two are finding to look at in there,' she said, with unsuitable coyness. 'It's only a room, after all. I'm off, anyway, down to the vicarage. We're rolling bandages. You'll find there's plenty of tea still in the pot.' She disappeared and then was back again, as though she was playing peek-a-boo with us. 'If you've got nothing better to do, Martin, why don't you show Laura your pictures from Egypt. She'd like that, probably, knowing it so well and all.'

'I don't think so,' said Martin, firmly.

'No, really, I...' I began, but she took me by the hand with a surprisingly determined grip and led me back into the sitting room.

'Now you just sit there,' she said, steering me to the sofa. She took down a portfolio from the bookshelves and laid it on my lap. 'There! I'm sure you'll find it interesting.'

And then, finally, she went off, carrying a basket of sheets, worn beyond repairing, to tear up for bandages.

Martin looked embarrassed. 'I'm sorry. She's not normally so ... so...' I sensed that he really wanted to snatch the portfolio back out of my hands.

'It doesn't matter.'

I flipped over a few leaves. Pictures leaped out at me, startling and immediate.

A column of soldiers, in solar topis and Bombay bloomers, on one of those terrible acclimatization marches, trudged along a dusty road and a column of camels swayed along in the opposite direction. Not one of the soldiers looked even vaguely interested.

184

A desert patrol brewed tea in a Benghazi cooker – a mess tin full of sand doused in petrol. Their faces were almost flayed by wind and sand, every crease filled with grit, noses, eyebrows, eyelashes; you knew that the tea would scald their cracked lips.

How strange that these black-and-white images were nearer to the truth than colour could ever be. They had a sharpness, a purity, that drew the eye and focused it on what was important, instead of letting it wander around a pretty coloured world. They had line and form and texture. I couldn't stop looking.

A column of tanks ran along the line between sand and sky, barely ahead of the sandstorm that you knew would catch them.

An ambulance was hopelessly bogged down, axle deep, while its crew sweated with spades and matting and its patients bled into the sand.

A dune was sculpted by wind, rippled like a beach, with a fringe of sand like foam scudding off the top. At the bottom lay all the detritus of war, inland beachcombings – barbed wire, shell cases, a spade, corned-beef tins, a helmet. A still life, meticulous, crisply shadowed, almost Dutch. Look again. There's a head inside the helmet.

Martin had left me. I could hear him tidying up his darkroom. I felt I ought to say something, but his view of war kept me silent and awed. I remembered the *taverna* in Alexandria and how Martin had scorned the set-up photograph. I had thought he was arrogant and now I knew that he was right.

'You don't have to do that,' Martin called

through. 'Stop when you're bored. I won't mind.'

A disabled tank, its tracks blown off. A soldier knelt on the turret and pulled one of the crew through the hatch. You knew he was dead. Dead is different from unconscious. Dead is empty. A soldier knelt on the turret and pulled an empty shell through the hatch. He put his hands under the dead man's armpits and strained to lift him. The body lay across his knees, arms outspread, a modern *pietà*.

The tenderness of the gesture transfixed me. The pity of it tore me. I closed my eyes and saw it still. The image was seared on my brain. Perhaps it always would be.

'Laura, are you all right?' Martin was talking to me and I couldn't answer. 'Laura? Laura... ?'

I couldn't breathe. My chest hurt. It was as though I had been squeezed dry. I began to shiver.

Martin took the portfolio from my fingers, closed it and put it back on the shelf. 'I'm sorry. I should have thought.'

I shook my head. 'It doesn't matter,' I said and the words came out more brusquely than I meant. 'I wish everyone would stop trying to protect me. I'm not the only woman in England to have lost her husband. Just ... just let me deal with it in my own way.'

'All right. I won't say any more. Is that what you want?' I nodded and he went on. 'Then come for a walk with me. I need to get the smell of hypo out of my nostrils.'

We climbed up on to the downs, up the zigzaggy path to the White Horse, faster and faster, Martin's long legs making nothing of the steep slope and my shorter ones going double time to keep up with him. Chalk powdered my shoes and dimmed the bright petals of poppies and knapweed.

There's a special kind of silence up there, a silence that isn't quiet. The wind that always blows across the top rustles the dried stems of grass, making them rattle. Up there, you can see the wind. It shimmers across the grass, flattening it like the pile of velvet when you sit on it. It turns up the undersides of leaves and flips them back again, a green and white flicker.

From the top, the White Horse stretched long, out-of-proportion legs back down the slope. He was tufted with neglect, shaggy with grass, needing a good clip, like an old horse in winter turned out in a field without a rug. His beady eye grew long, green tears.

We sat by his ears, on rabbit-nibbled grass that was starred with tiny flowers, sainfoin and bugloss, scabious and fairy flax, magical names. I tucked my knees against my chest and cradled my arms around them. If I looked towards the village, from here it hadn't changed at all.

Black and white walls, catslide roofs, thatch green with moss on the sunless slopes; redbrick school in black asphalt playground; church and vicarage rather aloof, making villagers come to God, rather than going to meet them; Ansty House looking the other way, as usual. From here, I couldn't see the struts that buttressed the corner of the Pocknells' cottage. A chunk had been knocked off by a tank that didn't quite make the bend. Old Mrs Pocknell had taken her stick to the driver when he called to apologize.

But if I looked beyond the village, the changes were plainer, The lanes had been widened to take the extra weight of tracked vehicles, the verges had been stolen to make passing places and the new concrete edgings were very obvious, very brash. The hedges were gone between Upper Horseleaze and Lower Horseleaze and between Great Croft and Little Croft, I suppose to make the fields easier to work with tractors. Lambpit Copse, that circle of elms in the middle of a field, had gone altogether. Where would the rooks build their nests now? And if I looked the other way, the Nissen huts of the American camp scarred the land irrevocably.

'I love it here,' Martin said, quietly. 'I love the space, the silence, the changing shapes of the clouds, the shadows running across the vale. This is the only place I want to be, when it's all over.'

'When it's all over ..' The words sounded impossibly good. 'I can't think that far ahead.'

A flight of C-47s, Dakotas, droned only a little above our eyeline, practising hedgehopping to avoid enemy spotters. I could see the first paratrooper balanced ready in the open door. Even bulked in all his equipment, he looked very vulnerable, waiting for the red light to turn to green. The plane would rise to dropping height over the practice DZ and the jump master would shout 'Go, go, go', pushing a man out into the rushing air with every shrieked word, whether he wanted to go or not. I imagined the buffeting slipstream, the jerk·of harness that swung men like dolls, the bone-jarring impact. This was Wiltshire on a sunny day. What would it be like jumping into darkness, into occupied territory?

The spiralling lark was silenced by the roar of engines.

'Not long now,' said Martin.

'They'll be dropping on the Plain, I suppose.'

'No, I mean, not long until they go. The training and the waiting will soon be over.' He looked at my face and gave a quick smile. 'Don't look so shocked. I know your work is hush-hush, but the invasion's not that much of a secret. Everyone knows it's coming. If I had a long-range weather report and a tide table, I could work out the exact day for you. Think about it. What else is there to do?'

I could have told him the reason for my shocked expression. I had suddenly realized that he would be going, too. I had seen his pictures and I knew that he'd be there, whenever, wherever the landing might be, as far forward as he could get. And I didn't want him to go. Not Martin, too.

Don't go, I wanted to say, please don't go. But I didn't. No-one ever said that. It wasn't – it wasn't *done*. So I shut my mind to my fears and smiled back.

'I'm secretive by instinct. Close as a clam. It's second nature. Once in Intelligence, always in Intelligence, they say. The trouble is that Germans have weather reports and tide tables, too.'

'Probably.' We were sitting so close, I could feel the warmth of his body seep into mine. 'Laura, I

189

wanted to say ... I wanted to tell you ... I'm sorry about your husband.'

I looked away and nodded.

'I should have written ... I meant to write, but ... but I thought about you. I'm sorry.'

'It's all right.'

'He looked a fine young man.'

'He was. He was a very...' I could feel my voice beginning to break up, like a fading wireless signal. I took a deep breath. '...a very fine young man.'

'You must be very proud of him.'

'Yes.' More deep breaths. I must be calm. I must... 'Martin – that night in Alexandria – it was ... it was all we had. It was...' He put his arm around me. It was all bone and sinew, but warm, strong, living. 'Oh, God, Martin, I didn't love him enough. We only had one night and I didn't make him happy and then he died. Oh God, oh God, he deserved to be loved...'

'Sssh. Sssh. It's all right.' His other arm came round me, sheltering, safe. 'There. It's all right, my love. Cry if you want to.'

He rocked me like a baby and murmured sweet, incoherent words. With one hand, he gently stroked my hair. And I wept at last for James, for all that he might have been, might have had. I wept for the waste and the pity. I wept for myself, for my loneliness and guilt, for all of us. Tears that had been dammed for two years were hard and painful, a storm of grief. My breath came in fierce gulps. And then, at last, I was exhausted.

I sat with my head on Martin's shoulder and

felt an immense calm seep through me. His fingers still stroked my hair, with a light, tentative touch. He bent his head and softly, so softly, kissed my hair.

His voice was husky, as though he scarcely knew how to use it for gentle words. 'Laura – my love.'

Amazed, scarcely believing, I looked up at him and his mouth came down on mine. Once, twice, he kissed me gently, then he pulled me against him. Thin and hard and fierce, he made a demand and I answered. I opened to him and tasted the secret sweetness of his mouth. He took my breath away and gave me his own in return.

For just a little while, it felt the only thing to do, the right thing to do. I needed his strength to support me. His kiss was all I wanted, had ever wanted. It was Martin, always Martin...

Desire flickered through me, lightning without rain, a summer storm. His body was beautiful, hard and without pity and I burned where he touched. He laid me down on the sunburned grass and his shadow fell over me. I reached out to him, folding my hands behind his head, drawing him down to me. Always, always Martin...

I felt all the untouched, empty places open for him to fill. I wanted ... God, I wanted...

Then I began to struggle.

'No.' I tried to draw back, but his arms were too strong. 'Martin, no. It's not right. Please. Please, no.'

'Why?' His lips trailed softly down my neck, down to the hollow at its base, as though he would drink from it. Very slowly, one at a time, he began to unfasten the little pearl buttons down the front of my frock and he kissed each newly naked fragment of skin as it appeared.

'I can't – don't make me...'

'I'd never make you do anything you didn't want to do. Don't you trust me, Laura?'

He was kissing my soul away, he was stealing my mind. I shivered with a burning chill.

'Yes. No. I don't know. Don't, Martin, please...'

'Laura, I know you too well.' And now he held my face between his cupped hands. His eyes looked into mine – who said that only pale eyes are cold? – and he wanted the truth. 'I could feel what you were feeling. That wasn't just a kiss between two old friends. You wanted me as much as I want you. You can't take back what you gave me just now.'

'I don't want'

He took his arms away from me suddenly. I felt as though I had been set adrift.

'What?' he demanded.

'I can't...' It was too difficult to explain. I turned my head away and looked out over the valley.

I felt guilty. That was what I was trying to say. Even with Martin's lips on mine, I could still feel a phantom kiss that slid between us. I could hear a voice I hadn't heard for two years and it was saying, *I love you, Laura.*

One man had loved me and I had given him nothing in return. God forbid that I should do the same to another.

'I don't believe in ghosts, Laura,' Martin said as

he rose to his feet. He put out his hand to help me up and, when I was standing, let me go again, as though I had bitten him. 'Neither should you.'

There had been such a long gap that I didn't recognize the writing. It was tidier, less spidery, as though the writer might be afraid that I would throw the envelope away unopened. I wish I had. I did open it and when I saw what was inside, I fished the envelope back out of the bin again.

There was a photograph of a gravestone. That was all. The print was poor quality, fuzzy, probably very old. I couldn't read the name on the stone, but, given what the sender had previously written, the implications were clear.

I was looking at a picture of my father's grave.

I felt sick. It was as though my head had suddenly become a balloon, empty and airy, larger than life, bobbing on rigid shoulders. I was aware that I had hands and feet, because they were so cold, but nothing else registered. There was the balloon head, painted with a mask, a grimace, and there was the photograph.

I tried to think. What sort of malice must the sender be harbouring? How long had it festered? And why now, after all these years, more than twenty-five years after the death of the man at whose nameless grave I was staring?

It was a standard British war grave headstone, pale stone, a narrow oblong with a slightly curved top, in a row that rivalled the Guards Brigade for perfection of line. On either side, between it and the two part stones visible in the frame, grew daffodils, formally planted. There were no other clues. The setting was anonymous. Somewhere along the line of trenches that had marked the Western Front, somewhere between the sea and the Swiss border, this photograph had been taken.

I didn't feel so sick any more. But now I was afraid.

I pushed Button A in as far as it would go and heard the pennies rattle into the box.

'Martin? It's Laura.'

'Laura? Where are you?'

'I need to talk to you. Urgently. Can we meet?' A three-minute time limit made calls admirably brief. No beating about the bush. Is your call really necessary? 'I'm off duty at eight in the morning every day this week.'

'Then I'll come up to London. Can you get there? Day after tomorrow? No, sorry, I can't make it sooner and I can only manage an hour or two, then. I've got a picture assignment in Southam – somewhere on the south coast. What train will you be on? I'll meet you at the barrier.'

I was afraid that I wouldn't be able to find him. There was such a scrum at Euston. Amongst all that khaki and navy and air force blue, how would I be able to spot one man? The only easily recognized figures were the military police in red caps and blancoed belts, patrolling in pairs up and down the platform, on the lookout for deserters. There were American MPs too, 'snowdrops' they called them, in white helmets, belts and gaiters, with dangerous-looking white

194

truncheons. Everyone who possibly could, seemed to wear initials on an armband, a way of looking important, perhaps. MP; RP; MTO; RTO; FSP; CD; ARP. It was bewildering, like walking Scrabble.

As the train slowed down, servicemen flung open doors and jumped out. There's no time to waste if you're going on leave, no time to worry that you might hit someone on the platform with your carelessly opened door. Life's too short to waste hanging around, being thoughtful.

Doors thumped. Whistles blew. Passengers struggling to get out met passengers struggling to get in, under a curved roof that trapped smoke and steam beneath blacked-out glass panels. I was so worried about missing Martin that I tried to walk more slowly, but the crowd caught me and spun me and hustled me along, making me run, whether I wanted to or not.

Then the stream pushed me off its flood into a backwater, so I stood there for a while, watching. My eyes were scratchy from lack of sleep and railway grime. I could feel my hair slipping out of its tidy knot. Behind me, a toothy skull adorned with a pink hat grinned from an anti-VD poster. *Hello boy friend, coming MY way?* asked the skull. I moved on quickly. I couldn't stand under that poster, like death's sister.

Then I thought I saw him ahead, a tall sergeant, dark-haired, walking the wrong way, walking away from me. 'Martin,' I called and waved my hand. 'Martin, I'm here.'

'I know you are,' said a voice from behind, and Martin took my arm. He bent forward as though he were going to give me a quick kiss of welcome, but drew back again sharply.

It was so good to see him. Amongst the hellos and goodbyes, amongst all the embracing couples, we stood formally apart, a respectable distance between us. But when Martin smiled, I found a great, big, answering smile on my own face and couldn't understand how it got there.

We went out through Euston's great Doric arch and into a drizzly, wind-scoured street. It felt more like March than May. The taxi queue snaked away for several hundred yards, so we just kept on walking.

'Where are we going?' I asked.

'I don't know. Does it matter? Let's walk towards the park.'

There was just enough rain to slick the pavements over with dirt. I could feel the backs of my stockings being spattered with every step. I'd left BP straight after my shift had finished, without waiting for breakfast. It seemed a very long time since I'd even seen my bed. Martin's strides were long. I half-trotted to keep up with him.

The streets were like mouths attacked by a manic dentist. There were gaps, rotten stumps, smashed remains. A sound terrace might have a void in the centre where someone's home had been plucked out, or a solitary house might be all that remained habitable in a square. Scarcely a building that I saw was undamaged. There were shored-up gables and cracked façades, boarded-up windows and sagging roofs. The streets were cratered.

People went about their business paying no

attention to the damage. Their faces had a grim, tough, surviving look. They had no option but to get on with things so they got on. The alternative was unthinkable. A shopkeeper in a long brown overall stepped out to hang an OPEN notice on the door, but there was no door, so she pinned it to the door frame, instead.

I gawped like a tourist in hell. Until then, although I knew about the Blitz, I had not really appreciated what Britain had suffered while I was sunning myself in Cairo. I'd had an easy war. It made me feel ashamed.

'Are you hungry?' Martin asked, suddenly stopping outside a café on the edge of Regent's Park.

'I thought you'd never ask!'

Martin ordered tea and toast. 'I'm afraid that's all I can run to at the moment,' he said in apology. 'Pay day's tomorrow.'

Embarrassment made me brisk. 'Come on, Martin,' I answered. 'This is the army, remember – share and share alike. But I'm afraid that I'm no better off than you are.'

The tea was hot and strong and a gritty National loaf had never tasted better. There was pale margarine, pure grease, and we were offered a choice between marmalade that was mostly carrot and raspberry jam that was all parsnip and wood chips. We both wolfed it down.

Martin let me finish the first cup in peace, before he said, 'Well?'

'Yes.'

'Well, I'm here. What next?'

The windows of the café were steamed up,

hiding the bombed desolation opposite. On the counter, an urn was hissing. Everything was so ordinary – thick, chipped china, clumsy knives, someone's initials scratched on the table. It made me feel warm and safe. It made my suspicions absurd.

'Martin, how much do you know about my father?'

'Nothing.'

'But you must'

'Why must I? I can only have been – what? – two or three years old when he died.'

'I mean... Surely you've heard people talking – your parents, perhaps – or gossip or rumour. Something.'

He shook his head. 'Nothing. And if I had, I wouldn't listen and if I did, I wouldn't tell you.'

'Stupid of me. I'm sorry. I hoped ... I knew you wouldn't keep secrets from me, you wouldn't fob me off with lies. It's just that no-one else will tell me anything. I know nothing, *nothing* at all.'

'And it's important to you.'

'More and more. I want to know. I *have* to know.' He spread the last piece of toast with the last scrape of marmalade, halved it and popped one half on to my plate, then leaned forward with his elbows on the table. 'Tell me about it.'

Someone was willing to listen to me. Someone wanted to hear what I had to say.

And so I told him everything – almost everything. I told him about the three letters and the accusations they made. I told him about the way everyone in my family seemed to evade my questions. I told him that my father seemed to have had no existence outside the fact of my own physical presence. Without that, no-one would suspect that there had ever been such a man as Edwin Ansty.

Then I showed him the photograph.

'I don't mind admitting, it ... it shook me up for a bit,' I said in as calm a tone as I could muster. 'You see, I don't know *why*, or why now, and that worries me.'

He looked at it for a long time, holding it at arm's length, as though it was something distasteful, between the forefinger and thumb of each hand. After a while, he laid it on the table between us.

'And have you brought the other letters?' Martin asked.

'I burned them. Yes, I know–' he'd made a little, tutting noise of disappointment '–it was stupid of me. But they were so awful, so vindictive. They made me feel sick. I thought if I got rid of them, I'd get rid of the feeling – but I didn't.'

'Did you check the postmarks?'

'One I burned, one was smudged and the last one was simply London. No use at all, I'm afraid.'

'Paper?'

'Woolworth's.'

'Ink?'

'Blue washable.'

'Handwriting?'

'Illiterate – or meant to look that way.'

'And there's absolutely nothing individual, nothing worth noticing about them? Think hard.'

'Do you think I haven't?' I snapped. 'Do you

think I haven't pored over the damned things until my eyes have gone crossed?'

'I wish you hadn't burned them.'

'So do I. But I did and that's that. I don't need you to tell me it was stupid.'

'All right. What do you need me for?'

Coming from almost any other man, that would have been a leading question. I would have had a smart answer handy – the sort of services backchat that keeps a girl out of trouble. I looked at him quickly to make sure that it wasn't necessary, but this was Martin and it wasn't.

'I need to talk to someone.'

'And I'm handy – I'm not sure that I find that particularly flattering.'

'Martin, help me – please.' He put out his hand and stroked one finger down my cheek. I gave a little shiver. 'Let's go through the possibilities,' I said, quickly enough to disguise my reaction. I ticked them off on my fingers as we went. 'Some disturbed person?'

'Oh, yes – that would wrap up everything nicely. You wouldn't have to worry about truth or motives or anything inconvenient like that. It's so tempting, we'd better not be tempted by it.'

'I was afraid you'd say that. So it's someone I know. Someone in the village?'

'Well, that's a pretty wide net. Practically everyone you know lives there – family, friends – about three hundred people, at the last count!'

'You're not being very helpful,' I said, acidly.

'You're not giving me much to go on. Let's be more specific. Is it your mother?'

'Don't be ridiculous!'

'I'm not. I just don't have any faith in the dotty stranger theory. I have the feeling that whoever is doing this to you is someone very close, closer than you'd like to believe. Your grandmother?'

'Absurd. My father was her only son.'

'Your stepfather?'

I thought a bit more carefully this time. Tom? No. 'Definitely not. My father was his best friend. They were as close as Pansy and me.'

'OK – it's your turn. Who do you think it is?'

'Oh, Martin,' I sighed. 'This is silly. It's getting us nowhere.'

'I admit it is a bit like playing Murder in the Dark.'

'I know. Only one person is allowed to lie and that's the one you're looking for.'

Martin checked his watch. 'I haven't much time left,' he said. 'Why don't you give the photo to me. I'll see if I can have it enlarged or enhanced or something.' He looked at it again. 'You could expect a life of about twenty years from a print, unless it's been carefully prepared. After that, they begin to fade. The paper is coated with gelatin and silver salts and pollution affects the silver. This one can't be much more than twenty years old – when were the war cemeteries laid out? – but it's very faded already. It can't have been properly fixed in the first place. Too short a fix and they fade. Too long a fix and the print is bleached. Still... There might be some sort of clue in the inscription. I'm sorry. It's the best I can do. I wish I could have spent longer with you.'

I felt a sudden panic flood me. So little time to

waste, so much already wasted. 'It's stopped raining – nearly. Let's walk for a bit.'

We walked through the park for longer than we had meant to, past the ack-ack gun sites and the barrage balloon winches and children who should have been at school sailing model boats on the lake. Perhaps there wasn't a school left for them to go to. Somehow it seemed quite normal for Martin to take my arm. Everyone else seemed to be doing it. Why shouldn't we?

'What will happen if the zoo is bombed?' I asked. 'Will there be lions roaming the streets, picking off the alley cats?'

'Snakes sliding down drains and coming up plugholes?'

'Vultures eating the pelicans in St James's?'

'Zebras crossing?'

Sillier and sillier, children again. But we had left those days so far behind us.

'Where are you going next?' I queried. 'No, don't say. Stupid of me. Will it be overseas? Can you tell me that?'

'I really don't know, but I do know that I'm fed up making propaganda points. I've had it up to here. I want to take pictures for tomorrow, not for today.'

'You used to say you wanted people to feel and taste your pictures – do you remember?'

'That was a long time ago. God, I was a pompous little ass, always talking through a hole in my ... sorry, darkroom language.'

'Don't worry. I've heard it all before – usually from women!'

'The daft thing is that I still believe it. I'm going

to wangle a trip to wherever it takes to get the images I want. One day, people will want to look back – hard to believe now, isn't it? – and they'll have a right to see what really happened, not what some bowler-hatted stuffed shirt in the MoI thinks they should be allowed to see.'

'You haven't changed all that much, you know, since you were sixteen. Still the bright-eyed idealist.' I laughed.

'Still tilting at windmills, you mean. Do you remember, you and Kate gave me a camera case just before I left home?'

'I remember. Kate and I fell out over it.'

'I wish I could say I'd treasured it ever since. It was stolen a week later. Someone must have thought there was a camera in it. What a nasty surprise to open it and find my sandwiches.'

'Do you remember...?'

So much to remember. So much we had shared.

And when we got to Euston, it would have been quite normal for Martin to kiss me. Everyone else seemed to be doing it. Why shouldn't we? But he didn't.

I let down the window with a leather strap that covered my fingers in grease, and ignored the glares and elbows of others who wanted to stand where I was. My turn this time. I hung out the window and tried to hear what Martin was saying.

'We've been looking at this the wrong way round,' he shouted above the hiss of steam.

'We have?'

'You'll never guess who's been sending these

letters until you find out what they're trying to tell you. So listen.' The train began to move, pulling away from the platform, slowly at first, as the engine gave its first explosive gasps of steam. The grinding of wheels was louder than all the other sounds. All along the platform, people began to run, trotting along beside windows, using every last moment before goodbye had to be said. Martin ran along beside me. 'Think about it. When you've worked out what it is, you'll know who it is.'

I gave a little laugh. 'Oh, simple!'

The train picked up speed. I held out my hand. He reached out. His fingers just brushed the tips of mine. People on the platform began to drop back, waving, waving. Martin was caught up in a group of crying women. He couldn't get round them.

'Laura...' I heard him call and then I couldn't see him any more.

No seats, of course. Either you hung out the window saying goodbye or you arrived early, found a seat and sat in it, keeping it against all corners. A sailor patted his knee in invitation. I just smiled and wedged myself into a corner.

I had been less than honest with Martin. I'd told him that I hadn't a clue who'd been sending the letters. Strictly speaking, that was true. But I didn't tell him what I feared – and hoped desperately was wrong: that the anonymous sender was James's mother.

For some reason, I expected Martin to get in touch with me very quickly. Silly, really – we were all swept up in the unacknowledged preparations for the invasion of Europe, so why shouldn't he be? Yet I watched the post, fearing for one letter, hoping for another.

It was a fortnight before his letter arrived and another couple of days before I even had time to break open the envelope. By that time, American, British and Canadian troops had landed on the beaches of France.

BP was working extended shifts, giving the commanders in the field up-to-date information on German plans and reactions. Even Hitler's personal messages passed through us on their way to France. People said it would have been quicker for von Rundstedt to give us a ring to get his orders than to ring Berlin!

Bleary-eyed after a double shift, I sat on my bed to read Martin's letter at last, too tired even to throw myself down to sleep. My ankles were swollen from sitting so long without exercise. After hours operating the keys of a cipher machine, spasmodic pains shot through my wrists. Sometimes I'd wake in the night with pins and needles in my hands. I'd tried to pick up a cup of tea and had dropped it when my wrist gave way, spilling the tea down my skirt. Just as well NAAFI tea was never made with boiling water.

'Dear Laura,' Martin wrote and the brisk beginning depressed me, but what did I expect? I'd as good as told him to treat me like a friend and nothing more.

I return the photograph to you. The quality is so poor that I was unable to take a very much clearer print off it. However, I called in a few (quite a few, actually) favours and was able to have it looked at by the RAF photographic interpretation people. There's a very helpful WAAF flight commander at Medmenham... Well, anyway...

Even with their specialized equipment, they've been unable to decipher the whole inscription. They are used to dealing with vertical exposures, that is, pictures taken from directly above the subject. Their system doesn't work so well on what they call 'obliques'. They put two of my copy prints into their stereoscopic lenses without much hope of success. However, we were lucky. Some of the carved letters cast a shadow. From those, they have worked out some sort of result. The stone is probably engraved A SOLDIER OF THE GREAT WAR. The two part stones seen on either side also seem to have the same thing carved on them.

That's all. Laura, I'm sorry. I'm not sure if that will be disappointing, or a relief to you. You've probably already realized that this is not a picture of your father's grave. It is a grave of one of the thousands and thousands of men of all nationalities who were unrecognizable when they were buried. There is no visible background in the picture, no way of finding out where it was taken.

Whoever sent this to you is playing with you very cruelly. I dismissed the idea of it being a crank, but now I'm not so sure. Someone is trying to hurt you – we don't know who and we don't know why – and I don't want him or her to succeed.

What next? You could tear it up and do nothing.

206

Burn any future letters without opening them and don't give the sender the satisfaction of upsetting you. Knowing you, I don't suppose you'll do that.

If you are still determined to carry on – and I really don't think you should – then perhaps your best bet is to write to the Imperial War Graves Commission to find out where exactly your father is buried. They keep very precise records. If he has no known grave, he may be commemorated in some other way. This will also reveal his regiment and give you another channel to follow.

Be prepared for disappointment. Sometimes men just disappeared in the quagmire of the trenches and were never discovered or even missed for a long time. Regimental histories often have unexplained gaps. And don't forget there's a war on! People might just be too busy to bother to reply.

My strong advice is that you should do nothing. Someone is going to a great deal of trouble to upset you. Don't give him or her the perverted pleasure of knowing that you care.

I won't be able to be in touch with you for some time.

Yours, Martin

Did Mrs Kenton really hate me so much? Poor, bitter woman. I pitied her. She acted as though I had taken her son away from her, but why blame me? Because there was no-one else nearby to take the responsibility, I suppose. Patriotism was an abstract. Hitler was far out of her reach (though retribution seemed to be on his tail). But someone had robbed her of her son and I stood conveniently close for her to lash out.

207

I remembered her glare at me as we had stood in the Palace yard, admiring the bronze bauble that we had been offered in exchange for James's life. I had been a symbol to her – a symbol of loss. Two generations of her family had been wiped out in that burning gun tractor – her only son and the children that he would have had, beautiful children, the grandchildren that I had denied her.

No wonder she hated me. The more I thought about it, the more I could understand her twisted viewpoint. She had been robbed by me, so she would rob me of something in return. She would take away from me the father I had never known, the soldier, the hero. An eye for an eye, one hero in exchange for another.

Her loss had deranged her. How could I blame her?

Yet I was not prepared to stop looking for my father now. All my life I had wondered about him, had asked and never been satisfied. The need to know was like a hunger, never assuaged. Now, at last, prompted by a sad woman, I was doing something about it. I would follow some of Martin's suggestions. Follow up the what, he'd said, and it will take you to the who. Well, I already knew the who, but I was still going to chase after any clue that would help me find my father.

I read again the last sentence of Martin's letter. It was his way of telling me as much as he could. He'd got his wish. He'd wangled his trip. I didn't need to guess where he had gone. I wished Pansy had been near to put up a prayer for Martin's safety on the `Normandy beachhead. When she hadn't been around, I'd failed for James, but I knew she'd succeed.

Now that the secrecy was over, our newspapers trumpeted the successes in Normandy, while underplaying the problems. Berlin by Christmas! Signal traffic through BP scarcely diminished at all and we were all working flat out. What a ridiculous time to catch chickenpox! Mrs Granby's nephew was to blame. I thought he was rather a spotty little boy and put it down to a poor diet, but his spots were nothing compared to those I displayed two weeks later.

Infections raced like wildfire through the cramped and overcrowded huts at the Park, so I was given the option of military hospital, but was discouraged, as most of the beds were occupied by Normandy casualties or reserved for future ones.

'Your landlady will take care of you, won't she?' asked the MO, with more confidence than I felt. 'It's not a serious illness for children, but at your age you ought to be careful. If your temperature goes up or you start to feel pain anywhere, come back here. Put collodion on the spots, or calamine lotion if you can't get collodion, and try not to scratch too much. Keep away from your chums. I don't want an epidemic on my hands. Have you been eating properly? No, I thought as much.' He pulled down my eyelids. 'A bit anaemic, I'd say. Run down, but who isn't? Tell your landlady to make sure you get plenty of spinach!' He signed me off on generous sick leave. 'And don't come back until you're spotless.'

'You'll get shingles,' screeched Mrs Granby when I arrived back at an unexpected time in the morning. 'That's what happens to grown-ups what get the chickenpox. And when the spots meet round your middle, you'll die. I can't be held responsible. I'm as reasonable as the next woman, but no-one could expect me to be responsible for a case of shingles. You'll have to go home.'

I didn't feel too bad when I left her, but by the time I reached home I felt as though Mrs Granby's predictions were about to come true at any moment.

Tucked up in my own narrow little bed under the eaves, with an extra pillow and a hot-water bottle, I thought even shingles would be worth while, since it had got me home. I slept and slept.

The trouble with chickenpox is that you're not actually ill for very long. You may have a face like a steamed pudding – and how long it had been since we'd tasted one of those, thick with sultanas, swimming in custard, the stuff of dreams – but you're not ill, just itchy and irritable.

On the first day, I lay in bed and was pampered by Mother. She ran herself ragged for me and got very little gratitude for it. On the second day, I got up after breakfast in bed and loafed around, getting in everyone's way and being thoroughly unpleasant. On the third day, Vee walked in the door.

'Well, you look like a wet washing day, and no mistake,' she greeted me.

She looked sleek as a pussycat, round in all the right places, her wild hair tamed under a pert hat. She wore an elegant, summer-weight tailormade, coral-pink, that must have cost whole barrowloads of coupons. Like many plump girls, she had beautiful ankles and they were set off by peep-toed wedges and nylons – real nylons. It was enough to make a girl's mouth water!

It was so wonderful to see her. I burst into tears.

'Dry up,' she said, putting her arms around me. 'I don't look that bad, do I?'

'Terrific.' I blew my nose loudly. 'You look simply terrific. Where on earth did you spring from?'

'From your gran's. She's a card, isn't she? I'm a married woman now, you know.' She held out her left hand. Her wedding ring was broad enough to fill the gap between the knuckles. Her nails were filed and beautifully painted. 'My Carlton was posted down here – the GI camp on the hill, you know – before D-Day and I thought, I'd better make the most of him before he goes, in case he doesn't come back again. Then I remembered what you told me about your gran taking in lodgers, so here I am.'

'I'm so pleased to see you,' I said and my eyes began to water again. 'Oh dear, what a drip I am. Sorry, I'm not usually like this.'

'You're tired out, I expect. Well, we all are, especially your mum, but having spots must be the last straw.'

'And you'll catch it too, now. Oh, dear.'

'I've had it already and the sooner Jennifer gets these things over and done with, the better, I say.'

'Jennifer?'

'She's down the vicarage playing with Pansy's Jonathan. Eighteen months old and another one on the way.' She patted her tummy. It didn't yet have the teeniest bulge. 'That's what comes of making the most of Carlton before he went!'

We both giggled. It was so good to see her. I began to feel as though I might live, after all.

'Jonathan's a lovely little boy,' Vee remarked. 'And doesn't he look the image of ... just like his mum.'

I thought it had been my imagination. I had seen it only because I feared to – or wanted to – I hadn't yet worked out which. But I knew by the way she blushed that Vee had seen the resemblance, too. Jonathan was beginning to look just like my dead husband.

I didn't get well as quickly as I'd hoped. I wasn't ill, but I just wasn't getting any better, either. I couldn't summon up the energy to do much more than sit in the sun and watch the children playing in the sandpit that Tom had made for them.

Jennifer, though younger, was bigger and more boisterous. She was a bouncy, fizzy replica of her mother, though Vee swore she was the image of Carlton. 'She's got his toes, bless her,' she said, with a soppy expression on her face.

Jonathan was small and slight, but with a determined manner that meant he more often got his own way than the bigger girl. Sometimes

I saw in him the young-old puckish look of Mr Millport, who had welcomed his grandson with love and understanding that was truly Christian. Sometimes he looked so like James, I couldn't bear to watch him. I felt bitterly betrayed.

If Mrs Kenton ever knew that Jonathan existed, if she had the smallest suspicion – no matter on what slender evidence – that James had had a son, nothing would keep her away.

Did Jonathan have a right to be introduced to two more grandparents? Would they make him happier? Did Pansy really need an ersatz mother-in-law? Did I have any justification to meddle? Maybe he wasn't James's son, after all, and the resemblance was only the one that all healthy, brown-haired young men have to each other. Maybe I saw the resemblance because it was what I feared – or wanted. Round and round like a wasp in a bottle. What was for the best? I sat in the sun and hesitated and nursed my sense of loss.

They were so beautiful, not because they were special, but simply because they were not special. Two ordinary toddlers, with sticky mouths and sand in their hair. They made me believe that the world might return to normal, one day.

The lanes were dusty green and quiet again. The skies were dusty blue and silent. The instruments of war had moved on and left Ansty Parva as peaceful as it had been before they came. When I closed my eyes, I could almost believe that nothing had happened at all. I could believe that Pansy was untouched and James was an unknown young man, something in the City, and I wasn't being tormented by a disturbed woman and Martin wasn't fighting his way through Normandy with a camera instead of a gun. But then the children would yell and I'd open my eyes again.

We three sat in the sun, lazy as cats, and pretended that we were busy watching the children. Most of my scabs dried over and began to drop off, leaving red marks that would fade in time, though they were hideous at the moment. I'd tried so hard not to scratch, but I was left with a little, pitted scar just below the hairline and another above my left eyebrow.

'Could be worse,' said Vee. She turned my face to the sun, pushed back my hair and stared intently. 'A blind man running for his life wouldn't notice them.'

'Think about all those Elizabethan ladies, slapping white lead on their faces to cover the pox holes. It killed them,' said Pansy, comfortingly. 'How odd to think that our children will grow up in a new Elizabethan age. Will it be another golden age, do you imagine? Will there be fine new houses to replace the bombed slums, and clean streets and fresh air and good food for everyone?'

'Fat chance!' laughed Vee.

'Or do you think that in another twenty-five years Jennifer and Jonathan and all their friends will be fighting for their lives?'

Pansy's eyes rested on her son with an avidity that was almost frightening.

'God forbid,' I said with a shudder.

'Well, if they are, we will be again, too,' Vee

214

reminded us. 'So we'd better make sure we finish the job properly, this time round. We might not get another chance.'

'The trouble with living in the country,' Vee announced a day or two later, 'is that it's too nice. I'm getting soft. There's nothing to bite on, if you know what I mean.'

'If you mean that it's more fun living in London and waiting for a doodlebug to drop on your head,' Pansy answered, 'then I don't believe you.'

'Don't be daft. I'm a lady in waiting now, don't forget. Bumps in the night are bad for my system. But I think I'm going to look around for a little job until Carlton comes back, just a few hours a week, maybe, if there's such a thing in the back of beyond. I've had enough of being Laura's gran's PG. I know she looks down on me—'

'Vee, she doesn't,' I protested, horrified that Vee might think it, but knowing it was probably true. 'What has she said to upset you?'

'Nothing, nothing ... it's just that – you know – all those pictures and medals and weapons and things, they weigh you down in the end. Those whiskery old men look down from the walls and say, "Who do you think you are, parading up and down my corridors, like Lady Muck? You may pay for your keep, but you'll never belong." Snooty old buggers. I'm sorry, Laura, but there it is.'

'Don't go, Vee, please,' pleaded Pansy, her pale eyes troubled. 'It's been so lovely, having you here.'

'If Grandmother's been rude to you, I apolo-

215

gize,' I said, stiffly. 'She doesn't mean half what she says. It's just her way. I'm used to it and it upsets me pretty often, too.'

'It's not just that. I don't feel useful enough, that's all. You're going back to playing soldiers, any minute now. Pansy practically runs her dad's parish for him, these days. Grace is driving fuel convoys in France. There's nothing for me to do. No GIs to make coffee and doughnuts for any more. No Carlton to keep happy. I feel like a ... a peapod, sitting in the sun, getting slowly bigger and bigger, until one day ... pop!'

She blew her cheeks up and made a disgusting noise. She looked so funny. 'Pop!' shouted Jennifer and blew a volley of raspberries, even better than her mother's. We all started to laugh.

'If it's a job you want, come and watch me sort out the attic,' I suggested. 'Grandmother's got another bee in her bonnet since the doodlebugs began. I tell her they haven't the fuel to get this far, but she's determined. She thinks that all that rubbish in the roof is like living with an incendiary device on top of our heads, just waiting to go off. One spark and...! Says she read in a leaflet that only two inches of sand spread on the attic floor will save her from being fried in her bed. She seems to think that Goering's got Ansty Parva marked on his list for the next big raid.'

'You'll never sort all that out on your own,' Pansy said. 'It'd take a regiment.'

'I promised her I'd take a look, anyway, and tell her what I thought. I just haven't had the energy until now. There's no saying what's stacked away. I haven't been up there in years.'

Vee looked along the length of the house, unbroken space, dim as under water. 'Dust of ages, spread for me...' she warbled, in a choirboy's treble. 'I think I'd better tell you, straight off, that if there's bats up here, you won't see me for dust!'

A row of bull's-eye windows, higher than our heads, lit the cobwebs that festooned their frames, lit the roofline and left the floor in shadow. A blocked gutter or a cracked downpipe, most likely both, had left a mildewed stain down one wall. White fungal threads crept along the floorboards, fanning out from the stain. Ivy had burrowed under the tiles and marched across the roof, sunless and bleached, a ghost tree.

We weren't able to raise our voices above a whisper.

'Laura – you can't,' said Pansy. 'It hasn't been touched for generations.'

'Spread two inches of sand on these boards and it'll end up in the cellar, quick as you like,' Vee commented, hacking at the floor with a heel.

'I can tell Grandmother that she's absolutely right – if Goering sends a thousand-bomber raid this way, we've had it! She'll be quite pleased, really. She always likes to be right. And if the bombers don't get us, the dry rot will. But there's nothing we can do about it, so let's go. It's stifling here under the tiles.'

'Oh, Laura, wait. Look at this.' Pansy stroked the mane of the rocking horse as though she'd found a real pony stabled under the roof. He was a spirited dapple grey, with a rolling brown glass eye – only one – the tip missing from his right ear and a bandage tied round one fetlock. His red leather saddle was crumbling round the edges, pitted with worm. 'He's so beautiful. You don't suppose... D'you think...?'

'You can have him and welcome. His name's Donald. But I'm afraid he'll probably fall apart between here and the vicarage.'

'No, he won't. I'll make sure of that.'

'I had all new for Jennifer, nothing but the best,' Vee told us as she ran a distasteful finger over the scarred body and, coming from anyone else, the remark would have infuriated me. 'You ought to get the Sally Ann in to clear this lot. *My* gran wouldn't give it house room.'

Pansy looked so embarrassed at having been caught coveting someone else's property. She seemed to class my grandfather's old rocking horse along with her neighbour's ox, ass, maidservant and wife.

'That's all very well for some,' I remarked crisply. 'We can't all marry Texan millionaires. I sometimes wonder if you've forgotten what it's like out here in the real world, Vee.'

But she wasn't listening. 'Here, just look at this,' she exclaimed. 'I can't believe women were ever so tiny. She only comes up to my shoulder. Isn't she cute?'

A dressmaker's dummy wearing a half-finished crinoline stood in a corner, a silent watcher. The colours of the gown had faded along one side, but towards the back they still blazed, arsenic green and royal purple plaid, fit for a visit to Balmoral. A veil of cobwebs, frail as old lace,

218

hung around her shoulders.

Vee's interest was caught by what she had thought was a pile of dirty old jumble. She began ferreting around in a corner. 'This is better than all those stuffy old warriors downstairs. Let's see what else we can find.'

'Vee, be careful,' I warned. 'I don't know how safe the floor is.'

'Nonsense, safe as houses. Give us a hand with this.'

The trunk was full of architect's plans. 'Look, it's here, it's Ansty House,' I said, holding up a linen page to catch the poor light. The ink was dimmed to sepia, the drawings laid out with a nib no stouter than a whisker. 'Here's the front – the steps and the portico –and here we are, behind this row of round windows at the top.'

'Then what's this lump at the top?' asked Pansy.

'It's some sort of dome. Isn't it hideous? We must have run out of money before it could be built. Just as well, really.'

The plans weren't interesting enough for Vee. She gave them a quick glance. 'Fancy that,' she said and then went on to something else.

There were chewed dog baskets and broken dog leads, thongless hunting crops and a hunting bowler smashed on one side – I wondered what had happened to the head inside it. There were alphabet bricks, but only nineteen of them, and headless dolls like guillotine victims. There was a cradle riddled with woodworm and a bicycle with pedals directly cranking the front wheel. There were stringless racquets and split polo sticks and handleless mallets. There were tea chests full of nameless horrors – moths, maggots, mildew, mice, shredded paper, chewed fabric. There were corpses of spiders, spindly husks. Where had all the living ones gone?

There were trunks and trunks of books, musty and spotted, some nibbled by mice, smelling, somehow, quite dead. They were so dull – sermons, bound minutes of meetings of the Wiltshire Archaeological Society, self-published adventures of various ancestors, with titles like *With Rod and Gun in Hindustan* and *Tales of a Simple Soldier.*

'It's so sad.' Pansy sat cross-legged on the floor, looking not much older than twelve. She had cobwebs in her hair, like a Victorian lace cap, but I didn't like to mention it in case it scared her. 'All these people have gone and this is all that's left.'

'That's normal,' I answered.

'Yes, but what's left is so dull. I don't mind dying and I don't mind people looking through my things after I'm dead, but I absolutely hate the idea of people saying that I must have been so terribly boring.'

'Oh girls, look at this. These aren't boring,' shrieked Vee. She held up a pair of enormous white cotton drawers. 'I take it all back. They weren't tiny at all. D'you think these belonged to the little lady over there when she got a bit bigger?'

The drawers would have wrapped twice round Vee in her early state of pregnancy. We lifted out cotton chemises and red flannel petticoats and

220

corsets with removable floral covers and quilted petticoats with stiffened hems padded with horsehair. Underneath were nightgowns and négligés, indecently filmy, and bed wraps with swansdown collars and Kashmir shawls, fine enough to pass through a wedding ring. There were dozens of linen handkerchiefs with an elaborate initial 'S' in one corner. There were stockings with embroidered clocks. Everything was beautifully preserved in a trunk lined with cedar wood and with all its seams made airtight with lead. Everything was new.

'It's a trousseau,' whispered Vee. 'And it's never been used. But they're all so enormous.'

'Even big girls get married.'

'But she didn't, did she? Oh, dear... Poor thing...' Vee's easy, ready tears slipped down her cheeks.

'Let's put them back,' suggested Pansy. 'I feel embarrassed. It's like being a peeping Tom.'

Sobered, we folded the garments back into the trunk and shut it carefully.

'There's no point in rummaging further,' I said. 'It's all rubbish – well, most of it, anyway. I'll tell Grandmother that it couldn't possibly be cleared, but if we keep some buckets of sand and some beaters up here, it should be all right. I can't believe there's any real danger.'

'The children will be awake and howling to get out of bed by now, anyway. We ought to go downstairs,' agreed Pansy. 'And I've got the Mothers' Union coming to discuss servicemen's wives' morals at four o'clock – boring old busybodies. What a cheek! I'd like to see them bring

221

up a family on twenty-five bob a week. They look at me and then at Jonathan and they purse their tight little mouths, as though they're choking on the words. I hope they don't expect any tea, because there isn't any.'

'Let's just have a last look over here,' Vee suggested. 'It doesn't look as old as the rest.'

She hauled out another trunk, a tin one, black japanned, very battered, but clearly more modern, and opened it before I had time to protest. On top was a uniform.

'It's not that old,' she said, holding up the tunic. A captain's service dress – three pips on the shoulder, not the cuff, so belonging to the second half of the Great War, and the collar dogs missing – and underneath lay a pair of riding breeches, paler in colour, buff not khaki. There was tissue paper between each fold and a strong smell of mothballs. 'D'you know whose it is, Laura?'

'No. No idea. Let's go downstairs.'

I didn't know, but I had made a sudden and unwelcome guess.

'I recognize this ribbon,' said Vee, pointing at a white-purple-white scrap above the left breast pocket. 'It's the MC. And it has a little silver rose on it. That represents a bar, doesn't it? He was a brave man, whoever he was.'

'Vee – I said, let's go,' I snapped and turned my face away from the startled looks of my two friends.

All these years, I had wanted to know, and now – now I wanted her to shut the trunk again.

It was like a magnet, drawing me to the attic. I

understood how Pandora must have felt. She could no more have ignored that box than she could have flown and then – and then we all know what happened.

I lay in bed, listening to the squeaks and scrabbles of the mice in the thatch. Double Summer Time twilight still lingered in the west. I could hear the crunch of Tom's boots on gravel, as he came in from a last visit to the lavatory at the bottom of the garden. He banged the back door shut, banged the windows shut, stomped upstairs. He wasn't drunk, but I wasn't certain that he was completely sober, either. He and Mother spoke quietly for a little while, high and low tones alternating, absurdly like a ventriloquist and his dummy. Then there was silence.

Under the roof, the heat of the day was trapped, like tea under a tea cosy. I got out of bed again to push the little window back on its hinges as far as it would go. The night was no cooler than the day. The garden was full of the noises of tiny creatures killing and eating and copulating. I took off my pyjamas and leaned, naked, head and shoulders out the window. Who would see me? Who cared?

Under the roof of Ansty House, in the musty, airless heat, the trunk sat, daring me to open it, daring me to question the past.

First the uniform. Not a shock, now – a known, anticipated thing, but still possessing the power to hurt. If I had ever suspected its existence, I would never have expected it to be so carefully packed.

I might have thought it would be hastily shoved into a trunk, out of sight, out of mind, like its wearer. It would have had a presence, then. It would have had creases at the elbows and knees, perhaps some stains – mud, the last meal, even (why not?) blood. It would have had bulk, would have held a shape, the last shape of the man who wore it. It would have told me something.

Instead, it had been meticulously laid away. Sponged, pressed, swathed in tissue, protected by camphor, all physical evidence of its owner had been expunged.

No chance that anyone, friend or foe, would see a light up here. I pulled the shielding tissue paper from my torch to take a closer look. The sleeves were slightly frayed at the cuffs. The suede knee patches of the breeches were shiny with wear. He had been tall and slight. Apart from that, the uniform was as characterless as though it had come freshly from the tailor. The tailor's label was still inside an inner pocket. *E J T Ansty* was written in indelible ink above an address in Dover Street.

I was like a sneak thief, like one of those villains who terrorize old ladies and escape with a sack marked SWAG. There was an intruder above my grandmother's head, prying into secrets she had shielded for more than a quarter of a century, rummaging and soiling and despoiling her perfect packing. I felt unexpectedly ashamed.

Beautiful boots, shining brown as conkers, still supple within waxed paper, kept in shape by hardwood trees that were slotted like a jigsaw puzzle, with little brass loops at the top to assist in their removal. These boots had been made for long, slender calves and long, narrow feet. I ran my fingers gently down the leather, trying not to leave sweaty fingermarks on their gloss. How had my dumpy grandfather and my petite grandmother made this long-legged boy between them? *Like you,* my mother had said, long ago, *or rather, you are like him...*

My father. I was getting a picture of him now.

And underneath, all the requisites of a military life: hat; gloves; cane; shirts with a Jermyn Street shirtmaker's label, soft collared, of a colour between cream and buff. Everything was marked, like a schoolboy's belongings. *E J T Ansty.* He was a real person.

I was sweating quite badly and my breathing seemed too haphazard to fill my lungs. I was beginning to be afraid of what I might find. I had a horror of finding something too intimate, something final.

Suddenly, there came into my mind two pictures of James: the well-dressed, well-pressed young subaltern in a Cairo nightclub; the dirty, smelly, unshaven soldier in a sheepskin waistcoat and dusty boots, driving straight out of the desert and into my arms.

I understood. These were not the clothes my father would have worn in the trenches. There, he would have been as filthy, as lice-ridden as anyone else. My grandmother had preserved the image of the soldier. She had not been able to lay hands on the man himself. I would not be shocked by anything in this trunk. He had not died in these clothes.

225

All the same, my hands were shaking.

And now, I seemed to have reached the bottom. There was a sheet of lining paper over a firm foundation. No, it wasn't far enough down. The trunk was deeper than that. I moved to get into a better position. My feet crunched a scattering of mothballs, releasing a smell pungent enough to make my eyes water. There was a fitted tray that could be lifted out.

I reached in and felt paper packets in a layer over the bottom. Neat bundles, all the same size, letters tied with faded tape, dozens of them.

I took out at random three or four of the bundles, then tried to fit everything else back into the trunk. I did my best, but it was impossible to fold and pack it all with the same accuracy. I felt vaguely ashamed of my slapdash efforts, as though I had defiled a sanctuary.

This was *my* family home. These were *my* father's belongings. Then why did I feel guilty, as though I were a little girl doing something that would make my grandmother very angry? She had wrapped her son in mothballs, stowed him away and closed the lid. There had to be a reason.

Dear Mother,

Nothing much happened this week. I was given Bene ++ for Latin. Mr Cartur askd if I copid. He is a swine. Thier are lots of conkers in Mr Butler's garden. I was beatten for being out of bed after ligts out, but it did not hurt much. Can you please send anothur cake. The chaps voted the last one ripping.

Your loving son,
Edwin

226

Dear Mother,

I hope you and Father are well. I am well. Not much is hapening here, but we all have to rite home on Sundays so that is what I am doing at the moment. Has Madge had her puppys yet? Father said I culd have the pick of the liter for my own. We had a run to Loader's Wood and back after lunch. It was kiling. There is a new boy called Tom Roding. His people live in India. He is a first class drip. Everyone says so, so it must be true. I woud like a penknife for my birthday, if you please.

Your loving son,
Edwin

Dear Mother,

Thank you for the jam. Mrs Ruggles makes the best jam in the world. Everyone says so, so she oat to be jolly pleasd. We had a mental arithmatic test on Friday. It was very hard and I came second botom. Tom was bottom and erned a beating. It was jolly hard luck. He is relly quite decent. The food is pig swill. We are going to run away. Please send Ruggles to meet us at the station. I am ink monitur this week.

Your loving son,
Edwin

Dear Mother,

It is ripping being in a senior house. We do not have to get out of bed so early. The sprogs bring us tea in bed. We had a hare and hounds chase yesterday. I was the hare. I led them a pretty dance, I can tell you. They lost my trail beyond Cooper's Farm and I was back at school with my feet up before the hounds

227

*found it again. We had toast and honey for tea. Tom
was flogged yesterday for persistent untidiness. I think
the Magister was very unfair, but Tom never minds a
flogging. He earns one nearly every week for
something or other. He is rather cut up about his
mother and not going to the funeral and all that. May
he come home with me at Easter? I find myself rather
short at the moment. Would you please send me a
postal order, for 5/-, if possible. I lent a chap some
money so that he could treat his cousin to tea and he
has not paid me back yet. I expect he will. Anyway, I
was invited to tea too, so that is all right. His cousin
is called Diana and she is not bad. Please give my
regards to Father.*

Your affectionate son,
Edwin

There were so many letters, all carefully arranged
in date order and tied with tape. Each bundle
was labelled with the year in my grandmother's
bold writing. Every Sunday, he had told her, we
have to write home and here they all were, not a
Sunday absent, not a week missing. The only
gaps were during school holidays. If I had crept
into the attic every night for the rest of the year,
I should not have been able to read them all.

The boy's voice filled my ears. He was so clear
in my imagination – tall, long-legged, captain of
the cross-country team, only moderately bright,
but generous and immensely good humoured. A
mother could be proud of a son like that. I could
almost see him. He was always just there, at the
corner of my eye, not quite in sight, not quite out
of sight. Look – there, just turning the corner.

And there, closing the door. I felt that if I turned round quickly, I would catch him before he disappeared. Yet I had never seen him.

It was a sort of haunting. I couldn't concentrate on anything else. Whatever I was doing, I wanted to be in the attic, reading the next batch of letters.

'You're not getting better as fast as I would like,' Mother said, with an anxious look at me. 'Laura? Laura?'

I was sitting in the garden, shelling peas. It was a rhythmical sort of job. Pop the pod, quick check for maggots, run a thumb along the peas, watching them plop into the bowl – one, two, three, four, five, six, seven if you were lucky – chuck the pod on to an old newspaper, pick up the next pod. You could do a lot of thinking, shelling peas.

'Sorry, Mother. I was miles away. What did you say?'

'I said ... Look, darling, are you still feeling awful? Why don't you go and see a doctor?'

'No need. I'm fine. Really.'

'You haven't seen Pansy or Vee for days. You were always together before. And your sick leave will be up in a day or so and I don't think you're fit to go back.'

'I'm fine. Don't worry.'

I don't know why I was so snappy. Mother looked hurt. She only wanted to mother me. She pulled up a chair and sat very close.

'Darling, I don't want to be nosy ... do tell me if it's none of my business ... but – but are you going to have a baby?'

'Good Lord, Mother!' I nearly dropped the bowl of peas and that would have had us scrabbling in the grass for ages. 'Whatever made you think that?'

'I didn't ... I don't ... just ... just ... well, there's a war on and girls are – are freer than they used to be in the last war, but even then – even then, girls ... you know...'

'Went to bed with a man before they were married.' I had to finish the sentence for her. Her face was scarlet, turned away from me. 'Did you, Mother?'

'Laura! What a thing to ask...'

'I'm sorry. That was an awful thing to say. I don't know why I asked. It's none of my business.'

'Exactly. Not that I mean ... and, of course, you have been married, so you're not ... and you must have – have needs that an unmarried girl wouldn't naturally have ... you must miss ... so ... I would understand, Laura, darling. It wouldn't be the end of the world.'

I could have told her then. I could have said *I don't even know what I'm supposed to be missing.* I ought to have said *How could I possibly have a baby, when I'm still a virgin?* I don't know what would have shocked her more – an illegitimate baby or my married virginity. On the whole, I think, probably, the latter.

I simply said, 'Mother, you can sleep comfortably. I am *not* having a baby. There. Does that make you happy?'

'Of course, silly me. I knew you weren't really,

230

darling. I just thought I ought to – you know – check that you were all right. Let me help you with those peas. Isn't it lucky that we've always been able to talk about anything?'

Dear Mother,

The Magister always starts assembly with the school casualty lists now. There were four names today. Farley, Bryce, Heatherington and Swindell. I remember them all. Bryce was quite old. He was a prefect when I first arrived here. He was gassed at St Julien. What a rotten weapon to use. Trust the Hun to have such a beastly idea. Heatherington was in the First Eleven and Victor Ludorum last year. They were all decent chaps. It makes us all quite mad to get out there and have a crack. Tom and I want to try for the same battalion. We shall not be able to escape from here until the summer, but it is never too early to start planning. Some people say the war won't last, but I think it will probably go on for a bit longer. We have both done well at OTC camp, so hope to get our first choice. Do you think Father could pull any strings? Would you ask him? I hope you and Father are both well.

Your affectionate son,
Edwin

He was getting closer. I could almost hear him breathing. If I put out my hand, I might even be able to touch him.

I had known that Tom and my father had been close, but I hadn't realized just how long they had known each other. My image of Tom was changing, too. Standing behind my gentle step-

231

father was a boy who was flogged almost every week, a boy whose mother had died in India, leaving him alone with his grief.

Why had he joined my grandmother's conspiracy of silence?

The army hadn't actually forgotten me. Nothing remained of my chickenpox spots except the two little scars on my forehead. Nothing remained, either, of my sick leave. I had never been so reluctant to go back to duty before. It was the most crucial and thrilling stage of the war. I ought to have been anxious to play my part. I went back to Bletchley with sticky kisses from Jonathan and Jennifer and a bag full of letters. Grandmother would never miss them.

Nothing had changed. Buses still rumbled round the lanes at shift change, picking up and dropping off staff. The night silence was still splintered by the coughing roar of motorcycles. Mrs Granby's cooking hadn't improved.

'I see you're back again,' she'd said as I walked in on my first evening back. She was gazing into the mirror above the mantelpiece, taking out her metal curlers (what a pity she hadn't given them up for salvage – now that would really have been patriotism) and fluffing up the resulting frizz. 'I've had my tea and there isn't a bite in the house. I'm off to the pictures. Don't forget to leave your ration card when you go off in the morning. TTFN, love.'

I could tell that she'd had her tea. The dirty dishes were still on the table – probably because the sink was still full of yesterday's. I'd promised myself a stand-up strip wash at the sink with the door locked and the blackout drawn. Now I'd have to wash up first or make do with a basin of water. The windows were shut fast, taped crossways against splinters and painted black round the edges because the blackout blinds didn't fit properly. The gloom hid the dust, at any rate. But at least the weather was warm and I didn't have to save shillings to keep that miserable little gas fire alight.

I was back at work with a vengeance. The temperature in 'E' block was as unbearably hot in summer as it was cold in winter. We could only open the windows the barest crack, because of the blast shutters. In quiet moments during night shift, and they were pretty rare, our wind-up gramophone used to grind away at Bing Crosby and the Andrews Sisters singing 'Don't Fence Me In'. We all knew how they felt! Kate had been posted to Portsmouth while I was away. 'Lucky me!' she wrote.

Life among the eggheads was a bit too serious for me. I don't know how you stand that place. Still, I suppose that all you want at your age is a hot-water bottle and a nice cup of cocoa before bed! I prefer something a bit livelier to keep me warm at night! Next time I write I shall tell you all about an absolute dreamboat of a first lieutenant who has his eye on me. Isn't that tantalizing? I'll bet you can't wait for my next missive...

There was only one other letter waiting for me. It was from the Imperial War Graves Commission.

Dear Madam

It is regretted that, due to the staffing position during the present situation, it has not so far been possible to answer your query regarding your father's grave.

Records may, however, be consulted, by prior arrangement, by application in person at the above address during office hours. Enquiries should include, where possible, the casualty's full name, rank and number; unit; age; place of birth; date and place of death.

Yours faithfully...

It was a bit of a blow. I'd no idea when I'd get time off to go swanning around on a search of my own. The office was near Beaconsfield, at Wooburn Green, not impossibly far away, yet I couldn't make it. We were working double shifts again and I was never free during office hours. I'd had too much time off sick to ask for any special favours. And if I knew the date and place of death, I wouldn't be asking, would I? No, that wasn't fair. They were only trying to be helpful, I suppose. The boy who had been my father was buried somewhere. I was determined to find out where. I owed it to him.

How strange to think that you're older than your father ever was. Fathers are supposed to grow old ahead of you, visibly and gracefully. They're not supposed to stay boys for ever.

'Vee – it's Laura.'

'Laura? Hey, that's great! Where are you?'

234

'At work. I haven't got long. Vee – will you do me a favour? Please?'

'Sure. Name it.'

'Will you pretend to be me? No, I haven't deserted and no, I'm not hiding from the MPs. I'm not as daft as all that. Not yet anyway. Will you go to the War Graves Commission offices for me? I want to know where my father is buried.'

'That's a pretty odd one. I mean – most people know where their folks have been put. What happened? Did you mislay him, or what? That's a bit careless, wouldn't you say?'

'Very funny. Catch me on another day and I might laugh. Look, it's very important to me. Vee, please?'

'I guess I could manage that.'

'You're wonderful. And there's just one more thing, Vee.'

'What?'

'Do you think you could possibly stop talking like a Texan millionaire's wife?'

'Get lost, Kenton!'

Dear Mother

You will be glad to bear that Tom and I have arrived safely with the battalion. We had a quiet crossing to Le Havre. The Channel was very still and the moon was so bright that we could see to read as we sat on deck. The shapes of our escorts were quite clear and very reassuring. Although all ships were darkened for safety, it made no difference. We could have been sailing in broad daylight.

So far, we haven't seen anything of the war. We had a pretty decent train journey, although the men were rather squashed in their carriages. France looks very peaceful so far. The only reminder of war was the hospital train that passed us travelling in the opposite direction. Quite a few of the walking wounded put their heads out of the window and waved to us as we passed. I must say, in spite of their bandages, they looked awfully cheerful. It is good to see such a splendid spirit.

The battalion is in the rest area at the moment. They had a bit of a mauling earlier and have been pulled back to recuperate. We are in a pretty village, just like a picture postcard. There is a church and a café (of course), a square with chestnut trees and a duckpond.

The men are billeted in a farmyard with two great stone barns. They have made themselves tolerably comfortable in clean straw and have been visited by a mobile bath unit, which was much appreciated. The farm is run by a very old man, his wife and their granddaughter, who is not at all pretty. I have not yet seen any French men under fifty years of age. The officers have taken over a large house at the edge of the village as the mess. The owner has moved to Paris in a funk. It has a pleasant garden and comfortable furniture. Tom and I share a room and a batman called Conibear, a good-humoured chap who makes a respectable cup of tea and keeps a miraculous shine on our boots. He used to work in an hotel in Harrogate. So it is quite like school again here. The sun is shining. You must not worry, everything is tickety-boo.

We are settling in well and getting to know our fellow men. The lads rather look down on two brand new subalterns, which is a bit of a cheek as half of them are nearly as new as we are. The second-in-command is an old regular, very down-to-earth, and

236

is, they say, the only officer still left of the original battalion. He doesn't talk to subalterns at all, or to anyone else below the rank of major until after breakfast. The adjutant is very quiet, with rather a board school accent, but seems quite efficient and has kept us up to scratch in our duties. He has a moth-eaten terrier called Rags that he found wandering around a deserted farm. It never does what it's told, but that's because it only speaks French!

I am told they are expecting quite a few replacement subalterns, so we shall soon not be the new boys. We have not yet met the CO, as he is on leave. He is said to be a bit of a disciplinarian. That seems to me to be only right and proper. A battalion needs a strong leader. Tom and I will get on very well. As I said to him, all we have to do is do as we are told and we shall be all right. We are both keen as mustard and anxious to get up to the Front.

Well, Mother, I must close now as it is my turn to examine the men's feet. That is one of the less pleasant aspects of a subaltern's life. You must not believe everything you hear about French food. So far, it has not come up to scratch and I am very tired of omelettes. Please give my regards to Father.

Your affectionate son,
Edwin

What a good boy. Not one word that he wrote would have to be obliterated by the censor. No place names, no regiment, no dates, no personalities. What use was that to me?

The last thing I expected was a posting, particularly at a time when we were working flat out, day and night, to keep encrypted signal traffic flowing to Normandy. Still, I suppose someone had to be at the other end, to decrypt back into plain language. Once in, never out, they used to say at Bletchley Park. Once you were in intelligence work, you learned so much that they couldn't afford to let you out again. Brickfield Cottages for ever and ever. What a thought! A life sentence couldn't be any more depressing.

Thank goodness it was just a rumour. When I walked down Mrs Granby's path for the last time, with my posting documents and travel warrant buttoned safely in my pocket, I could have thrown my cap in the air and given three cheers.

All she said was 'Never again.' Her voice followed me, persistent as a bluebottle and twice as irritating. 'I've been at my wits' end to satisfy you. Lady Muck. Don't like this and don't like that. Coming and going at all hours. It's not decent, young women gallivanting about after dark, war or no war. I'll look for a nice commercial gentleman next time. They're ever so much less trouble – more grateful for the least little thing you do for them.'

She'd miss my rations, though, and the twenty-five bob a week the army had paid her to keep me.

With a mixed draft of drivers, telephonists, cooks' clerks and ack-ack girls, I sailed to France to join Rear HQ 21st Army Group, sick all the way – and we'd been fed bully beef and treacle tart in Southampton – in the teeth of a summer gale, landing at Arromanches. Was it worth four shillings a day to hang over the side, heaving all the way to France? If this was what a third stripe entailed, they could keep it!

The girl in front of me balked as she clambered into the LCI – Landing Craft Infantry. 'After you, Claude,' she muttered. And for once the ITMA catchphrase didn't seem funny. No-one quipped back, 'No, after *you*, Cecil.'

'Get a move on, that woman,' yelled a petty officer.

We squeezed in as well as we could, kitbags slung over our shoulders, clutching our tin hats, looking about as warlike as though we were wearing saucepans on our heads. What a ridiculous shape they were. They never stayed on unless you fastened the chin strap tight enough to throttle you. The ship pitched and rolled as we were swung out on davits. The sea looked a horribly long way down, heaving with a smooth, glassy, hungry swell. Unidentifiable things – sharp, sloppy, spiky, squidgy, smelly things, things we didn't want to know about – bobbed against the ship's sides. Up here we were safe. Down there was – oh, God ... We all squealed as the LCI dropped towards the waves with a sickening swoop, worse than any lift, and splashed down. The landing craft surged towards the shallows, dropped its bow door and we were in France.

The tide was a long way out and we paddled across firm, rippled sand to the pontoon footbridge that connected the beach to the land. We were just beyond the western edge of the landing beaches codenamed Gold. The beach was littered with the debris of invasion. Massive poles, once angled into the sand and armed with anti-landing mines, Rommel's asparagus, had been disarmed, dug up and shoved aside by tractor. Barbed wire had been cut and torn apart like hopelessly tangled knitting. There were burnt-out vehicles, abandoned hulks, their smell dissipated by the seasidy scents of salt water and seaweed. The pleasant little family resort was shattered, fought through street by street, its houses roofless, windowless, fought through room by room.

The massive bulk of the Mulberry harbour, with its protecting sunken blockships and its floating quays, stretched back out to sea behind us in a pattern that must have made sense to someone. A complicated network of pontoons allowed vehicles to roll right up to the ships for offloading. There were lighters and barges hurrying backwards and forwards through the shallows. Cranes rose and dipped. The heavy swell made the whole harbour pitch and roll giddily. It looked dangerously unstable, yet it had survived the storms of 18–22 June that had destroyed the other Mulberry harbour off St Laurent.

The sand was scored with deep tyre-tread patterns that filled with water, were washed away every tide and churned up again. Everything an army could need to sustain it was being landed on the shores of France, a monstrous shopping list. Vehicles. Tanks. Guns. Ammunition. Spades and pickaxes. Bridging equipment. Demolition equipment. Signalling equipment. Food. Cookers.

Tents. Medical supplies. Men. And women.

It was a scene that would have been impossible if the *Luftwaffe* had been any sort of danger. We controlled the air and with it we held the sea and the land. The earth was ours and the dominion thereof. So many people were doing so many things, I couldn't tell whether this was the most efficient invasion since William the Conqueror went the other way or whether it was complete chaos. A regiment of tanks was being landed, diesel engines growling, tracks squealing like pigs on the way to slaughter. They heaved up on to the cobbled street and headed inland, leaving only their smell.

The street was lined with lorries, picking up parties of soldiers. It echoed with revving engines and slamming doors. The air was acrid with engine fumes. Up and down the street, in and out of the vehicles, played the children of Arromanches. Bad luck, kids. If this had been the American sector, you'd have been showered with gum and Hershey bars.

If we'd had any sense, we should have been able to recognize our own tac sign painted on the lorry that was going our way, but we stood about, wondering what to do next, as military as a party of Girl Guides in search of a handy campfire.

'Going our way, girls?' asked a driver with a cheeky grin. 'Next stop Berlin.'

A whole truckload of Highlanders hung out and whistled at us as we passed.

'You women – what're you doing there? Over here at the double.'

We were scooped up and sent on our way by a

241

harassed MTO. Our lorry crunched and ground over shell-pitted roads. A feeling of desolation persisted throughout our short journey along Norman lanes to a camp outside Bayeux.

It was high summer. There should have been crops ripening in fields bordered by ancient hedges. There should have been trees, burdened by little unripe cider apples, shading red and white spotted cattle. There should have been dog roses and honeysuckle and poppies in verges powdered with chalky dust.

But the verges were churned to slurry by tracked vehicles. The ditches were filled and obliterated, the hedges holed. Tanks had torn their own muddy roadways through fields that wouldn't be harvested this year. Ansty Parva might have looked like this. Sometimes there'd be a cow, legs in the air, stiff as fenceposts above a bloated body. Scattered along the roadside were hastily erected crosses, marking bodies awaiting collection and decent reburial. British, Germans, Canadians – who were they? How easy to miss one. How easy to lose a husband, father, son.

There wasn't much giggling amongst the girls in the lorry. In England, we'd have been chattering and laughing, weighing each other up. New faces – will we get on together, who will be the clown, who will be the natural leader, who the rebel, the good soldier, the toady, the bully, the misfit? Instead we were silent. Some of these girls had worked gun sites throughout the Blitz, some had carried messages through bombed streets or manned telephone exchanges throughout air raids. Some were conscripts, who never wanted

242

to be in uniform at all and would do anything rather than be a soldier. They would be trouble one day, I thought, but not today. None of us had been anywhere near the front line before. It was different, somehow, frightening and exciting at the same time. We were awed into silence.

Home was a camouflaged tent in a field. The stormy summer and hundreds of army boots had destroyed whatever had been growing there. The farmyard ought to have been deserted. Its barns were roofless and the cattle sheds looked as though they had been used as machine-gun nests. A neatly walled little farm like this, properly organized with overlapping fields of fire, could hold up a battalion for hours, maybe a day or two. In the end, someone had popped a grenade into each stall and blown the machine-gunners apart. They wouldn't have been able to sort out who was who after that.

Yet there were still a few straggly chickens picking about the yard. A thin woman milked a thin cow, her head tucked into the hollow in its flank. The beast's hip-bones were like coat hangers. The farmhouse chimney had gone, but a wisp of smoke rose from a hole in the roof.

Now that I had my third (still very new) stripe up, I was living in a bit more comfort. Instead of having to sleep with the junior ranks in the huge marquee dormitory, there were only eight of us in a bell tent, although the women's ablutions were in another tent half a field away. We ATS senior NCOs were allowed by the men to share (with a welcome half gallant, half resentful) the

243

sergeants' mess, but our quarters were as segregated as though we were a ravening pack of man-eating maenads.

Heavens, we were far too busy to bother about sex!

We were well behind the front line, but the war wasn't far away. Stubborn German resistance and the difficulties of fighting tank battles in hedge-and-ditch *bocage* country meant that Allied armies had made nothing like the strides across France that had been planned and hoped for. There was still a pocket of the enemy at Falaise, only a few miles away, like a big bite out of our advancing line.

Straddling a ditch at the far end of the field, just beyond the canvas screens of the DTLs, the deep trench latrines, was a brewed-up German tank. The trees around it were scorched and scarred by anti-tank fire. You could squat in the latrines, primly peeping over the top of screens that were never quite high enough, feeling like Aunt Sally at the fair, and look at the peeling black-and-white cross that still marked the tangled metal. Anything movable had been stripped off for souvenirs. In the salty air, the tank was beginning to rust already.

Morning and evening, the line of ambulances rolled in, carrying the wounded from casualty clearing stations to the field hospital. For the first few days I stopped whenever they appeared, unable to work until they had gone by. How many this time? Who were they? What would happen to them?

Soon I didn't even look up.

Dear Mother

I am snatching a moment before going out to inspect the guard to thank you for the parcels, which arrived, more or less intact, yesterday. The fruit cake and cigarettes have gone into mess stores (a tin box suspended from the ceiling, out of reach of the rats – we hope). It's share and share alike here. We all do pretty well out of each other's parcels. However, I have been rather selfish and kept the soap for myself One day, I may actually have a bath and the opportunity to use it. We are all so caked with mud that even our mothers would be hard pressed to recognize us. I was especially glad of the extra socks. It's impossible to have them washed or dried properly here. We just wear them until they dissolve. It's a schoolboy's idea of paradise. No-one checks whether we have washed our necks or behind our ears. Imagine, or try not to imagine, the atmosphere in the dugout. After a walk down the trench on a frosty night, the smell of socks, gumboots, cheese, paraffin, tobacco, whisky, wet wool and badly cured sheepskin waistcoats hits one like a sledgehammer.

You'd be amazed at the practical ideas we have for getting round shortages. If we are short of wood and there are no handy ammunition boxes to break up, a dozen or so army biscuits make a reasonable fire. If there are no biscuits, the men boil water for tea by firing off a few belts of machine-gun ammunition in the general direction of the enemy. The guns are water cooled and by the time they've been fired, there is enough boiling water to make a decent brew.

I am getting on tolerably well. We went through rather a sticky patch a fortnight ago, but things have

245

quietened down now. We seem to have reached an agreement with the Hun not to bother each other. The front line trenches are so close that we can hear each other snoring. We stand-to like good little soldier boys at every dawn and dusk, ready for an attack, but nothing happens. A few starshells go up, just to remind us that there is an enemy out there, but that's all.

Even their artillery is silent. They sent so much over a week or two ago that they probably have to save up for the next big strafe. All their shells have their own sounds, a sort of signature tune that we learn to recognize pretty quickly – or else. Their 77mm whiz-bangs spark like giant fire crackers. The 5.9s bark out the shells that whine and growl their way across the lines. If there is a roar like an express train speeding through a station, then we know that some poor devil behind us is being pounded by heavy artillery. Minenwerfers give a cough and spit out a black ball that wobbles over to us in a visible curve, giving us time to duck, and gas shells land with a soft plop. Everything is quiet at the moment, however. A sensible fellow, Jerry. He doesn't make trouble and neither do we.

The CO is not at all happy about this state of affairs. He has a bee in his bonnet about taking the offensive. Have you seen the cartoon that shows a subaltern in a frightful state of dress, hair too long, trousers too short, hat on the back of his head and a golf club in his hand? The caption is: Questions a Platoon Commander should ask himself – Am I as offensive as I might be? We all had a jolly good laugh over that one. The old man takes offensiveness very seriously, however.

The divisional commander has presented a hand-

246

some cup, to be awarded each month to the battalion with the most points – just like house points at school – one point for enemy identification by articles taken from dead bodies, two points for each live prisoner (three for an NCO, four for an officer), three points for each enemy trench mortar or machine gun captured and so on. I suppose anyone who captured Crown Prince Willie would win it outright. Our colonel is determined to have the battalion's name on that cup, every month, if possible. He tries to drive us over the top on any pretext: wiring patrols, mapping patrols, trench raids, bombing parties, prisoner-catching patrols, any excuse for a spot of offensiveness. I think that if he ever met a Hun, he would probably tear the poor fellow apart with his teeth. Life has been much quieter since he went on leave. He'll be back soon and I suppose things will start humming again, but, fortunately, by then we ought to be back in reserve. We're overdue a spell.

Tom tells me that he will write as soon as he is able to thank you for his parcel. He never normally gets one, as he has no people to speak of, so he was jolly pleased with yours. It was a kind thought, Mother. Could you possibly do it again some time? I know you are very busy with all your committees and every-thing, but spare a thought for two old soldiers!

Tom has been having rather a rough time. For some reason he has got on the wrong side of the CO, which is jolly bad luck for him. I think it all began on the day that the colonel decided to open up a listening post that had been closed down by the last battalion because it was too bloody dangerous (sorry for the language – but it was). Tom was the unlucky chap selected for the honour of spending a day in a hole that was well marked out by an enemy sniper – one twitch and he spots you, two twitches and he aims, three twitches and you're dead. Tom crawled out in the darkness just before dawn. He got there, all right, although it was a bit dicey when a flare went up just as be was ducking under our wire. We all held our breath for him and he just froze, hoping to look like a corpse. A couple of hours after daybreak, Tom came back – crawled back in broad daylight, if you please, though he was damned lucky it was too foggy to see the end of your nose – saying that he couldn't hear a thing because the post was just too far from the German lines. The CO didn't believe him, accused him of being in a funk. It was probably true, but so would I have been, stuck out alone for hours in that Godforsaken hole, and so would anyone with an ounce of common sense. The mist lifted about an hour later and, if he'd still been there, he'd have given the sniper a decent spot of target practice.

Since then. Tom has been put in charge of every single party sent out to do stupid things in sight of the enemy. He never gets a night's sleep. Poor blighter. I don't know how he bears it. I know I couldn't. The company commander tries to stand up for him, but it's like trying to stand up in a blizzard when the CO gets in one of his bates. I don't see any way out of it for Tom, except to get himself killed – or hope the CO gets bagged first.

I don't suppose it would be possible to send out some records? Probably not. I can't imagine how you would pack them. We are badly in need of some variety in the mess. I think that if I hear 'In a Monastery Garden' (the MO's favourite) just once more, I shall throw it on the ground and jump on it – or him. Something

248

jolly would be nice, but not too patriotic or we shall all be sick!

It's the little things that get on one's nerves. The big things are too awful to worry about. Dick Chambers whistles hymns through his teeth all the time. He used to be a chorister, but he sounds more like a groom. Frank Maitland does nothing but play patience and if anyone else wants to use the table, all Frank's cards have to be moved carefully off and then moved back again. Clive Vernon files his nails as often as a French madam and when he clips his toenails, the bits fly out across the dugout. It's enough to make me volunteer for the next trench raid. Silly, really, to allow myself to get so irritated when we could all be blown to kingdom come by the next big one. Tom is far more tolerant than I am. He just laughs and tells me that I should get my own back by practising golf swings or fly casting at every opportunity. He's so good humoured and I'm an insufferable little prig.

I had a letter from Diana Lampard the other day. That was a surprise and a very pleasant one. She told me at Christmas that she would write, but I hadn't really expected it. Girls often make promises that they don't keep. She writes very sweetly about life at school and says that she intends to become a VAD when she is old enough and if the war goes on. I hope she doesn't. There are things that any woman, especially a young one, should not be obliged to see.

My regards to Father
Your affectionate son
Edwin

Our little intelligence section was shift-working as frantically as any at Bletchley Park. The signal

249

traffic flowed both ways. Messages to and from our commanders in the field required encryption or decryption. The text of enemy messages, their codes broken at BP, were received by us and decrypted for onward transmission to the staff of the Commander 21st Army Group, General Montgomery, at his headquarters in Creully.

On my fourth morning, I answered the phone in the approved manner.

'Int section – Sergeant Kenton speaking, sir.'

'Hier ist Funf spikkig!' a husky voice replied.

'Who?'

'Funf, dummkopf!'

I giggled. It could have been anyone. The ITMA spy, Funf, always answered the phone that way. The voice on the other end of the phone burst into laughter, rich and promising all sorts of naughtiness. I knew that laugh!

'It can't be! Grace – that can't be you!'

'Oh, yes it can! I'm in the transport pool. When're you free?'

She breezed into my tent/office, bringing with her the smell of engine oil and Rochas *Femme,* and everyone stopped scribbling to stare. Her overalls were filthy and her nails painted. She had a spanner in the breast pocket and her hair tied up in a turban, but her lipstick was fresh.

'Oh, my,' she exclaimed in mock admiration of my stripes. 'Oh, my.' She breathed on them and polished them up with her sleeve. '*Sergeant* Kenton!'

'Idiot!' I put my arms around her and gave her a hug.

'Mind out – you'll get that smart battledress

250

covered in oil.'

I took a quick step backwards. 'What're you doing here?'

'Driving fuel tankers. We go from the Rear Maintenance Area at Bayeux to front-line fuel dumps – up and down, up and down – it's a bit like being a tram driver. Well, someone has to. The Americans have theirs piped in. Imagine – I thought that PLUTO was a chum of Mickey Mouse and now I find that it stands for Pipe Line Under The Ocean. You live and learn.' She pushed all my papers to one side of the desk – secrets, secrets, I rushed to turn them face downwards – and perched on the corner, swinging her legs. 'What about you?'

'Oh, still driving a desk.'

'Close-mouthed as ever. Honestly, you make a clam seem positively chatty.'

'Grace – I'm so glad to see you.'

'Won't we just paint the town red. Meet you in the village tonight. Café des Bons Amis, eight o'clock – OK?'

It was easier for us, now different in rank, to meet on neutral ground. Most of the camp seemed to have squeezed into the little café, anyway. The smoke was thick enough to have alerted the fire piquet. Someone was thumping an old piano in one corner, vamping his way round the sticking keys, telling us all what he was going to do when the lights went up in London. His voice was like a tomcat on a garden wall.

In another corner, a man was twiddling the dial on a wireless. There were howls and squeals as he

251

whizzed through the stations – Hilversum, Luxembourg, Toulouse. No-one paid any attention.

'Laura. Over here.' Grace stood up and waved across the room. She was hanging on to the back of a chair. A stocky soldier in a Highlander's Glengarry was trying to take it away from her. 'Hands off,' I heard her snap. 'Didn't your mother ever tell you that it's good manners to give up your seat for a lady?'

There was a carafe of sour red wine on the table. Grace poured me a tumblerful. The first sip made my mouth feel as though it had been scoured with Vim. The second was just about bearable, and by the time I took a third sip it was beginning to taste quite nice. We had so much to talk about, so much to catch up on.

'I've had three stripes up, too, you know,' Grace confided in me. 'But they'd only give them to me one at a time!' She gave a little whinny of laughter at her own joke. 'Every time I got caught sneaking in after lights out, my stripe was taken away again. I ought to get some press studs put on my sleeve. It'd be quicker than all that sewing and unpicking!'

A bunch of lads dragged their chairs over and sat at our table with hopeful smiles on their faces – they looked just like dogs waiting to be thrown the scraps from a sumptuous meal. You could almost see them drooling.

'Shove up, girls,' said a burly sapper with a gappy grin. 'There's plenty of room for another little one. Can't have pretty girls like you sitting all on your lonesomes. What'll you have?'

'Sorry, boys. Put your tongues away,' said Grace with a smile as promising as a whole book of sweet coupons. She patted me on the hand. 'There's nothing here for you. We're dykes. Aren't we, sweetie?'

'Bloody hell. Wouldn't you just know? Sodding queers.'

They were off. They picked up their chairs and scarpered, far quicker than they'd come, to another table where the pickings were richer.

'Grace, how could you?' I protested, embarrassed into a weak whisper.

'You'll learn. It's the best way I know to guarantee a bit of privacy. Anyway, half the men think we're raving nymphomaniacs and the other half think we're all screaming queers.' She shrugged. 'Who cares? So, what about Vee? Have you heard from her lately?'

So I told her all about Carlton and Jennifer and the coming baby.

'No! A Texan millionaire? Called Carlton?' shrieked Grace. 'I don't believe it. Tell me you're joking!'

'Well, so far there's no proof that he's actually a millionaire, but he's certainly a Texan and Vee acts as though money's no object.'

'Lucky girl. She's got the right idea. You don't suppose he's got any pals, do you? Preferably, but not necessarily, single. In fact, I wouldn't turn a man down even if he'd got a whole harem stashed away. I'm rather in need of a handy millionaire myself, at the moment.'

'Aren't we all!'

The soldier on the piano seemed to be gaining

on the one with the wireless. He plonked the keys inaccurately but noisily enough to attract a group around him. He was already as lit up as the lights he was singing about. They all were.

'Now, Laura, tell me...' Grace leaned forward, her arms folded on the stained table, her voice dropping to a sympathetic whisper. 'How are you?'

'Fine. Of course. How are you?' I answered in a tight little voice.

'You know what I mean. Are you happy? How's your sex life? Is there a man on the horizon? Come on – tell!'

'There's nothing to tell.'

'I thought as much. You look pretty frightful. You look in need of a good ... a good man!'

'Thanks awfully. It's so nice to have friends!'

'Don't mention it. It's what friends are for. Silly. You look rather ... rather lost, that's all.'

'Well, I'm fine,' I snapped. 'So let's talk about something else.'

'If you say so.'

Grace topped up my glass. I hadn't realized it was empty. She took an elegantly engraved cigarette case from the breast pocket of her battledress blouse, offered a cigarette to me and, when I shook my head, lit one for herself. She sat back with a sigh of contentment, blowing twin columns of smoke through pinched nostrils.

'Ah, that's better. You've no idea how I suffer when I'm driving tankers. One of these days, I'll just light up and to hell with the consequences. Better go out with a bang than a whimper, eh?'

Freshly set hair, freshly made-up face, tailored

and pressed uniform – how did she manage it? She looked very like that ATS recruiting poster – the cool blonde in profile – the one that had been withdrawn at the beginning of the war because the woman looked too elegant. Don't want to give the wrong idea to impressionable girls, do we?

'I saw a friend of yours the other day,' said Grace, with a knowing, come-on-why-don't-you-ask-me look on her face. 'A very good friend, so I'm told.'

'Oh?' I replied calmly, not rising to her bait.

'Go on. Ask me who. You know you're dying to.'

'You'll tell me, anyway.'

'Martin Buckland, that's who. He's rather a dreamboat, isn't he?'

'Who told you ... I don't ... I've never...'

'Oh yes, you *have*,' Grace insisted. 'Don't come the innocent with me. Pansy may get away with it, but you certainly can't.'

'Martin is an old friend. I've known him since I was five. And that's all,' I said firmly. Grace's coyly cocked head and disbelieving expression infuriated me. It was none of her business, anyway.

'Old friend. Of course. That's why you're blushing like a bride.'

'Shut up, Grace. Where did you ... where did you meet him, anyway?'

'In hospital. Hey, steady on. It was only a scratch. Here – drink this.' I saw her reach over to the next table and pick up a bottle of cognac. She sloshed some into my glass and rather more into her own, then put the bottle back with a sweet smile for the surprised owners. 'Medicinal purposes. Thank you so much.'

I felt very cold. Not again. Oh, please, not again, I prayed. Don't let me lose Martin, too.

I hardly dared to ask. 'What happened?'

'He picked up some shell splinters during the breakout from the bridgehead. That's all.'

All. *All?*

Grace tipped up the wine bottle. Somehow, it seemed to be empty. How surprising. She trotted off to the zinc-topped bar, came back with another one and filled our glasses.

'Whoops – that's a bit full. Steady as she goes. Anyway, some of the girls decided it would be good for morale to go hospital visiting – you know, cheer the boys up with a spot of feminine charm – and he was there, looking frightfully pale and interesting with his arm in a sling. We had a bit of a chat. In fact, we had quite a long chat.'

'Oh.'

'About you – you goose! You know he adores you, of course. Not that he said so. Well, he wouldn't, would he. Men don't. Damn them. But I could tell. Really, I don't know how you do it. There you are – a scrawny chit of a thing – and you marry one lovely man and have another one dangling on a bit of string. Honestly. It's not fair.'

'That's not funny, Grace.'

'Oh, God, I know it's not. I'm sorry, darling. I'm such a bitch.'

'I know.' Then I giggled. 'That's why I like you.'

That's what friends are for, I thought, hazily. You can say what you like to each other and know that it will still be all right. You can lean as

256

hard as you like and know you won't be let down. Pansy, Vee, Grace and me – we needed each other.

And their children. And their children's children. Grace's hair had a sort of misty aureole. She wore a halo of light. Anyone less deserving of a halo … she was saying something, but I wasn't sure what. I saw Jennifer and Jonathan and Vee's unborn child and Grace's children – lots of them, she'd have lots, I was sure. She'd treat them like puppies and train them up like young hounds.

And I saw myself as a sort of benevolent aunt to them all, a maiden aunt – that wasn't right, how could I be a maiden? – but I was. I would preside over their marryings and christenings and their Christmases and seaside holidays. There would be peace and sunshine and crisp white winters and nights without bombs and plenty to eat and … and we'd always be friends.

'Aunt Laura?' the children would say. 'Oh, we must ask Aunt Laura. We can't have Christmas/New Year/Easter or … something … without Aunt Laura.'

I could feel the smile growing wider and wider. It was splitting my face.

'Laura? Laura?' Grace was saying anxiously. She was staring at me, leaning forward.

It's all right, Grace, I tried to say, but the words wouldn't come out right: don't worry, we'll always be friends.

And young men won't be burned to death and wives will still have husbands and children will have fathers and...

And I wasn't smiling any more.

Grace shook my shoulder, none too gently. 'Laura. Come on. Time to go.'

I think I answered, but I'm not certain. At any rate, I didn't move.

'Laura. Get up. You can't stay here. There's going to be trouble. Get up, blast you.'

Then noises did begin to penetrate the haze. There was a splintering of glass. A woman shrieked and jabbered in French. *'Salaud!'* Someone overturned a table. A whistle blew an urgent blast and was answered by another. Grace grabbed my arm and pulled me after her. We squeezed into the empty space left in the wake of the military police patrol as they began to clear the room. Their sticks whistled through the air, cracked off tables and heads. Boots met flesh with a sound that reminded me of a butcher's shop, a soft, succulent thud, meaty and yielding, oxtail being chopped. The quarrelling soldiers were rounded up into a corner, meek, now, as sheep. The headquarters clerks would be pretty busy writing out charge sheets in the morning.

There was dead ground between the MPs and the door, so Grace and I used it to slip out. The lads were good. No-one turned us in. Then we ran.

We ran until we couldn't run any more. Then we stood under a tree, leaning against it for support, sucking in the soft, sweet summer air. Far away, farther than the muzzle flash would carry, the sound of guns made the night tremble.

'All right?' asked Grace at last.

I nodded.

'It wouldn't do your shiny, bright new stripes

any good to be rounded up by the MPs, now would it?'

'You really are wonderful, Grace. You think of everything.'

'I know! Now – straighten your tie and pull your hat down a bit. Perfect. We can stroll into camp as innocent as though we've just come from confession.'

We linked arms and strode off, singing.

'Ven der Fuehrer says "Ve iss der Master Race",
ve Heil! Heil! right in der Fuehrer's face.
Not to luff der Fuehrer iss a great disgrace,
So ve Heil! Heil! right in der Fuehrer's FACE!'

Dear Mother

We've had a bit of a mauling, as you will have heard, while trying to break through to the Belgian coast, so I write to reassure you that I am quite well. You must have read all about it in the newspapers at home and probably know more about events than I do. At least that means that the censor will leave this letter undecorated by his blue pencil.

Dear God, this is a horrible place. A slough, a stinking morass, the bottom of the pit. Every natural feature has been blasted away. The only reference points are shattered stumps, like rotten teeth, or upturned wagons or bloated corpses. At home, we direct travellers by pub signs. Over here, we have different landmarks. Turn right by the Legless Machine Gunner. Straight on to the Forgotten Fusilier. Then left at the Dead Donkey. A merciful God will never send to hell the men who fought their way to Passchendaele. We have been there already.

The lads suffer terribly from mud and cold. They all have chilblains and raw feet. They sleep in shelves dug into the rear of the trench, like a human dovecot. I am wet and miserable, but they are ten times more so and we are all desperately short of sleep. We came up from reserve just in time for the last big push. The battalion we were supposed to relieve passed us going down the line at the same time, so there was no proper handover. They left us with one guide. I don't blame them. What did they have to tell us? We had reached the end of the world.

We were all wet and bad-tempered by the time we arrived in position. I don't know how it is, but duckboards seem to have a malevolent sense of humour. We were tipped off them into foul water every few yards. At one point we passed through an appalling stench. Word came back that an entire mule team had sunk into the mud there about ten days before. They called it Dead Mule Alley. A cartload of chloride of lime wouldn't take the stink away. Every few moments, a soldier would become wedged by his pack at a corner and have to be shoved from behind to free him. I'm sure the guide sent down his warnings about wire, but like Chinese whispers, by the time they reached my platoon at the end of the line, they bore no relation to where the wire actually was. I would duck where there was nothing and a few minutes later be practically garroted. It was a tedious night and we were all exhausted by the time we'd covered the five miles.

The trench is a wretched one, shallow and wet, with firesteps cut too narrow to stand on and the parapets blown to smithereens, but since we were not here to defend, but meant to attack and take the slope in front of us, it didn't seem to matter too much. Now we're

260

back where we started, only there are not so many of us as there were when we arrived.

Did you ever go into the kitchen at home, Mother? I don't suppose you did. Mrs Ruggles always came to you for her orders. I remember her, standing at your little desk at the window of the morning room, where it catches the sun. She carries a fat notebook and pencil and has her sleeves rolled down for once, covering her red arms. You're turning over recipes and frowning and biting your lip. You know that whatever you order, Father will grumble. She has a machine, you know, that she fixes on to the edge of the kitchen table with a big butterfly screw. Into one end she feeds recognizable pieces of meat and out of the other end comes pulp. I can see her standing there, turning the handle, making the remains of the Sunday beef into Monday rissoles. 'Now then, you, Master Edwin,' she'd say, 'you keep your fingers out of that there, you'll lose them, else.' And I'd make her show me the finger that had lost its tip. It has a blunt end, stitched like a star. Did you know we had eaten a bit of Mrs Ruggles? The staff feeds the battalion into one end of their machine and we come out as rissoles, but not so neatly shaped.

And so here we are, still facing that wretched little slope that passes for a hill in this drowning land. We have been marched up to the top of the hill and marched down again. And there are precious few of us left. I know the others are out there somewhere. They are lying at the bottom of crump holes, their mouths and nostrils packed with mud. They are the human rags that hang on wire like washing on a line. They are turned to spray that spatters our faces and our clothes. We inhale them. We paddle in them.

261

Oh, Mother, don't read this. Why should you know what I know? I'm being selfish to write it. Or maybe the paper will be so scrawled on by the censor that there will be nothing left for you to read.

I was put in charge of a mopping-up party the other day. When a trench has been taken, then any remaining pockets of resistance must be 'mopped up'. What a cosy, roast beef and Yorkshire pudding, Sunday lunch after matins sort of phrase that is. You take half a dozen men and stand outside a dugout and throw a few smoke bombs down, so that the poor blighters inside must suffocate or run out. You station your men outside the entrance and wait for the enemy to appear. They come out, coughing and streaming with tears, hands in the air or rubbing their eyes. But you only have half a dozen men, not enough to spare to escort prisoners behind the line, so you bayonet them. A neat solution. Suppose that had been suggested before the war? What an outcry there would have been, what accusations of Hunnish practices and Prussian frightfulness. Yet here we are, the British army, refusing to take prisoners. The only way to win this war is by being more frightful than the other side. The idea frightens me.

The CO tells me I am to have a medal, but I'm not sure what for. I must have done something to please him at some time. Heaven knows what. Bravery is simply a matter of survival. You and your friends live, or the other chap and his friends. Them or us. That's all there is to it, really.

Tom is in hospital. He was buried under a collapsing dugout. It wasn't hit by a shell, it just fell apart in a muddy landslide and Tom and Sergeant Clapton were underneath it. We dug as fast as we could, scrabbling with our hands, afraid to use spades in case we should hit their faces. It was like clearing away black porridge. Sergeant Clapton was dead. Tom began to breathe again when we cleared the mud from his nose and mouth, but he was very confused and couldn't stop shaking, so was sent down the line for a few days. I miss him, but I hope he doesn't come back too soon.

Do you think you could be especially nice to Diana? I know you are not very keen on her, but she can't be held responsible for her parents and she really is a very sweet girl. We have quite a jolly correspondence going. She lost her cousin a week or so ago – I'm a bit vague about time at the moment – and she will be dreadfully cut up. They were very close. Cranford-Lewis. Do you remember him? We were in the same form and once you took him out to lunch after Sports Day. Well, he's in a hole in Sanctuary Wood now. I don't suppose there will be much point in having an Old Boys' Reunion after all this is over. I may be home for a little while soon. My name was a long way down the leave roster, but now I see that it has crept up towards the top. No, that's not right, my name hasn't moved. The others have gone.

Edwin

P.S. I see that the censor will never pass this letter, so I am giving it to our CSM to post on his way home. He is a decent fellow and will make sure you get it. Someone has to know.

I lay in my canvas camp bed and listened to the rain splatter off the tent like pebbles thrown against it. We ATS sergeants lay in a circle with our feet to the central tent pole. Myra Compton was just going out on shift and Doris Aitken had

263

just come off shift in the field telephone exchange. She was asleep already. I angled my shaded torch down further, so as not to disturb her.

A bit of a mauling at a place called Passchendaele. He was becoming more real. Here, in France, I heard what he was trying to say and understood. The sponged and pressed uniform still lay in mothballs in the trunk in the attic at Ansty House, but I had the man here, in my hands, in his own words. The serious boy was growing into a man with a wry sense of humour and a touching concern for his friend. Poor Tom. No wonder he screamed in the dark. I was beginning to understand my stepfather better, as well as my father.

I heard from Vee at last. *'Here, were you pulling my leg, or what,'* she wrote,

sending me on a wild goose chase all the way to Wooburn and me in an interesting condition, too! I've turned into a real roly-poly with this baby, blown up like a flipping great barrage balloon overnight, and so when a nice young sailor stood up to offer me his seat in the train, I couldn't fit into it and his mate had to stand up as well. Who says chivalry is dead?

Well, I won't keep you in suspense any longer. I couldn't find hide nor hair of your father in the Imperial War Graves Commission records. The clerk there, an old biddy with a moustache, had the cheek to ask me if I was certain that he really was dead – as if you wouldn't know! They did their best, but everything's at sixes and sevens, all the records are stuffed into fireproof trunks, just in case, but it makes it very hard to turn up anything useful. Don't tell me, I know, I said to her, there's a war on.

Of course, it doesn't help that you don't know his rank or his regiment or when he died or where. Not much to go on, is it? Funny old family you belong to, I must say. How can you just lose somebody? My Uncle Jimmy was killed at Wipers and we all know exactly where they've put him. It's ever so nice there, lawns and flowerbeds and all. Aunt Dot went on a sort of pilgrimage and took a picture of his grave to put on the mantelpiece and keeps a pressed poppy from France in her bible.

So, armed with just a name and initials, this is what I found. There's an Ansty in the Hampshire Regiment buried near Loos, but he died in 1915, so he can't be your dad. There's an Ansty buried at Tyne Cot, but he was an Australian. There's an Anstey at Telegraph Hill, but he has an 'e', so that's no good. There's an E Ansty at St Julien, but he was a private and your dad can't have been an OR because we saw his uniform. There's an E G T Ansty at Château Thierry. One of the initials is wrong, but the dates fit. Could that be him, do you think? Probably not. He was a rather old major, much too old for your mother, unless she was looking for a father figure. I see your dad as young and handsome and glamorous, like Leslie Howard only darker, a real lost hero. I'm sorry if that sounds flippant. It's not meant to. But it is all rather romantic, don't you think?

Well, that's it. Not much to go on. Thank heavens your name's not Smith! Maybe you'll never find your father, Laura. Does it really matter? I'm serious. Think about it. You've got a mother and a terrific

265

stepfather and a lovely gran and a sister who isn't half as bad as my sisters. What more do you want? Hankering after two fathers is a bit greedy.

I had a letter from my Carlton the other day. So at least I know he's safe so far. He sounds as though he's having a whale of a time, living it up among the mademoiselles. He's supposed to be fighting a war not fighting off the ladies. I'd have his guts for garters if I ever thought he'd two-timed me. He sent me the cutest little pair of white satin shoes for the new baby, with tiny blue forget-me-nots – French, of course, you can always tell. I wonder where on earth he found them.

Lots of love,
Vee

P.S. Jennifer sends a big kiss. She's growing into such a little madam and needs her dad to keep her in order. I know 'it' will be a boy this time because he's kicking the hell out of me already. Would you like to be godmother to Carlton H. Riversdale III? Say yes.

P.P.S. For heaven's sake, why don't you just ask your mum? She must know everything. Or if you think it would upset her – but it is twenty-five years ago – why don't you ask Tom or your gran? Seems to me you're making an awfully big secret out of something when three people already have all the answers.

Did Vee think I hadn't tried? Things weren't that simple. All three had shut up as though they were under a holy vow of silence. It seemed as though just saying the words *my father* gave my whole family the jitters. They'd talk any old twaddle rather than answer me.

Not much to go on. Vee was right. But in another way she was wrong. It did matter. It seemed to matter more and more.

We followed the war and moved from one farmyard to another, scarcely distinguishable from the last. Same broken walls. Same gaping roof. Same scrawny cows and chickens barely worth killing. Same dour, tough, hardy women, making do, hanging on grimly for a peace that would be long in coming. They were used to us now. The first rapture of welcome had passed. No more flags and flowers and kisses. Bent over the scarred earth, repairing the ravages of liberation, they barely raised their heads as we passed.

And when we got to Caen, it wasn't there any more. I had seen London and I had seen Southampton, but nothing had prepared me for this. The city of William the Conqueror had been all but removed from the map. The smell of destruction still lingered, thick as fog, of crumbled, ancient masonry, of fractured sewers and seeping gas and the sickly, vinegar-and-sugar smell of corpses decaying under the rubble.

We did that, I thought. On 7 July we destroyed Caen. We flew over and hurled thousands of tons of TNT on to it. We turned our guns on this city and blasted it, while its citizens crouched in the shelter of the Abbaye des Hommes and prayed for a deliverance that was slow in coming.

I don't suppose anyone wanted to do it. I don't suppose anyone felt proud of it afterwards. It was a cruel twist that we came to deliver France and brought death with us.

'Grace, if you wanted to find someone, where would you look?'

'What? My ears are full of soap.'

Grace shook her head and bubbles flew around. The basin balanced on a packing case wobbled. I picked up the jerry can of ice-cold rinsing water and sloshed it over her head. She shrieked with shock.

'Steady on. You'll drown me.'

'I said, where would you look if you wanted to find someone?'

'Is it squeaking yet?' she demanded.

I soused her again, then ran my fingers through her hair, listening for the squeak that would tell me it was clean.

'Clean as a whistle.'

Grace knelt on the grass, towelling her hair vigorously. Her voice was muffled. 'Who're you looking for? A long-lost aunt who's got a fortune to dispose of?'

'If only.'

'Well, who, then?'

'It doesn't matter. I was just curious.'

It sounded so absurd. Where should I go to look for my father? No wonder Vee thought it was all so funny.

'Look, I've a date with a gorgeous airman tonight. Absolutely scrumptious. All big blue eyes and wandering hands. He's bound to have a chum just right for you. Why don't we make it a foursome? Go on. Say yes, Laura. It'd be such fun.'

Thank goodness I had a cast-iron excuse.

'Sorry. I can't go out. I'm orderly sergeant tonight.'

'Are you? Oh, goodie, what timing. Be a darling and make sure you turn a blind eye if I don't quite make it back in time tonight, won't you!'

'Laura – you're orderly sergeant, aren't you?' Marjorie Halse, admin sergeant for the ATS, looked as though she was cooking up something. 'Got a little job for you.'

'Mmm?'

'Regimental bath.'

I gaped. 'What?'

'Regimental bath. Five o'clock. Private Madigan. Hasn't washed since we arrived and God knows when before that. We have to do something.'

That sort of thing didn't happen. Surely? I mean, we all heard stories in training that girls who didn't wash were *made* to do it, but surely they were just the usual barrackroom rumours.

'You can't do that.'

'Oh yes, I can. I've already spoken to the company commander about it and she said she'd turn a blind eye – as long as the orderly sergeant went along. I need you as witness that there wasn't any funny business.'

I tried to think of something, anything, any urgent job that would keep me in my office all evening, but she wasn't having any excuses.

'It's got to be done. At least if we're there, it'll be done properly. Otherwise the girls'll take things into their own hands and use pot-scrubbers and Vim on her. Who's to blame them?

You imagine sharing a tent with someone who hasn't washed since the midwife washed her. But there'd be hell to pay if they went for her.'

Somehow, I'd imagined a miserable little creature, but Private Madigan was a big, bold girl, brassily attractive, with greasy hair done in elaborate pin curls, chipped paint on her nails and a tidemark of dirt around her khaki collar. She was an orderly GD – general duties dogsbody – which meant she did any unpleasant task that was left over when everyone else had finished their work. The orderly private, the orderly NCO, the medical orderly carrying a bottle of nitkiller, Marjorie Halse and I all turned up and told her to come with us. She went quietly enough. Just as well. She was bigger than any of us.

Quietly, anyway, until she was marched into the bath-house and told to take off her clothes.

'In front of you lot? Not bloody likely!'

Marjorie Halse looked at her watch. 'You've got one minute to get started, otherwise we'll take them off for you.'

'Bloody cow! You'd like that, wouldn't you? You'd love to get your hands on me!'

'Thirty seconds.'

'You lay a finger on me and my mum'll write to our MP. You see if she wouldn't.'

'Fifteen seconds.'

She looked wildly around at the five grim-faced women between her and the door and began to pull off her tie. She smelt like a billy goat. It's just about the worst smell in the world.

Yet I felt sick with shame.

Her clothes were picked up with a pair of laundry tongs by the orderly private and stuffed into a sack. The collapsible bathtub was already filled with hot water and milky with a liberal dose of Dettol. Madigan stood shivering and naked on the wooden slatted floor, pathetic and somehow smaller. 'That'll take the skin off me, that will.'

There was shuffling and giggling on the other side of the canvas. The orderly NCO stuck her head out. 'This isn't a party. Push off, you lot,' she ordered, 'or I'll put you all on a charge.'

'Like what?'

'I'll think of something.'

'Get in,' Madigan was ordered, 'or we'll put you in.'

'You and whose bleeding army?'

She sneered as she swung a leg into the water. Oh, she was dirty, all right, she was filthy, her skin was scaly with ancient dirt, her heels and elbows wrinkled and grey as an elephant, yet her neck was ringed with love bites and there was another on her left breast. I felt soiled. I was repulsed by her squalid habits and disgusted by my own silent part in this vigilante squad. It wasn't to persecute ignorant girls like Madigan that I had joined the army. Sergeant Halse tossed her a bar of carbolic soap.

'I don't want to be a fucking soldier, anyway,' shouted Madigan, kneeling in the disinfected water so that it barely reached the important places. 'I hate you all and your fucking uniforms. Stupid bitches, stamping about and pretending to be soldiers. Bunch of bleeding dykes.'

'Will you do your back, or shall I?' asked

271

Sergeant Halse, calmly.

Madigan began to scream as the medical orderly got to work with the nit paste, a revolting mixture of coal tar, paraffin and cottonseed oil, black and sticky. I wouldn't have given much for her chances if anyone had struck a match.

'If you think you're going to get me back into that fucking uniform again, you've got another think coming. It's off and it's staying off.'

And when it was over, when the shivering girl had been handed a coarse bath towel to cover herself, I found that I was trembling almost as much as she was.

'Proud of yourselves, are you?' she demanded. 'Think you're proper little soldiers? Proper cows!'

She sprang with fingers hooked and slashed four bleeding lines down my left cheek. I gasped with shock and recoiled as the four other women grabbed Madigan and dragged her out, still screaming and cursing.

'You ought to get that looked at, Laura,' said Marjorie Halse later. 'Lucky for you she did it after the bath, though, and not before.'

'What will happen to her?'

'For striking a senior NCO? If she was a man, court martial and the glasshouse. Striking, using or offering violence to his superior officer, contrary to Section 8 of the Army Act, in that he ... blah, blah, blah. But since she's a woman, we can only get her under Section 40, conduct to the prejudice of good order and military discipline. They'll kick her out, though.'

'But that's what she wants.'

'Of course. And that's what the army wants, too, so we're all happy, aren't we?'

And that justified everything? I held my handkerchief to my bleeding cheek and wondered.

I sat outside a café in a village street, with my scratched cheek turned away from the sight of people at the other tables. The elegant, stone-fronted buildings had been pale honey coloured before they'd been blackened by smoke. Most of the windows were cracked or broken and boarded up. The frames hadn't been painted for years. Yet it was a fine street, wide and dignified, with broad pavements on both sides. Overlooking the village was a château that had been a German headquarters and was now a British one. Its outer walls plunged down to the bridge across the river and the graves of the men who'd died to liberate this place.

It was a town getting back to living. Stalls lining the street sold the rich dairy products of Normandy – straw-coloured butter, so fresh that droplets of moisture still oozed from it, and cream, crusted with globules of yellow fat, and cheese – Pavé d'Auge, golden-ribbed, packed in little, wood-chip punnets, smelly Pont l'Évêque and soft goat cheese, white as chalk, laid on bright green leaves. Works of art. We hadn't seen anything like it in England since 1939, and not then, not ever probably, in Wiltshire.

I sat in the sun and revelled in the smell of my coffee, dense and black and bitter, a smell almost as good as its taste. It was real coffee, not NAAFI sawdust and gravy browning, or treacly Camp coffee from the bottle with the kilted officer and his Indian bearer on the label.

Housewives with baskets, as shabby as any at home, headscarves and bare legs and wooden-soled shoes, were bargaining their way around the stalls. They pinched and poked and squeezed and sniffed and turned up their noses with knowledgeable disdain. I thought of the patient, plodding British housewife, grateful for what she could get, ready to join any likely-looking queue, not to be budged even by an air raid,

There was one young woman who turned away with an empty basket and, as she went, the stall holder spat, just missing his artichokes. The woman might have been pretty, but her eyebrows had been shaved off, brutally, leaving nicks in her skin. Her headscarf was pulled down and tied tightly. I was pretty sure she didn't have any hair under it. Nothing here for her. Nothing until her hair grew again and she could move away to a place where her past wasn't known and resented.

How different was her treatment from what we had done to Private Madigan, I wondered? And what would we have done if the Germans had come to Britain? Pansy would have had nothing to do with them, of that I was certain. But how would I have behaved, or Vee, or Grace? Resisted? Collaborated? Kept our heads down and our noses clean and pretended everything was normal. Would Britain have been any different from France? Thank God, now we'd never know.

Grace was bargaining with a *marchand des brocantes* over a set of majolica asparagus dishes with matching jugs for melted butter. The plates

274

were decorated with moulded china asparagus stalks, coloured an improbable green and purple. They had little hollows to hold the butter. How extraordinary, I thought idly, how French, to have special dishes for a food that was only available for a few weeks every year. Asparagus plates, oyster plates, strawberry plates, snail plates...

I watched Grace turn them over to look for a mark, run her finger round the edges to check for chips, then shake her head, begin to walk away, change her mind, reluctantly walk back... Anyone would think she was back in Cairo, bargaining in the bazaar of Khan el Khalili. Stall holders really understood bargaining there. What did she want them for, anyway? I didn't know anyone at home who hadn't dug up their asparagus beds to plant potatoes. Still, one day...

I turned my face to the sun and closed my eyes. I could still see its brilliant disc on the backs of my eyelids. My nose was freckling and beginning to peel and the scratches stung, but the sun felt too good to turn my back on it. For the first time since ... oh, for a very long time, I felt relaxed and – very nearly – happy.

France. Twenty-five years ago – or a little longer, to allow for the months of my gestation – perhaps my father had sat at a café table in a village like this, farther north, but not so very different. If I opened my eyes I might catch him there, that tall, thin, gawky boy. He had sat on the sunny side of a battered village street, sipping coffee, watching life go on, in spite of war, in spite of hardships and loss. His legs were crossed, his tin hat out of the way under the table. His war was as near to ending as, perhaps, this one was. He would be able to see the finish not so very far ahead, to anticipate, to hope. He was a married man, with a wife who adored him, a child on the way and everything to live for.

And then he had risen from the table, paid his bill, gone back to war and vanished.

Grace plumped into the chair beside me and set the three-legged table rocking. She put her bargained-for plates on the empty chair.

'I don't know why I had to have them. The asparagus season's over until next year. Coffee? Wonderful. *Encore deux cafés, s'il vous plaît, madame.*' She stretched out her legs and admired her trim ankles in their tightly laced brown boots. They didn't look like army issue to me. She reached over and turned my cheek towards her. She ran a gentle finger down the four red lines.

'I heard what happened,' she said.

'I don't want to talk about it.'

'Please yourself. *Merci, madame.*' She spooned sugar, real sugar, into her cup, sipped and sighed with delight. 'Mmmm, wonderful. What will you do when the war's over, Laura?'

I closed my eyes again and gave her question the consideration it deserved. Well, what would I do? Stay in the army? The episode with Madigan had convinced me that there wasn't a place for me. Go back to working in a solicitor's office in Salisbury? Settle down to be the unmarried daughter at home? Unthinkable.

'Laura? Are you asleep?'

'I'm thinking.'

'And?'

'I haven't a clue. Everything seems impossible. What about you?'

'No idea. But whatever it is, it'll sure as hell be boring after this.'

Scrappy bits of paper torn from a notebook and written in spindly handwriting with indelible pencil. A muddy thumbprint. No envelope. Perhaps it had never been written as a letter. Perhaps it had just been amongst my father's effects – effects, that innocuous, catch-all word that meant the heartbreaking bits and pieces forwarded to relatives – a pen with a crossed nib, a watch with broken glass, a few Egyptian coins, a scorched photograph.

The Germans have made a push for Paris. So far we are holding them, but only just. One way or the other, I think it will end the war. I don't know how they have done it, but they have really caught us napping. We knew there was going to be some sort of attack, but there has never been anything like it. Two weeks ago we were in Flesquières and now we are forced back nearly as far as Arras. We haven't been anywhere long enough to dig in or consolidate. Snatch a breath, a cup of tea, bind up the wounded, count the dead and move again. For the moment, we have stopped falling back, but I don't know how long we can hold the line here. 'Gott Mit Uns,' they say, God With Us, and wear the words on their belt buckles. Who knows, perhaps they are right. Mr Millport will know. We prayed for the rain and the mud that has baited our own offensives every time, but it didn't come. Instead, the ground was firm and the air was dense and white and woolly. Ludendorff can even organize the weather to suit himself. Gott Mit Uns. We were deafened and dazed by their first bombardment. They opened up with six thousand guns. Six thousand. Where did they come from? Guns don't just appear overnight. It takes time. They have to be hauled in, manhandled. They leave tracks. They scar the ground. Why did our Intelligence not warn us? Why did our aircraft not see the wheel tracks, not spot their camouflaged positions? Why didn't we know? The earth rocked and shook under us. We crouched with our hands over our heads while fountains of earth and stones and rotting remains and fence posts and old tin cans were hurled at us. We were sick with the noise. We couldn't think or breathe or stand or sit or lie or help each other. We weren't men, we were less than worms. We could only cringe close to the earth and whimper and wait until the enemy had finished with us. They blew up gun positions and ammunition dumps. The roads were torn apart. The signal wires were tossed into the air and came down like string. The air vibrated and solid objects seemed to dance and flicker. The fog was yellow and crimson and orange. It sparkled and fizzed and blinded us with its brightness. The bombardment ranged backwards and forwards, choosing where to blast and where to spare. God forgive us, we were even glad when some other poor devil was getting it. We knew it was nearly over when their engineers fired the charges they had laid in what was left of our wire. And when it stopped, we waited for them to come out of the mist. But we couldn't see them. The Germans call them Sturmabteilung, Storm Troops. They raced through the fog, smashing through the forward positions with bombs and flamethrowers, never waiting to see the effect, overwhelming everything in front of them. What they couldn't subdue, they bypassed and cut off. They don't reinforce their weakest points, as we do, but their strongest ones, cutting and stabbing and forcing a breach, then widening it and consolidating. It's a new concept and a terrifying one. They even knew where they were going. Dear God. When I think of the muddle and confusion of our own attacks, when we can scarcely find our way over the parapet of our own trenches, it's hard to believe that the Germans could find their way through and round our defences so quickly. How is it possible? We fell back and then back again, further and further, though never so far or so fast as on the first day. Now we have stopped, simply because we can't go any further. We are exhausted. Our backs are to the wall and even the staff must admit it. Our only hope is that German exhaustion is greater than ours. They must halt soon. Surely they can't continue the attack with such fury for much longer. Their losses are terrible. The war must end after this. One way or another. How can any country expect its men to do more?

'Laura?' The MT sergeant put his head round my tent door. 'Are you busy?'

'As ever, Stan,' I answered with a smile. 'Who isn't?'

He was a decent man, quiet and hardworking, the best sort of NCO, always coaxing more out of his engines and their drivers than they thought they could give, always ready to take the snaps of his family out of his pocket and pass them round.

279

I knew them all by name. Ivy, who worked shifts in an aircraft factory and still managed to keep the family together. Little Valerie, with straggly pigtails tied with floppy bows. Barry, who just couldn't seem to get the hang of reading, somehow. Clive, who was almost old enough to be called up, God forbid.

'Can we talk?'

'Of course. Do you mind if I come out to you? I'm afraid I can't ask you in. There's paper all over the place. It seems to multiply every night.' I slipped out of the tent, away from the clacking machines, but their noise followed me out, tireless, voracious for information, clattering night and day.

'I'd rather stand anyway, if you don't mind.' He stood by the flap of the tent entrance, almost at attention, thumbs in line with the seams of his trousers, as though he were on a charge. 'There's bad news, I'm afraid. Private Westonbirt – she's a friend of yours, isn't she?'

I nodded. Knowing. Funny how you always know.

'There's been an accident. Her tanker went up. She's asking for you.'

I didn't stop to ask for permission. I ran and, as I went, I heard him say, 'I'm sorry, love.'

Out of their grey and scarlet, in khaki shirts and slacks, with their hair tied up in turbans, the nurses looked much more approachable than they did in England. I stopped one and asked where I'd find Grace.

'The ATS driver? Down there. She's in a side

280

tent off the main burns ward.'

'May I see her?'

'Any time,' she said, with a smile that told me more about Grace's condition than I had asked.

It was a long walk down the length of the marquee. My right boot squeaked with every step. I'm sure it didn't usually do that. The brailings were rolled up to allow a breeze to pass through, but the smell was still there. It reminded me of the smell in Martin's darkroom, but underneath the cleanness of chemicals was the whiff of decaying flesh. Scarlet-covered beds lined each side, several with drip stands by their sides, two completely curtained. I didn't know whether to look and smile at the occupants or whether they'd think I was gawping.

One lad raised his bandaged hands in a clumsy wave. 'Hello, gorgeous, come to visit me?'

Nineteen, was he? Twenty? Sunken eyes in bruised sockets. A wire cage lifted the bedclothes off his legs. I smiled. 'Not today, I'm afraid.'

'Don't leave it too long. I might have my clothes back on by then!'

Whistles and waves followed me down the ward.

'Over here, sarge.'

'Blow us a kiss, darling.'

But some were silent and motionless, their eyes turned towards the canvas ceiling. And in the side ward, a swathed body, long and bulky and shapeless.

I stood by the bed, hesitating and helpless, sick with selfish fear of what I might be forced to see. She was my friend and I was afraid to look at her.

281

No need. There wasn't very much of Grace to see.

The mummies in Cairo museum looked like that, human but not human, mutely self-contained, set apart, untouchable. But this one was wrapped in cleaner bandages. It was breathing, slowly, painfully, the air rasping through passages seared by heat. Saline mixture dripped from a bottle, down a tube and through a needle inserted into the only patch of visible Grace.

A nurse looked through the curtains. 'She's just had a hefty shot of morphine, I'm afraid. She'll be out for the count for a long time.'

'I hope so,' I whispered.

The nurse came in and drew the curtains closed behind her. She put her hand on my shoulder. 'It's marvellous what they can do with burns these days, you know,' she said brightly, in answer to a question I hadn't asked. 'They're learning all the time. Look at all those poor burned pilots at ♥East Grinstead. They're almost...'

'...almost normal. I'm not sure that Grace would like that very much.'

Grace without eyelids. Grace without nostrils, without lips. Beautiful Grace.

'We'll do our best to stabilize her condition here,' the nurse continued. 'If she does well, she'll be flown back home.'

'May I touch her?' My throat felt tight, my voice wobbling out of control, like a growing boy's.

'She won't feel anything, dear. We've knocked

her out for a good, long sleep.'

'I see. Of course... Do you know what happened?'

'Sorry, no. An accident, a crash, I think. That's all. Well – this won't get a wardful of dressings changed. No peace for the wicked. I must get on. Stay as long as you like, dear.'

And that told me all I needed to know.

I put my hand on the place where Grace's ought to be. I had expected it to be soft. The firmness of the dressings surprised me. She felt like a well-upholstered sofa. Braver, I began to stroke the hand.

'Grace,' I whispered. 'I know you can't hear me, but I'm here anyway.'

I'd like to imagine she heard me. I could pretend that there was the faintest twitch of recognition, a sign, anything. But I'd be fooling myself. There was nothing. Just as well, really.

I had to go back to work, but I slipped back again, to the hospital just after dark. Tilley lamps hung, hissing, from the ridge of the marquee. They cast bright pools of light that turned the beds into shadowy, painful mysteries. Moths batted against the lamps, fizzed, flared and dropped to the ground. The smell of paraffin was added to all the unnameable hospital smells and the heat from the lamps hung in a dense layer below the canvas. A soldier behind drawn curtains was making a faint, repetitive sound. I couldn't tell if he was groaning or weeping or laughing.

The night nurse sat at a table at the end of the ward. The lamp lit up the forms she was filling in, her hands – red and rough, with clipped, clean nails – and a fringe of fuzzy fair hair.

'Hello,' she said with a smile. 'You can go on through, if you like.'

Nothing had changed. As far as I could see, Grace had neither moved nor been moved, but a new bottle of saline dripped into her veins. I pulled a chair closer to the bed. I leaned forward and stroked where her forehead would be. What had happened, I wondered. Had she hit a mine? Taken a bend too fast with a laden tanker? Had she finally risked that cigarette she'd always said she was gasping for?

'Hello, Grace,' I said softly. 'I'm back again.'

And she twitched. I swear she twitched. Then – nothing.

Far away, much farther than when I'd first landed in France, I could hear the sound of guns, a sort of background mutter, like soldiers on parade complaining beneath their breath. The battle was moving on, deeper into France, towards Paris, towards Germany. Soon the headquarters would pack up again and follow.

Behind the curtains it was very quiet, but it wasn't peaceful. There was a struggle going on. I could sense it, almost feel it, but I had no part to play in it. Grace had to fight alone. She loved company, adored crowds, but she was on her own in this. All I could do was be with her and try not to think of the body beneath the wrappings, skinless and raw, a carcass.

James had taken three days to die. Please God, please God, let Grace go quicker than that.

I sat with my hand on hers, listening to her

breathing – so shallow, how could she draw enough air into her lungs? – until the night nurse came to change the drip bottle. She threw me out, but kindly.

Next day, there was a minor flap on. Signals flew backwards and forwards, all to be encoded or decoded and interpreted. It was late afternoon before I got a moment to slip over to the hospital.

There was still a bandaged body in the bed, but enough was visible to show me that it was a man. I smiled at him, a thin, unkind smile that he was too sick to return. 'Sorry,' I said, 'wrong place.'

The nurses on duty were busy, going from bed to bed doling out medicine. I hung around until the ward sister reached the place where I was standing.

'Grace ... my friend ... Private Westonbirt ... has she...?' Of course, I knew the answer. I wasn't stupid. All the same, I had to ask, I had to be certain. I cleared my throat and tried again. 'Has she been transferred back to England?'

The woman turned to me and I could see how tired she was. Her nose was pinched round the nostrils and her lips were pale. A wisp of greasy hair had escaped from her khaki turban. Her shirt was patched with damp under her arms and across her collarbone and in a line down her spine. You'd think she would have run out of compassion by now, but she hadn't. Her eyes were still kind.

'I'm so sorry. We made her comfortable. That's all we could do.'

I nodded and turned away. 'Thank you.'

She caught my arm as I went. 'It was the best thing for her. Really.'

'I know.'

As I walked back down the ward, a lad whistled. From the next bed, a voice said, 'Shut up, you. Show a bit of respect.'

I ducked through the canvas door flap and into Martin's arms.

'I've been looking for you,' he said. He took my hand and led me away.

There was so little privacy in camp that we walked towards the little wood, in the opposite direction from the village. From a distance, the wood looked ravaged. Trees were splintered and tanks had gouged tracks where none had been before.

Now that we were closer, I could see that the wood survived, no matter what had been done to it. The tank tracks were edged with growing grass. Shattered stumps were already putting out fresh shoots. While the top growth had been destroyed, all the low-growing, creeping, humble plants carried on in the way they always had done. A blackbird was sending out its silly, evening message that told every predator exactly where he was going to roost. The sounds of the camp were a very long way away.

I think I'd have walked off the edge of the earth with him that day, if he had only taken my hand and asked me to follow.

'I'm sorry I wasn't in time,' said Martin softly. 'I wanted to be with you.'

I didn't feel much like talking, but just to be

near him was comforting.

'I ought to write to her parents,' I said, trying to be practical. 'I know the army will notify them officially, but I ought to write. They have a right to know what happened, what it was like.'

'Don't be too hard on them,' Martin warned me. 'Write if you must, but don't tell them ... everything. What good would that do?'

I nodded. He was right, of course. Their daughter was dead. Why add to their grief by telling them how? 'Then what can I say?'

'Tell them about your friendship, about the four of you and what you mean to each other. Tell them why Grace was special. Tell them about the laughter and the mischief. Tell them that she was beautiful and funny and that she made everyone feel good.'

'I remember...' I smiled. 'I remember she read the whole of *Gone with the Wind*, hidden under a truck, with her boots sticking out. It took her a week and everyone who passed thought she was working on the engine. She was under there snivelling over Bonnie Blue's death and no-one noticed.'

Martin laughed. 'Typical army – no-one worries where you're going or what you're doing, as long as you march smartly, salute everything and carry a broom.'

It was good to laugh. It was good to remember the funny things, the happy moments. With Grace, there had been so many. 'But Martin ... oh, Martin, every time I close my eyes, I see Grace in flames...' I began to shiver again.

He put his arms around me. 'Sssh. Sssh. It's all

right. I'm here.'

What he said didn't make sense, but I didn't care. His being there didn't make things all right, but it made them bearable. Just. His khaki tunic was rough beneath my cheek. The buttons pressed their pattern into my skin. His arms were hard and strong, their grip fierce. It was what I wanted, what I needed. They made me feel safe and, at the same time, very vulnerable.

'You know that I want to look after you, don't you?' Martin went on, softly. He laid his cheek against my hair. I was cold and his breath was warm. 'Always.'

'There doesn't seem to be much of an always to look forward to.'

'Things will change.'

'I know. It just doesn't feel that way just now.'

'It will get better. I promise you.'

I looked up into his face, that dear, disfigured face that had been part of my life for as long as I could remember. When had I not been able to turn to Martin for safety? I reached up and touched his cheek, his nose, his strongly marked eyebrows. He was warm. His skin was supple. He was so alive.

'Oh Martin,' I sighed and shuddered. 'Touch me. Love me. I need you so much.'

For the second time in my life, I woke up in the same bed as someone else. I lay with my eyes still closed and felt the unaccustomed warmth of another human body pressed against mine. The ornate iron bed sagged in the middle and rolled us as close together as we could be. We lay in the dip in the mattress, tumbled together like a pair of puppies. Martin's legs, long and muscular, were entwined with mine. His arm lay heavily across my waist, awkwardly comforting.

I knew what I would see when I opened my eyes. Not a stranger. My friend. His dark hair would be tousled, sticking up in startled peaks, in the way it used to be when he'd towelled it dry after a swim. His eyes would still be closed, fringed by dark half-moons of lashes, but when they opened I knew they'd be bright as China tea with lemon, like dry sherry in firelight, like last year's leaves on a woodland floor dappled by sunlight.

'Un lit de mariage?' the landlady had asked coyly. She'd looked down at my hand, quite openly. I still wore a wedding ring, James's ring. It had nestled comfortably into the flesh of my finger over the years. No curtain ring donned for one night only, she could see that.

She'd shown us up winding stairs, along a corridor that sloped at an angle that threw you into the opposite wall. *'Le lavabo,'* she'd announced, throwing open a door that seemed to lead into a black box. *'Et voilà...'*

An enormous room, full of evening sunshine, lit by tall, narrow windows opening on to a minute balcony. White starched curtains looped back and a white starched counterpane on the bed. Pale, painted furniture, soft grey and green, blue and yellow, faded and scratched, but very beautiful. Tiny squares of sunlight, like a mosaic of gold, were scattered across the bed.

She'd smiled at us knowingly and handed

Martin a key that might have come from the Bastille.

He had been part of my life for as long as I could remember, yet, when the key was turned in the lock, I was scared and shy as I hadn't been with James on that brief, long-ago wedding night that had ended before it began. We'd stood in the sunlight, facing each other. I didn't know what to do, how to act.

Slowly, Martin had pulled off my tie and collar, taken out my collar studs and laid them on the table, opened the first few buttons of my shirt and spread the edges wide. Keeping his eyes on mine, he'd laid his hands on my naked shoulders and caressed my collarbones with his thumbs, gently and firmly smoothing the skin. His hands were trembling as much as mine.

'Laura, are you sure? Tell me now, before it's too late.'

I nodded briefly. 'I'm sure,' I'd said. But I wasn't. Not really. Not then.

I'd unbuttoned my cuffs and Martin unfastened the remaining buttons on my shirt, then peeled it back and off. Quickly – rather adeptly, I thought – he unhooked my regulation brassière. He cupped his hands around my breasts, taking their weight, cradling their fullness. They looked very small in his long-fingered hands.

'So beautiful,' he whispered and brushed his thumbs across the nipples.

A spasm shot through me, fierce and sudden. It was so unexpected that I jerked back and away from him. I felt my eyes widen with shock. I wasn't even sure whether I liked it or not. Martin laughed with delight and touched me again. The shock ran through me once more, like an electric current, taking my breath with it. I wanted him to do it again and again.

'Your turn,' said Martin quietly, holding out his wrists for me to deal with the buttons.

Clumsily, I unfastened them all, while he stood quite still. His rough shirt slid to the floor. The sun was warm on my back, making me feel very relaxed, very languorous. Everything seemed to be happening very slowly, as though time had turned his back on us. The light gilded each separate wiry hair on Martin's chest, except where my own body shadowed his. A line of dark hair, finer and finer, ran down to his waistband and beyond.

A seam ran from his shoulder, down the left arm, to his elbow, beautifully stitched, a work of art. One day it would fade, but now it was angry still, the stitch holes dull red, the bottom pair oozing slightly. A bruise spread right round and under the arm. I touched the top end of the scar with a fingertip.

'Does it hurt?'

Martin lowered his head and kissed the finger. 'Not now.'

For a moment, we stood very still, facing each other, scarcely breathing. All the sounds of the evening – traffic in the street, clattering dishes in the dining room, a dog barking – faded away. Nothing mattered but Martin, here, now. Martin didn't take his eyes off mine. I couldn't look away. It was as though each waited for the other to call a halt. If you're making a mistake, now's the time to say so. Last chance, Laura.

But for me there was no turning back. And there never would be again.

I could scarcely stand. My thighs felt heavy, my knees weak. I tipped forward and my breasts brushed lightly across his naked chest. Martin gave a gasp and, bending over, picked me up and laid me on the bed. He lowered his head and took my nipples in his mouth, one after the other, teasing, lightly nipping.

'Laura,' he whispered hoarsely, looking up, and his eyes were hazy with emotion. 'Laura, I never thought you'd come to me.'

I'd never imagined, I'd never dreamed how beautiful he would be...

He'd entered me quickly and fiercely, with all the urgency of the little time we had together driving him on. The force of his thrust hurt me, parted me like a knife, so that my muscles spasmed in self-defence. I clamped down hard on him. He stopped.

'Laura ... darling ... ?' he'd begun to say, then he'd shuddered, shuddered again, driven on, unstoppable, until I'd learned the rhythm from him and joined him and matched him.

Martin opened his eyes.

'Good morning,' I said and kissed the place where his nose altered direction.

He propped himself up on one elbow and looked down into my face. 'Still here? I thought I'd been having the sort of dream that no-one wants!' He gave a soft laugh and ran his fingers gently down over my face, my throat, my breasts. My skin tingled wherever he touched. I ached, but it was a delicious ache. His hand smoothed over my stomach and he laced his fingers in the crisp hair below, giving it a gentle tweak. 'No, this is really you.'

'Mmmm. It's me all right.' I nestled closer and rubbed my face against his chest like a spoiled kitten.

He kissed me very slowly, caressing my lips, tasting all the soft, secret places of my mouth. Low down in my belly, something kindled and spread wide fingers of fire.

When we stopped for breath, Martin propped himself up on one elbow. 'I'm very sorry,' he said.

'Sorry – what for?' I asked, with more calmness than I felt. Don't, don't say you're sorry for what we've done, Martin, I don't think I could bear that.

He looked deeply embarrassed. 'I hurt you. I didn't know, didn't expect that you ... that you hadn't...'

'It doesn't matter.' And, at last, it was true. I listened for James's voice and he was silent.

'I was in too much of a hurry. I'm sorry.'

'It doesn't matter,' I answered again, coaxing him back to kissing me.

'I won't ever hurt you again. I promise.'

His hand was still entwined with my body hair and he slipped his fingers lower still, finding the warm, secret spots that no-one had even told me about. Subtly, sensitively, he took possession of every hidden place. My body took control. It jerked and arched against him. I felt as though I was melting, dissolving.

Just in time, he rose above me and slipped into

place. No pain, no resistance. I opened up and received him.

And afterwards, we lay so still and close that I wasn't certain if it was my own heart or Martin's that I felt thudding against my ribs. It didn't matter. He laid his lips quietly against the angle of my jaw.

'Laura,' he whispered. 'I love you, Laura.'

Just for a moment, I thought there was an echo in the room, the same words but another voice, far away and fading. I strained to hear. No, it was gone.

The morning light was grey. Another rainy day. The room that had been bathed in evening sun looked shabby and worn by day, its paint chipped, its walls cracked. Who cared?

I watched Martin dress. Everything he did fascinated me. I loved the way his muscles moved, the long, lean line of his naked body as he stooped over the washstand to shave in the half-pint of hot water Madame had thought sufficient. I loved the quick neatness of his fingers as he tied his tie. I loved the curve of his back as he bent to tie his bootlaces.

How odd it felt, not to be diffident to dress in front of him. It was ... it was natural.

'Goodness, I wish I wasn't wearing passion-killers,' I said with a laugh, quickly pulling up my skirt to disguise them.

'They didn't kill my passion.' Martin gave a grin and patted my bottom.

I buttoned my waistband and picked up my crumpled shirt. 'How long have you got?' I needed to know and dreaded the answer.

'I haven't. I should have gone back last night.'

'What will happen?'

'I'll think of something.' He sat on the edge of the bed and pulled me beside him. Then picked up my right hand and tucked it into his battledress tunic. 'You're not sorry, are you?'

'Sorry?'

'No regrets?'

'No regrets – not now or ever.'

I smiled the bright, tremulous smile of every woman who sends her man back to war. Then I finished dressing and went back to war myself.

Dear Mother

I didn't want to part from you with such harsh words, but you gave me no choice. Forgive me, then, for the words, but not the meaning. Nothing is certain these days. I may not come back. I don't say that to demand your sympathy – that would be despicable – it is simply a fact and we would all be very stupid to ignore it. You ought to know that Diana and I were married yesterday. We have cared for each other very deeply for a long time. You have no right to try to stand between us. Whatever your prejudices – and I can't understand them – we have made our own decision. She is a good, sweet girl and I don't deserve her. I pray that I will never cause her any unhappiness. The war must end soon and I will do my best to come back to her. I have such a good reason for living. Diana is expecting our child in February. I only hope that I will live to see him or her. If I don't, for my sake, Mother, look after my wife and be kind to her.

Edwin

Who could blame them for snatching a little happiness? Only a short time ago – a month, a week, yesterday – I might have been shocked to discover that I had been conceived outside marriage. My mother, so faded, so gentle, and the man I ought to have known, but didn't. They had loved and they had made me. Was that wrong? Why is it so difficult to imagine that one's parents have ever been young, ever felt passion? How sanctimonious. How was it in any way different from what had happened between Martin and me?

And had they managed to see each other again? Had my father been able to scrape another leave, maybe just a 48-hour pass, before he died? Or had those few moments of love been all they had been allowed? I hoped they were happy, in the little time they had together.

And the letter raised another, even more personal concern. Like mother, like daughter. Supposing I mirrored my mother and found myself expecting Martin's child. What then? I didn't even know where he was. He drifted in and out of my life, turning up at unexpected moments, but where he went in between, I never knew. I didn't blame him. I blamed the war, but all the same, supposing...

But I only had a week – it felt much longer – to indulge in worries like that, before becoming certain that I wasn't pregnant. I didn't know whether I was relieved or sorry.

The war moved on. We followed.

By 1800 hours on 19 August, the Americans and Poles met at the biting end of the pincer movement that had closed the Falaise pocket. Although their generals escaped, the German Seventh Army and 5th Panzer Army were annihilated. Ten thousand died and 50,000 were captured. The roads around Trun and Chambois were jammed by German convoys, stationary now, blasted by bombing Typhoons and artillery. The verges were littered with bodies, decaying, stiffening, bloodstains turning black on dusty grey uniforms, a feast for flies. Horses, trapped in their harnesses, crawled on shattered legs. The stench rose so high that even the pilots of observation planes recoiled. For days afterwards it was impossible to move, they said, without treading on human flesh.

Seven days later, Generals de Gaulle, Leclerc and Koenig, at the head of Free French soldiers of the Division Leclerc and the *résistants* of the city, marched from the Arc de Triomphe to Notre Dame to give thanks. The Parisians went crazy with delight and relief. The fight for Paris had cost the lives of a thousand Frenchmen, but Paris was liberated and intact. The time for settling old scores had arrived.

By 3 September, we'd reached Hitler's new standpoint on the Somme-Marne line and passed through it as though it had no more significance than a pencil line on a map. On 4 September, having advanced 110 miles in two days, the Allies entered Brussels to scenes of rejoicing as wild as those in Paris. Nothing like that mad speed had been seen since those long ago days when we'd pushed the Italians across the Western Desert.

People were beginning to believe again the old saying – all over by Christmas. Winter and the Germans had other ideas.

My dear Mother

There's so little time left, not enough to explain or complain. By the time this letter reaches you, you will know what has happened to me. I want you to know that I haven't done anything that I am ashamed of, or that would make you or Father ashamed of me. I've done my duty, as I saw it had to be done. Not everyone agrees with that. They've all been very kind to me here since the verdict was confirmed. There are no grudges, or, if there are, they will soon be settled in a final fashion. I don't think I'm actually afraid of dying. I've seen so many men die and the way of their dying was far worse than the one I shall face. The RSM will pick the best shots and the lads will do a good, clean job for me. I trust them to do that. It will be the last kindness. The MO has pumped me full of something to take the sting out of waiting. That was good of him. I don't feel sleepy, just rather drowsy and calm. If it's any comfort to Father, tell him that I won't have to be dragged out. I won't let him down. The MO has promised me another shot of his magic potion in the morning, so I shall be all right when the time comes. He's a good chap. He'll be with me in the morning and the padre, too. I shall make my communion before I go. I'll have plenty of company. The whole regiment will be drawn up on parade to watch – a sharp lesson for them all. Poor Tom. I wish he didn't have to be there, but the CO will take no

298

excuses, particularly from Tom. He visited me this morning and told me he'd have to get very drunk before he'd be able to watch. Better not, I told him, you're in enough trouble, anyway. Everyone is doing their best to make me comfortable tonight, as comfortable as anyone can be in a French auberge with no roof. There's a subaltern with me all the time – the newest one in the regiment, poor devil, what a job and he's only been here two days – to make sure that I don't take French leave through the roof and that I don't cheat the firing squad by doing their task for them. Why do they think I should want to do that? If I have to die, far better to be finished off quickly and properly than to make a hash of it myself. How odd, to be able to write so calmly. Perhaps it's because there's no way out. If there was the slightest chance of escape, I'd be begging for it, but, since there isn't... Tell Mr Millport that I put myself in God's hands, knowing that I've done nothing wrong. I have plenty of regrets. I would like to have had the time to come home again and make my peace with you. I wish I could see Diana again. I wish I could see our baby. I know it will be beautiful, if it is anything like its mother. I would like to have one more chance to climb on to the downs above Ansty Parva and feel the wind and hear the grass whistle. I don't want to die in this Godforsaken, muddy country. I've asked you once before to look after Diana. Now I want you to do more. I want you to love her – for our child's sake, if not for hers or mine. Tell Father that I did my duty.

Your loving son
Edwin

I sat with the yellowing sheet of paper in my hand

for a long time. The nib had been scratchy. It had blotted several times. And my father's hand had not been steady. Whatever the doctor had given him, however he tried to comfort his mother by pretending an unnatural calm, his writing told me that he had been terribly afraid. You see, I knew it so well by now. I'd seen it in messy schoolboy's letters, in cocky young subaltern's letters, in the letters of a man dazed by shellfire and exhausted. I could recognize the difference.

The last letter.

Of all that pile in the trunk in the attic at Ansty House, this was the last and nothing that I had learned so far had prepared me for it. I had read them all and it had been like listening to a voice, a voice that had become very dear to me. Now that voice would be silent for ever. I knew, of course, that I would reach the end of the cache of letters, but not like this.

I folded the sheet of paper and slipped it back into its place in the bundle. I didn't need to read it again. I felt as though I could recite every word and that, if I never saw it again, I'd still be able to repeat every word of it on my own dying day.

What you know, you can't un-know. What you've learned, can't be un-learned, no matter how hard you try.

There was a king who visited an alchemist who could turn base metal into gold. 'It's quite simple,' said the alchemist. 'Anyone can do it. Just follow this formula. The most important thing to remember is that while you are making the gold you must never, ever think of a hippopotamus.' And, of course, the king never made gold, because every time he tried, he couldn't get the hippopotamus out of his mind. I felt like that.

I couldn't think of anything else. It was like saying goodbye. It was like taking a long journey with an old friend and reaching a crossroads where your ways parted. It was finding out that everyone you have trusted, everyone you have respected and loved for as long as you can remember, has been cheating all the time. It was a shock.

And yet ... of course ... it wasn't. It all made a dreadful sense.

Asking ... telling ... my mother was the cruellest thing I have ever done in my life.

I understand now why men and women go absent without leave. Something happens that is so momentous that they feel they can't cope with everyday service life any longer. A husband or wife dies, a child is in hospital, a lover writes that cruel, final letter – and suddenly the life of kit inspections and parades and petty tyranny can't be suffered any longer. They could ask for help, but they don't believe they'll get it. So they just push off and the Redcaps follow and drag them back and then everything is worse than it was before.

I nearly did that. I lay in my comfortable billet in Brussels, listening to the sounds of husband and wife making love in the next room and I thought: that's enough, I can't stand it any longer, I have to know and I'm going home.

I wanted to. But I didn't, of course. There's

301

such a thing as self-discipline and responsibility and all the other high-sounding qualities they try to drum into you on promotion courses (but if you haven't got them already, they'll never teach you). And when something has been kept secret for more than twenty-five years, it can keep for a day or two longer. Certainly until I managed to wangle a spot of leave.

So I went home and I told her about my father's letters, about the anonymous envelopes, the photograph of the grave, everything. My mother looked as though I'd said something utterly indecent, as though I'd stood in her kitchen and opened up at the top of my voice with every disgusting word the army had taught me. She cradled the newly warmed teapot against her chest. The kettle lid began to rattle as the water reached the boil.

'Laura! Whatever made you think...'

'I don't think. I know,' I snapped. 'And I want to know why.'

'I don't know'

'I don't believe you. I want to know why. I need to know.'

Water spurted from the kettle spout and bounced like silver beads across the hot surface of the range.

'I don't know...'

I felt such rage. Dear God. I could have shaken the truth out of her. 'You must know. He was your husband. You were carrying his child. Me. Didn't you care?'

'Oh, Laura. How could you ask that?' Her eyes filled. She was thin and worn down and the hands that clutched the teapot were swollen and painful looking. The freezing weather had split her skin and the cracks had become infected. 'You don't understand. I was very ill. I thought I was going to lose you. I'd already lost Edwin, but I made up my mind that I was going to hang on to his child. And your grandmother...'

'Ah, yes. Grandmother. She wrapped him up in tissue paper and locked him in a trunk.'

'She what...?' The kettle lid blew off and boiling water deluged over the stove. There was a tremendous cloud of steam. Mother turned and grabbed at the handle without waiting to pick up a cloth. She screamed as water spat up.

'Mother! For heaven's sake...' I plunged her scalded hand into the bowl of cold water that held peeled potatoes on the draining board. 'I'm sorry. I'm so sorry...'

'It's all right, darling.' She leaned against me, trembling with pain and shock. 'I know you didn't mean it.'

That evening, I watched my mother knitting a jersey for Tom. It had to be a striped one, because the wool had been unravelled from several old things and there wasn't enough of one colour. The wool was squiggly and wouldn't run smoothly, but she plain-and-purled stubbornly on, her bandaged right hand getting in the way of every stitch.

I could see that her hand hurt. Her lips were compressed, as though she was afraid that, if she relaxed, she might cry out. Burns or secrets. She was very good at keeping her mouth shut.

I felt so ashamed. I had done that. She would

never have scalded herself if it hadn't been for me. She'd have made that pot of tea, as she'd made thousands, probably, before that. I might as well have picked up the kettle and poured the boiling water over my mother's hand in an attempt to force her to speak. That's what the Gestapo would have done. Was I any better than that?

I got up and stood behind her chair and put my arms around her shoulders and kissed her cheek. 'I'm sorry, Mother,' I whispered.

She secured her knitting carefully, then reached up with her good hand and patted mine.

'What's that?' asked Tom, looking up suddenly and catching us. 'What's that? Girls' secrets?'

In the morning, my brief leave was up and I had to go back to Brussels and my billet with the middle-aged couple who treated me like a daughter, back to walks in the parks and coffee in tiny cafés and Christmas dinner in the Bon Marché department store, a special 'Liberation' Christmas party put on in thanks by the Belgians.

I had achieved absolutely nothing at home, except to scald my mother. And I thought how absolutely impossible it is to force someone you love to do anything at all.

But, before I left, she wrote to me. She must have written that night, because I found the envelope slipped under my door in the morning. Can you believe it? We were talking about the man who was the link between our two lives and she couldn't bear to face me and talk. I was her daughter and she couldn't tell me about my father.

My darling Laura

We've always been such good friends, you and I. We've always been able to talk, haven't we, about anything. Not many mothers and daughters can say that. No matter what, we've been able to talk it through and appreciate, if not agree with, each other's viewpoint, the way friends ought to do. You have always been and are very dear to me. I love you very much.

I want you to try to remember that as you read the rest of this letter.

This time, I can't talk to you. I don't have the courage to face you. I have tried, but I'm just not brave enough.

I wish you didn't have to know. There's never a right time to be hurt and there's no way to make the truth easier for you. The letters are true. I don't know who sent them or why they were written – malice, envy, grief, who knows. It doesn't matter really. Not now.

Your father was executed by firing squad in 1918. That's really all there is to say. I don't know why. Court-martial records are secret, even now, and will be so until I am long dead. They can legally only be shown to the accused – who is dead. How bizarre, how cynical. Not even your grandfather, with all his influence, was able to find out what happened. So now that I've told you that one, horrible fact, you know as much as I do.

We didn't mean to keep secrets from you. We just thought, your grandparents and I, that you didn't need to know. What good would it have done? I had to live with the knowledge, but you were only a child

305

and I couldn't bear to burden you with this horror. Losing your father was bad enough.

There wasn't any more to say – then. As you grew older, you had a right to be told, but it just got harder and harder to talk. I still can't.

I wish I didn't have to tell you now. Please, please, please ... don't try to ask me about it. I don't know any more. Maybe I don't want to. I can't face the thought of opening such cruel, old wounds and Tom, I know, would be so distressed to have it all out in the open again. He and your father were such good friends and went through such awful times together.

Tom mustn't be upset and I can't allow you to do it. He couldn't cope. I will protect him against anything and anyone – even if that means you, Laura.

Don't let this change your thoughts of your father. He was quiet and kind and strong and very brave – no matter what they say – and he would have adored you. Let that be enough.

Forgive me.

But I owed it to the boy who had been my father to find out why he had died.

1945

I sat, one of a long row of women on wobbly benches in a freezing Nissen hut. Under our greatcoats, we were all ǀnaked except for our khaki knickers. Under each chair was a little jar of urine. What a waste of time. Heaven knows what it would take to test the urine of every demobbed servicewoman. I was pretty certain the country didn't have resources on that scale. And why do it, anyway? Still, if that was what it took to get into civvie street...

When my turn came, I accidentally kicked the jar as I stood.

'Oh, blast, now they'll never let me go.'

'Here, have some of mine, love,' offered the woman next to me, tipping some from her full jar into my empty one. 'Plenty more where that came from!'

A weary doctor listened to my chest, tested my reflexes, peeped into my knickers (and I *still* hadn't found out what they were looking for) and passed me as fit.

In a chattering line, shrill as parrots, we filed into the clothing stores and handed in our kit. The stiff serge tunics were a bit more woman shaped than they had been when they were issued, the caps squashed into an amazing variety of non-regulation shapes. All along the long counter, women were dipping into the pockets and taking out nipped-off cigarettes, old bus tickets, cinema stubs, wash-basin plugs (very desirable possessions), kirby grips, lighters made from polished brass ammunition cases, odd earrings. We were allowed to keep a pair of shoes. Useful, that, with so much still on coupons.

And that was that. Feeling oddly naked in a Utility frock, a hand-knitted cardigan and no hat, I hefted up my cardboard suitcase, collected my last ever railway warrant plus £12.10.0 and fifty-six coupons for civilian clothes (no baggy demob suit for us, thank goodness – but with a tailored costume costing £4.15.0, shoes around 15 shillings and a pair of stockings at ten bob, that wasn't going to go far) and walked out of the gates. In my bag was a 14-day ration card and two weeks' worth of sweets. I had fifty-six days' leave to look forward to, plus an extra day for every month spent abroad. oh!

I could go wherever I wanted for the first time in five years.

'Well, darling,' asked Grandmother after I'd been home for a few days. 'And what are you going to do with yourself now?'

'Do?' I echoed, dully.

'I hope you're going to be sensible and stay at home. You've done quite enough gadding around lately.'

'You sound as though I'd just spent a winter sunning myself on the Riviera.'

'There's no need for that! It hasn't exactly been fun at home, while you've been globe-trotting,' she remarked, acidly. 'I suppose you have looked at your mother – actually looked? Five years of make-do-and-mend and growing vegetables have worn her out. She's done night fire watch twice a week on top of the church tower. Every Thursday she's pushed a trolley of tea and sandwiches for servicemen round Salisbury station. She's organized village salvage drives, raised money for Spitfires, fed the pigs and chickens, cleaned her house, done her laundry – and mine – and kept a drunken husband out of trouble. Now ... what are *you* going to do?'

308

Grandmother handed me the soap cage with a nearly threatening gesture and click-clacked on her neat little shoes out of the kitchen. I whisked the handled wire cage with its distasteful little bits of soap around in the washing-up water. The water went cloudy. It didn't look as though it was going to shift much grease, but washing soda was like gold dust.

Grandmother certainly hadn't changed. If anything, she seemed younger. She looked ravishing in slacks and, from behind, she could easily have been mistaken for a woman on the right side of forty, rather than nearly seventy. In many ways, she looked younger than her daughter-in-law.

She was right. In an odd sort of way, I'd had an easy war. I had to admit it. Cairo had been like the promised land. Good weather. Good food. Lights. Music. Dancing. Behind the lines, Normandy had been no worse than a wet Guide camp. The kindness and hospitality I'd enjoyed in Brussels had been delightful. And if digs at Mrs Granby's hadn't been exactly palatial, at least I'd had the consolation of knowing that I was doing interesting and important work. Not that salvage and fire-watching and canteen work weren't important, of course. I mean ... oh, dear, what did I mean?

I mean that I'd had a good time. There'd been terrible moments. I'd been widowed. I'd lost a good friend. I'd seen other girls mourn parents and husbands and friends. The grief of war, the sheer waste had touched me and changed me. It had matured me, which is a kinder way of saying that it had aged me beyond my years. And like all soldiers, I'd groused over the pettiness of service life. But – but it had all been so worth while – and it had been fun...

Now? Well, what now?

Jonathan had grown so much. I said so to Pansy.

'Of course he has,' she laughed. 'I'd be really worried if he hadn't. But he is enormous, isn't he? It must be all that extra government milk and rosehip syrup.'

'Last time I saw him he was still a baby, now he's turned into a real boy. What is he – about three?'

'Three a month ago. Isn't he gorgeous? I think so, anyway.'

'Come on, Jonathan – come to Laura.' I held out my arms to the chubby little boy. Laughing and confident, he ran to me. The feel of him was delicious. Unexpectedly solid, soft and yet firm. Defenceless yet surprisingly strong. I lifted him on to my knee. His delightful podginess made me want to squeeze him.

Pansy had been rather sentimental about cutting his hair. Toffee-brown and sun-streaked, fine as gossamer, it curled round his ears. His eyes were bright blue, startlingly direct, guileless and sweet. He was so beautiful.

I knew, of course. You only had to look at him. This was James's son. I'd wondered before. No doubt, now. The question was – did Pansy know? Just how naive was she? Had she known all along? Had she guessed later? Had she still no idea?

The other question was – did it matter any longer?

Jonathan began to squirm. 'My want down,' he said. 'Let my go now.' He slithered on his tummy off my knee and on to the grass. He knelt down beside his mother and began to dig in the vegetable patch. Earth flew around. He tunnelled furiously, far too busy to allow me to cuddle him for long.

I looked over at Pansy. She was pricking out carrots, handling the feathery, fragile seedlings with long-fingered delicacy. The sun was merciless. It pointed out the skimpiness of her frock, how faded the pattern was, how worn under the arms. If she stretched too far, the material would never stand the strain. Pansy herself, however, looked brown and healthy, thin and fit, where my mother was thin and ill.

Pansy knelt up and put a hand to her lower back with a groan. 'Well, that's that. I wonder who'll get more of them – us or the carrot flies?'

'Mothballs. I seem to remember Tom swears by mothballs to keep away carrot fly. You sow them along the row with the carrots. Or do you put them down molehills? I wonder.'

'And who has mothballs these days? If I had, I'd put them among the winter coats. I really don't know how we can expect them to last another year.' She rubbed her muddy hands on the grass and picked up her basket of tools. 'Come in and say hello to Father. He'll be waiting for his tea and he'll be so glad to see you.'

Shouting 'Grampa, Grampa, where are you?', Jonathan ran ahead of us on sturdy legs. Pansy seemed sublimely ignorant of my suspicions. Better to keep it that way. What was there to gain?

311

I watched the little boy dash down the gravel path to the kitchen and couldn't keep a fond, foolish smile off my face. His fat little knees rubbed together as he ran. All that energy, all that beauty, how marvellous.

'Sometimes,' I said with a laugh, not taking my eyes off Jonathan, 'and only sometimes, mind you, I really envy you, Pansy.'

'Do you?' she queried, crisply. 'I wonder.'

She saw me watching him and I saw her watching me, watching him. So – now I knew – Pansy was as aware of the identity of Jonathan's father as I was.

Jonathan was a lovely child who'd given great joy to his mother and grandfather. Did it matter who was his father? Did I care? Why, then, did I feel as though, a very small light had finally gone out?

Later, I remembered something else about the way Pansy had watched me. She looked ... she looked hungry. The usual bland sweetness of her expression had looked pinched and greedy. She had her son, yet she looked as though there was something else she coveted, something I had. Or rather, something I once had. A husband? Surely not. And I wondered – God, no, it couldn't be true – I wondered if I had wronged James's mother, after all.

Supposing Pansy had written those anonymous letters that had pointed me towards the truth about my father. Supposing she wanted to take something away from me. She couldn't have my husband, so she made do with depriving me of a different man. She had a possible source of knowledge – her father, who had known the young Edwin Ansty. And she had a possible motivation, however unlikely.

Simply thinking such thoughts about Pansy made me feel guilty.

'What does it feel like to be a civilian again, Laura?'

'Very odd, Mrs Buckland. A bit like a snail without its shell.'

'You'll settle down again in no time, I'm sure. I expect your mother'll be so glad to have her daughter safely back in the nest again.'

'I suppose so.' A dutiful daughter might feel happier about that prospect. For some reason, I didn't. So I asked the question I'd been longing to ask since I came home. 'How's ... how's Martin?'

'I wish I knew, my dear.' Mrs Buckland sighed. 'I had a letter from him just the other day – I'll show it to you if you pop round some time. It seems he's still in Germany with some commission or other. He has a nice little job with *Picture Post* waiting for him to come back to, but I don't know when. You'd think they'd send our boys home as soon as, they could, wouldn't you, not hang on to them. He signed on for the duration and, as far as I'm concerned, the duration's over.'

Damn it, damn it, they were trying to put women back in their places again. And those places were in the kitchen, by the hearth, in the marriage bed and in the nursery. But definitely not in paid employment.

Give us a job to do and we'll do it, we'd shouted in 1939. And we'd done it, willingly and ably, for five and a half years. We'd tilled the land and unloaded ships. We'd ferried aeroplanes and driven ambulances. We'd taught the children and manufactured ammunition. We'd swept chimneys and spotted fires, made vehicles and serviced engines. Some of us had been killed doing it.

Now there were men coming home who'd want those jobs back. Of course they did. And women were told that motherhood was the most glorious career open to them. Women's magazines emphasized how important it was to help the men to readjust to their new civilian world. Never once did I see it suggested that returning servicewomen might also feel disorientated and puzzled.

Without a husband or a child, I was surplus to requirements, a spare woman, a waste of the nation's rations. So I stayed at home – I didn't have the heart to walk out on my mother again so soon – and applied for every possible job within range. I spent a small fortune on stamps.

And when – if – I was called to interview, old men would purse their lips. 'Oh, ATS,' they'd say, as though I'd mentioned something not quite feminine, not quite nice.

Perhaps it was my fault. Perhaps I expected everything to fall into my lap. Perhaps I was wrong and not the system. But I didn't think so.

I had plenty of time to spare, a lot of energy and a burning passion to find out what had happened to my father. 'Just ask – why not?' Vee had said, a

314

long time ago, but I was equally determined not to cause my mother any more pain than I had to. Now that the rage I had felt on first discovering the manner of my father's death had mellowed – no, perhaps matured is the right word – I realized what a terrible burden my mother had been carrying for so long. She simply had to look at me to be reminded of the man she had been married to for such a short time.

Rightly or wrongly, she had tried to shield me from the distress she must have suffered. Was it right that I should add to it?

The first I knew of Martin's return was when Mrs Buckland knocked at the door as we were having breakfast. She had taken off her hairnet, but hadn't spared the time to comb out her careful pin curls. They coiled like flat grey snakes around her head, giving her the look of Medusa off duty. No-one had ever seen Mrs Buckland beyond her own gate without a hat. She was wearing fluffy pink slippers. Something was definitely wrong.

A few months earlier, the sight of Mrs Buckland looking so unkempt, at that time in the morning, would have been enough to set off an invasion scare throughout the village. Nothing less than a regiment of German paratroopers could have stirred her.

'Mrs Buckland, how nice,' said Mother, with the merest quiver of mirth detectable in her voice. 'Won't you have some tea?'

'Well, I ... no, I can't stop.' She'd been – almost – running. Her breath came in short puffs. 'I just wondered if Laura was in.'

'Where else would she be at this time in the morning?' muttered Tom. Morning was never his best time.

'Laura, dear, I wonder if you would...? Do you think you could possibly...?' Her hands fluttered up to her lips to still their trembling.

'Of course,' I answered, rising from the table. It wasn't an invasion. So it had to be Martin. I looked at Martin's mother, at the slippers and the uncombed hair, and felt a sickening spasm of fear. Martin. Not Martin. Not now. Not when it was all over.

She trotted beside me as fast as she could along the lanes, taking two steps to every one of mine. I wanted to shriek at her. I wanted to run, to outdistance her plump little legs, but I didn't have the heart to leave her behind. Her agitation was so comic and yet so serious.

'I don't know what to do. He won't stop working, Laura.'

'That doesn't sound too terrible. Martin always works hard.'

'Yes, but don't you see ... oh, good morning, Mrs Attwood, yes, lovely morning, isn't it ... don't you see, he won't stop. Ever since he came home. He won't come out.'

'Not ever?'

'Well...' She blushed. 'Sometimes, at night, I hear him come out for the ... you know ... necessary. And I hear the kettle rattle ... no, Ted, of course there isn't a fire, and I'll have less of your cheek, young man ... but if I come downstairs, he locks himself in again. I can't so much as get at my own scullery – I should have done the wash yesterday – and heaven knows what he's eating ... Laura, you'll have to do something. Perhaps he'll listen to you.' Just as she had the last time I'd visited the cottage, she scratched with her fingertips on the locked door. 'Martin, Laura's here. Martin.'

Last time he'd told me to go away, but he hadn't meant it and he'd come out a few moments later. This time there was no answer. I heard him moving, heard a tap slowly running, but he paid no attention to us.

'You see? He won't talk and he won't come out. It's not normal.'

'What's happened to him, Mrs Buckland?'

'How should I know, when he won't talk to me? Don't ask silly questions, Laura.' The answer was a measure of her distress. I'd never known Mrs Buckland to snap. 'Oh, I'm so sorry, dear. I shouldn't. It's not your fault. But I just don't know what to do.'

'Why don't you...' I thought quickly. 'Why don't you pop upstairs for a bit, Mrs Buckland, have a rest and I'll make you a nice cup of tea.'

'I couldn't, I shouldn't...'

'Of course you can. I'm here now. Leave everything to me.'

Reliable Laura. Worth every one of her three stripes. But it was only the sound of Martin moving beyond the door that kept me calm.

'Oh, I don't know...'

'Off you go. I know where everything is kept.'

And when the tea was made, I called to Martin on the other side of the locked door. 'Martin,

317

there's some fresh tea, if you want it.' But I didn't knock and I didn't ask or tell him to come out. He'd always been stubborn. Tell Martin he had to do such-and-such and he'd think of a hundred reasons why he shouldn't. Tell him he couldn't possibly swim to the other side of the lake and he'd drown himself to prove he could. I tried to keep my tone light and unforced. I left the choice to him.

Then I took a pot of tea upstairs to Mrs Buckland along with some thin toast, laid out prettily on a tray, the way I knew she liked it. There was just a teaspoonful of marmalade left in the bottom of a jar, but I put it into a scalloped glass dish. The teapot was under a patchwork cosy.

She was sitting on the edge of her bed, dithering. 'What you really need, what you deserve, Mrs Buckland, is a day in bed. You've been very brave, but I'm sure you're tired, aren't you.' She nodded. 'Look, I'll put the tray here by the bed and pull the curtains – like that – so the sun doesn't shine in your eyes, but you can see what you're eating.' I plumped up the pillows and smoothed the eiderdown to make her bed look more inviting.

'No crusts, dear,' she said in accusation. 'You've cut off the crusts. What a waste.'

'Ah, but I know that's the way you really like your toast, isn't it?'

She nodded again, with a guilty duck of her shoulders.

'And nothing's wasted. You can always dry them for raspings, or something. So you just enjoy your breakfast and don't worry about a thing.'

I left her tucked up, sipping tea and reading the first episode of the new serial in *Woman's Weekly*. Downstairs again, I took two chairs into the garden and poured myself some tea. I browsed along the two bookshelves, looking for something to read. It might be a long wait.

Every Woman's Flower Garden by Mary Campden. Warwick Deeping's *Sorrell & Son*. A whole row by Ethel M. Dell and Annie S. Swan. Heavens. Mary Webb's *Precious Bane*. That was strong meat for Mrs Buckland.

I settled down with *The Big Book of Great Short Stories*. It looked as though it would put me to sleep faster than Martin's mother. Then I went into the garden to wait for him. I thought I saw the blackout curtains twitch over the window of Martin's darkroom. Then nothing.

At about half-past twelve I whipped up some mushrooms on toast, with stewed plums to follow, for Mrs Buckland and took it up on a tray.

'Oh, how lovely, you shouldn't, dear,' she said, with a greedy look at the plates. There wasn't much on either, but I'd made them look attractive.

'Have you had a little sleep?'

'I had a lovely snooze, thank you. So restful. Now I really should be getting up. Lots to do and no time to do it in, you know.'

'There's no hurry. I think you ought to spoil yourself today.'

And I didn't want her pottering around, chattering and meddling. How arrogant. It was her house, after all, and her son I was waiting for.

All afternoon I sat in the garden, waiting

patiently, hoping. Some time around three, I think I fell asleep. I woke with a jerk, imagining I'd heard the scullery door key turn in its lock. No. I was wrong. Everything was quiet. The vicarage doves went off with a flapping of wings like applause. Some children were playing a skipping game in the lane. Salt, mustard, vinegar, pepper. Salt, mustard, vinegar, pepper.

No-one else was awake, it seemed, though I knew that couldn't be true. Michaelmas daisies, dusty blue, yellow-eyed, were just coming into flower below the thatched catslide roof. A peacock butterfly was dipping into them, unrolling and re-rolling its watchspring proboscis. Everything was dusty, hazy, shimmering.

I could wait. I was prepared to wait all day for Martin. If, by evening, he still hadn't come out ... if I couldn't keep his mother upstairs any longer (there was, after all, a limit to the amount of sleep she needed, a limit to the number of enticing little trays I could carry upstairs) ... then I didn't know what I'd do next. I hadn't thought beyond one day.

He knew I was there. He knew I was waiting for him. I wasn't going to knock and shout for him. He'd never liked fuss. And he'd come. Or he wouldn't come. That was all.

He came out when the shadow of the tall hedge at the bottom of the garden had been thrown right across the grass. I was sitting in the shade, watching the daylight turn blue and the blue of the Michaelmas daisies turn luminous. I'd just

320

about given up.

I heard the rattle of the key, but I didn't turn round. I let Martin come to me. He dropped heavily into the chair by my side, moving stiffly, seeming older, far older, than he ought.

We sat in the lessening light, silent as an old married couple, as far apart as lonely people can be. Something terrible, something private, had happened to drive Martin into retreat. I didn't feel I had the right to force him to talk about it. Yet, if I didn't, who did?

I didn't even dare to stare. But it's amazing what you can see without seeming to look. Women are good at that. The spark had gone. His eyes had glazed over. All the vibrancy and humour that made his plain face remarkable had dried up. He was an empty sack in the shape of a man. I could have wept for him.

He'd been in that little room all day, all the night before and all the day before that and – I didn't know how long. I could, at least, be practical. I could begin to cure the body, if I couldn't touch his lonely mind. I went back into the kitchen, rummaged around, and discovered three slices of bacon under a muslin canopy. I hesitated – Mrs Buckland would never forgive me if I used it all – what the hell, this was an emergency. The smell of frying made me drool, but I managed to resist it. I made a thick bacon sandwich and carried it, with a bottle of Bass, back to the garden.

He took it with a half-smile of such poignancy that it hurt more than if he'd ignored me, or stormed or sworn. Those I could have dealt with.

321

This withdrawal ... I didn't understand the meaning of it.

His eyes were dry, yet they glittered as though there ought to be tears. Still, no doubt, he looked better when he'd eaten and drunk.

'Sensible Laura,' he said, softly. 'You think that anything can be cured with a sandwich.'

I didn't know what to say, didn't know what he expected me to say, so I kept quiet.

'Well, why not?' he went on. 'Some things are so dreadful that you either have to curse God and give up living, or decide to get on with it one day at a time. I think I've just decided.'

We sat silently. The evening grew darker. Children were called in from their games. Oil lamps were lit in the cottage next door, giving a soft, bloomy light that didn't reach out beyond the windows. Martin didn't talk, didn't move. I wish I could have comforted him. When I'd needed him, he'd been there. He'd given me the physical warmth that I longed for, when words wouldn't have been enough. I could have done the same for him, if he'd let me.

I ached to touch him. I wanted to put my arms around him and take away the pain. I didn't need to know what was wrong. I loved him. You don't ask questions when you love someone. It was enough to know that he needed me. But Martin had put up a barrier between us. I couldn't reach him.

A bedroom window was closed and the curtains whisked together. A lamp was lit and travelled around the house. I don't think I really registered what that meant, but Martin did. He leaped out of his chair, knocking it backwards.

Mrs Buckland popped her head through the kitchen window. 'Laura, I thought I smelt bacon. Whatever are you two doing out there in the dark? Can't you feel the dew falling? Anyway, it's nice to know I can have my scullery back at last,' she scolded cheerfully.

'Get out of there!' he shouted and ran towards the house, but stiffly, like someone whose limbs are not under control.

Mrs Buckland stood very still, with her hand on the scullery door latch. Her other hand rested on her chest, where her heart might have been felt under the sturdy corsetry.

Over her shoulder, I saw shapes, patterns, black holes in white – or white on black, a jumble, shading, stripes, angles. A puzzle. Then I recognized what I was seeing.

Faces looked back at me, terrible faces, scarcely human. No, that was wrong. Once I'd identified the key to the pattern, they were inescapably human. Gaunt faces, sunken pits where eyes ought to be, gashes where you'd expect to find lips. Shaven heads, skull-shapes unsoftened by hair. Everything opposite, turned inside out. Man, woman, child, old, young. No human diversity. Every single face reduced to its basics.

The faces accused me. More shocking than the pits carelessly piled with bodies, the jumble of naked limbs, more horrifying than the chimneys still smoking, the faces that looked through the wire blamed me. I had not done enough. None of us had done enough.

But I didn't know, I wanted to cry. How could I help you, when I didn't know?

We tried to tell you, the faces replied, we tried to tell you but you wouldn't listen. You wouldn't believe.

Martin stood across the door, a fierce guardian. 'I told you!' he shouted. 'I told you not to go in.'

Beneath my hand, I could feel Mrs Buckland shaking. I took her by the arm and led her away.

'Martin,' she whispered. 'Oh, Martin, what have you done?'

'There will be trials,' Martin said, dully. 'There must be trials and the evidence – some of it – is on those walls. I have to go back. No-one could believe...' He was still shaking. 'It was a job. I was told to do it and I knew it had to be done. It was right to record what we found at Belsen – wasn't it? – or the world would never have believed it. We couldn't – nothing in heaven or hell had prepared us for that.'

'Martin,' I whispered. 'You're tormenting yourself.'

'Why shouldn't I hurt? Why shouldn't you? Or my mother? Why should we be different? We drove along a narrow road through pinewoods, dark and dense, Hansel and Gretel woods. There was a smell, hideous, a charnel smell, and we looked at each other and wondered where it came from – and yet, you know, I think – maybe – we guessed. Soldiers who'd fought their way from the Channel, hard men, who'd maybe had to pick up the pieces of friends, vomited when

324

they reached the wire and saw what was on the other side. Ten thousand unburied dead, long dead some of them, dissolving ... and then the living dead...'

I couldn't stop him. I wanted to put my fingers in my ears and scream at him to stop, but I couldn't do it.

'We were so angry – mad with anger – we did things we shouldn't have done. I didn't think British soldiers would behave like that. We made the camp guards bury the dead, made them run backwards and forwards, lugging their victims, and when they dropped with exhaustion, we kicked them back to work, or shot them if they wouldn't. Kinder, perhaps, than letting the inmates get them... I came round a corner and found two soldiers beating a guard, whacking him with their rifle butts. I should have stopped them. I had three stripes up, it was my job to stop them. But I turned my back. I walked away. There was typhus, no wonder, the place was crawling with lice ... people were free and still dying, what a terrible thing, to die just when you are offered life... We moved the sick into the SS barracks and then torched the huts. Even the smoke stank. There were British nurses with us. One of them gave me a container of water and told me to go down the lines of mattresses and give water to all the sick. I held them in my arms – so light, they were, like bundles of sticks, loosely tied together – and trickled the water into their mouths, because they were too weak to take the cup. There was one man – he had no teeth and no hair – he said "bless you, bless you" and then he died. He died in my arms and the water dribbled out of his mouth. His face is there on my wall, look, there. How could anyone believe, without having seen...? Laura, tell me I was right to take those pictures...' I nodded. 'But oh, God, Laura,' Martin went on and his voice was a hoarse whisper, 'I dream ... I dream...'

The early stars still shone. The summer evening air was still soft and warm, but the sweetness had gone from it. Perhaps for Martin, it might never come back. I put my arms around him and he began to weep, a hard, dry sobbing that brought no relief. But then he pushed me aside and wouldn't let me comfort him. There was nothing I could do.

Now I had time to spare and time to think. I wrote to the headquarters of our county regiment, reasoning that it was a sensible place to start the search for my father. He had been an infantryman, the letters had told me that. And although the collar badges on his uniform had been missing, it would be logical to assume that he had joined the regiment that had its links closest to home.

A courteous reply told me that there was no trace of Edwin Ansty in the regimental records. Damn, damn, damn – *another* blank. I crumpled the letter in frustration and then smoothed it out again, alarmed by my own fury. I was becoming obsessed and I didn't like what it was doing to me.

Anyone would think that Edwin Ansty was an elaborate myth. There was the uniform. There were the letters. But of the man there was no trace. He had left no shadow. Whichever way I looked, there was only empty space. He was nobody.

And then there was me. I existed. But if I wasn't Edwin Ansty's daughter – then who was I?

When Kate was demobbed, she didn't dither, like me. She knew exactly what she was going to do. She arrived home with a set of new leather luggage. Inside were silk lingerie, shoes, stockings, hats ... my teeth ached with envy.

'Who've you got involved with now, Kate? Aladdin?'

'Someone rather like that,' she admitted. 'His name's Geoffrey. He's ... he's a businessman.'

'Sounds good. And what does he do?'

'Oh, this and that, here and there,' she answered airily. 'There are so many opportunities after a war, you know, for a clever man.'

'I'll bet.'

'Someone has to put things back together again,' she answered, but her tone was defensive.

'And?'

'I'm sick of Utility this and Utility that.'

'And?'

'He's very fond of me.'

'And?'

'He's a bit older than me.'

'How much?'

She looked straight at me with that defiant stare I remembered so well from our childhood. 'Thirty-seven years, actually.'

'Kate! You're joking! That makes him ... sixty-one. He's an old man!'

Older than Mother. Older than Tom. As old, almost, as Grandmother. It was indecent.

'Rubbish. He's very ... very virile...'

'...for his age,' I finished for her. 'So whatever happened to what's-his-name, the first lieutenant, the one you were so mad about?'

'He was married. Aren't they all?' She gave a little laugh that was one of the saddest things I'd ever heard. 'Senior Service Satisfies. All lonely, all misunderstood...'

'And all very firmly hooked.'

'His wife was having a baby. And he said that they weren't ... that he didn't any more ... "Darling, it wasn't supposed to happen,"' she mimicked bitterly, '"but I can't leave her now, not with the baby and everything, you do see, don't you..." Oh yes, I saw all right. Bloody liar.'

'Oh, Kate, I'm sorry.'

'So what? I'm tired of young men, anyway. All they want is one thing and I'm fed up with *that*. It's highly overrated. All that heavy breathing and pawing in back seats and watching the clock and the calendar and cricks in your neck and grass in your knickers and a quick thrill at the end of it – *if* you're lucky. No, I'm perfectly happy to be cherished. In fact, I love it. Here–' She rummaged in her suitcase and pulled out a night-dress, champagne-coloured satin, barely there, slithery and incredibly sexy. It was new. The label still swung from it. *And* the price tag! 'That's for you. I bought it the other day and when I got home – silly me – I found I'd already got one exactly like it. Go on. Take it.'

'I'm not sure...'

Such generosity. Such careless, thoughtless, *easy* generosity.

'Oh, don't be so stuffy. Darling Laura. Someone has to profit from Geoffrey's ill-gotten gains. So why not you and me?'

She thrust it into my hands. It felt gorgeous. It had to be wrong to enjoy it.

'And where do these ill-gotten gains come from?' I asked, primly.

'Well, at the moment – between you and me – he's buying up bombed sites in London.'

'Bombed sites?'

'Silly! They won't *always* be bombed sites, you know.'

Much to my surprise, Geoffrey and my grandmother got on together like a house on fire. They were two of a kind, I suppose. Charming. Ruthless.

When Kate announced, rather defiantly, that Geoffrey was 'just passing through' – as though anyone just passed through Ansty Parva! – and might call in, I found that I was bursting with curiosity. My expectations were embarrassingly predictable. At least, I gave Kate the credit for having the good taste not to bring home a barrow boy – wide tie and Max Miller moustache and smutty jokes. But he'd be rather florid, I imagined, probably overweight, a paisley cravat and a belted camel-hair overcoat and driving gloves and – yes, definitely – suede shoes, crêpe-soled. And he'd drive a car that was all chrome and white-walled tyres and that gobbled up black market petrol. Such a little snob, Laura!

Tom was very acid. 'So you're bringing your spiv to see us, are you, Kate? Showing him how the country bumpkins live? Decent of you. I suppose he'll come, if only to check on what the house is worth. He'd buy and sell you like a shot.'

'Daddy ... it isn't like that...' Kate began and then looked away because she couldn't stop her lips from trembling. I could see how much he'd hurt her. Why couldn't Tom?

'Well, what am I to think when my daughter comes home flaunting her new clothes and her makeup and her flashy jewellery? Like a rich man's whore. But no ring, I see. He's not decent enough to give you a ring.'

'That's not fair, Tom,' I said quietly, but I hoped he would take warning.

'Isn't it?' He turned on me with a sudden ferocity that made me realize that Kate and I had both better just walk out the room, quickly and quietly. Sometimes – more and more often – Tom was impossible. He could scarcely get the words out. They tripped over each other on the way past his tongue. Little stalactites of spittle gummed his lips together. 'Go on, then. Take her side, as usual. The little trollop. After all, what do I matter? I'm only her father!' He shouted again as I closed the door: '–only her father...'

I couldn't have been more wrong about Geoffrey Paxton. I was right about the black market petrol, though. How else could anyone drive a Daimler, black, sedate, positively regal? And from it stepped a quiet man, soberly dressed in a pin-striped suit, immaculately tailored. His shirt was white. His tie looked as though it ought to be regimental. His hands were white and smooth, with finely manicured nails, shell pink. What a surprise. He could have been a judge or a banker or, with those hands, a gynaecologist. Not a spiv.

Not unless you looked at his eyes. They were bright blue, scarcely faded at all, snappingly shrewd, and they saw much farther than most people. As I said, he and Grandmother were two of a kind. They looked at each other, summed each other up, and respected what they saw.

And when he spoke, his voice was pure Wiltshire, rolling and rich. What a surprise. He could have come from any of the villages for miles around, or from Ansty Parva itself, for all its voice told us. I liked it. It made him seem more human, somehow, made Kate's choice less inexplicable.

Grandmother whisked Geoffrey off on a tour of the mouldy old generals and their medals. She pattered along, chatting easily, as though to an old friend. Beside him, she looked so much more suitable than Kate, so much more appropriate, in age and style. They made what Vee might have called a lovely couple. Kate hung back, uncharacteristically silent, her hands behind her back like a gauche schoolgirl. I gave her a little squeeze, meant to be encouraging.

'He looks nice,' I whispered, and he did. 'Where ever did you meet?'

'It's not such a coincidence as all that. I was touring Swindon on a Battleship Week drive – they always try to get a glamorous Wren on those tours, helps no end, especially if she's a local girl – and Geoffrey is on the Wiltshire committee for just about everything.'

'I'm sure he's a darling. He'll have us all eating out of his hand in two shakes – you'll see.'

We had tea in the garden, as far away as we could from the pig pens and the hen runs, but that meant inconveniently far from the kitchen, too. Grandmother had insisted on what she called a proper tea, at last. So the bread was cut thin enough to see the pattern of the plate through the slices, even though there was only margarine and carrot jam to spread on it. There were sandwiches with ghostly slivers of cucumber in wafers of crustless bread. The fatless, sugarless, eggless – practically flourless – cake sat on a comport of Limoges china, gold-rimmed, ornamented with poppies. You *could* make meringues with powdered egg and, if you were rash enough to risk it, the result would be like the soggy objects sitting on the wire cooling tray. I decided to call them drop scones instead.

And then – at the last possible moment – there *was* butter and enough sugar for everyone and China tea, pale and fragrant, just as Grandmother liked it, all produced with utmost tact by Geoffrey.

'Offended? Oh, Geoffrey...' Grandmother had given the little, tinkling laugh she always used when she had a man in her thrall. 'Nonsense. You're the soul of diplomacy–'

I balanced the tray against my hip and staggered across the grass, trying to avoid the tussocky bits, cursing the pride that had made us place the table and chairs so far from the house. From here you could almost – almost – forget the sycamores sprouting in the gutters and the broken window in the attic where the bats flew in and out and the mould spreading behind each downpipe.

Grandmother and Geoffrey were chatting – or rather Grandmother was telling some frightfully complicated tale and Geoffrey was nodding. Kate sat to one side. She was gnawing the quick around one scarlet nail. Mother seemed to be dozing in the sun, taking a chance to rest.

It's funny how you can see someone every day and only now and then really notice them.

Tom looked ill. His red-brown, countryman's complexion had become yellow. There were broken thread veins in his nose and cheeks that gave the appearance of rosy good health, but it was an illusion. As I came closer, I saw that his head and hands trembled, very slightly, but constantly. It was a vibration rather than a shake, like a just unmoulded jelly.

'Of course, I'm only a local lad, really,' Geoffrey was saying, with a smile that didn't match the modesty of his words. 'I've been lucky – couldn't settle to anything after the Great War – spotted a few opportunities –bought here, sold there – you know how it is–'

I was amazed that Grandmother didn't bristle at his assumption that she shared his background, but she just smiled and nodded.

'I didn't sit on my backside – not like some thinking that my country owed me a living, just because I'd been in the trenches. I bought a batch of worn-out lorries from the War Office and turned them into charabancs,' he went on. 'People were going to want bright lights and holidays after the war, I thought – and well, there you are. You won't travel a road in Britain today without spotting Pegasus coaches. And then I bought a few aeroplanes–' He looked over at Tom, who, with skinny legs stuck out, was admiring the shine on his shoes. 'I'm being boring. You don't want to hear this, I'm sure.'

'Nonsense, Geoffrey,' said Grandmother, briskly. 'Pay no attention to Tom. He's very naughty, sometimes.'

I put the tray in front of Grandmother and passed round bread and butter while she poured the tea. There was a vacant chair for me on her other side. When we were all served, Geoffrey leaned across Grandmother and said to me, in his rich, surprising voice, 'I've been looking forward to meeting you, my dear. I knew your father very well.'

No-one screamed or fainted or dropped a teacup. We all behaved very well. But then, we always did.

'Tell me,' I demanded.

'I shouldn't think I could tell you anything you don't know.'

'But I don't know *anything*.'

Geoffrey looked rather startled. I could almost hear what he was thinking. He was wondering how he'd allowed himself to be separated from the after-dinner coffee drinking and walked off into the night by a determined young woman who wasn't going to let him go again until he'd satisfied her!

'It's a long time ago...'

I took his arm and steered him towards the seats we'd left out after tea. The sky had clouded over. The night was dark and starless. A fringe of brightness around a cloud showed where the moon ought to be. I knew the way, but Geoffrey stumbled as he tried to keep up with me.

'Tell me everything,' I insisted.

'Your father and I were in the same regiment – you know that, don't you – Princess Augusta's Own – it's amalgamated now, I think, like so many old regiments – 8th battalion. The same company, too. He was a newly joined subaltern and was promoted as dead men's shoes became empty. I was a sergeant and later company sergeant major. I kept an eye on the young officers. It was part of my job. They needed someone to keep them straight, to tell them what was what. I remember your stepfather, too. He doesn't seem to remember me, though. Still, it's not up to me to remind him. As I say – it was a long time ago...'

'What was he like – my father?'

Geoffrey stopped and thought. He gave my question careful consideration. 'A fine young man,' he said, slowly. 'Good. Now, don't mistake me, I don't mean goody-goody. He had a temper and no excuses. But he was cheerful – most of the time: thoughtful, kind, he cared about his men.'

'Did you know him well?'

'Pretty well. As well as an NCO can know an officer. At the start of the war, that would have meant not at all, but life in the trenches broke down all sorts of barriers in the end. You can't squat in the mud with a man for weeks on end and not talk to him. First you share the lice and then you share other things, too. Cigarettes. Gripes. Jokes. Pretty soon, you know each other's families as well as your own. It's funny, you know. I look at you and remember things I haven't given a thought to in years. I can see your father in his rain cape and gumboots, squelching along the trench, checking that the lads had all got a hot drink and a splash of rum to go with it, when he could've been having his own tea, snug in the dugout. He was like that, always made sure they were all right first.'

I sat quietly, waiting for Geoffrey to remember more. He opened a plain gold cigarette case, offered me one and, when I shook my head, took one for himself and lit it. In the brief flare of the match his face looked younger, tenser.

'Clear as clear.' He made a little noise that was half laugh, half grunt. 'The smell's the last thing you forget. Khaki serge that's been worn so long it could stand up on its own. Gumboots. Chloride of lime. Tobacco. Lyddite. Dead men... You had to smoke, the stronger the better. And drink, whenever you got the chance. We all drank too much and who's to blame us. But some didn't stop when it was over.'

Everyone else seemed to be going to bed. I could hear Tom and Mother on the gravel path to the cottage. Tom's voice was high and querulous. I couldn't hear the words, only the tone, and Mother's soothing answer. I wondered why Tom didn't seem to remember his own company sergeant major. A long time ago, yes, but CSM was an important appointment. They'd have had regular contact, talked to each other, discussed problems. Why didn't Tom remember?

'I don't know why you want to be burdened with my memories,' said Geoffrey. 'I'd've thought you young people'd have plenty of your own by now.'

'They're different.'

'I was there when your father won his MC. Took out a Jerry machine-gun post all on his own, when we were pinned down and taking heavy casualties. You wouldn't think it to look at him – long, skinny lad – but he was a terror when he got going. Fair mad, he was. Over the top and through the wire like greased lightning. The rest of us were pushed to keep up with him. He used to say, the faster he went, the less likely he was to catch a bullet. Who'd've thought...'

'What happened?'

'Every man has his breaking point. Sometimes brave men get there sooner. Courage is like a bank account. The more often you go to the bank, the quicker you're broke.'

'Geoffrey – what *happened?*'

'I don't know, my dear. I wasn't there.'

Oh, the disappointment. I couldn't bear it. I could have screamed. I'd thought – I'd really thought that this was the time when I'd find out at last.

'We were back in that bloody Flesquières salient again. I'd stopped one in the leg – a nice Blighty one – and it gave me six weeks at home.

When I came back, it was all over. Your father was – I'm sorry, my dear, I don't like to have to say it to you – your father was dead. It was all such a muddle. No-one in the sergeants' mess could make head or tail of it. There were lots of rumours, of course, about who'd done what and when. They said that young Mr Roding–' He stopped and cleared his throat. 'I'm sorry, Laura. You don't want to hear this.'

'I do. I must.'

'I never listened to rumours. The only facts were that your father had been found guilty by field general court martial of "misbehaving before the enemy in such manner as to show cowardice" – that's how the Army Act puts it, I seem to remember. The sentence was death and it was confirmed by the C-in-C. But who'd've thought...'

He sat quietly, thinking his own thoughts, for a long time. I thought he'd finished.

'I'll tell you this, though,' he began again. 'Our lads didn't shoot him. Now, usually, executions were carried out within the unit. The firing party – poor sods – would be detailed by the RSM and the rest of the battalion formed up to watch. A parade, you see, to make sure the lesson sank home. But that didn't happen. I don't suppose they could find a single man who'd lift a weapon to your father, not for fear nor favour. Anyway, in the morning – the morning it was due to happen – he was taken off somewhere else, so that he could be shot by strangers. And only two months or so of the war left. A crying shame, that was.'

'Thank you, Geoffrey. That's such a relief.'

338

He looked at me with curiosity. A relief? To be told about her father's death?

'You'll think this sounds so stupid. I was beginning to think that there never was such a person. That – that Edwin Ansty was fiction.'

He laughed softly. 'No need to worry about that. You're the very image of him.'

We walked slowly back to the house. There was one lamp left burning on the hall table to light Geoffrey to bed. The shadows clustered closely around it.

'Goodnight,' I said, 'and I'm so glad you've met Kate.'

He turned back at the foot of the stairs. The lamplight wasn't kind to him. 'I think the world of her. I'll be good to her, you know.'

'I know you will.'

'Perfect. Absolutely perfect,' declared Grandmother after Geoffrey had left, taking Kate back to a life of luxury and sin. Lucky Kate! She had been going to stay at home for a few days, but, as Geoffrey drove off, she'd pulled open the car door and hopped in beside him.

'Tell Daddy I can't stand his grousing a moment longer,' she'd yelled out the window at me. 'Or on second thoughts – don't!'

Mother looked rather put out at Grandmother's judgement. 'Perfect? I wouldn't quite say that. He's nicer than I'd feared, of course – he'd almost be eligible, if he were even ten years younger – but...'

'Oh, but – don't you see – he's the answer. The answer to an old woman's prayers, I might say.'

She paused fractionally, as though waiting for someone to say that she wasn't really old. She was too proud to wait for long. 'How else are we going to put Ansty House back into shape? We'll never get a building licence for the work without some clout. Timber and bricks are like gold dust. There's the roof ... the gutters...'

'No!' Mother shouted – actually shouted – and to Grandmother.

'Now, don't be silly, Diana. I should have thought it was obvious enough, even for you. Kate must marry him.'

'You are not going to sell her to the highest bidder. Kate is *my* daughter and – as you've never tired of pointing out over the years – she is *not* an Ansty.'

'Then she is the next-best thing. She has been reared here. She has a duty to the family. And if Kate won't marry him, then I shall have to do so myself.'

Grandmother knew when to make an exit. She left us gaping. But she was only joking. Wasn't she? At the door, she turned for a final dart. She was famous for them.

'The Anstys have a long history of sons. What a pity, Diana dear – I've thought it so often – what a pity you couldn't contrive to give my son a son of his own.'

A few days later, an envelope with a London postmark arrived for me. There was a letter inside and I guessed that Geoffrey had sent it, but I didn't take time to read it. It wasn't important.

There was a photograph, spotty, faded. I pulled it carefully from the envelope.

Half a dozen men sprawled under a pear tree. They were all scruffy, boots filthy and unlaced, hatless, jackets unbuttoned, collars open. It was summer. Three of them had cut off their trousers at the knee to make unorthodox shorts. One had a ratty little terrier yawning on his lap. Another was stroking a kitten. A couple were smoking ridiculous pipes that made them look like schoolboys experimenting behind the cricket pavilion. They were all smiling. And they were all so young, years younger than I was.

One of them was Tom. He seemed to be about to go somewhere. His boots were laced up. Clay was caked on them, bulky as an extra sole. He was bending forward, trying to wrap his puttees and looking up at the camera, making a silly face.

The man next to Tom was my father. I knew that. Thin, rather bony face. Narrow nose. Stubborn chin. He'd caught hold of the loose end of one of Tom's puttees and was trying to persuade the sleepy dog to grab it. He was laughing.

I had never seen him before, but I knew him. It was like looking at a picture of myself, if I had been a man. I was blood of his blood and bone of his bone. This person had made me in his own image. It was a disturbing thought. He had never seen the result of his love for my mother.

I sat in my bedroom with the photograph in my hands. I sat for a long time. It was difficult to put it away.

Lieutenant E J T Ansty, MC, Princess Augusta's Own.

341

There he was at last. Son of Lieutenant-General Sir Hubert and Lady Ansty. Husband of Diana Lampard. Father of Laura Kenton.

I had seen him. The uniform had flesh.

I didn't get round to the letter until later. 'We had rather a sticky journey back,' Geoffrey wrote,

that included a nasty prang at Bullington Cross. We seem to have been dripping brake fluid all the way from your house. I can't understand it. I make sure that car is properly looked after. My mechanic will have some questions to answer. My poor Kate banged her head and needed a few stitches, but is nicely on the mend now. She's worried there will be a scar, but I tell her that I shan't care if there is. It could have been so much worse. I should like to talk to you again. Could you come up to town somewhen? Kate would be so glad to see you. Let me know and I'll send you a ticket. Or perhaps we could meet when I come to pick up the car.

I sent an immediate telegram to find out how Kate was. I'd decided to wait for the answer before telling Mother and Tom. Mother had enough to worry about. The reply was short:

BLACK AND BLUE BUT FINE STOP DON'T WORRY MUMMY AND DADDY STOP LOVE KATE

'I don't understand it. I've given them his name, rank and unit and approximate date of death and the War Graves Commission *still* can't find him.

342

He must be somewhere. Someone must have buried him. He wasn't like the bodies that were blown up and disintegrated. If you shoot someone, you have a corpse. They must have put him somewhere when they'd finished with him.'

'And what will you do when you find him, Laura?' Pansy asked, a little voice of common sense.

'I don't know.' I stopped pacing round the vicarage kitchen and thought. 'I don't know. I simply need to find him. I need to know that he hasn't been just ... just thrown away.'

Pansy shuddered. 'Don't say that! Look – I'm sorry – I have to dash round to the church. Mrs Attwood has her twinges again and *someone* has to fill the vases for the flower ladies or there'll be ructions. Do you think you could sit with Daddy while I'm out? Would you mind? He's feeling a bit tired today and I don't like to leave him for too long.'

Mr Millport was in his study. Outside, it was still summer and he had a meagre fire burning, yet the north-facing room was cold, the air heavy and still. Nothing ever warmed it. I could remember my confirmation classes, after tea on winter Sunday evenings. We'd all put extra coats and scarves on to come in, and taken them off to go out. He wore a plaid blanket around his shoulders and his scalp was hidden beneath a knitted tea cosy of a cap. His chair was pulled up to the big desk where he'd written forty-six years' worth of sermons. Today he wasn't writing. His head drooped over his chest. I thought he was asleep, but he looked up as I tiptoed into the room.

343

'Ah, Laura,' he said with a tremulous smile of greeting. His voice was like a breeze through a drift of dry leaves. 'How nice of you to come and see me. I find it a little difficult to get around my parish now, I'm afraid. So kind to come to me...'

'I didn't mean to wake you.'

'Not asleep – no, not asleep, my dear. Just thinking. There's a PCC meeting tonight. So much to do. New rotas for readers and sidesmen ... all in a muddle ... oh dear ... and the church-wardens at loggerheads, as usual ... we must have the war memorial newly inscribed. All those young men. That's not on the agenda. I must bring it up under AOB. So much to do...'

I hadn't thought about it until that moment. Of course. It was so obvious. This is what I had to do.

'Mr Millport – will you put my father on the memorial, please?'

He pushed his spectacles back up his nose and they slid down again. 'Your father...? Oh, my dear Laura, is that really such a good idea?'

'I know now – everything. You don't need to pretend any more.'

'I'm not at all sure – I don't think I could go against Lady Ansty's wish.'

'My grandmother's wish?' I queried, more sharply than I'd meant.

'She was quite specific. The cross was put up in 1920 and she came to see me before the masons began work. She funded a generous proportion of the cost, of course. I remember the day well. No name, she insisted. I had no objections to your father's name, of course ... though some

344

might... Who is to say what perils and dangers he passed through? "The pains of hell came about me: the snares of death overtook me ... I am poured out like water, and all my bones are out of joint: my heart also in the midst of my body is even like melting wax..." It is not our place to judge, Laura... "my strength is dried up like a potsherd, and my tongue cleaveth to my gums: and thou shalt bring me into the dust of death..." Yes, yes, it must have been like that for him ... poor boy.'

'And what did my grandmother say?'

'A strong-minded woman. She said that she did not wish her son's name to appear on the memorial. Feelings ran very high, then. I don't think you'd understand, Laura. Your war has been different. There is compassion for men like Edwin, men who couldn't take any more. But at the time, no-one realized. There would have been talk...'

'What did that matter? People are always talking.'

'Perhaps even desecration of the monument, who can guess. There was so much bitterness. Your grandmother is a proud woman. Stubborn, perhaps – it's not for me to comment. She felt that there were – matters – that were better forgotten.'

'Oh, yes. I can believe that. How could she treat her son's memory like that? How could she just pretend that nothing had happened. She wiped him away. I'll never forgive her for it. Never.'

'But you must. Child, you must. You couldn't be so cruel. She is your grandmother.'

'And she is Lady Ansty. She is patron of your living, after all. What was your conscience compared to that?'

'Laura...'

His hands came up as though to ward me off. They made me feel guilty. The tip of each finger was quite bloodless. The nails were ridged, tinged with blue.

'I'm sorry, I'm sorry. That was thoughtless. I didn't mean to hurt you.'

'You may be right. Who is to say? And was she entirely wrong? I'm not certain.' His lips fluttered with a little, rippling sigh. 'I'm certain of so little now, Laura. It's very confusing. Is it time for tea, yet? Where's Pansy?'

'Pansy's popped over to the church for a moment. I don't suppose she'll be long.' I felt a deep sense of shame over my outburst. 'Would you like me to make you a cup of tea?'

'That would be nice. How kind. I may work for a while on my notes for tonight.'

He'd fallen asleep again by the time I came back. I didn't like to wake him. The tea would keep warm under its cosy for half an hour or so. The room was very peaceful. I sat and thought about what he had said until Pansy came back.

So much revolved around my grandmother. The cache of letters, the preserved uniform, the missing name. The silences. The denials. The betrayal.

He was her son, for God's sake.

What a secret woman. What a strong woman. Unyielding. Adamantine. I had a ferocious desire to lock myself in a room with her and *force* her to

346

talk to me. No matter how long it took. How foolish. I could batter myself against her resolve until I was bloody. She would never weaken.

Pansy put her head around the door. I held a finger up to my lips. No need to waken Mr Millport until he was ready. Then the quality of the silence made me think again. The clock was still ticking. The ash of the dying fire trickled through the bars of the grate. Pansy's father wasn't breathing.

Kate came down for the funeral, but, wisely, left her lover in town. She had cunningly arranged her hair to hide the cut on her forehead. She looked like a classier Veronica Lake. As long as the wind didn't blow, Mother would never notice.

Tom noticed, however. He pushed back the curtain of hair and looked in shock at the red, stitched gash. It was longer and deeper than Geoffrey had let on. 'Sweetheart – what happened?'

'Just a bump, Daddy. Don't fuss.'

'If that man laid a finger on you'

'Of course not. Don't be silly. Just a bit of a smash in Geoffrey's car. Killed someone's dog, I'm afraid.'

'Oh, God...'

Fiercely, he clasped her and laid his lips on the scar, then let her go, leaving Kate to stare after him as he slammed out the door.

'It's not that bad,' said Kate, with a shrug.

After the funeral, Kate and I helped Pansy move

347

from the vicarage. Grandmother was letting her have a couple of rooms until she could find somewhere to live, and a job. It was a distressing task. Pansy had been born there.

'We shall be busy,' Pansy declared. 'That's a blessing. And all the furniture was here when Daddy arrived. That's something. We shan't have to think what to do with it. I suppose the new incumbent will want it.'

'What do you know about him?' asked Kate.

'Only that he's been a varsity Blue before the war and a forces chaplain for the duration. A muscular Christian, I imagine, a bible tucked under one arm and a rugby ball under the other.'

With the energy of a squirrel, Pansy stacked clothes, papers and books. 'Salvation Army, I suppose,' she said, adding to a pile of clerical grey suits of Victorian cut, shiny at the elbows and knees. 'I wonder who could possibly want old surplices? Do you imagine there is a clothing fund for distressed clergymen?'

In a rusty dustbin in the garden smouldered parish paperwork that had accumulated since 1899, when young – but already middle-aged – Mr Millport, the new bachelor vicar, had arrived to care for the souls of Ansty Parva. Surely, he had thrown nothing away since then. Amongst the rubbish, we could have been burning heaven knows what valuable records. The spiral of smoke, flecked with charred specks of paper, reminded me of Ash Wednesday in Cairo. We ought to have put it by for salvage, I suppose, but the effort was just too great.

Still, Pansy rushed round with a smile that might have been set in plaster.

There were crates of books, most of them unimaginably dull. 'Perhaps that bookshop in Salisbury might take them as a job lot. You know? The one near the Close gate. I must ask.'

'But you ought to check. Some of them might be worth something,' suggested Kate.

'I don't think so. Daddy didn't have a thing that was valuable. He didn't believe in property.' Pansy said it proudly. It was almost a boast.

And every time Kate or I suggested that Pansy might keep such-and-such a thing, she'd brush the idea aside.

'I won't have room. I won't have room,' she'd say and rush off to clear somewhere else.

Kate pulled out a drawer in the hall table. 'Good Lord, Pansy,' she exclaimed. 'Your problems are solved. You can open a shop.'

It was full of spectacles. Gold-rimmed pince-nez. Sturdy tortoiseshell frames, the legs elastic-looped for sport. Sixpenny ready-mades from Woolworth's.

Jonathan grabbed a pair. 'Grampa's,' he said and trotted off into the study. 'My bring them for Grampa.'

Pansy looked down into the drawer. 'Daddy could never find a pair that suited him.'

Then she began to cry. I held her in my arms and let her cry on until she couldn't do it any more. When she lifted her head, the right shoulder of my blouse was sodden. Pansy's skin was blotched and her nose had a drip on the end.

'I'm not sad,' she insisted, wiping her nose with

a man's big, white linen handkerchief. 'It's just that I miss him so dreadfully. I'm not really sad. Daddy was tired. He'd had enough living. He'd been here long enough. And I know he's happy now, with Mummy. It's just selfish to cry.'

And when we'd finished, the vicarage looked as unlived in as a film set for *Gaslight*. The late Victorian furniture was lumpish and unlovely, but gleaming with polish. The rugs had been beaten. The curtains had been brushed. All the traces of Pansy's past had been burned or carted off. We wandered from room to room.

'Well, I hope the new man likes it,' I remarked. 'And I hope he can stomach Mrs Attwood's cooking.'

'He won't care,' answered Pansy. 'Clergymen never do. It's only their wives who care where they live. It's funny, but I always used to think that this was my home. Now I realize that it was no different from a farm tied cottage. I never had any right to live here.'

I picked up her suitcase. Pansy took Jonathan by the hand, tucked her father's huge bible under the other arm and left, without locking the door.

'Such a pity,' Kate remarked. 'I always hoped that Mr Millport would hang on long enough to marry Geoffrey and me.'

'Kate! That's an appallingly selfish thing to say.'

'I know. But it's true. Someone new won't be the same at all.'

'You are getting married, then?'

'I suppose so. Some day.'

She held out her left hand. On the fourth finger sparkled a diamond solitaire of gorgeously vulgar beauty.

The Belsen trials began in Lüneburg in September. Martin was spared that. His photographs were evidence enough, though other men had to stand in front of a court and testify to what they had seen and heard and done in that nightmare place. Martin was posted to Aldershot, to a holding unit, and expected a posting back to Germany later in the autumn. In the meantime, he came home as often as he could.

We spent hours just walking. He didn't mind my being with him. He didn't shun me, as I'd feared he might. We walked. We talked a little. We sat on the grass with our faces turned to the sun. He seemed to need me near. But he never touched me with love.

I ached for him. He was so close and the memory of the night we'd spent together was torment. What you've never had, you never miss. How true. But now I knew what I was missing. Martin and I had shared something beautiful and I longed for his body. More than that. I longed for evidence that we still meant something to each other. A look. A word. A touch. Was that too much to hope for?

It was as though we were separated by a glass partition. Martin looked through it and saw me, but I was as unreal as a reflection. It seemed as though he couldn't understand what he was seeing. I was there and my presence didn't make any sense to him. He wandered alone on the other side, in a fog of memory. His gaze was focused on his own horizon and I didn't know where that was.

Martin had seen things and done things that set him apart from day-to-day life. The evidence was in his eyes. He had looked into the pit and the darkness was still there. I could sense his pain – see it, feel it, touch it – but he would not let me share it.

'Let me carry it with you,' I would have begged. 'That's what love is all about.'

But the words stayed in my head. He didn't want to hear them.

We must have looked, as we strolled in the early autumn sunshine, with eighteen inches of space between us, like two old friends. If that was what he wanted, it would have to be sufficient for me. I was too proud to complain. No-one who saw us together would have guessed how much I wanted him.

But I had all the time in the world. I could wait for Martin for ever, if I had to.

Princess Augusta's Own, I discovered, had been amalgamated in the military upheaval of 1924, with the Duke of Clarence's Loyals, to form a new regiment, Princess Augusta's Loyals. Then again, in 1937, they had been reformed, with Queen Caroline's Royal Regiment, to become the Queen's Loyal Regiment (Augusta's Own). Good grief – what a ridiculous muddle! Who, after all these changes, could possibly recall one man, more than a quarter of a century ago? The trail was stone cold.

With more hope than faith, I wrote to the regimental headquarters of the Queen's Loyals, asking for details of my father's service. The reply, from the regimental secretary, was polite but unhelpful. He confirmed the dates which I had given, and no more. What he had not written lay like a stain across the page.

'They're embarrassed, of course,' Geoffrey said with a snort, when I told him. 'They don't want to admit what happened. It was barbaric. Thank God, in this war, doctors showed more sense and senior officers more compassion. At least, I hope they did. Mind if I have a look at the letter?' He was quiet for a moment as he read it. It didn't take long. 'Well, well. JSP Carterton, Major (Retired) – still around, eh? I remember the bugger well. Thick as two short planks. He was a member of the field general court martial that tried your father.'

'Don't be daft,' Martin argued, when I told him. 'Go and see him? What good would that do?'

'None, probably. But I'm going.'

'All the way to Bedfordshire? Good God – what a waste of time. Is your journey really necessary?' He quoted the propaganda slogan with a wry grin.

'That's what Tom said. He thinks I'm looking for a job. Said it would be a waste of time and money, chasing dreams, only end in tears, blah, blah. He actually forbade me to go – can you credit it? He tried to act the heavy father. How ridiculous. He seems to think I'm still ten years old.'

'I suppose you want me to go with you, damn you.'

'Of course not. I can manage better on my own. Anyway, Carterton will probably throw me out on my ear.'

'Then I'd better be around to pick you up.'

I looked for the spark of humour that might once have accompanied those words, but it wasn't there.

He kept me waiting and that annoyed me. Martin and I had had a pig of a journey. Anyone would think there was still a war on. The sooner Mr Attlee's government kept its promise to nationalize the railways, the better, if that journey was anything to go by. It certainly couldn't be any worse.

I was in a fever of impatience to meet Major Carterton, to talk to him, to make at least *some* progress. And he couldn't be bothered to get back from lunch in time for our appointment. The clerk in the orderly room took one look at my expression and decided that it wouldn't do to keep me hanging around, so he showed me into the office and made me a cup of sticky army tea to keep me occupied.

I had a good nose round while I was waiting. The cubbyhole of an office that Major Carterton's relatively humble status as a retired officer allowed him was, decorated – practically wall-papered – with regimental pictures. Behind his desk was a print – probably taken from a gigantic and hideous oil painting in the officers' mess dining room – of some bloody last stand on the

354

North-West Frontier. The attacking Pathans were fiendishly ugly and the last British soldiers, back to back in their broken square, preternaturally calm, considering they were about to be disembowelled. Why do all regimental paintings depict great defeats?

Hung three deep around the remaining walls were photographs of his serving days. The army had been his life and it still was. Afraid to let go, he'd found himself a little retired niche in this military backwater, spending his days doing damn all.

Here was the football team of '27, the year they'd won the army cup. Only soldiers play football, but there is always an officer in the centre of the pictures. There was the polo team, runners-up to the 9th/12th Lancers. Here the colonel-in-chief, the Princess Royal, presented a new standard. There the officers and sergeants posed outside an ivy-clad building. Year after year. The buildings changed. The faces changed. The images were the same.

There was my father. January 1918. Regimental officers posed outside a château whose walls were pocked by machine-gun fire. Captain now, I see. Dead men's shoes... He wasn't the laughing boy who'd tried to feed Tom's puttees to a dog. Perhaps the formality made him look older. Hat on straight. Immaculately fitting tunic. Polished Sam Browne belt. He was standing towards the back of the group, but I could imagine the boots and breeches. Conibear had kept a miraculous shine on his boots, I had read, but Conibear had been gutted by a shell splinter.

355

Poor devil. I wonder who kept a shine on the boots after that. The hat peak shaded his face, but it wasn't the shadow that had made the hollows below his eyes and the lines around his mouth.

I read the names printed beneath the picture and counted along the rows, second row, fifth from the left. And there – I looked at the man just coming through the door and then back at the picture – oh, yes, there was Major Carterton, who had sat in judgment on my father.

He was exactly as I'd imagined from Geoffrey's description. That is, he was completely nondescript. He hadn't changed all that much from the pictures behind him, either. A little jowlier, not much. Middle height. Thin, sandy hair. Pale eyes. Tweed jacket with leather elbow patches. Regimental tie. It was like talking to a military puppet. I could imagine the Chief of the Imperial General Staff with his hand up the poor man's vest, making him move.

'My dear Mrs Kenton, you've been kept waiting.' He said it as though someone else entirely was to blame.

'Yes,' I answered shortly.

'Do sit down.' He indicated a chair that placed me across the desk from him, like a supplicant. 'As I understood your letter, you're enquiring about an – an episode...'

'Episode? You mean my father's death?'

He shuffled his bottom on his chair, fiddled with a pencil, straightened his blotter, as though we were discussing some indecency.

'A regrettable episode... It was – it was a very

356

long time ago.'

'I know that. It was before I was born. My father never saw me.'

That really made him squirm.

'I don't think I'm in any position to help you.'

'You tried him. You condemned him.' Damn – I hadn't meant to be so aggressive. Not at first, anyway, not until I had to be. I'd meant to get him on my side, win him, not alienate him, but, somehow, it hadn't worked. I couldn't stand the sight of him.

'Not alone. You talk as though it was my sole responsibility. I can't be blamed. I was merely a member of a properly constituted field general court martial. There were no irregularities, let me assure you.'

'But why? What happened? No-one will tell me why.'

He stood up and, walking over to a glass-fronted cabinet, pulled out a fat, red-bound book. 'You've had a wasted journey, Mrs Kenton. Before you set off, it might have been sensible to have consulted a copy of the *Manual of Military Law.*' He flicked through. 'Read this.'

'"You–, do swear that you will well and truly try the prisoner [or prisoners] before the court according to the evidence,"' I read, following where his finger pointed, '"and that you will duly administer justice according to the Army Act now in force, without partiality, favour, or affection, and you do further swear that you will not divulge the sentence of the court until it is duly confirmed, and you do further swear that you will not, on any account, at any time

357

whatsoever, disclose or discover the vote or opinion of any particular member of this court martial, unless thereunto required in due course of law. So help you GOD."'

'Rules of Procedure, 1907, para. III. That is the oath I swore when the court martial was convened. So you see, Mrs Kenton, there's really nothing I can tell you.'

'I *can* read,' I snapped. 'There's nothing here to say that you can't at least tell me what my father is supposed to have done. There must be papers, written records. Where can I see them?'

'I think you'll find that you can't.' He thumbed through that hateful book again. 'Ah, yes, here we are, paragraph 98 – preservation of proceedings...'

I read for myself again. '"The proceedings of a court martial (other than a regimental court martial) shall, after promulgation, be forwarded, as circumstances require, to the office of the Judge-Advocate-General in London or India, or to the Admiralty, and there preserved for not less, in the case of a general court martial, than seven years, and in the case of any other court martial, than three years."'

'There are no records, Mrs Kenton. They are long gone.'

I could have wept. Or screamed. Or throttled him. Possibly all three. Instead, I picked some imaginary fluff off my skirt, looking down until my trembling lips were under control. 'I see. So the army wins again.'

Just for a moment, the puppet showed some humanity. 'I didn't make the rules. I'm only a

358

simple soldier. I merely followed orders.'

'That's an excuse used rather too often these days, don't you think – in Germany, for example.'

'It's all in here.' He waved the red book. 'All in here.'

'What a waste of time,' I ranted, 'and money. You were right, Martin. I should have stayed at home.'

'Not exactly,' said Martin. 'While you were banging your head against a brick wall...'

'Not a wall. A jelly. Every time I hit him, he just wobbled and carried on.'

'...I was chatting with the clerks in the orderly room. Good lads. They didn't see any harm in letting me have a look at the regimental history volumes of it, but I was only interested in a couple of months. Apart from Carterton, the other members of the court are dead. But I've got the names of the padre and the medical officer here. Let's hope they're still alive.'

The old Martin would have grinned in triumph. Clever old me, he'd have teased, getting more by the back door than you with your frontal assault. And I'd've punched his arm and called him a clever clogs.

The new Martin just stuck out his arm to flag down the bus.

The bus bounced along a dreary road, past a brickworks, a deserted airfield, a sprawl of prefabs on the outskirts of town. I looked out of the window because I – we – had nothing to say. We seemed to have lost the habit.

In the centre of a scrap of paper, I scrawled his name. Edwin Ansty. In a circle around him, I wrote the names of the people who knew what had happened to him. My grandmother, his mother. My mother, his wife. Tom, my stepfather, his best friend. Those three, the closest, would say nothing.

But the circle was wider than it used to be. There was Geoffrey Paxton, his sergeant-major. That name went down on the paper. Who else?

J S P Carterton, second-in-command of the battalion. Judge and jury – or one of them. For that is the fault of the court-martial system. The same men – and, in the case of a court martial in the field, only three men – are accusers, jury and judge. Just three men are responsible for the convening of the trial, its conduct and its outcome – even if that should be death. And in seven years, all record of what they have done has disappeared. Could that be right?

I looked at the circle of names. Two more places were filled by question marks, the other members of the court, but Martin had already discovered that these two were dead. I stared so hard that the names began to blur.

A sudden squall spattered off the window panes and shook them in their warped frames. I got up and pulled the curtains. There was no-one else at home. Mother had gone up to spend the evening with Grandmother, picking over tattered curtains and reputations. Tom was out, probably treating his chums at the Green Dragon. Yet the cottage wasn't quiet. The wind boomed in the chimney, a hollow, lonely sound. The door between the kitchen and the dark sitting room rattled. The range gave a comforting hiss. I'd stoked it up well – spoiling myself, when fuel was so short – but the night was cold and I was feeling rather low. Anyway, I could argue that I was saving fuel, by sitting in the kitchen rather than lighting the sitting-room fire. Tom had pulled in an easy chair for me, to make it feel cosier.

Perhaps I'd overdone it. As I walked back to the table, I realized that I was feeling very sleepy. Absurd. It was only half-past seven. I went back and opened a window, just a crack, but the wind was coming from that direction and the rain forced itself in, so I closed it again. Typical autumn gale, I thought; tomorrow the first of the leaves would litter the grass and Tom would begin the bonfires that seemed to last until Christmas.

Yes, I really was feeling overpoweringly sleepy. And my head was pounding to an uncomfortable rhythm. I coughed a couple of times, soft, wheezy coughs. Perhaps I was going down with something. Drat. That was all I needed.

I began to draw a chain that linked all the names on the paper. But it was a chain that didn't have a beginning or an end. Then I realized I'd left out a name – no, not a name, because I didn't know it – but there was someone missing. I'd left out the person who'd sent me those anonymous messages, the ones that had arrived early in the quest to find my father. I still couldn't guess whether the sender was vindictive or just disturbed, whether he or she was attempting to encourage my search or frighten me off, but whoever it was deserved a place in my plan.

Who?

At one time, I'd thought it might be James's mother, but I'd discarded that idea long ago. I realized, now, that I'd been making them fit my own imagined pattern. No matter how plausible their motives, I could no longer see any connection. They had had no access to the information. Or, if I still believed they had, I would also have to believe that I had – by chance, and thousands of miles from home – married a man whose father had – by chance – known my own in France; no, more, known him in the last few months of his life. I couldn't accept that coincidence, even if I still wanted to.

Pansy? I'd certainly suspected her. I was ashamed of that now. I'd imagined that Pansy – Pansy, of all people – had been so jealous of my marriage to the man who just might, possibly, be the father of her child, that she'd ... Pansy? Absurd.

God, my head was thumping.

Then, who? Who had known enough?

Mr Millport? He'd known what had happened to my father, of course. He'd connived with my grandmother to ensure that my father was denied his proper place amongst the remembered dead. But to suspect him of further malice was like imagining Saint Nicholas stealing toys from children.

If it came to that, the whole village seemed to have known, or why did Grandmother fear that the memorial might be vandalized? But they'd all kept their own counsel for twenty-five years. Country people have long memories, but surely a quarter of a century was enough to soften old grudges. This vindictiveness was irrational. It had been especially targeted at me.

In fact, I was probably the only person in Ansty Parva who had not known what had happened to my father. If I suspected one person, I might as well suspect three hundred. Martin had said that once and I had not listened.

So why? And why now? There had to be a reason.

Round and round, round and round ... if I could just close my eyes for a moment...

I drew a large question mark on an outer ring and chained it into the circle with bigger links. And then I stopped. That was all I knew.

I stared at my scribbled diagram. The marks blurred and then merged together. Dots and dashes. Squiggles. I blinked to try to clear my vision, but that didn't work. Sleepy – I felt so sleepy – no, sick...

What a waste of time ... I'd think again in the morning ... I'd understand .... in the morning...

And the rain was failing on my face and the stones were pressing into my back and legs and I was cold, so cold, and someone was shaking me...

'Laura, Laura. Oh God, Laura, wake up...'

Sleep ... let me...

'Laura, please ... breathe...'

No ... I could drift... go away...

And the rain was like needles on my skin, a cruel way to wake, and he wouldn't leave me alone and I hated him for bringing me back. He shook me and shook me and wouldn't let me go. Couldn't he see how much it hurt?

So I took a breath. And then another. Cruel... Damn him... From some hidden reserve of army language I dredged up a word I'd never used in my life before. 'Bugger off.'

'Laura, thank God, darling Laura, I thought I'd lost you...'

And Martin laughed and cradled me to his chest until the coarseness of his sweater rasped my cheek and I could smell wet wool and sweat and fear. And I could tell the difference between his tears and the rain because the rain was cold.

'The fire cement has just crumbled away.' Tom's voice was muffled because his head was squashed into the gap between the range and the chimney breast. He backed out into the open. There was coal dust in his hair. 'There's no seal left between the range and the flue.'

I nodded. What a silly way to nearly die.

'The fumes must have been leaking for ages, but we wouldn't have noticed it with windows and doors open all summer. I suppose you closed everything up last night because of the weather?'

I nodded again.

'Carbon monoxide,' said Tom with chill precision. 'I saw a chap once who'd gassed himself. His skin was cherry pink. Couldn't get over how well he looked. Not a bad way to go, on the whole, I thought. If you have to. You looked like that – pink, very. No pain, I suppose?'

It took me a moment to realize he was asking a question. 'Only coming back.'

'Thought so. Ah, well.' Tom nodded. 'How amazing – Martin coming round like that. Were you expecting him?'

'No.'

'Lucky, then. Anyway, I'll have it fixed in a jiffy. No more accidents.' Tom delved into his pocket and brought out a crumpled piece of paper. 'You were clutching this. Hanging on for grim death. Your mother found it when she put you to bed.' He smoothed it out on the kitchen table and read it. 'Awful lot of question marks, old girl.'

I used to think that I was a patient person. Fairly. As a child, I knew that everything would come, if I just waited long enough. Christmas. Birthdays. A pony. All in their own good time and much more exciting because of the anticipation. Imagine how dull we would be, if we could have everything we wanted whenever we wanted it. Now my relationship with Reg Shellard, the postman, was in danger of breaking down.

He couldn't help it if no-one did write to me, he protested, why blame him? And no wonder, when I had a face that'd curdle the milk. I was persecuting him. He only carried the post, he didn't make it. So leave off.

But he did, eventually, bring me the answers I'd been expecting.

From the office of Crockford's, I learned that the Reverend W S Mantell, chaplain to Princess Augusta's Own between 1916 and 1918, had died in 1929.

From the British Medical Association, I learned that Dr Humphrey Whitlock, medical officer to Princess Augusta's Own from May 1918 to the end of the war, still practised in Camberley.

'Another job interview?' questioned Mother. 'Laura, dear, why can't you be content with a local job?'

'Because I can't find one,' I answered, truthfully.

'But there was that trip you made last month – where was it, Bedfordshire – the fare was so expensive. And it all came to nothing in the end. Your demob grant won't last for ever, you know. You ought to put something aside for a rainy day. Besides, it's so nice to have you at home'

'Camberley isn't Darkest Africa, Mother.'

'I suppose I'd better go with you,' said Martin.

'Why? I don't need anyone to hold my hand.'

'Who was it, last time, went in with all guns blazing and stirred up the military shit?'

'Me.'

'And who was it quietly winkled out some useful information from the clerks?'

I laughed and punched his arm. 'You.'

'See. Besides, I don't think I dare let you out of my sight.' He put his arms round me and drew me close. 'I thought I'd lost you, Laura. Don't do that to me again.'

It was so long since he'd touched me. He was stiff and awkward, uncertain of his welcome. I

366

drew his lips down to mine. I'd forgotten...

I'd forgotten the taste of him, the way I had to stretch to reach his face. I'd forgotten the feel of his body, whipcord and wire. I'd forgotten how right I felt, how safe, when I sheltered within his embrace.

I knew that I was wanted and the knowledge was powerful and exciting. If decent women don't feel desire, then I am not decent and I'm proud of it.

It was Martin who had the common sense to call a halt. We were in his mother's garden, for heaven's sake. She'd have had a heart attack to see me there, like a harlot, with my lips rosy from Martin's kisses and my blouse unbuttoned.

His fingers trembled as he tried to fasten my blouse. 'Bloody buttons. Why are your buttons always too big for the holes?'

'They're not. It's you.' I fastened the last three to prove my point.

'I haven't been fair to you, Laura,' Martin said softly.

'No, you haven't,' I agreed, briskly. I don't know if that was what he wanted, but that was what he got.

'I came back and – I can't explain...'

'Try.'

'I couldn't connect. Does that make sense? Everything I saw was distorted. I looked around at my home and nothing was the way it ought to be. I walked down the road and I smelt smoke. I woke in the night and I heard the sound of digging.'

I listened, aghast, with a growing sense of

367

shame. Martin said that he'd not been fair to me – and that was true – but how fair had I been in return? I realized that I had not made the slightest attempt to understand him. I had looked, but not seen. I had listened, but not heard. Where had I been when he had woken to the sound of digging? What sort of love was that? He had needed me and I had failed him.

'I looked at faces,' he went on; 'people I'd known all my life, people I'd been to school with, you, Laura, even you – and behind them all I saw the other faces, the hungry, the pleading, the dying...'

He turned his face away, but I could still see the jumping nerve at the angle of his jaw. I touched it, gently, as though it might hurt him.

'Martin, I'm sorry, I never guessed. I didn't understand what had happened to you. I'm sorry.'

He looked back then, and stroked my hair away from my forehead. 'And then I nearly lost you. God, I can't think of my life without you in it. And I realized that it was time to come back and live in my own world again. So, Laura, when will you marry me?'

'As soon as you ask me.'

'Then I'm asking you now. When, Laura?'

'I don't know...' It was difficult to look at his eager face. 'Soon, Martin, soon.'

I didn't realize then, but later I understood why I hadn't answered him. I had something to do first.

Dr Humphrey Whitlock practised from a bay-windowed Victorian house in Camberley's respectable Park Street. Martin and I were shown by Mrs Whitlock through a hall booby-trapped by bicycles, alphabet bricks and a one-legged teddy bear. You'd think a doctor could have stitched the leg back on. From the hesitant way she opened the consulting room door, I guessed we were a nuisance, a break in a packed appointment book.

He wasn't as old as I'd expected. He was a brisk, late-middle-aged man with spectacles and a straggly moustache and the pink, rather soggy hands of someone who washes too often and doesn't take time to dry properly. There was only one chair opposite his desk, the patient's chair, so I sat in it. The sun shone straight into my face, leaving Dr Whitlock as an intimidating black bulk.

Martin stood behind me. His hand was on the back of the chair. If I leaned back, I could feel the pressure of his knuckles. I was scared – of what might be said, of what might not be said. Martin moved his hand to the back of my neck and gave it a quick, encouraging squeeze.

Dr Whitlock said, 'Well? And what can I do for you?' in the way that doctors do, the way that makes you want to say, 'I don't like to trouble you, but...'

'I think you may once have known my father.'

He was writing, giving me only a fraction of his attention. 'Mmm?'

'Edwin Ansty.'

'I don't think...'

'It was a long time ago.' I could hear myself,

breathy and apologetic: '1918. France. Edwin Ansty.' Now I had his attention. He screwed the cap back on his fountain pen and laid it on the desk. 'You were battalion MO and he was...'

'No, really, I don't think–'

'I *know* you knew him. I've got letters.'

'I don't want–'

'He said ... he said you were a good chap.'

He pushed back his spectacles and massaged the bridge of his nose. 'What do you want to know?'

'Something. Anything. Why did he die?'

'I don't know why he died. And that's the truth.'

What a literal-minded man. I phrased my question a different way. 'What had he been accused of?'

'Of ... of cowardice in the face of the enemy.'

'Tell me about it.'

'I can't be expected ... it was a very long time ago ... how can I remember...'

'Please.' I put my hand out and it nearly touched his across the desk before he pulled his back into his lap. 'Please.'

'I wish I didn't have to ... I wish you hadn't come ... these things are better left...

'I remember ... it was late August and we were beginning to roll the Germans back, taking control of almost all the ground we had lost in the enemy spring push. It was the beginning of the end of the war, though we didn't know it. The soldier on the ground never sees the great plan. I suppose there was one. All you see, all you really believe in, is the few hundred yards spread out in front of you. All you care about is what happens today, or maybe tomorrow. All you think about is surviving until the next leave. Everything else is as remote as the moon ... or the commander in chief.

'The battalion was facing a German strong point – twenty yards of wire and concrete bunkers – that could be dominated from one of those bloody little hills, you know, hills with numbers that told you how far above sea level they were – Hill 60, Hill 62, I forget what number this one had. Molehills, really, you wouldn't even notice them on a stroll across the common. But they were so *bloody* important. We had orders to take this one.

'I was only the doctor, remember. I wasn't there. I didn't really know what was going on. I just patched and stitched – and hacked, if I had to.

'Only a little hill, but we took it and then they threw us off it and then we took it again, up and down ... a messy, messy business, close combat, cut and stab. I had a busy day. At the end of it, just before dark, your father crawled back into the lines. No-one had seen him since morning. What had happened? Where had he been? He wouldn't say.

'So of course, there was talk. Men who go missing during bloody battles do get themselves talked about. He was placed under arrest and court-martialled – but you knew that – and he never said a word. Never excused himself. Never explained.

371

'No, not even when they passed sentence. I don't suppose he had time to draw breath, it was all over so quickly. Only three officers are needed to hold a field general court martial, instead of the peacetime five. The CO appointed himself president of the court – I don't know, I'm only a doctor, look it up in the *Manual of Military Law*, can't you. He seemed to take it as a personal affront that he had to try one of his officers. Not many officers were shot, you know. Only another three, throughout the whole war, and one of those was sentenced for murder. Not that officers were more or less cowardly than the other ranks, just that their pals covered up for them more efficiently, I suspect. No-one covered up for your father, but then no-one could. No-one knew where he'd been.

'We took over the upstairs room of the local *estaminet* – bit of a squeeze to hold a court martial in a dugout. They had to shove an iron double bed against the wall to push in a trestle table and a few chairs. What a farce. Trying a man for his life with a potty under the bed and a woman's nightie hanging on a nail on the door. The three officers sat in a row at the table, hats on, swords in front of them. The CO, Major Carterton – he was second-in-command – and one of the company commanders, Handsworth – he was killed the following week, I seem to remember.

'The adjutant prosecuted. Open and shut. Your father went out on the attack in the morning and no-one saw him until he came creeping back in the evening. No defence. No mitigating plea. He had a prisoner's friend, of course, to speak for

372

him. Rules are rules. A subaltern – Roding – Tim, or Tom, I forget. He was useless. A gibbering wretch. Couldn't string two sensible words together. Not that a QC could have done any better, I imagine. Not when there was nothing to explain. What on earth can you do with a man who refuses to talk?

'I was called to testify. I'd examined him, you see, to find out if there was any medical reason for his behaviour. The CO was fair, give him his due. I did my best. I reminded the court of your father's exemplary record, of his MC, of how long he'd been in France, under what terrible conditions. But so had we all. There was no getting away from it – he was as sane as anyone in that room, whatever that might mean. I couldn't fudge that.

'So the trial ended. I remember looking across the room and realizing that your father really didn't *believe* that it could happen to him. He was so calm. He still had faith in the system, in the good will of his fellows – amazing, isn't it?

'I don't know what he expected. A slap on the wrist. Prison. Not death, I'm sure.

'To pronounce a sentence of death, the court has to be unanimous. But how could it not be? With the CO as president, Carterton licking his ... boots ... and a junior officer imagining what his life could be like if he held out on his own, perhaps salving his conscience by relying on the commendation to mercy.

'A court martial works in a peculiar way. If the finding is Not Guilty, or a punishment within the authority of the president, the prisoner is told straight away. Anything else – cashiering or long imprisonment or death – and the sentence has to be confirmed by a higher authority. For the death penalty, only the commander-in-chief's signature will do. If you're lucky, the court will add a commendation to mercy and so will the reviewing officers, all the way up the chain. If you're lucky. So, at the end, if you're not told what's going to happen to you, you know it's something serious. And you have to wait. A couple of weeks, perhaps. In the summer of 1918, a new procedure was introduced – the secret envelope.

'Secret envelope? Don't you know? The court couldn't state outright that the sentence was death, because it hadn't been confirmed, so a secret envelope was slipped to the prisoner telling him that he was going to be shot. Can you imagine – the suspense, the fear, until confirmation came through? When perhaps it wasn't going to happen at all. It was meant to be kindness, but it was pretty near to torture. One poor devil cut his throat while he was waiting – before the verdict was quashed.

'And *still*, I swear, Edwin didn't believe it could happen. He knew what penalty is laid down for cowardice in the face of the enemy – death or such lesser punishment as the Army Act sanctions – and he didn't believe...

'I was with him the night the sentence was promulgated. The doctor gets called on for all sorts of unsavoury tasks. In this case, I think there is a fear that the prisoner will faint or have a fit or something. Got to keep the victim healthy, so you can shoot him in the morning.

374

The adjutant read out the sentence and he was crying. "I'm sorry, Edwin – I can't believe it's come to this – I'm so sorry."

'And then your father knew – not until then, I swear – that it was hopeless. The heart went out of him. He rocked, I remember, as though he was going to fall. I put out my hand to catch him, but he held on to the table instead. "Not your fault, Jack," he said to the adjutant. "No-one to blame but me." I gave him a shot of morphia to take away the shock, with the promise of another one in the morning. It was all I could do. That's what doctors are for, isn't it? To make the best of things? Patch up other people's mistakes?

'My God, he was only a boy. But they were all boys – how many? – three hundred odd over the four years, I think, dragged out into a cold dawn and hooked on to a post or tied on to a chair, so that they couldn't move and spoil the firing squad's aim. It's a sort of common sense, I suppose. Much crueller to make a mess of it.

'No, I didn't see it. They took him away. Just before first light, a party arrived with a closed vehicle – two provost sergeants, a provost officer and another doctor from the headquarters staff. They took him away. I don't know where. No-one ever told me anything.

'And when it was over, the ... the proceedings were usually published in Routine Orders, to make sure everyone knew. No, I didn't actually see it myself. I had better things to do than scrutinize bits of paper.

'That's all. I don't know. No, there's nothing more I can tell you. I'm sorry, it's distressing for you. Look, I don't know... Will you see yourselves out? I wish you hadn't come. What good does it do...?'

On the way home, I stared out of the train window, reluctant to face Martin, reluctant to face the truth. I'd come to the end of the search. I knew as much as anyone, as much as anyone still alive, that is. And that wasn't enough. I knew what, but I didn't know why. I knew how, but I didn't know where.

I stared fiercely at the blurred, passing countryside. If I closed my eyes, I could see my father being led away to his death. Just before dawn, as the cocks were crowing.

'Guess what?' Vee wrote. 'I'm still here. Carlton is doing his best to get me entry to the US of A, but his government certainly is picky. Tidworth is a Godawful hole. Come and see me, before I go round the bend...'

Standing at the top of Station Road, looking down the slope of shabby shops towards Tidworth, I could see exactly what Vee had meant. On the opposite side of the Salisbury-Marlborough road, beyond the handful of thatched cottages, the line curved, red brick and blue slate barracks, each one identical to its neighbour, unchanged since the early days of the century. A banner hung across one door – BRIDE RECEPTION.

'Lovely, isn't it?' snorted Vee. 'A real gateway to paradise.'

'There are so many women,' Pansy remarked as we walked down the hill, and so there were – pregnant women, women pushing prams, women leading toddlers – scarcely a man in sight. A few GIs, rootless and jobless, mooched around with cigarettes drooping from their lips and their hands in their pockets. There seemed to be a baseball game going on in the stadium by the main road. As we passed, a couple of small boys disappeared down a culvert that led under the stadium wire. The Yanks were still good for a spot of free entertainment.

'There's thousands of us – GI brides. We're all waiting for Uncle Sam to decide whether we're fit to be allowed into his country. Only he's very particular. He doesn't want bad girls trapping his boys into marriage. So we have to wait while our morals are dusted down and inspected. Lectures on this. Lectures on that. Leaflets on how to behave ourselves when we meet our in-laws. Pep talks on how we mustn't all expect an icebox and a coloured maid. It's called processing and it makes me feel like a tin of corned beef. Tidworth is the waiting room to the promised land, yessir. They even inspect us for VD, because everyone knows there's no such thing in the land of the free.'

I looked at Vee, trying to decide whether she was being flippant or bitter, but I couldn't make up my mind. She was much the same – a little plumper, perhaps (she'd still not quite managed to lose the weight she'd put on before Carlton junior's birth), glossy, well groomed from her permed curls to her painted toenails. Pansy and I looked like a pair of country bumpkins. Yet there was an air of discontent about her, a restless, challenging swing to her walk. It didn't suit her.

'Christ, this is a real hole. Miles away from anywhere. Hardly any shops. Even two boiled eggs for breakfast is no consolation. It's like being back in the bloody army again – rules and regulations – go this way, don't go that way. If there's one thing worse than living with a pack of women, it's living with a pack of women and their squalling brats. Two of the girls in my barrack-room have already run back home to Mother. I tell you, if Carlton doesn't pull a few strings soon and get me over the pond double quick, I'll find myself another man who can. Only joking, love,' she said quickly, seeing Pansy's shocked face. 'Tell you what – I'll stand you coffee and dough-nuts, how about that?'

We strolled along the lime-edged avenue towards Tedworth House, under a portico that led from a carriage turning circle, and into an elegant entrance hall with a sweeping staircase leading from it. The paintwork was scarred by careless boots. Initials had been scored into the plasterwork. The cornice had been stained by an upstairs flood.

'Pretty nice, huh?' said Vee. 'Wonder what it was like to live here in the good old days. Fancy me moving in such grand circles. I tell you, I think about my gran's shop in Leathermarket Street and then I look round here and I have to pinch myself. Come on, I could kill for a coffee.'

A room with sash windows to the floor and views across the park had been converted into a canteen. We queued at a long table where young men in overalls served coffee from an urn.

'Morning, Heinz,' Vee greeted the one who handled the milk jug. 'How're you today?'

'I am very well, thank you,' he answered in careful English. 'How are you?'

He was squat and dark, not the least bit Aryan. Pansy was gaping and I suddenly realized that, despite five years of war, she had never actually seen a living German.

'PoWs,' Vee informed us in a loud, careless voice. 'Rather sweet. Bit like prison trusties, I suppose. Still, they've got to earn their keep somehow.'

'But why don't we send them home?' queried Pansy, looking back over her shoulder with sympathy. 'Surely we can't keep them now the war's over.'

'I expect we would if we could,' I reassured her. 'But we still haven't managed to demob all our own men yet, let alone the enemy. And things are in such a mess in the east, some of them have nowhere to go, anyway.'

At the end of the trestle, Vee collected a plate piled high with doughnuts and took it to a free table. We all sat down and Vee offered the plate around. Pansy just stared at it.

'Do you think,' she asked in awe, 'I could possibly take one back to Jonathan?'

'Sure. Look, there's plenty.' Vee raised her voice. 'Heinz, can we have a paper bag over here?' She tipped half a dozen doughnuts into the bag. 'Now make sure he eats them tonight. No saving them for tomorrow. They'll be stale by then.'

'Oh, we can't ... he couldn't...'

'Why not? Let the kid get sick if he wants. He won't get the chance again, not for a long time. I'd send him back some ice-cream if I could work out how. Has he never tasted ice-cream? Jennifer just loves peach. Peach for a little peach, I tell her.'

I made a pig of myself. When we'd eaten three doughnuts each, Pansy and I licked the sugar off our fingers. We looked at each other and laughed.

'You've got cinnamon on the end of your nose, Laura.'

'So've you. Why go to America, Vee? Seems to me you've got everything you want here.'

'All except Carlton. I've got a sneaky feeling that if I don't get myself over there quick, he'll find some nice down-home girl to console him. Shouldn't be long now, though. I've got my name down on the first ship out.'

It was such fun to see her again. We walked round the park, pushing little Carlton in his pram and playing hide and seek through the trees with Jennifer. We laughed a lot and cried a little and hugged and laughed again.

And we all knew that we would probably never be together again.

There were so many questions I ought to have asked Dr Whitlock. I had been so distressed by his memories that I'd been unable to put my thoughts together in a logical manner. Now, too late, they buzzed around my brain.

Taken away by a doctor on the headquarters staff, he'd said. Who? Did he know him? Which headquarters? Where had they been based? What had been their authority? Who else had seen them? What did other people say? What did they guess?

But when I'd telephoned, Mrs Whitlock said that her husband was too busy to talk to me. When I'd suggested calling back at a more convenient time, the poor woman had ummed and aahed, but quite clearly gave me the impression that there never would be a convenient time for me.

I'd gone a long way along the road with my father, but now it seemed as though I had reached a point where I could accompany him no longer.

Dear Madam

I am informed by Mr Paxton that you are looking for men who knew your late father Captain Ansty. Mr Paxton and I are old pals. We signed on together in August 1914 and did our basic training together. Then we were posted together to the same regiment but he became a sergeant major and I never did get further than corporal. Well he had the brains and I had the brawn. That is what I always used to say anyway. After the war he was kind enough to see that I got a job with the Corps of Commissionaires. Well life was hard then and too many old soldiers looking for a job. Mrs Maltby and I were living in an old railway carriage in a field no life for a wife and the little ones always coughing. So now I am his doorman and have been these nineteen years past and when I have to salute him in the morning we have a good laugh about it. I was on guard outside

381

your late father's door all the night before he was taken away. An awful job but the good thing was that the RSM would not pick me for the firing party as I had been up all night and would not shoot straight. No-one wanted to be picked well no-one ever does and we all tried to find jobs out of the way of the RSM's eye but someone has to do it in the end. Well your father was a gentleman and well liked by the rank and file and none of us thought it was right and I know the 2i/c was afraid there might be trouble so the clerks heard but there were orders so there you are what can you do. Lots of things happened in war that I would not care to put a name to now. Now just before it got light a truck comes up and two officers and two provost sergeants went in to see your father I don't suppose he was asleep I don't suppose he had closed an eye all night poor boy. I got talking to the driver the way you do and we had a cigarette together and I remember he told me that he was detailed to drive to some hospital. I remember this because I thought it was odd and I said are you sure and he said don't you think I know where I'm supposed to be driving. I am sorry to say that I don't remember the name of the hospital because it was not a place I had been to and all French names sound the same to me and anyway it was a long time ago but I am certain that is where they were going if that is any help to you. I was sent on leave that day which was a nice surprise as I was not coming up on the roster for a long time and our second made his appearance in the world due to that leave which all goes to show these things are meant to be. After that I was posted away and that is all I know. I hope you will be kind enough to pass my respects to Mr Roding who I

382

understand is now your stepfather. He will remember me just say my name.
Yours truly Stanley Maltby
(ex-corporal Princess Augusta's Own)

'A hospital?' Martin read the end of the letter again. 'Why?'

'I don't know. I can't think.'

'What would be the point of taking away a condemned man? At the last minute?'

'To avoid trouble? The letter says that the second-in-command – that beastly man Carterton again thought there might be trouble.'

'So they bundled him away, before anyone else was up. That makes sense. They could have taken him to another unit, to strangers.' Martin shuddered. 'God, how vicious. But to a hospital? You don't send men to hospital to be killed.'

'And they sent the guard on leave – that day, too. And then he was posted.'

'So that he wouldn't be able to gossip? I think we're reading too much into this, Laura.'

'I know, I know. I just can't help it. All my life, my father has been a ghostly figure, someone I had to believe in, because everyone has a father, but I was supposed to believe in him like Pansy believes in the Holy Ghost – she doesn't need to see Him to know that He's there. She has complete faith, but I wanted more proof. I always had a sneaking sympathy for doubting Thomas. Now, in the last few months, people who knew my father are practically falling out of the trees. And we've heard the same story twice. My father was driven away from the regimental lines one morn-

383

ing and they never saw or heard of him again. And no-one asked where or why. It frightens me. Martin, think of a reason.'

Martin wedged his back more comfortably against the tree trunk and drew me close to him. I fitted perfectly into the crook of his arm. He kissed the top of my head, but absentmindedly, without passion.

'Well, then – they may have taken him to another unit and shot him.'

'No known grave,' I countered.

'The vehicle may have been blown to smithereens on the way there – wherever *there* might be.'

'That's possible,' I acknowledged, reluctantly. 'It would make a convenient explanation. Or?'

'They may actually have taken him to this supposed hospital, after all.'

'But why?'

'I don't know. You didn't ask me that, remember?'

'I'm asking you now.'

Martin was quiet for a while. He didn't hurry to soothe me, to find an answer that would shut me up and make me happy. He would never take the easy way. I could trust him not to do that.

'Supposing...' he said, slowly, at last, 'supposing the death sentence had been confirmed – for the sake of example – and the execution arranged ... supposing someone wanted to avoid killing him...'

'Who?' I demanded. 'Why?'

'I don't know. Don't interrupt. Supposing someone wanted to halt it – what would he do?

384

Persuade the C-in-C to change his mind? Possibly. Someone very influential might be able to do that. The messenger on a white horse comes galloping in waving a pardon just as the rifles are raised – very Hollywood. Dicey. There might not be time. How awful if the C-in-C was having dinner with the King that night and didn't get home until after midnight and the messenger galloped in just as the rifles were lowered. Or again – and it would still have to be someone who could pull strings, someone of sufficiently high rank to be above question – it might be possible simply to spirit your father away. Order out an escort, give them an appropriately signed piece of paper – who's going to question it? the corporal on the door? a subaltern who's been in France for two days? – and the prisoner is whisked away to ... ah, well, that's the problem, isn't it?'

'That's ridiculous,' I scoffed.

'Well, you asked me a silly question. What sort of answer did you think you'd get? But you could make it fit, if you wanted to badly enough. What do we know? Barely an hour before he was due to face a firing squad, your father was carted off in a closed vehicle and disappeared. The implication is that the execution has taken place elsewhere. So the battalion is given its terrible example, the CO's bloodlust and the regimental honour – which, in this case, might be the same thing – are (presumably) satisfied, but the mysterious meddler gets what he wants and the victim just disappears. I know it's far-fetched, but it's the best I can do.'

'But ... disappears for a quarter of a century?'

385

'No. It's too ridiculous.'
'I want to believe you, Martin.'
'I know. That's what worries me.'

I'm standing with my back to the school play-ground railings. They crowd me against the bars. I can feel each iron rod pressing into my back and the gap between each. They're all there. Dennis Rudge. Billy Kimber with only one leg now. Josie Pocknell with her children, one white, one black. The two Thurlow boys.

'Le's see you run, then,' they chant. 'Le's see you run like your old man.'

'I haven't got an old man,' I answer.

And they all laugh. I'd said something funny. It must be a joke, then, and they aren't really going to hurt me. But they push and poke and jostle. They're trying to pull the petals off the poppy in my buttonhole. It's as big as a dinner plate and there are hundreds, thousands of petals. It'll take all day to pluck it. They love me, they love me not.

I look round for Martin. I know he should he there. I've reached the point in my dream when he ought to appear. He always does. Petals fall at my feet, swaths of scarlet, countless, and each one has a name on it.

'Stop, stop!' I shout. 'Give me time. I can't read them all.'

I'm down on my knees, frantically picking up petals and throwing them down again. There are so many. How will I ever find the one I want? James's name is inscribed on one. Grace's name is there on another. I knew they would be. I put them in my pocket. When I get home, I'll look for an eraser. I can rub their names out and then everything'll be all right. My father's name isn't there, though. But he must be somewhere. I'll find him, I know I'll find him. If only I have the time, if only I look hard enough.

I look and look, but the pile of petals is so deep and more are falling all the time.

And then, at last, Martin is there. He takes my hand and pulls me to my feet. He takes the petals from my grasp and drops them to the ground. He brushes them from my hair.

'He isn't there,' he tells me. 'You're looking in the wrong place.'

Of course...

All along, I'd been making an assumption. I'd assumed that my father had died on the day that was appointed for his death. But what did I have to prove that? Nothing. No witnesses. No record of burial. No grave.

There were plenty of people who could say to me, 'Your father was shot.' But I had not yet discovered a single person who could say, 'Your father was shot on such-and-such a day, at such-and-such a time, in such-and-such a place.'

Only an assumption. Supposing, for some reason, I wanted to prove his death. I could go to court and ask a judge to pronounce. Do you think he would? What evidence could I offer? Where was the death certificate? Who had seen him die?

Yet my mother had married Tom. She could have had no doubts.

This made no sense. It was madness.

Yes, I could make myself believe. I could squeeze and trim and shove until, like the slipper on the feet of Cinderella's sisters, the story had to fit.

'Pay no attention,' Martin had said. 'I was just thinking aloud. I didn't mean it. I wish I'd never started the stupid idea.'

But he had. And now he'd put it into my head, I couldn't think of anything else. That hippopotamus, again.

My bed seemed too narrow, the ceiling too low, the mice in the attic too active, Tom's snores too loud, my pyjamas too scratchy. My thoughts spiralled and jinked like planes in a dogfight.

Martin and I both knew how muddled the simplest thing could become on active service. SNAFU. Situation Normal All Fucked Up. Units were moving in and out without proper hand-overs. Messages were being delayed. You'd have weapons without ammunition, ammunition without weapons. People were being killed, for God's sake. How easy it was to lose something.

Lost half your kit or flogged it to the locals for souvenirs? If you had a chum in the stores, he'd see you all right, for a consideration. Pranged a staff car? The MT corporal would swear blind it had been hit by a divine thunderbolt and certify it BER – Beyond Economic Repair – if you chatted him up nicely.

Lost a man? Not really. Not if you had a signature for him.

As long as you had a signed and stamped chitty, you could sell the regimental silver on a market stall. No-one would notice or care. The paperwork was the important thing.

Given that, where would he be taken? Where could he be hidden? The war had been almost over. Supposing he had been in hospital in France, by November, December at the latest, they would all have been closed down. Anyway, there were no long-term occupants of beds in overseas hospitals. Men either died, or were cured, or were shipped back to England.

So what about military hospitals in England? There were so many, in all the major garrisons - Aldershot, Tidworth, Colchester, Catterick. All crammed with men. All with archives that must go back to the Boer War or further, perhaps right back to the days of Florence Nightingale. I couldn't search them all. And there had been so many other hospitals, only temporary, set up in large houses to deal with the surges of casualties that followed each major offensive. What had happened to their records?

I couldn't think how or where to start. I sat up, pummelled the pillow, and lay down on my stomach. The familiar shape of the mattress I had slept on for twenty years seemed to have altered. There were dips where there should have been lumps. There were hummocks where there should have been hollows.

So I crept downstairs, keeping to the edge of each step, avoiding the third tread from the top. I didn't want Mother and Tom to wake just because I couldn't sleep. The kitchen smelt of the marrow bones that had been set to simmer for stock all night on a cooling fire – lucky to get those, Mother had said, you'd scarcely believe the war was over. It smelt of grease and the soda I'd used to wash up, and cold ash. There was just enough glow in the embers to catch the kindling I fed to the range. And while I was waiting for the slow kettle to boil, I opened the back door and stood on the step, letting the stone draw the bedtime warmth from my feet, watching the sun rise and listening to the waking song of a sleepy wren – what a huge noise for a tiny bird – and working out what to do next.

The only place to start was at the beginning.

The military hospital at Netley was both impressive and immensely depressing. I remembered looking over the ship's rail as I'd sailed to and from France and being grateful I wasn't a nurse there. I'd wondered how many miles a day a nurse had to walk. What a relic, as externally magnificent, as internally impossible as the age in which it had been planned, the Empire's answer to the squalor of Scutari. The building must have been impractical from the day it received its first patient, in March 1863. For more than a quarter of a mile, the Royal Victoria Hospital lined the eastern bank of Southampton Water, redbrick, faced with Portland stone and corniced with Welsh granite, with rows of windows drawn up like a battalion on parade, and the central domed chapel that was a landmark to vessels entering and leaving port.

The major part of the British forces on the Western Front, the returning casualties, the prisoners of war, all came and went from Southampton and past the Royal Victoria. From

Southampton Docks, a train carried the stretcher cases the few miles to Netley. It was the staging post for the lucky men with a Blighty one, their first treatment in a permanent building, before, perhaps, being sent on to other hospitals throughout the country. Some would never leave it. It was the place to begin my search.

I walked through pleasant grounds that stretched down to the shore. Men in military hospital blue sat in the sun or were pushed in wheelchairs along a promenade by the water's edge. Not so many now as there had been. The war had ended five months ago, but there were men here who might never go home. I didn't know which door to go through, didn't know where to look, didn't know who to ask.

It was impressive. It was monstrous. The corridor stretched ahead of me, a quarter of a mile of highly polished lino that squeaked under my feet. About a hundred yards away, a nurse in scarlet and grey was squeaking along in front of me – walk, don't run, nurses never run, even when they work in a hospital where a patient could die of a heart attack before anyone could reach him. The nurse certainly walked fast, though. She outdistanced me and turned off into a ward. Further away still, a porter was pushing a trolley. From where I stood, it looked as though the figure on the trolley had a blanket pulled over his face.

Closely ranked windows made up the left-hand wall of the corridor. It was like walking the length of a particularly badly designed greenhouse. No, plants would never have survived in that dry, dead atmosphere. The sun was scorching. It could have blistered the paint and melted the polish on the lino. Yet, I imagined, in winter it was probably bitterly cold. Not a single blue-bottle buzzed against the acres of glass. The smell of Lysol caught at my throat. A germ wouldn't have dared raise its head.

Somewhere there must be an archive store. Feeling like a sneak thief, I set off down the corridor, past doors labelled Surgical, Ortho-paedic, Pathology, Officers Only. Yes, this was definitely a military hospital. Officers and soldiers couldn't possibly lie in bed next to each other or use adjacent urinals.

I tried not to look through the many doors, but it was difficult to avoid getting glimpses of the dark interiors of the wards. Orderly rows of beds. Starched sheets. Hospital corners. Patients lying at attention. And I thought that the architect of this ridiculous building ought to have been made to spend a few months in bed here. He might have learned a lesson or two. The hospital was in a perfect setting, with sea breezes and views across the water to the margins of the New Forest, yet he'd wasted all that on a pompous façade and corridors, while the patients had to endure a view of the clutter of stores, kitchens and canteens at the back.

When I'd explored about three-quarters of the ground floor, I was cornered by a woman wearing the three-cornered starched veil and scarlet cape of a QAIMNS, sister.

'No visiting until 1400 hours,' she informed me, crisply.

'I'm looking for your records office.'

'Top floor – but you can't go up there–'

When I saw the RAMC sergeant sitting at his desk, reading the sports page of the *Daily Sketch*, cigarette stuck to his bottom lip, mug of tea comfortably within reach, I wished I was back in uniform. It would have given us a starting point, a bond of experiences shared. We would have known at once what to make of each other. It would have been 'us', the senior NCOs, the backbone of the army, against 'them' – meaning anyone and everyone else. Now, to him, I was just a nosy civilian.

'1918? Well, now,' he said, slowly, 'I don't know. I really couldn't say. I can't let just anyone poke around in confidential records.'

'It's terribly important.'

'Can't be that important if it could wait nearly twenty-seven years.'

'It's about ... about my father. I never knew him, you see.' I could scarcely recognize the breathy, feminine voice as my own. Good heavens, I was actually manipulating the man. I might have been ashamed of myself if I hadn't wanted something from him so badly. 'And he might have been here. I've just found out. And I do so need to know ... to know *something*.'

'Medical records – confidential,' he reiterated. 'I'd be for the chop if it got out. It'd be more than my stripes are worth.'

'Please. I could make it worth your while.'

'I didn't hear that, love.'

'Please.'

'Well, I don't know. I suppose I could just tell you if he was here. Would that help? I can't let you look.' He got up and went towards a door on the other side of his office. '*If* he was here. *If* I can find anything, which isn't likely, considering. *If* it hasn't all been eaten by mice or rotted in the rain or...'

I could see his point. Racks and racks of shelving stretched off into a dusty distance. Each rack was packed with paper: splitting brown envelopes spilling paper, paper shoved back and jammed at the back of shelves, crumpled, stained, spotted, nibbled paper. Here and there, buckets and basins stood on the floor to catch drips from the roof. There was no water in them at the moment, but they were tidemarked by past rainy days.

'Good Lord,' I gasped.

'Not a pretty sight, is it?' he agreed cheerfully. 'It's all here – right from the days when Florence Nightingale was lighting her little lamp – somewhere. Falling to bits, this place. All swank on the outside and a leaking roof. All fur coats and no knickers, as my old granny would say. They'll have to pull it down, if something isn't done soon. Now, what name are you looking for?'

'Ansty. Captain E J T Ansty, Princess Augusta's Own.'

'Well, that's a mercy, anyway. Narrows things down a bit. Officers' documents are separate from ORs. Bad for discipline to have them hobnobbing on the same shelf.'

'Alphabetic or date order?' I asked brightly, trying to encourage myself that the task wasn't hopeless. But it was, I thought. Hopeless. A needle in a haystack would be child's play compared to this.

'Wouldn't you like to know? I've been here seventeen years and I'm only just getting the hang of it.'

'Seventeen years?' He was joking – wasn't he?

'That's right. 1928 I came here, straight out of basic training. Sometimes I think the army's forgotten me. Still, suits me. Nice cushy little number. Wife and kiddies, married quarters and all. Mind you, the hospital's not what it was.'

I could only nod my encouragement. He was raking through a filing cabinet as he spoke and I didn't want to distract him.

'Before my time, of course, but would you believe that in the last lot, there was patients overflowing into the corridors and huts and tents all over the grounds. Stands to reason that some of the paperwork went missing. Beds everywhere. Germans, too. Kept them on the middle floor, where they could be guarded proper, while our lads were in tents, until the shop stewards in Thorneycroft's heard about it and organized a protest march. Then it was Germans outside and Tommies in again, quick as you like. Not this war, though, not so many patients. Too near the docks and they had a pasting, I can tell you.'

I watched his sifting fingers, afraid to stop his flow of talk and searching – willing him, willing him to find something.

'Look, love,' he said, raising his head from the packed drawer. 'Why don't you take a little walk outside for half an hour or so. Give me a chance.

Have a look round the cemetery, why don't you? It's very nice, very tasteful. And you never know what you might find.'

There is a path that leads through neglected woods. Still, heavy shade, dark and brambly, weighty. Then you come out into the dappled sunlight of a grassy knoll and you're dazzled by the brightness of the neat rows of headstones. White, uniform, impersonal you think, until you read the few words on each, words of farewell, pride, regret, hope, chosen by the families of the men who came back from the war only to die. Among the stones are more angular ones carved with the names of the German wounded who never went home.

I read them all. Then I moved slowly up the slope, through the less-regimented ranks of older graves, the soldiers of the Queen-Empress who had carried back their tropical diseases halfway across the world to Hampshire.

Down the slope again and another handful of tombs, belonging to officers of the Great War, more ornate, grander than those at the entrance to the cemetery, divided even in death. I read the name on each one.

Edwin Ansty was not there.

I didn't know whether to be relieved or sorry. Both, perhaps. I had followed the trail for so long, with such intensity, that it would have been almost a respite to have reached the end. I longed to know, here, now, whatever it was that I had to face.

I wanted it to be over.

And when I went back to the sergeant clerk's office, he had found nothing either. A waste of a day. A waste of *another* day.

'Sorry, love,' he said. 'I did my best.'

'It was kind of you to try. I'm sorry to have wasted so much of your time.'

'That's all right. I was only picking the winners at Kempton on Saturday, anyway.' He held out his hand to shake mine. 'Good luck. I hope you find him.' Then, as I went out the door, he said, 'I don't suppose ... he wouldn't have been in the Asylum, would he, your dad?'

I sat and waited this time, while he fetched another bunch of keys and opened a different door. Behind it were the same racks of shelving, the same fruity smell of decay, but the number of documents was smaller. I felt very frightened.

Asylum. It was such a Victorian word. It stood alongside workhouse and pauper and poor law – and lunatic. No-one used it any more. No-one *modern* said it. But whatever you called it, it meant the same thing.

'No need to look like that. It's not as bad as you think,' the clerk reassured me, as his fingers riffled through a card index. 'They were mostly shellshock cases in there. The odd queer fish, of course, no getting away from that. D'you know the one about the loony looking over the wall, watching this feller scooping up the horse's doovers from the road ... no? ... and the loony says ... oh well, p'raps not. And there was always one or two who thought it was a quick way to get out of soldiering. Silly sods. They were soon

397

given the old about-turn, quick march. But mostly, they were lads who couldn't take any more. Well, they were either shot or sent to Netley, depending on how lucky they were.' He slammed one drawer shut and opened another. I felt very cold. It was as if ... as if I knew. 'Take your pick which you'd rather. Those were the bad old days, weren't they? We're a bit more sensitive now, I like to think. It's not so bad, though. "D" block. Its own grounds, pretty little summer-house to sit in. Nice and secluded behind the wall. You can go and have a look if you like. Aaaah...' He gave a long-drawn sigh of satis-faction and pulled out a card. 'Here we are. There's no-one can find their way round my filing system like I can, though I say it myself. Is this who you're looking for? Here until May 1920 and then transferred to a nursing home in Surrey. Before my time.'

1920. He was alive in 1920 and so was I. But we never saw each other.

By May 1920, my mother had married Tom.

I couldn't look at them. I couldn't talk to them.

My gentle mother – wispy hair always escaping, long hands always on the move. Always trying to make sure that everyone was happy and failing because what she tried couldn't possibly be achieved, ever, only she hadn't worked that out yet, so she kept on trying. I wondered what she had been like, in the days before I could remember her. Eighteen years old and a widow with a child on the way. Supposing my brief moments with James had left me in that

398

situation. What would I have done? Would I have grasped at the next man who showed me kindness? But I had been older, stronger, altogether tougher than my mother ever had been.

Tom, whatever his faults – and who was I to criticize a man who had come back from the trenches with shot nerves and a taste for whisky? – had been the kindest, most generous stepfather anyone could have wanted. He had cared for me, played with me when I was small, supported me. He had never, not once, made me feel that I was any less his own daughter than Kate.

Both of them had loved Edwin. And when Edwin died, they had filled the void where he had been in the most natural way. But Edwin had not died, not then.

'You're not going down with something, are you, darling? I do hope not. There's an awful fluey bug going round.' Mother put her hand on my head and it was all I could do not to jerk away. 'You're rather hot.'

'I'm fine,' I lied, ungraciously. 'Just a bit tired.'

'Too much gadding round the country,' Tom remarked, irritably shaking out the pages of the *Daily Telegraph* – yesterday's – he always had Grandmother's when she'd finished with it. She didn't even leave him the crossword. 'I don't know what you think you're doing. Bedford. Camberley. Southampton. Where next?'

'I'm looking for work,' I answered, as calmly as I could.

'Work? Then I can find plenty for you. That's the one thing we're never short of here. I can scarcely see the leeks for groundsel. You can make a start on that whenever you like.'

'I promised to help Pansy with the potatoes for the harvest supper.'

'That's right. Promise to help everyone but your own family. Your mother's run off her feet, while you gossip with your chum.'

'That's hardly fair, Tom,' Mother pointed out, mildly. 'There are half a hundredweight of potatoes to peel, before the WI can cook them. Pansy can't possibly do them all on her own.'

'I won't be late,' I said, rising and giving my mother a quick kiss on her cheek.

I felt like a traitor. I felt as though I was letting Edwin down. But I couldn't tell my mother that her second marriage had been bigamous.

'Just like the army all over again,' Pansy giggled, stabbing a muddy potato. We sat outside the kitchen door of the Memorial Hall, a galvanized tub of potatoes in front of us and another one full of water for the peeled ones. Pansy whipped the skin off the potato she was holding and tossed it into the water.

'You're a lot quicker than I am,' I said, with admiration.

'Practice makes perfect. Don't forget I served my country by peeling spuds when you were in charge of the nation's secrets.'

'And you can see which turned out to be more useful,' I sighed, picking up another.

The pile didn't seem to be getting much smaller. My hands were slicked with that white scum that lies just under the skin of potatoes and that makes them so slippery. They kept jumping out of my fingers and on to the gravel. Yet it wasn't unpleasant to be perched on a stool in the late afternoon sunshine and to have a legitimate excuse to sit and gossip. In the hall, Abbie and her Frank were moving tables. The trestle legs screeched across the lino and set my teeth on edge.

Abbie's too, by the sound of things, because she never stopped scolding. 'Pick it up, Frank, don't drag it. You can manage that, can't you, a big boy like you. How many times do I have to tell you – not there – there. Not like that. For goodness' sake, get out of my road, can't you.' Poor Frank.

'The first harvest of peace,' said Pansy, her knife still at last. 'Just think. Mrs Thurlow is baking one of her plaited loaves with the shiny crust for the altar. And Stan Rudge is making the straw dollies for the pew ends. And the church will smell of sunshine and earth and ripeness. And there'll be bells. We've so much to be thankful for.'

'Oh, Pansy, there you are.' The new vicar hurried round the corner. 'I just wanted to ask your opinion on... My goodness, look at all those spuds. Aren't you girls marvellous.'

He was a bouncy young man, a bit like an enthusiastic Labrador, with fair hair that he tried to tame with Brylcreem to make him look more dependable (he couldn't and it didn't) and an engaging grin. Everyone liked him, although all they said was, 'He'll settle hisself down in time, like enough' or, 'He's not like Mr Millport, but he'll do well enough, I suppose.' That was high praise indeed, from the people of Ansty Parva.

And when I saw the way Pansy smiled in response, it was clear why she'd decided that her fetching sunflower-yellow frock was suitable wear for potato peeling. Goodness, I'd been blind. I noticed for the first time that she'd started to wear her hair longer and softer and that she'd put on a little weight, making her look rather less like an undernourished twelve-year-old.

Just perfect!

I walked home in the twilight, still grinning to myself at the memory of Pansy and the Reverend Peter Sutton earnestly discussing parish business, while staring at each other like the starving at a feast. Pansy deserved all the happiness she could get and I wished with all my heart that she would find it with him.

There would be a real old village scandal if the vicar married an unmarried mother. But, having seen them together, I was in no doubt that it would be a tragedy for both of them if he didn't.

It was still fairly light when I left the village hall, but I wasn't walking fast and by the time I reached the short cut home that led through the old shrubbery, it was nearly dark. The path was so overgrown that it was overhung by straggly laurels. It smelt of cats. Or was it foxes? Anyway, horrible. Just a strip of sky showed overhead and that was losing its colour. The only possible reason for using the path was that there was a hole in the park wall just there, where children had broken in to play, so I didn't have to walk the extra mile round to the gate. The dew was heavy and my shoulders and hair were damp as I brushed through the leathery leaves.

It would have been nice to have had a harvest moon, I thought, looking upwards at the anaemic last quarter. It would have been traditional and, somehow, I felt in need of tradition again. Perhaps we all did. We needed to stop watching the sky, except to guess if there would be rain next day. We needed to stop guarding our tongues, watching for the telegraph boy, listening to every news broadcast. It was time to get back to the quiet, sure rhythms of every day.

After the last war, people said they'd wanted excitement and music and dancing – anything to make them forget. This time it was different. I felt we'd all had quite enough excitement. I certainly had.

And then someone shot at me.

I felt the passage of the bullet almost before the sound. It whipped through the leaves and the air was somehow empty behind it. There was a noise like tearing leather and then a crack, sharp and unmistakable.

I knew what it was. I dropped to the ground. Brambles caught at my wrists and snagged in my hair. Leaf mould, inches thick, generations old, smelt of graves and decay. I lay quite still, while every instinct told me to get up and run. My skin tingled as though I'd rolled naked in stinging nettles and I could smell my own sweat. I couldn't hear anyone, coming or going. There had been the shot and then nothing.

How absurd, to be lying under a bush in the

dark, waiting for – for what, for someone to kill me? Here? I felt so stupid. My reaction had been so melodramatic. Too many nights wasted at the pictures. Too much Edward G. Robinson and George Raft. It was a car backfiring. It must have been.

But I couldn't quite convince myself of that and I didn't get up. I may never have been a frontline soldier, but I'd heard enough firing to recognize the sound, without a doubt.

I lay for a long time, long after reason had told me that my attacker had gone. And when I stood up at last, I thought that I was going to faint and sat down again quickly.

My mother made an awful fuss about the state I was in.

'I tripped, that's all. I tripped over a root and fell into the brambles. Stupid of me.'

She made me sit by the lamp while she took the prickles out with tweezers and dabbed the scratches on my hands and face with iodine. I'd look a perfect fright in the morning, not only scratched, but daubed with bright yellow.

'You ought not to go that way in the dark. You ought to stay in the open. A woman on her own. It's not safe.'

'Mother – this is Ansty Parva, for heaven's sake, not wildest Southampton. No-one's been raped here...'

'Don't say that word!'

'...since the Stone Age. Anyway, it was light when I started.'

'Still, you never know. There are funny people around everywhere. War brings them out.'

'Your mother's right,' put in Tom, who was in the kitchen washing his hands. He sounded very angry. He had reached that stage in his night's drinking, talking with slow, clear, exaggerated diction, when a very little opposition might push him into a rage. We both knew it. I decided, for Mother's sake, not to say any more. 'I don't want you out in the dark again,' Tom commanded.

She set on me with the iodine again and made me squeal.

And in the morning, I couldn't quite take it seriously. This was Ansty Parva, as I'd said to Mother, I'd lived here all my life and no-one had ever before complained of being shot at, except George Blackdown and that had been in 1916. He'd blown his own toe off. Cleaning the gun, he'd said, but everyone knew he was trying to avoid being called up.

Martin took it very seriously. He prowled through the shrubbery looking for – something.

'Perhaps it was a poacher,' I suggested, rather lamely.

'Hardly. There are easier places to take pot shots at pheasants than from the middle of a laurel bush. Look, here, where everything's trampled down. He stood there, waiting for you.'

'Not necessarily for me,' I said quickly, because the idea of someone lying in wait frightened me badly. 'Maybe I just happened along.'

'Maybe. But who else takes a short cut to your house after dark?'

'Well ... Tom does most nights after he's been to

the Green Dragon. But he was at home last night.'

'And who would want to shoot Tom?'

'Who would want to shoot me? I'm sure it was just a poacher and I strolled between him and his pheasant at the wrong moment.'

But Martin was poking around with his knife in the thick stem of the bush under which I'd fallen. 'Poachers don't use pistols,' he said, holding out his hand. The bullet lay in his palm, rather squashed, but quite recognizable and definitely not from a poacher's shotgun.

'I'm not an expert, but someone will know what sort of pistol fired this.' Martin wrapped the bullet in his handkerchief and put it in his pocket. 'I suppose it would be silly to ask if you're going to the police.'

'Yes, it would. I'm certain there's no-one here who could possibly want to hurt me. So what's the point of stirring things up?'

'Only that this is the second attempt and that next time he might kill you.'

'Martin! That's ridiculous!'

'Is it? Do you think that the stove in your kitchen accidentally chose to release its fumes on an evening when you were alone in the house, and known to be alone? I'd swear the fire cement had been chiselled away.'

'It was an accident. Anyone could have been at home.'

'But no-one else was. And anyone could have been shot at last night?'

'Yes.' He was frightening me and it made me angry. 'Yes. Yes. Yes. Anyone.'

406

'Laura, you've been within moments of death – twice in a few weeks. That isn't normal. Are you really so stupid that you can't see what's going on?'

'No. I won't believe it.'

'And Kate. Do you think that Geoffrey Paxton's car – a car carefully maintained – dripped brake fluid all the way to Bullington Cross by accident? They could both have been killed.'

'Accidents happen in threes. Everyone knows that.'

'Stop being so bloody stubborn.'

Martin took me by the shoulders. His fingers hooked into my flesh. He gave me two quick, sharp shakes. Twice my head snapped back on my shoulders. Then he pulled me close against him and kissed my hair, my eyes, my lips with short, hard, fierce kisses. I tasted blood, his or mine, salty and metallic, delicious.

'Laura ... darling...' There were kisses between the words. He never gave me a pause to answer the kisses or the words. 'God, you look awful ... yellow warpaint ... if you won't look after ... yourself I'll have to ... do it for you.'

Next day, Martin showed me the bullet again. He unrolled it from his handkerchief. Somehow, it seemed diminished. It lay in his hand, not much bigger than a decent-sized pebble, and no longer looked as dangerous as when I had first seen it. But his words changed my mind.

'I've had it looked at by a chum of mine,' he said. 'It's from a Webley service revolver, 1914 pattern, .45 calibre. No-one fires one of those by accident.'

'Who...?' My mouth was too dry to finish the question.

'There must be thousands that should have been handed over at the end of the last war. Somehow, they weren't. They went home in trunks and kitbags and there they are, still dangerous. Every other ex-officer might have one somewhere.'

'I mean ... who would want to...'

'I don't know who. But I know why and so do you.'

I nodded, suddenly certain. 'I'm getting very close to him now. It won't be long before we know – who and why.'

'Laura, give up,' Martin said suddenly.

I looked at him in amazement. 'Give up?' I echoed stupidly.

'Give up before you get hurt.'

'But – but I can't. Not now. I'm getting so close. I can feel it. Martin, I'm almost *there*.'

'Where? Have you thought? How much do you bloody think at all?'

I had never seen him so angry. He'd said he wanted to protect me, but he looked as though he wanted to hurt me. All the harsh, hard lines of his face were back. His nostrils were pinched and white and there was a thin, white line around his mouth. He was standing very close to me, too close. I felt as though his anger was pushing me back against a wall and I resented it. He was leaving me with only one way out and that was forward.

'I have to know,' I said, with dangerous

stubbornness. 'I need to know.'

'You're obsessed. You know that, don't you? Obsessed. Christ, it's not normal. The man's dead, Laura. He's been dead for a quarter of a century, for God's sake. Why can't you leave him in peace?'

'Because someone has to care about him!' I was shouting now, too, and our voices were matching each other. We were spitting and glaring, like two cats on a wall. I hated him then, I hated anyone who got between me and Edwin Ansty. 'No-one else does, but I do. Someone has to love him.'

And I saw the fight go out of Martin. He stepped back and pushed a strand of hair out of his eyes. I was suddenly shocked to see that it was streaked with grey.

'And you're prepared for what it costs?' he asked, softly. 'You're prepared to turn your mother's life upside down, to crucify Tom, to hurt Kate? To be hurt yourself?'

'Yes.' I wasn't certain that it was true, but I was damned if I was going to admit it to Martin, or to anyone. 'Yes. I am.'

'Then I'm sorry for you, Laura.'

He began to walk away, stiffly, as though he'd just been beaten, and there was such weariness in the droop of his shoulders.

'Martin?' I put out my hand to touch him in a gesture of peace, but he was already beyond my reach. 'Martin, don't go.'

'I have to go back to Germany in a few days. Come with me, Laura. Marry me.'

'I can't. Not yet.'

'I don't understand what's happening to you ... to us.'

'I don't understand myself. I just know that I have to go on.'

'I can't fight a ghost. I'm not going to try. I won't be able to see you again before I go. If you need me, Laura, I'll get back to you somehow. I hope you find what you're looking for – but I hope you never have to regret it.'

And when he had gone, I stayed in the wood until the marks of my tears had faded, so that no-one would ask me questions.

Martin was right. I was going to hurt everyone I loved. But I didn't seem to be able to stop myself.

In his own territory, Geoffrey looked different. On the far side of a walnut desk big enough to hold a respectable little bachelor's dinner party, he looked unexpectedly remote, disturbingly powerful. His welcoming smile showed none of that eagerness to please that I remembered from his visit to Ansty Parva. He moved more deliberately, with sure strength, in conscious knowledge of his own position in his own scheme of things. The effect was – I was taken unawares – surprisingly sensual. For the first time, I appreciated what Kate had said about her lover. If power is sexual, he was, indeed, a very virile man.

'Laura, this is nice.' He shook my hand firmly. 'Am I allowed to kiss you?' He didn't wait for my answer, which would have been 'yes' anyway. 'You'll be my sister before too long, I hope, so

410

that's all right. Miss Acott, we'll have that tea now, please,' he called and, keeping hold of my hand, drew me to the window. 'Let me show you my view.'

The window looked over piles of crumbled brick and splintered wood, all the detritus of the Blitz, tumbled haphazardly, as though the hand of a giant, petulant baby had swept across the City and knocked it for six. It was becoming possible to date the ruins. The newer ones, the work of the V1s and V2s, were still bare and black, still acrid with smoke. The older ones, the relics of the Blitz, five years old now, were softened by a haze of pink and purple, colonized by rosebay willowherb and buddleia. Already, the hairy seeds of willowherb were floating on to the newly bombed sites. In a year or so they, too, would have been taken over. Smoke-blackened, water-stained, impossibly beautiful, the bulk of St Paul's rose above the destruction.

'Marvellous, isn't it, a sort of miracle. God's answer to Goering's *Luftwaffe*. I waste far too much time just staring at that. But in a few years' time, I won't be able to see it from here. See that hole down there?' asked Geoffrey, pointing in the direction of a row of adjacent bomb craters.

'Which one?'

'That one. Look. The one behind the one in front.'

I laughed. 'Oh, *that* hole.'

'That used to be my office. I only rent this one and the rent is bloody sky high. So, I started thinking – sooner or later, all those bombed-out businesses that moved away for the duration are

411

going to come back. There'll be clearing, building – all new, glass, concrete, daylight and space. In a few years' time we'll stand here and look at a bright new City, you'll see. So I've bought all the holes I could lay my hands on. I own holes in Cheapside, holes in Poultry, holes in Cornhill and Old Jewry, bloody great holes all over the square mile. The owners can't believe their luck.' He grinned. 'Some people think I've lost my marbles!'

'I don't. I think you're very clever and very ruthless.'

'Amn't I just! Not bad for the bastard son of a housemaid, eh? Kate'll be a very rich young woman when I go to meet my Maker. Then she can take her pick from all the men younger and better looking than me.'

I gave him a quick hug. 'She couldn't pick anyone nicer.'

We were meeting Kate later in the evening, perhaps going out to dinner together, but I'd asked Geoffrey if I could see him earlier and alone. Over the pot of tea that Miss Acott brought in – mahogany coloured, thick enough for a fly to leave its footprints, stiff with condensed milk, just the way Geoffrey liked it – I told him everything. I told him about my trip to Netley and what I had discovered there. I told him about Martin's fears for my safety, about the faulty flue and the shot in the shrubbery. I reminded him about his dripping brake fluid. It sounded more like St Mary Mead than Ansty Parva. Miss Marple would have solved everything in a flash of intuition.

But I was beginning to treat Martin's theory seriously. I had laughed at him, yet I found myself now looking over my shoulder, listening, waiting. Geoffrey didn't dismiss any of it. He listened quietly until I'd finished.

'It's the not knowing. Who or why. The waiting. I don't think I can go on any longer,' I said.

And suddenly, I knew it was true. I hadn't thought it before that moment. The words had just come to my lips.

'Because you're afraid?' he asked gently.

I considered his question carefully. 'No,' I said at last. 'I don't think so. Not because I'm afraid. Well, I am, of course. Afraid. It's hard to imagine that anyone wants to hurt me. It's different from war, somehow. The *Luftwaffe* may have been tossing down bombs willy-nilly, but no-one ever thought that it was personal. Bombs and bullets didn't really have people's names on them. Now, I find the idea that someone may be waiting round the next corner for me – and only me – rather frightening.'

'I wouldn't believe you if you said you didn't. Then why?'

'Because ... because I don't want to know any more. Not now. I thought that I wanted to know everything – every last detail – it was like a puzzle, a quest for my personal Holy Grail. Edwin Ansty – funny, I think of him more often as Edwin, now, than as my father, as though he was a friend – was unknown and my family had made him unknowable. I wanted to change that, to challenge their right to decide what I knew. But now I'm afraid to find out. It's all gone too far. I started out to discover who my father was. Well, I've done that. I know who he was. I've seen what he looked like. That's enough. If I go any further, I'm going to hurt so many of the people I love.'

All the things that Martin had said – had shouted at me – made sense, but I still hadn't admitted as much to him. I hadn't even seen him since that day. Mr Millport would have said that we were both suffering the effects of the deadly sin of pride. He'd have made us see sense. But Mr Millport wasn't around any longer.

'And you don't think you owe it to your father to carry on?'

'Oh, Geoffrey, don't confuse me. I used to think that. It was all I thought about. But don't I owe my mother anything? She doesn't deserve to be hurt and I don't see how I can avoid that, if I go on. How can I tell her that she and Tom were not properly married? She would be so distressed. And Tom. He's a very conventional man and he's been good to me since I was a child. How can I tell Grandmother that the son she thought had died in 1918 was still alive, for at least another two years? She's an old woman, nearly seventy. The shock would be too much for her.'

'Lady Ansty is tougher than you think, Laura.'

'It would be cruel. And Kate. How will Kate feel when she finds out she was born to unmarried parents? I'm sorry – I shouldn't have said that – I know that you ... I didn't mean to...'

'Kate doesn't need you to protect her. She has me now.'

414

Lucky Kate. He said it so quietly, so confidently. After all her years of flitting from man to man, never secure, never finding one she could rely on, she had finally met the strong man she had been looking for.

'Let me show you something. This may change your mind.' Geoffrey unlocked a drawer in his desk and pulled out a folder. He pushed it across the desk to me. 'I've been putting out a few feelers myself, through the regimental association and the British Legion. It's a cross between an old boys' club and the Mafia, the Legion. If a man's still above ground, they'll find someone who knows someone who's seen him. I wasn't certain what to do with this. I wasn't sure whether I ought to show you. But who am I to take decisions for you? Perhaps you have a right...'

Inside the folder were a couple of dozen letters, some very short, some rambling, probably full of long-remembered anecdotes. Geoffrey picked out one, on lined paper torn from an exercise book, written in blue indelible pencil. The writing was large and loopy, filling the space between each line. It was difficult to read.

I don't suppose you'll remember me after all this time, Mr Paxton, but I was a machine-gunner in A Company and I remember you well. Now I am a storeman at Harvey Nichols Furniture Repository in Westbourne, as you'll see by the address, which is a very nice job, though heavy and we had a very nice class of furniture in during the war due to all the London houses closing for the duration. I like to keep

415

up with all my old pals, well, the old pals are the best ones I always say. I met Chalky White (ex regimental boxer, bantam weight, you'll recall him I'm sure) at the Legion the other night and he said he'd been talking to Percy Lowe who told him he'd heard you'd been making enquiries about Captain Ansty. Now there's a name that rang bells, I said. I hadn't thought about him in a long time. You probably already know this, as it's very old news, but I last saw him in a nursing home in Surrey, near Hindhead, very nice place, very select. I was in furniture removals then and delivering a piano, if I remember rightly. Well, that was a surprise, I can tell you. A bit of a shock, in fact. Not that I believe in ghosts, of course, but it certainly makes you think. If ever a man ought to be a ghost, he ought. We were all sure that he'd bought it, one way or another. And here he'd been tucked away in a – here there were a couple of words crossed out – *asylum all along. He looked well on it though. Better than I did, I must say, though we'd be about the same age at a guess. I made myself known as soon as I could. He was quite friendly, though a bit vague. He didn't seem to remember me, but it was him all right. It takes them all ways, I always say. Not everyone cares to remember the war and not all the lunatics have been put away, for that matter. I used to go to all the reunions, wouldn't miss one if I could help it, excepting only for bereavement, but there's some that want nothing to do with it and I don't blame them. It takes all sorts, as I say. Shortly afterwards I met Mr Roding at a reunion and I mentioned to him that I'd seen his friend. Well, I could see he was shaken and no wonder. He was very interested of course and asked where and said that he'd make a point of going to see him which I'm sure he would have done as they were such pals. If you want to know more, then Mr Roding is probably the best person to ask, but I can't help you to get in touch with him, as I never saw him again at any other reunion since. This was in 1927 or maybe early 28. I know that because I left that job shortly after to come down here because of my wife's chest. The sea air did her a lot of good until she was taken from me nine years ago come November, but it was a mercy she didn't last longer as her suffering was cruel. Please excuse the writing as I am putting pen to paper at work hoping to catch the post on my way home...*

Geoffrey let me sit for as long as I wanted, thinking.

Tom had known. Tom had known for almost nineteen years where my father had been taken and had kept the knowledge to himself.

To protect my mother, my grandmother and my sister, Tom had kept his secret. And keeping it had almost destroyed him.

If I were going to be shut away for the rest of my life, in a place of someone else's choosing, I might have done a lot worse than Greentops.

Geoffrey travelled slowly up the long drive that finished in a circular gravel sweep before an imposing front door. It was painted a glossy and satisfying seaweed green that rather reminded me of the colour of American military vehicles, but when paint was in such short supply, who would ask questions? The door knocker was well polished. It was a good sign. Once, long ago, before wars and death duties had made it

417

impossible, a family might have lived here very comfortably, supported by a huge staff to run the house from cellar to attic.

It was better and worse than I had feared.

Better because it wasn't obviously a lunatic asylum. There were no barriers, no wire – not to be seen, anyway. I'd stood outside the high wall at Netley and tried to visualize the pleasant garden on the other side that the RAMC sergeant had told me about and the little summerhouse, where patients could spend their long, empty hours. But all I could imagine was a long corridor lined by the steel doors of padded cells. Greentops wasn't like that.

It was worse because the painted door and polished knocker gave an impression of un-yielding competence. I couldn't understand why anyone who wasn't kept by force would want to stay in an institution, however pleasantly it was disguised. An efficient management would know all the other ways of keeping a man in one place for years and years. oh oh

The step was scrubbed and the doormat brushed. I had the feeling that not many people passed through the door – in or out.

'I'm scared,' I said, sitting in the car with my hand on the door handle.

'Of course you are,' Geoffrey agreed, cheerfully. 'Come with me.'

'No. I can't do that. You'll manage better on your own. But I'll be here when you want me.'

Inside, the hall looked again like the hall of a well-run country house. Against one wall stood a carved oak chest and on it, catching the light

418

from the open door, stood a jug of copper-coloured chrysanthemums, not the shaggy, ear-wiggy, comfortable kind, but the perfect spheres, like toffee apples on spindly sticks, the kind that always win the prizes at flower shows, groomed and waxy. Their funeral smell lay on top of all the other smells – beeswax and turpentine, distant gravy and nearby dog fart. On a faded rug, a black Labrador lay, too old and fat to do more than raise his head and wag the very tip of his tail to acknowledge my entrance. Somewhere, a wireless was playing modern dance tunes.

There were no notices, none of the expected arrows on the walls to point me to Reception or anywhere else. There were no rules pinned up, no numbers on the doors. Nervously, I looked through a couple of open doors. Through one, I could see into a conservatory where four people were playing a game – ludo, I thought, although I couldn't clearly see from that distance. It was, I reluctantly admitted to myself, quite pleasant – for what it was.

I don't know what I'd expected. Not this. I hadn't anticipated, either, the very ordinary woman who came along a passage towards me. She was plump, untidy, with greying fair hair caught up by slipping combs. She had a sweet smile.

'Heathcliff, you naughty boy,' she scolded, 'you know you're not supposed to be out here. Off you go. I'm so sorry, Heathcliff is awfully old and smelly, but he can't help it. Now, can I help you at all?'

'I'm making enquiries about one of your...' Oh

419

God, what should I call him – patient, guest, inmate? I ought to have worked out what I was going to say before I opened my mouth. '...one of your past ... about Edwin Ansty. I understand he used to be...'

'Oh, Edwin. You'll find him in the church. Just pop out of the french windows and turn right. You can't miss it.'

So here I was, at the door of the little mock-Gothic church and at the end of my search.

It was very cold inside, full of dead, still air that scarcely stirred as I passed through it. In the eastern wall, a coy Victorian stained-glass window told the story of Mary Magdalene in the garden on the first Easter Day. In the morning, with the sun behind it, it might have lit the chancel. In the afternoon, it was only dull slabs of colour, shapeless and ugly. Mary's red hair, badge of her shame, looked like rusty barbed wire. The chrysanthemums on the altar didn't have to compete with the smell of old dog.

I stood for a moment, to allow my eyes to grow used to the gloom. Then I saw that the whitewashed walls were patched with memorial tablets of all sizes. Methodically, I began to work my way round them.

Some of the tablets, those nearest the altar, were as old as the house and commemorated the family.

Eugenia Mary and Edith Elizabeth, aged 3 years 2 months and 1 year 4 months, infant daughters of grieving parents, called to their Saviour... Suffer little children...

Robert Cranley Stokes, aged 88 years, in sure and certain Knowledge of the Resurrection of the Body...
Then there were smaller plaques, dating from the years of the Great War and immediately after, marble or brass, simply worded with names, dates and regiments. The house must have become a hospital then, I imagined, or a convalescent home, like so many at the time. Here, among these memorials, dated some time after 1927, I would finally find Edwin Ansty.

And when I had read them all, I went back to the beginning and read them again. I pulled back the curtain that shielded the bell tower, but there were none in there. I looked in the porch, but there was only one, above the inner door: *Remember before God the Men of this Estate who went to War in defence of Honour, King and Country and who never came Home.*

I sat on a bench in the porch and wanted to cry, but the effort was too much. It was the end and I hadn't expected to reach it so soon. I was drained. I had followed up hearsay, listened to gossip, rummaged through papers, travelled miles, talked, pleaded, cajoled, argued. For nothing.

Yet the woman in the hall had been so positive. Perhaps she'd been thinking of someone else, of a similar name. Perhaps she hadn't really been listening to me, but thinking about something more important – the dog's walk or evening meal. Greentops must have regular visitors, looking for lost relatives or friends. And it had all been so long ago.

I could go back and search the tablets again for

421

a name that could have been confused with the one I'd been looking for. But I didn't have the heart to try. It was too late.

My instinct to stop had been the right one. There had been nothing to gain by following a letter from a man who'd spoken to a man who'd heard from another man... But Geoffrey had been very persuasive. No, it was wrong to blame him. I'd been easily persuaded. Too easily.

I'd wanted too much for too long. It had taken over my life. I'd been living in a curious, self-imposed limbo since the end of the war. I had thought about nothing else. I had no job. My army terminal grant was running out. My mother was wearing herself out trying to keep things going. And Martin was waiting for me to make up my mind to marry him, but he wouldn't wait for ever. I'd already kept him waiting for a lifetime.

It was time to see sense. It was time to stop.

When I came out, the afternoon was past its best. The sun had hazed over and there was a new nip in the air that smelt of bonfires and blackberries. I thought of Geoffrey, waiting in his car, and knew that I didn't want to talk to him. Not yet. I needed more time to myself – just a little longer, I promised myself – but away from that ugly, empty little church.

I walked on, aimlessly. Like most gardens, this had been dug up during the war for vegetable production, but it had been converted with an eye for beauty. The old herbaceous ribbon borders, planted with cabbages, purple and iridescent blue, with wigwams of runner beans for focus, were sheltered by a mellow brick wall. The lawn had been dug into a chessboard of squares, edged with dwarf espaliered apples and pears, with grassy paths between them. Onions, their necks twisted, their roots pointing towards the sun, lay on the surface to dry for storage. The beetroots were ripe. Their purple shoulders pushed through the earth. Someone had been digging up carrots. The fork still stood at the end of half a row of feathery leaves.

A ha-ha, crossed by a narrow, gated bridge, divided the garden from woodland. There, the trees were widely spaced, allowing plenty of light and air, and formally planted. Some were quite tall and well grown; others had been more recently planted. None seemed to have reached its full height. I could see there was a pattern, but it didn't make itself clear to me.

A man was digging a hole. For a shocked moment, I thought it was a grave, but then I could see that, although it was an imposing hole, it was nowhere near long enough to hold a coffin. He had a barrowload of rotted manure, gently steaming, beside the hole. I leaned on the gate and watched him.

He worked slowly, handling the spade easily and steadily, with none of the energy-wasting attack of a novice. He looked as though he could have kept up that bend, stretch, toss all afternoon. When he was satisfied with the size, he half-filled the hole again with manure mixed with some of the earth and a couple of handfuls of white powder that I knew, from watching Tom, was bone-meal. Then he picked up a small tree that had been leaning against the wheelbarrow and heeled it into the hole, backfilling and stamping down until he was content with the planting.

The little tree added to the pattern that I still could not understand.

And when, pushing the barrow with the spade balanced over it, the gardener passed me, he smiled and asked if he could help me. He had a shy smile, slow, as though rusty from lack of use.

'You look unhappy,' he said. It was an oddly innocent remark, unexpected from a stranger. People don't usually comment on what they see. It isn't considered polite to notice. Only children and madmen really say what they think.

'Thank you, but I'm all right,' I answered. There are rules, after all. Just as it isn't done to mention a stranger's sorrow, it isn't expected that one should confess to feeling anything at all – not to a stranger, not even to a friend. Emotion is embarrassing and best kept secret. 'I'll go in a moment. I was looking for someone's memorial in the church, but I couldn't find him.'

'That's not the church,' he replied. 'That's just the chapel. This is the church.'

I looked around, but saw nothing.

'Here. Look.' He sounded impatient, as though talking to a rather backward child.

But I only saw trees.

'Come with me.'

He led me through the great west door. A pair of holly trees, small yet already formally clipped, guarded its portals. We walked down a nave of lime trees. Their leaves were yellowing and spinning down like coins. In the early summer, greedy bees would burrow into the scented blossoms. Their branches would, one day, interlace overhead, complex and perfect as fan vaulting. The transepts were marked by a double row of horse chestnuts. Conkers split beneath my feet as we walked. Spiky shell, glossy seed, white heart crushed into leaf-spangled grass.

And the pattern that had evaded me from a distance became clear at last. A tree church. A tree cathedral.

'The walls are oak, English oak. And here is the oldest,' the gardener told me, 'here, the yew, the altar. I planted it in 1921. It might live for a thousand years. And the youngest you saw today. That won't live so long. Long enough, though. A little pear. For Clive.'

'Clive?'

He looked at me and smiled. 'Clive who used to cut his toenails in public and let the pieces fly across the floor. Sometimes I was unkind to him. I laughed at him. He didn't deserve that. The trees all have names, you know. Does that make me sound utterly batty? Each one is a memorial to someone I knew, once, a long time ago. Come into the porch. I'm rather pleased with it.'

And on the southern side, where a porch ought to be, laburnum had been trained over hoops to make a tunnel that would drip golden rain in May. It would be grossly, vulgarly, gloriously beautiful.

Trying not to look as though I were looking, I

425

searched each tree for a plaque or a label. He saw me and guessed what I was doing.

'No, no, they don't actually have names. I'm not as mad as that. Some people said I was, but they were wrong. But I *know* who is represented by each one. And when I'm gone, it won't really matter, will it? People can put their own names to each tree, remember their own friends. I won't mind.'

He was very odd, but nicely so. We were well out of sight of the house, yet I didn't feel afraid. I'd have thought I'd have been scared out of my wits, wandering through a wood with a stranger who was – well, unbalanced. I mean, it wasn't *normal,* his obsession – he was planting a forest single-handed, for heaven's sake – though he seemed harmless enough. But he didn't scare me. We were comfortable together.

He was rather long, rather thin, rather bent. Middle-aged, not old, but with hands already knotted by arthritis, like so many gardeners – all that digging and damp. I had the impression that he was very strong, tough and knotty – like one of his trees, perhaps – but that didn't worry me. He was curiously gentle, unworldly as a hermit.

I walked back into his church, back into what I supposed he might call the south chapel. The grass was patterned with shadows, long, reaching, twining shadows. The smell of decaying leaves was sweeter than incense.

'It must have taken you a long time,' I said, rather fatuously.

'A lifetime.'

'Have you lived here always?'

'A lifetime.' He looked up at the sky. 'It's very clear. There might be a touch of frost tonight. The first of the autumn. That'll bring the leaves down. It's beautiful when it's bare, too, you know. Sparse. All bones and no flesh.'

And I knew him.

He looked down from the sky, across to me, with a smile that was as familiar as my own. How could I not have noticed at once? Perhaps I had been fooled by the grey, thinning hair and the swollen finger joints. I had looked, but I had not really seen.

I had expected that something would call to me. But it had not. I had expected some communion, some link. There had been none, except the friendly empathy of strangers. A changed angle, a tilt of the head, a trick of the light. Dear God, I might have missed it.

In twenty years' time, I would look like this man.

The jolt of recognition was less of a shock than I'd expected. His was the face that had stared back at me, unrecognized, since I was old enough to stand on tiptoe to peer into the looking-glass.

'I find that a comforting thought, don't you? That something can be beautiful even when it's dead.' He held up his hand towards the dropping sun and turned it back and forth. The light shone through the loops of skin between his fingers, glowing red, full of life and blood. He clenched his fingers and opened them again, several times, seeming fascinated by the interplay of skin and tendon and bone. I thought he'd stopped speaking, but after a while he seemed to notice me again. 'For ever and ever. Constant renewal. Eternal life. Now that's where the trees score over us, don't you think? If I had buried Clive in that hole there, instead of a pear tree, do you think that he would have risen again? Do you?'

He seemed to expect an answer. I shook my head.

'Of course not. There would have been no new flush of life in the spring, no rising of his sap. Imagine – if he sprouted. You do understand – he's not actually in that hole there. None of them are. You would need to be very stupid to think that. In fact, he's in the bottom of a shell hole somewhere, drowned, not enough to piece together to bury. So are they all.' He turned in a slow circle on the spot, looking at the trees, and I felt a flicker of fear, but his mind was not concerned with me. 'Every one. Shreds. Blasted. Rags on the wire. But they tell me the grass is growing there again. And trees. I don't know what to think. We only saw stumps, you know, half-buried, splintered and scorched, like broken fingers sticking out of the earth. Black and birdless. But it's different now, they tell me. Green. Do you think so?'

I nodded.

'Really? People tell such lies. One never knows who to trust. They should grow well, then. I always take care to put a good handful of blood and bone in the planting hole. It makes such a difference. They don't thrive without it. You said you were looking for someone here? Who was it?'

'I was mistaken.'

'Pity. I know them all. I could have helped you.

428

Come back and have tea. My wife and I always have tea together at this time of day. No? Then do come again. Won't you? I have so much to show you.'

'Did you find out anything?' asked Geoffrey, as he accelerated down the drive, leaving tyre tracks in the raked gravel.

I shook my head. 'He wasn't there.'

He wasn't a fool. He knew that I was lying and I knew that he knew. But we agreed to leave it that way.

I went to find a martyr and I found a man who had chosen the place where he wanted to be. I went to find a young warrior, crusader knight, and I found a lost, gentle man with dirty hands. I came carrying the flame of vengeance and found that my zeal wasn't wanted.

I couldn't. I couldn't tell him. It would have been grotesque.

Why did I go?

Because ... so that...

So that I could throw my arms round him, shouting 'Daddy darling, I'm your long-lost daughter'?

Don't be absurd.

Then if I wasn't looking for a father, was I trying to bring back my mother's husband?

She's got a husband. She may not be legally married to him, but she thinks that they have already celebrated their silver wedding anniversary.

Then, for Christ's sake, what was I doing there – just meddling? Satisfying my own selfish curiosity?

I was looking for a ghost. Don't you understand? I didn't want to find a real man, a man with grey hair and arthritis and a woman he calls his wife. He was a person, not an icon, unexpectedly human. I had been prepared to pity him. I had longed to love him. I didn't expect to *like* him!

'Mother, did you love my father?'

'Darling, you do ask the most personal questions.'

'I asked you once before and you didn't answer.'

'Because I think that the answer is my business, not yours.'

'But I need to know. Stop it. Stop being so busy.' I took the iron from her and propped it upright on its asbestos stand. I took her moving hands within my own hands and held them tightly. She struggled for a bit, not too seriously, and then gave up. 'Don't hide from me, Mother, please. Please...'

'Yes. Then, yes, if you have to know, I loved Edwin Ansty.'

'Very much?'

'Laura, please...'

'How much?'

'Laura, you're hurting. Let go ... I loved him ... oh, you wouldn't understand how much I loved him.'

'Why not? Am I so different from you? Why

430

wouldn't I understand?'

Mother sighed and rubbed her wrists. 'Because you're older, a woman and I was a child. Because nothing hurts so much, nothing is so wonderful, nothing is so terrible, nothing passes so quickly, nothing lasts so long as when you're young. Let me work, Laura. I couldn't talk to you if I thought you were looking at me.' She unrolled one of Tom's shirts and sprinkled water on it from a jam jar with holes punched in the lid. It steamed as she slid the iron across the first sleeve. 'It's no criticism of you if I say you wouldn't understand. The world was so different then and girls had such different lives.

'I was fifteen when I first met your father, fifteen and living at home, the only child of elderly parents, a father away at war, a vinegary spinster for a governess. The only male I met, very occasionally, was my cousin Victor. He was quite sweet to me, but very boring and spotty. Edwin was still a schoolboy, too, but to me he was like a young god. He was tall and handsome – everything an impressionable girl might dream about – but he was kind, too...' She smiled, with her face turned down towards the half-ironed shirt, but I could see the way her left cheek curved. 'He didn't tease, or mock, or make me feel stupid because I was only a girl and didn't know anything. Victor took me to tea and Edwin came too. I remember ... I remember everything. I remember the way he leaned forward to listen to me, as though everything I said was important. I remember the way his hair would flop forward as he leaned and he'd push it away impatiently.

431

His hands were beautiful, narrow and long-fingered. His eyes were hazel, flecked with light, green and gold and grey. I thought he was wonderful. I remember... Oh, darling, why do you need to know these things? It was all so long ago.'

'Please...'

'And then he went away to war and I knitted socks and packed little parcels and hoped – prayed – that he wouldn't forget me. And that first Christmas he was away – 1916 – he sent me a little brooch, a copy of the regimental cap badge, silver, worth nothing, but priceless to me and I wore it on my vest, because I knew that my mother would not approve. I was so young, you see. And silly. It was all so exciting. Secret letters. Photographs. It made me feel very grown-up. I kept his picture in my prayer book.' She folded one shirt, flattened it and ironed in the creases, then began on the next. 'We didn't meet again for a year and a half. His letters were changing, I realize that now, but at the time, I never noticed. I thought that he would still be the handsome boy I remembered. Well, he was still handsome, of course, but not a boy.

'Edwin came back for seventy-two hours. I told my mother that I was staying with a friend in Richmond, a girl I'd met through Victor's sister. So deceitful. I don't know where I'd learned to tell lies like that. But the thought of *not* seeing Edwin was more than I could bear. He was so different. Quieter. Harder. Older. He laughed a lot at things that weren't funny, but wouldn't tell me anything I wanted to know. He took me to

432

dinner at the Berkeley and I had to wear my best dress – brown velvet with a lace collar – that made me look about twelve years old, even with my hair up. All the men were in uniform, but Edwin's medal ribbon made him special, and all the women seemed too glamorous to be real. We had champagne. I'd never tasted it before. There was an orchestra, playing songs from *Chu Chin Chow*. It was so exciting. If it hadn't been for the uniforms, you wouldn't have known there was a war on. We were going to go dancing afterwards, but Edwin was very tired.

'He was staying – camping, really, there was only one servant left – at a house belonging to the parents of a chum of his. The furniture was in dust covers and the chandeliers in holland bags, looking huge and ghostly. It was cold – our breath made puffy clouds around our lips – and we were still hungry. We rummaged around and found some sardines, a couple of apples and a half-full decanter. Edwin lit a fire. We sat on the hearthrug with blankets around our shoulders, eating sardines with our fingers and drinking whisky, watching the flames, making plans, never once mentioning the war, talking, talking, and I missed the last train to Richmond...' She was looking over my shoulder towards the window, but I knew that she saw nothing and her hands were still at last. '...I was so young and he was so unhappy...'

And then there was me. I didn't say that, of course. She was silent for a while.

'Is that what you wanted to know?' she asked, briskly shaking out a pyjama top. 'I hope you're

433

satisfied at last.'

'But you married Tom.'

'Of course I did. You still don't understand, do you? Sometimes I think you were born without normal human emotions, Laura. You have to have everything laid out neatly in front of you. Love isn't like checking off a laundry list, you know. Oh, darling, I'm sorry. That was cruel. Your father was a knight in shining armour. I'm not sure I'd have been able to live up to that. I'm rather dull, you know, and very ordinary. Tom has been faithful, kind, considerate – not always sober, I know – but always loving for twenty-five years. If I had to decide between the hero and the ordinary man, I think I'd have to choose Tom.'

Tom had kept his secret for nearly twenty years. I had kept mine for two days and I wasn't certain how much longer I could cope.

Greentops was like a magnet. It called me like the siren song that lured Odysseus's crewmen. If stopping my ears with wax would have drowned it out, I would have done that. I could sense it drawing me so strongly that I felt as though I would soon be forced to hang on to the door lintels by my fingernails.

I had found my father.

He wasn't the man I thought I'd been looking for. We'd stood in the enchanted circle of trees and everything he'd said sounded perfectly sane – then. Now, I wasn't so certain. But he was alive and well and I couldn't just turn my back and forget him. I hadn't thought about what I was going to do next. The quest had been enough. I'd made no plan for the future. Now, I could see that I had reached a fork. Without my realizing it, my path had led to this.

I could choose to admit that I had reached the end. I'd found what I had been looking for and that should be enough. All Pansy's useful little sayings – least said soonest mended – urged me to take the safe course, the sensible one. Or I could pursue the other path to the bitter end – discover why and by whom my father had been left to fester since he was twenty years old – in the knowledge that the end might be very bitter indeed.

I was too close to the problem to be able to see clearly. I needed someone else. If I could only have talked to Martin. But Martin was back in Germany and not expected home, his mother told me, until Christmas.

'And not for long, then,' she complained. 'He's got himself a job with *Picture Post*, starting in America in the New Year, and it'll take him all over the world, he says. I don't know. You'd think he'd've had enough gadding about by now. You'd think he'd be glad to settle down, at his age, with a nice wife and kiddies.' And she glared at me, accusingly.

I deserved that.

I wrote and told him what I'd discovered, but it wasn't the same. I had such an ache to hear his slow, soft, Wiltshire voice. He didn't answer my letter. I hoped until I grew weary of hoping. What did I expect? He had a life to lead. How long did I expect to be able to dangle him on a string?

When Vee came back, I selfishly thought she'd been sent from heaven.

'He divorced me, the bastard!' she spat, slinging her expensive leather luggage on to Kate's old, protesting bed. 'Straight off the boat and into the divorce courts. I blame his mother. Right battleaxe. She thought that there wasn't an English girl born that was good enough for her Carlton. Dammit – he was *my* Carlton by then. She said I was a hooker, only after his money and why couldn't he have settled for a nice, clean American girl. The bitch. She'd poisoned his mind before I even arrived. I didn't stand a chance.'

'But the children? Surely she must have loved them when she saw them? They're her grandchildren, after all.'

'Oh, Laura, they looked so sweet. Little Carlton had his sailor suit on and looked just like Swee'Pea and Jennifer had bows in her hair and I'd taught her a little speech.' Vee began to cry and brushed the tears angrily away with fingers still dirty from travelling. 'I'd taught her to say, "Hello, Gran, my name is Jennifer" and then to go and give her gran a kiss. And the bitch said, "How do you do, little girl?" just like she was the Queen or something. And Carlton gave a sickly grin and I knew then ... And that night she said ... she said how did Carlton know they were his children. From what she'd heard about English girls, they could be anyone's. Hell's bells and buckets of blood! I swore I wouldn't cry any more.'

'But how could he divorce you, just like that?'

'Easy. If you're rich and your name's Carlton H. Riversdale II you can do anything you bloody well like. His mother had already got a nice little blonde lined up for him – sweet and suitable and biddable – and no tits.'

I put my arms around my friend and let her have a good cry. It might not do any good, but it'd make her feel a lot better. She rocked in my arms and howled. Poor Vee. She'd adored her Carlton and she'd have made him a fine wife – funny, loving, sexy, motherly, efficient. I hoped with all my heart that he'd regret what he'd done. But I don't suppose he ever did. I hoped the biddable blonde would lead him a dog's life. I began to cry in sympathy. After a while, the sobs became sniffs and sighs. Then Vee sat up and blew her nose violently.

'Bloody Uncle Sam. The only good thing the American government ever did for me was to give me a return ticket.'

'That's the spirit. How long can you stay? Make it as long as you like.'

'Well, with my mum and gran in a prefab in Rainham and my sister Beryl's kids in the other room and Beryl and her husband sleeping on the floor and my sister Brenda and *her* husband staying with his mum and dad... We'll try ever so hard not to get in your way, Laura.'

She rummaged in her case and pulled out a bottle of Jack Daniels. A quarter of it was missing already. 'Now the kids are asleep, why don't we give this a thrashing? I could do with a good sleep myself tonight.'

437

So we made off to Tom's potting shed and locked the door, like a pair of naughty school-children with their first cigarettes. And I told Vee about everything she'd missed.

'And Pansy's going to marry the new vicar.'

'Never! That's just perfect. When?'

'Well, she doesn't know it yet – and neither does he. But they will.'

We clinked toothmugs. 'To Pansy and Peter.' Vee laughed. 'Pansy and Peter – they even sound right together, like children in a story book.'

The fruity smell of whisky mingled with the scent of over-ripe apples, dusty cobwebs and potting compost into a rich, desirable aroma. You could have spread it on bread. You could have chewed it. It was comforting, secure, as soothing as a cup of cocoa. Yet, for the first time, I felt uneasy. Under the familiarity, I was aware of something disturbing, something that brought out a prickle on the back of my neck. And I couldn't think what... Silly...

We pulled the sacking over the window, as though blackout was still enforced, but really we were trying to hide our lamp from the house. It was very cosy, very intimate, an ideal place to swap secrets.

'And what about you and gorgeous Martin?' she asked, with a wink. 'When're you two going to name the day?'

I gave her a little smile that was supposed to be enigmatic and courageous, but now I suspect that it just looked tipsy. 'Oh, Martin?' I said, coolly, as though I scarcely ever gave him a thought. 'Maybe Martin's got tired of waiting.'

438

'I don't believe it. I always thought you were made for each other.'

'Well, you were wrong.' I reached over and poured another slug into both mugs. 'He's in Germany now and everyone knows there are plenty of *Fräuleins* desperate for a British passport, then it's off to America. Land of the free and home of the brave. Without me.'

'Better off without him. Believe me. In America, the mothers get the balls and the sons get the...'

'Vee! Your language!'

'What'd I say? Tell the truth and shame the devil, Pansy always reminds us. Here's to men...' She leaned forward and our toothmugs clinked again.

'Who needs them?'

'The bastards! What'd we do without them?' She laughed and cocked her head on one side, cute and knowing. Jennifer might have got away with the gesture, but not a grown woman. 'I really did hope that you and Martin ... So why don't you just run off with him? What's keeping you?'

'I've found my father.'

'No!'

And I told Vee everything.

'Honestly, I can't understand what all the secrets are about. Your family is very odd,' she said when I'd finished. 'Why don't you just up and tell them – straight out. I would.'

I looked across at Vee and realized that she didn't have a clue. She was so honest, so straight-forward. She'd have done what I could never do.

439

She'd have thrown her arms around any long-lost relative and hugged him.

'You don't understand. No-one in my family ever – *ever* – says what they really think.'

'Well, it's about bloody time they started.'

And in the morning I looked and felt terrible. The tiny, age-spotted mirror above the wash-stand showed me bleary eyes and puffy lids. My tongue seemed to have grown in the night. It didn't seem to fit into my mouth properly. Vee looked as bright as a button.

'Practice makes perfect,' she trilled.

I stuck out my furry tongue at her and she pedalled off on my bike to look for work around the village.

I tried, but I couldn't stay away.

I went back to Greentops, alone this time, no Geoffrey waiting impatiently in the drive. I'd thought about asking Vee to go with me for comfort, but Vee was never the person to trust with a secret. She knew enough already. If I'd been sober, I might not have told her the half of it. Besides, with two children and a job as general dogsbody at Thurlow's farm – a three-mile, uphill bike ride – she had more than enough on her plate.

The autumn was further on its way to winter. The trees were closer to being bare. Their bones were beginning to show. The chrysanthemums in the hall had been replaced by a vase of burnished leaves. The game of ludo in the conservatory seemed now to be Monopoly. Nothing else had changed. Smelly old Heathcliff still lay on the rug and looked up at me with white, filmy eyes.

'Now, we've met before, haven't we?' asked the plump woman who was my father's wife. 'Haven't you been ... yes, weren't you here a few weeks ago, asking for Edwin? Didn't you find him?'

'Yes, thank you. Yes, I did. And he ... he promised to show me around his tree church again. It was so interesting.'

'But he's out. Was he expecting you? He does forget things, rather. Come and have some tea while you're waiting. I don't suppose he'll be long. He's just popped down to the village for some screws. There's always something that needs mending. But my husband is very good with his hands, thank goodness. He keeps the old place together somehow.'

She showed me into a comfortable drawing room, shabby in the right way, with patched armchairs drawn up to a fire and a tabby cat curled up on a hairy cushion. A man was sitting by the fire, not reading, not doing anything that I could see, not even thinking, just staring. He had a disturbing, young/old look, untouched by time, yet worn to transparency. When I came in, he got up and tried to rush past me.

'It's all right, Keith,' the woman said as he passed us. She held out a hand that didn't touch him, but seemed to halt him, all the same. 'No need to go. Miss – er, Mrs – er...'

'Laura Kenton.'

'Mrs Kenton has come to see Edwin about his trees. That's all right, isn't it?'

But he jerked his head and kept on going, out of the room.

'Oh, dear,' she sighed, 'he really can't cope with strangers.'

'I'm sorry. I didn't want to upset anyone.'

'It's not your fault. He's always the same. Now, sit here. I won't be long.'

I sat by the fire, wondering what on earth I had been thinking of, to come back. Once should have been enough. I'd found what I'd been looking for and that should have been sufficient. I ought to have gone away and kept my recognition to myself. But I'd come back. I was meddling again. I could never let well enough alone. I'd come back with fierce curiosity and a lame excuse.

The cat climbed on to my lap and began to knead my thighs with her claws. I stroked her head with absentminded kindness and wondered how I could get out before my father came home.

'Here we are.' She laid a tray on the low table in front of me. Heathcliff lay down with a grunt beside her and laid his heavy head against her legs. His jaws left saliva streaks on her skirt, but she didn't seem to mind. 'It's such a walk from the kitchen. Whoever designed this house ought to be made to work here. Funny, when I was a girl, no-one gave a thought to how many miles a day the maids had to walk.'

'You lived here as a girl, then?' I asked.

'Yes. Milk or lemon?' She passed me a wide, rose-garlanded teacup with a twiddly handle, difficult to hold. 'I was born here. Oh, it was so different, then. Full of people. Aunts, uncles, masses of cousins every summer. Full of fun. Still, we do our best now. No-one can keep up these old houses as they used to be. My father was a consulting psychiatrist – quite a daring thing, then – and during the first war, he joined the army as a senior medical officer. The house became a convalescent home for cases of neurasthenia – you know the old joke – officers had neurasthenia, NCOs had shellshock, other ranks were shot – not such a good joke, after all. Sugar? Do have a biscuit. Some of the boys here don't take sugar in their tea, so I find there is enough to make them a little treat now and again. And after the war – well, some of them had nowhere else to go and I had to earn a living after my father died or sell the house, so they're still here. Like Keith. His family pays to keep him out of sight. He's very sweet, but he can't stand change. Everything has to be in the right place, at the right time. Furniture. Ornaments. People. Or he gets very upset. He's managed to get a job once or twice, but people can't stand it when he spends all morning arranging the paperclips and shouts if someone uses up a stamp. Richard is younger. He was in the navy, Atlantic convoys, and his ship was sunk in 1947. He is quite an ordinary young man, until he hears a bang – a door, a car, thunder, it's surprising how many bangs there might be in one day – and then he dives under the table and won't come out for a long time.'

She was a comfortable person to be with. Untidy in a way that set you at ease, a very English, droopy cardigans and animal hairs sort of way. Slightly overweight, but with generous curves still in the right places and a sweet smile. Twenty years ago, she might have been quite pretty.

And I suddenly wondered – why hadn't I thought of it before? – if I had any unknown brothers or sisters. The thought scared me and excited me at the same time.

'And your husband...' I began, putting the cup carefully back in the saucer, trying not to rattle it. 'Did you meet him...?'

'Edwin? Yes, Edwin was a patient here. He was... he is... he has difficulties. He digs holes, as you know. They interest him, for ... various reasons. And when he has dug them, he obviously can't just leave them. I suggested filling them with trees. I don't mind. I love him, you see.' She looked at me across the hearth and the firelight flickered on her skin and revealed the tension in her jaw. She smiled. For the first time, I saw the hint of steel within her softness. 'You're so like Edwin, as he was when we met.'

I stammered something. Whatever I'd expected, it wasn't this.

'I've been waiting for you for so long. Expecting you. Goodness. Did you think I didn't know?' She gave a little rattle of laughter, sharp and sudden as hailstones against a window. 'How blind you must think me. You are his image. And to see you together – why, you might as well put an advertisement on the front page of *The Times*. No chance that he would recognize you, because he hasn't been looking. But I have. I watched you both walking across the garden last time you

444

were here and I thought – here is Edwin's daughter come to claim him at last. Have you?'

'No,' I answered slowly, and I thought carefully about my response. 'No, I don't think so. I don't know why I'm here. When I last came, I didn't even know he was alive. I came to look for his grave.'

She shivered. 'Not yet. It's funny. I've been afraid of you for so long and now that you're here, I find that I'm not afraid any more.'

'I didn't know anything, you see. I didn't know who he was, or where he was or why...'

'But surely... There, darling...' She took the last biscuit off the plate and tossed it to Heathcliff. His slobbery jaws snapped round it. 'Is your grandmother still alive? Surely she told you... No, I can see that she didn't. How cruel.'

My voice came out as a whisper. 'She doesn't know I'm here. No-one knows I'm here.'

'Oh, my dear,' she said softly. 'I'm so sorry.'

'Tell me.'

'Must I?'

'Tell me. Please.'

'There's so little I can tell. All I really know is that Edwin arrived here as a patient in 1920. He'd come from Netley, I believe, but then so had many of our convalescents. Edwin was very withdrawn. He wasn't interested in anyone or anything. He didn't seem to have any memory earlier than Netley. But that wasn't unusual. As my father frequently observed, the treatment he called electrical suggestion often did more harm than good.

'I was twenty years old, rather spoiled, the

445

darling of an elderly father, and surrounded by hosts of damaged young men, but this was the one I wanted. This was the one I fell in love with. He was ... he still is a very handsome, a very gallant man, intelligent, very quiet ... but he was damaged and I thought – with the arrogance of youth – that I could cure him. And I suppose I have – in a limited way.

'A year later, my father died and we were married. The two events were connected. My father would never have allowed the wedding. Never. He told me so.' She smiled and again I caught the glint of something unexpected, something flinty. 'I've always known what I wanted. Without my father, it was even more important to keep our patients and I was determined to run the house as it ought to be – I wouldn't allow standards to slip – so easy to become shoddy. I took over the paperwork myself and it wasn't until then that I found out that it was Lady Ansty who paid Edwin's bills. I wrote to her, to tell her of our marriage. And it wasn't until then that I found out that Edwin was already married.'

She paused and looked over at me for my reaction. I just nodded, encouraging her to go on.

'That's all,' she said, simply.

It was nowhere near enough.

The old dog began to thump his tail.

'Edwin's back,' she said. 'Heathcliff always knows.'

There was the sound of footsteps in the hall and then his voice. 'Angela? I'm back. Angela, where are you?'

'Here, darling.'

We both stood and suddenly she gripped me around the top of my arm, with fingers that dug deep into the flesh. I knew that I would carry the marks of her nails for days. I squirmed and pulled back, but she would not relax her grip.

'Stop it. You're hurting.'

'He must not know,' she hissed, with her face inches from mine. 'I warn you. He must never know.'

But by the time my father came into the room, we were standing apart and both smiling. He was parting down hair ruffled by the wind and his cheeks were reddened by the cold. He brought in with him the smell of soap and frost and wholesome earth.

'Edwin,' she said, 'do you remember Mrs Kenton?'

'Oh, yes, I remember you,' he replied. 'I showed you my trees and you promised to come back. I'm so glad you've kept your promise. Delighted.'

And, keeping my jaw rigid to hide the trembling of my mouth, I shook my father's hand.

Alone with the portraits and medals, my grandmother has sat, manipulating, pulling the strings and watching us dance. She has watched and said nothing. She has seen my mother marry again. She has seen Kate's birth. She has seen me struggle in pursuit of the truth.

She has known everything and said nothing. She is the silent canker that has lurked at the

447

heart of this family for three generations.

So I cornered her. I chose my time carefully. I waited until Mother and Tom had gone to Devizes market. They'd caught the early bus and wouldn't be back until evening. It had taken a bit of persuading to get Tom to agree to go. I suspected that only the thought of the extended market day licence in the surrounding pubs had persuaded him.

I found my grandmother in the morning room. She was balanced on top of a stepladder, taking a duster to the pelmets. I had always seen her as indestructible, glamorous and ageless. Now I saw how stick-thin were her arms and legs, how hunched the top of her spine had become in the last few years. The room was so high that, even from the top of the ladder, she could barely reach the pelmets. With one hand clutching a curtain for balance, she flicked the duster over the top of her head.

'For heaven's sake, Grandmother,' I blurted. 'What do you think you're doing?'

She wobbled and I caught my breath and wished I'd said nothing. Then she turned carefully. 'Oh, it's you, Laura. What a silly question. What does it look as though I'm doing? There are generations of spiders up here building absolute palaces.'

'Do come down. Slowly. If you really insist on having that done, why didn't you ask me?'

'Because you're never here to ask.'

She felt her way cautiously down each step. When she reached the bottom, I realized for the first time that she had shrunk a couple of inches. How odd, that I had never noticed before. She had always been a small woman and now she was a tiny one.

'How nice to see you, Laura dear. You should have warned me. I would have killed a fatted calf! You're such a rare visitor, these days.'

She whipped off her turban and shook out her perfect perm. That was another shock. I'd expected it to be grey and I saw that it was white. I hadn't looked at her properly for a long time.

'Come along, then. If you want to be useful, you can make me a cup of tea while I wash my hands.'

She trotted off in front of me and I was relieved to see that her pace hadn't slowed a jot.

'Well, now,' she said, as we sat comfortably around the kitchen table. The Lady Ansty of pre-war days wouldn't have dreamed of sitting in the kitchen – I wonder if she could even have found it; Mrs Ruggles had always come to her – but it was the only warm room in the house. 'This is cosy. I've missed you, Laura. You haven't had much time for your grandmother in the last few months.'

Damn, damn, damn. I felt bad enough already. Now she was putting me thoroughly in the wrong before I'd even begun.

'I've been thinking,' she went on, all sugar and spice. 'Wouldn't it be splendid if you could move in here permanently? It would make space in the cottage and we would be company for each other. We'd have such fun.' She gave an unsuitable, girlish grin. 'Two girls together. And one must be realistic about these things – I'm seventy, after all. The house will be yours before too long.'

The house. And the portraits. And the medals. And the weapons. And the burden of history.

'And now that awful Buckland boy has stopped hanging round you. Thank goodness you had the sense to send him packing. He was only ever after what he could get. I could see that, even if you couldn't. I know they all say that class doesn't matter a jot these days, not now we have a Labour government, but really – there are limits. It's bad enough to think of Kate involved with that man – although he does have a certain rough charm – but you, Laura, you are an Ansty, after all.'

'Grandmother, if Martin crooked his little finger today, I'd go running, but he won't. And that's my loss, not his.'

'More fool you, then. Quite ridiculous. A woman should *never* let a man think she's interested in him. The trouble with you, Laura dear, is that in many ways you are too like your mother. She has always allowed her emotions to overrule her common sense.'

'As when she conceived me?' I queried, acidly.

'Exactly. A little irregularity that could so easily have been avoided. Not that ... oh, darling, don't look like that, I didn't mean that you should never ... we all loved you, the moment we saw you. You were so bright, so quick. And we were always so close, you and I. Do you remember? When you were a little girl, you were always up here and I'd show you around and you'd patter along behind me in your little sandals and ask such intelligent questions. I knew then that you loved this place and I've always wanted it to go to you one day.'

I didn't want it. I didn't want it with a sudden passion that amazed me. I'd sell it to an institution, pull it down, leave it to rot, set fire to the damned thing, if I had to. And it ought not to be mine. There was an earlier generation still living. It should belong to my father. In fact, in law, it should already be his and she must know it.

My grandmother didn't seem to notice my silence. But then, she never had before, either. She hadn't changed all that much, then. When had she ever noticed what anyone else said or did?

I felt sick, really sick. Dear God, what am I about to do? Stop me, before it's too late.

But it was already too late.

'Don't you think that my father ought to be allowed to make that decision for himself?' I asked, quietly and calmly.

And she shrivelled, before my horrified gaze. Her voice was breathy, as though a chill wind had blown across her vocal cords.

'You know?'

I nodded.

'How much?'

'I've seen him.'

And to my horror, my grandmother stretched out her hands in a plea that was both tragic and distasteful. Her rings swung loosely on desiccated fingers and the stones slipped in towards her palms.

'You've seen my son? Is he well? How does he look? My son?'

And I wanted to say, what did it ever matter to you? You put him there. Go and see for yourself what your beautiful boy has become.

Instead, and I scarcely recognized the icy voice as my own, I said, 'You wouldn't know him. He's a middle-aged man. And he wouldn't know you, because he doesn't seem to know anything – or want to know – I'm not sure which. But he would still fit the uniform you have folded into the trunk upstairs.'

And she gave me a sharp, assessing look, with a revival of her old spirit. 'You know that, too, do you? Quite the little detective. Didn't you find it loathsome, grubbing around in private lives? What else do you know, Laura? What other secrets have you dug out of their graves?'

'Enough to know that there are more to come.'

'Oh, yes. There are plenty. You will wish you had never begun to dig. And all of them have been a burden to me for a quarter of a century.' She gave a short, hard laugh, quite unlike the feminine tinkle she had cultivated for years. 'Confession is said to be good for the soul, isn't it? I wonder if you will agree with that when I have finished. No, sit still. This won't take long. And it's far too late now to be sorry...

'You have been married. I can speak to you without embarrassment. And I wonder sometimes... I wonder if you have allowed the Buckland boy more liberties than you ought. I've watched you. I've seen you, sometimes, with your face rasped and your lips swollen and your eyes heavy and languorous. You have the look about you of a woman who has been well loved. You will understand what I mean when I tell you that marriage to an old man is hell. Your mother would never understand. She has never, I'd swear, felt desire. But we are alike, you and I, we are both passionate women.

'Your grandfather was forty-one years older than I – I wonder if Kate really understands what her married life will be like when her husband becomes a shuffling dotard? – he was born before Victoria was even crowned, he was already a young man during the Crimean War, he fought at Delhi and Lucknow. Imagine that. And I thought I was a modern young woman. Hubert had lost his first wife and had no children. I was young, presumably fertile, and I was an Ansty, too, some sort of obscure cousin, closely enough related to care deeply that there was no-one to carry on the name and traditions. So suitable. I had been brought up here. As a child, I'd been dandled on Hubert's knee. I'd been petted, fed sweetmeats, spoiled by him. He would give me things that my parents could not afford, the pretty things I craved, ribbons and gloves and bracelets, a little enamelled watch that hung from a tiny gold pin ... and, as I grew older, I was expected to pay for the gifts. We had secrets ... no, don't shudder.' Her tiny hand closed over my wrist and pinned it to the table. 'Better an old man's darling than a young man's slave – that's what they say, isn't it? He gave me pretty baubles and, in return, I gave him pleasure. That was fair, I thought...

453

'When I was seventeen, Hubert and I were married. I was very silly. I imagined – without knowing how – that we would have a fine young family and I would dote on them all. I would have pretty girls and strapping sons. After a year or two of marriage, it became clear, even to me, that there would be no children. I won't talk of that. It's quite unnecessary to elaborate. I used to pace the corridors and think – I should have been a boy, this should have been mine. I would never allow the roof to leak and the gutters to fill. I would never have sold the farms or cut down the woodland. I felt a sort of fury, to think that if I had been a boy I could have had everything and would have been forced to give nothing in return...

'Does this distress you? You didn't have to meddle. You didn't have to poke around, like a child with a stick in a muddy pond. Some things are better decently hidden. Sit down. I haven't finished yet.

'I wanted children. The Ansty name needed sons. So I produced a son. I wasn't cheating. My husband and I had an agreement. Hubert's only proviso was that I should be discreet and not involve the neighbours. So I chose my mate with care. He was an intelligent man, a gentleman, a doctor who had been introduced to us by friends who were involved with a charity he ran. I was a young, passionate and – I like to think – attractive woman and he was middle-aged and flattered by my attentions. It worked very well. I was pregnant within a fortnight and the doctor went back to Surrey. We both agreed that we wanted nothing more from each other.

'Hubert – dear, doting Hubert – was thrilled. He adored Edwin. The boy was the light of his life, the solace of his old age. How could that be wrong? We were a happy family, I think.'

She smiled and her sharp-featured face softened at the memory. I wished she would stop. I didn't want to hear any more. It was none of my business. Ham, son of Noah, was cursed because he saw his father naked. I sat and listened to my grandmother uncover her own nakedness and I was afraid, because I knew, now, that there had been too many shameful secrets.

I pushed back my chair and tried to escape, but the hand she had clamped over my wrist was more powerful than mine. Her little hand was bony as a bird's claw and strong as a madman's. I was afraid to hurt her.

'He was a good boy, none better, but stubborn. That was his only fault. Once he had made up his mind to do something, nothing would deflect him. Like you. When that silly girl, Diana, became pregnant, he *would* marry her, no matter what I said. She wasn't good enough for him. No-one was.

'When I heard that my son was to die,' she went on, in her cracked, old woman's voice, 'I thought that I would die, too. The news reached us, discreetly, through old friends of Hubert, before the sentence was confirmed, but we were told that it was a foregone conclusion, that there was no hope. I shut myself in my room and wept and paid no attention to my husband's pain. What was his grief compared to mine? Who had carried

455

the boy in her body? Who had endured the pangs of his birth? Who had suckled him? Not you, Hubert. So I shut my door and shut my husband out.

'And then I thought – no, I won't allow them to do this. The *waste*. His beauty, his loving nature, all that promise to be wantonly destroyed. It made me so *angry*. I can't expect you to understand, Laura. But when you are a mother, you will know what I felt. I was so *furious* – that some dunder-headed oaf should dare to condemn my son to die. If I could have laid hands on that man, I would have torn him to shreds.

'So, for the first time in twenty years, I contacted Edwin's father. By then, he was a very senior army medical officer, a psychiatrist, a rare bird indeed, then. I went to see him at the War Office. I smiled and shouted and cajoled and bribed my way into his office. He was horrified to see me. What man likes to be reminded of his indiscretions? And when I asked him to save our son, he told me that it was quite impossible, out of the question. I wept. I pleaded. I reminded him of how we had made Edwin between us. I offered him anything – anything... But he said that no-one could halt the process of confirmation.

'So, do you know what I did? I got down on my knees and followed him around the room. And when he tried to escape, I followed him, on my knees, out of the door and into the corridor, slithering down the black and white marble, so that he was obliged to rush back in again, in case anyone saw us. I hung on to his coat tails until he prized my fingers off. Then I clung to his high, polished boots and he realized that he would have to break my wrists to make me let go.

'Edwin's father saved his son. He chose his moment wisely and whisked him out from under the very rifles of the firing squad. So clever, so neat. The correct paperwork is everything in the army. Edwin was lost in the flood of maimed bodies being transported back to England and his father had him admitted as a psychiatric patient to Netley and, later, to a private nursing home, Greentops, which he owned. It was his own home, I believe. I never saw either of them again.

'I made a decision and I kept to it, no matter what it cost me. I have been silent since then. It has taken courage. And in your eyes that makes me a twisted, vindictive old woman. You still don't understand, do you? I have never thought you stupid, Laura, but now I'm beginning to wonder.

'For the first year or two, I said and did nothing for fear that Edwin would be snatched back and the sentence carried out. I realize now that I was being illogical. But at the time, it seemed a very reasonable fear. What did I know? I had so nearly lost my son. I bullied Tom, until he told me the little he knew. No-one else would talk to me. Edwin was sick. He must have been, to have done what he had done. He was an Ansty. He was born to be a soldier. He seemed to have lost all connection with his home and his family, with everything that mattered. It was as though he had passed on to another world, a lonely world

457

inhabited by ghosts, where we could not follow. So I kept my silence.

'By the time I was certain that Edwin was safe, your mother had married Tom and Edwin had married the daughter of the owner of Greentops. He had married his sister.'

Old age doesn't qualify anyone for sainthood. Sweet old ladies are a rarity. The years simply exacerbate the qualities we start out with. My grandmother had been a ruthless young woman and had progressed to becoming a ruthless old one.

Sometimes I really believed that. And sometimes I thought – well, what would I have done? Enmeshed by lies and secrets and self-spun half-truths, would I have handled things so very differently? We were alike, she and I, in so many ways.

I wanted to talk to someone so badly. No, specifically, I wanted to talk to Martin. I needed someone to tell me to stop. I needed someone to tell me to shut my mouth, go away, find a job, travel, make love, forget...

I sensed that, if I stayed, there would be a tragedy. Yet, on my own, I didn't have the strength to avoid it.

But Martin wasn't there. And there was no-one else to shake some sense into me.

So much was now clear. I knew the how. I knew the where. I knew the when. But why? The last piece of the puzzle was lying close to my hand. And I'd make it fit, even if I had to break it first.

Just before Christmas, at the darkest time of the year, just when you think that there will never he light again, Pansy and Peter Sutton were married.

It was supposed to be a quiet wedding, suitable for two quiet people, especially since there had been a lot of gossip, not all of it charitable, about their marriage. It wasn't unexpected that the parish biddies would shake their heads and tut-tut and predict disaster, but Pansy was still hurt by their attitude.

Peter's widowed mother was there, and a sister whose husband had been in a Japanese PoW camp since the fall of Singapore and was still too weak to travel. Pansy invited Vee and me, of course. And that meant Jennifer and Carlton, too, with picture books to keep them amused during the quiet parts. I was supposed to keep an eye on Jonathan and stop him rushing round the church pushing a toy car that Peter had given him. My grandmother and mother were there, too, with Grandmother wearing a splendid toque that she'd retrimmed using the sable collar from a coat that had caught moth.

She quite outshone the bride, who'd only just been dissuaded by Vee from wearing her Sunday-best costume, six years old and too good to retire, serviceable pigeon-grey, with a useful box-pleated skirt and a just-not-quite-fitted-enough jacket.

'Not on your nelly,' Vee had warned her.

'But it's all I've got. I could smarten it up with a frilly blouse or something.'

Vee shuddered. 'You'd look like the WI speaker, who'd blundered through the wrong door.'

'Well, I'm certainly not going to wear cascades of white. That wouldn't be at all decent – considering...'

I lay on my tummy across Pansy's bed, swinging my heels over the edge, one shoe off and the other shoe on. 'Things were a lot easier when we all wore uniform. No worrying what to wear, no worrying if we grew out of something or it wore out, no worrying that your shoes or bag didn't match.'

'Oh, those were the days,' mocked Vee. 'Pansy'd look gorgeous waltzing up the aisle in her cook's overall and turban!'

Pansy was beginning to look alarmed. 'Really, it doesn't matter. Do let's get on. It's going to be a very quiet wedding, anyway.'

'But it's also the only one you'll have – I hope – so make it a good one. Now...' Vee opened the suitcase she'd brought with her and displayed the treasures she'd managed to bring back from America. 'What about this? No? You're probably right – a bit flash. Even I wouldn't get married in magenta. Well, then, this... oh, yes...'

The ice blue costume was just right. Modest, maidenly, but charming – most unlike Vee! Peter would be knocked out by it. But it made Pansy look like a child who'd been raiding her mother's wardrobe.

'It's no good, Vee,' she'd wailed. 'I haven't got your... your...'

'Bosoms,' I'd finished for her.

'Bust, I was going to say. Well, I haven't, have I?

460

And don't you *dare* suggest stuffing me like a goose! Please don't think I'm not grateful – I am and it's lovely – but it doesn't fit and that's that.'

Vee's mouth was already full of pins. 'It will,' she'd muttered. 'It will.'

And it did. Nobody would have guessed that Vee had had to take the suit apart and put it back together again, three sizes smaller. She'd only finished at midnight. Pansy looked like an ice maiden. Her usually pink cheeks were drained of blood, but she must have bitten her lips in her nervousness, because they were a startling slash in her pale, un-made-up face. She carried a tiny posy of sweet white narcissi that Tom had forced especially for her.

She walked towards the altar with her hand tucked, like a trusting child's, into the crook of Tom's arm. And when Tom had given her away and returned to his seat, he left her looking even smaller beside her muscular Peter.

Vee nudged me. She'd not put on any mascara that morning, because, as she'd said, it would be all down her cheeks before the first hymn, so her eyes looked like peeled boiled eggs. Just as well. The tears were already streaming down her face.

'Bless her,' she whispered. 'I just hope she makes a better job of it than you and me.'

And when Pansy said, 'I, Pansy Aurora, take thee, Peter John, to my wedded husband...' in a voice that startled us all with its clarity, she looked at her new husband and the colour flooded back into her cheeks. He gave her hand a little pat. I was suddenly certain that it was going

461

to be all right.

A quiet wedding, Pansy had said, but when we left the church we found the back pews were full of women who'd come to wish the vicar and his new bride well. Abbie was there, and old Mrs Pocknell and Josie and Mrs Attwood with her brass-polishing duster hanging out of her pocket, both Colebecks because the pub was closed, Mrs Treadwell in WVS uniform ... they were all there. Pansy had been forgiven.

'Sanctimonious old cows,' Vee hissed in my ear, but loudly enough to be heard as she passed Mrs Treadwell. 'They don't deserve her.'

There was a splendid lunch that lasted all afternoon at Ansty House – smoked salmon (Grandmother must have worked extremely hard on her black market connections), roast pheasant (several, shot by Tom) with braised celery, watercress and those wonderful, traditional breadcrumbs fried in butter (more black market activity). And Pansy and Peter sat amongst their friends and saw only each other.

Then Tom, who'd carefully reserved his drinking for the toasts, drove them to Salisbury station in the doctor's car to catch the Exeter train. Their honeymoon was to be a few days in Dawlish. We watched the car disappear down the drive. I'm as bad as Vee, I thought, as the rear lights seemed to waver and blur. I blinked hard, but by the time my sight had cleared, they were out of sight.

'Perfect,' I heard Vee sigh. 'Come on, Jonathan. Time for your bath. You can share with Jennifer tonight, if you like. Let's see if you can sink her ducks.'

Tom was very late back. Mother looked exhausted, so I'd sent her to bed and waited up for Tom. He was still in the morning dress he'd worn for the wedding, exaggeratedly upright, ostentatiously steady, with his back collar stud adrift, revealing an endearing gape of skin at the nape of his neck. I'd already decided that it would be better not to say anything, but Tom must have read my disapproving expression.

'Now, don't be cross,' he wheedled. 'I just met a few old chums in Salisbury. We had a glass or two in the Chough. Just one or two. You surely don't grudge me that, do you?'

'Of course not,' I lied.

'I don't get out much these days, don't see my chums as often as I'd like.'

'It's all right, Tom. Really. Anyway, it's been a long day and I'm off. Goodnight.'

'Yes. It's been a splendid day, hasn't it? Splendid.'

'Lovely. Goodnight.'

'Splendid. Nice to see little Pansy looking so happy.'

'Yes, isn't it.'

'I'd like to see you happy and settled, Laura. I'd like to see you with a good man.'

'Thank you.'

'No chance of Martin, I suppose?' he asked, coyly. It didn't suit him.

'I don't think so.' And saying it, aloud, in front of a witness, made me realize how true that was.

'Pity. Pity. I like Martin. He'd be good for you.'

'Goodnight, Tom, sleep well.'

'Don't go. Not yet.' He was in front of the door and he pushed it shut. 'It's early yet.'

'Not any more. It's nearly midnight.'

'Really? Are you sure? Well, anyway, it's early yet. Special occasion. Not every day we have a wedding in the family – well, as good as... Lovely girl, Pansy. We should drink her health.'

'We have already.'

'Nonsense. We should drink the health of the happy couple. Come on, Laura, don't be stuck-up. It's not asking too much, is it – to drink the health of your best friend?'

I could see that Tom was swinging between the truculent friendliness and the friendly truculence that distinguishes the true drinker from the amateur. In a moment, he'd be weeping or shouting at me. So I stayed. Tom poured a couple of stiff brandies.

'To Pansy and her new husband...'

'To Pansy and Peter...' I held up my glass. I shuddered as I sipped. I really didn't want it. I'd had enough already. At that time of night, I'd rather have had a mug of cocoa. 'I hope they'll be very happy.'

'It's a happy state, marriage,' Tom declared. 'I've been so blessed in mine. Diana is a wonderful woman. Wonderful. You ought to try it... marriage...'

'Tom...' I smiled and kissed him on the cheek. 'I'm going to bed. Sleep well.'

'I'd like to see you settled, before your mother and I go.'

'Silly. You've both got years yet.'

'You never know. You never know. Things happen. I wish you'd make up your mind about Martin.'

'He's made his mind up about me, I'm afraid.'

'What? Jilted you?'

'No, no. Nothing like that.' What an old-fashioned term. I hadn't realized anyone might still use it. 'Just ... moved on ... we've both – both...'

'Oh, my dear – tell Tom.' He put an arm round my shoulder and I wasn't certain who was supporting whom. 'You're too good for him, of course. There's something rather low about him, I've always thought. You've made the right choice. I'm so glad... You know I've always loved you, don't you, Laura? You've always been my little girl... Always.'

Embarrassed by his emotion, I gave a little, awkward laugh. He made me feel in the wrong, obscurely guilty, and I wasn't even sure why.

'Do you love your old Tom?' he queried, pressing me, physically and emotionally. 'Say I've been good to you.'

'No-one could have been nicer,' I answered and meant it. 'You've really been my father.'

'You were Edwin's child and I've always loved you.'

'You never talked about him, Tom.'

'Didn't I?'

'No-one did.'

'No ... well ... well, what could we say?'

'You could have been honest with me.'

'You look so like him, you know. So like. Well, I dare say you're right, old girl. It's been a long day.' He took his arm from my shoulder. 'Off you go. I'll just bank up the fire for the night. Don't wake your mother.'

The temptation was terrible. I could simply say – Tom, I've seen him. And wait and watch. But I couldn't do it to him.

Tom was riddling the fire in an enthusiastic way that meant it would probably be dead by morning. He heaped a few shovels of damp slack over it. The smoke twirled up, grey and dense, finding a tortuous escape route around the mean little beans of coal.

He didn't notice that I hadn't gone. He pottered around a bit, locking the door, turning down the lights. Their wicks glowed for a while in the dark. Then he sat down before the fire, unlaced his shoes, and, in the sudden way that people who drink do everything, fell asleep. He looked quite safe.

I look and look, but the pile of petals is so deep and more are falling all the time. James is there, Grace is there, but Edwin's name is not there and now I know that I'll never find him.

It should have been Martin who took my hand and said, 'He isn't there, you're looking in the wrong place.'

Of course...

The dream came more and more often, getting in the way of my sleep, disturbing my peace. I always knew when it was coming. I don't want to dream this, I'd think, twisting my head right and left, I don't want to dream this, but it paid no attention...

Only this time, it wasn't Martin who led me away from the bleeding heap of petals, but Tom...

I was coming back out of the dream, not deeply asleep, but still fuddled, halfway between sleep and reality. It was the sound of the bolts being drawn roughly back that woke me. Then the front door was opened so quickly that it banged off the wall.

Sleepy and bemused, I jumped out of bed so suddenly that I staggered on my way to the window, bounced off the chest of drawers and rocked the swinging glass that stood on it. It fell and cracked across. Seven years' bad luck...

When I looked out of the window, Tom was striding off down the path towards the walled garden. If it hadn't sounded too fanciful, I'd have said he was marching.

'Tom? Laura?' My mother's voice was plaintive. 'Where are you? What was that noise?'

'It's all right, Mother. Tom's just gone for rather a late walk. Don't worry.'

'At this time of night...?'

And I was worried. Tom had seemed so purposeful. He hadn't looked like a man going for a stroll to clear his head. I pulled on an old mackintosh over my pyjamas and gumboots over my bare feet. There was an icy puddle at the bottom of the left one.

Perhaps I ought to have run after him. I ought to have caught up with him and put my arm round his shoulders and turned him round and said, come on, Tom, time for bed.

I wish I had.

Instead, I followed, closely, but not too closely. Curiosity, I suppose. Where would anyone be going, at that speed, at that time of night, in Ansty Parva, of all places? Hardly a hotbed of vice, Ansty Parva.

Purposefully, Tom headed towards his potting shed, his sanctuary. Out of sight and out of earshot, intrigued by his determination, I hung back. I watched him shut the door, light the lamp, pull the sacking over the window. He left a narrow gleam of light down the right-hand edge. I perched on a fallen trunk and waited for him to come out again. It was a raw, damp, misty night. I blew puffs of breath, like a horse in a field. The cold made my nose run and crept up through the soles of my feet and invaded the network of my veins. It was so still that I thought I could hear the ice growing across the surface of the puddles.

I began to think about blankets and hot-water bottles and hot milk with nutmeg grated over it. Good grief. What on earth did I think I was doing, lurking in the shadows, spying on my stepfather, on a night cold enough to splinter glass?

But I knew that Mother would worry about Tom. She'd fret and get up herself and not bother to put on her dressing gown and catch a chill that would turn to pneumonia and then she'd die and it'd all be my fault, because I didn't have the courage to haul Tom, drunk or sober, back to bed.

I pushed open the door of the shed.

'Tom, it's awfully late...'

Ludicrously childlike, a naughty boy caught in the act, Tom's guilty face gaped back at me. I'd have laughed if there had been anything to laugh at.

In that fanatically neat shed, with its tools hung on nails, its pile of scrubbed pots, its stacked fruit boxes, the scatter of paper on the bench demanded my attention. Tom had been cutting paper, snipping letters out of old newspapers and reassembling them into words ... into lies. There was a pot of gum, with its handy brush combined with the lid. There was an envelope, already addressed. I couldn't see that far, but I knew it was addressed to me.

And the fertile, decaying, tobacco-and-cobwebs, dust-and-damp smell would have been transferred to the contents of the envelope. When I'd opened it, the smell would still have been there, lingering, reminding me of something, and I wouldn't have been able to remember what.

But now I knew.

'Tom, why...?'

And all the questions I wanted to ask were encompassed in that. Why you? Why me? Why him? Why then? Why now? I already knew the when, the where and the how. Only the why had eluded me. Until now.

Tom seemed to wake up. 'Laura, my dear.' He made an ineffectual attempt to scoop the snippets of newsprint into the envelope. Some of them fluttered to the earth. 'What on earth are you doing? You'll catch your death.'

'Why, Tom?' I bent and picked up a few of the letters that had spun to my feet. There was a D, a W and an I. I passed them to Tom to stuff into the envelope with all the other evidence of his guilt.

'Just tidying up, you know. Bit of a mess in here...'

'I've seen him, Tom. He's very well. He sends his good wishes.'

A lie, that. But there had already been so many lies. Tom put his head in his hands. His fingers were laced into the thinning, sandy hair, snatching, tugging, hurting.

'I didn't think ... he didn't believe ... we never meant it to come to this. Whatever else ... you have to believe, Laura, whatever else...'

'I *do* believe you, Tom.'

'I still wake up suffocating, you know, with the mud clogging my nose, blinding me. I can taste it, grind it in my teeth and I know I'm going to die. In a funk, the CO used to say. Roding's in a funk again. Roding's in a blue funk. And I was, of course. Edwin knew that.

'The listening parties were the worst. An extra tot of rum didn't go amiss before you climbed over the top. Just you – only it was always me – and an NCO. Over the firestep and through a gap in your own wire and into the mud. Silent, you had to be silent, but the rum made you clumsy, only you couldn't do it at all without the rum, without the trickle of fire that coursed down to your guts. And the mud was like badly made porridge, cooked too quickly, full of lumps and grit and nasty, unidentified things. If you stopped to work out what you were crawling through, you'd scream. And that wouldn't do, because it was a listening party and you had to be quiet.

'You'd had a good look at a trench map before you went over – no point in taking a map with you, because just a pinpoint of light would bring fire down on you – and you'd fixed a landmark in your mind – maybe a hundred yards to the left of the tree that looked like a hunched bird. But when you got down to the ground, down on your belly, everything was different. The tree stump didn't look the same. It wasn't there any more. The mud was deeper. Perhaps we'd churned it up ourselves with an artillery pasting that had lasted two days. The enemy lines had moved. The distances were all wrong. It took twice as long, three times as long to crawl through human soup as you'd estimated, so you thought you'd got lost. And then you'd start crawling round in circles and sometimes the sun would be coming up before you found your way back, having dis-covered nothing. And only a couple of stiff ones would stop you shaking. Roding's in a funk. Send him out again. Make a man of him.

'And then the next night – off you'd go again. And you'd stretch out your hand in the darkness and touch teeth, but the teeth wouldn't bite because they were detached from their head. Or you'd put your weight on something that moved and belched. Christ, you'd think, the poor beggar's still alive. Then the stench would hit you and you'd realize that it was only the escaping gases that had made him sit up and fart.'

'Tom ... Tom, you don't have to tell me this. Enough.' I put my hand on his shoulder, very gently. He didn't seem to notice it, but I could feel the quiver, strong and sustained, that was running through his body. He'd forgotten I was there, but now that he'd begun to talk, he didn't seem to be able to stop.

'Offensiveness. The CO was hot on offensiveness. We had to be as offensive as possible, all the time. One day, near the end, when the enemy was already on the run, he hit on the idea of really rattling the Jerries. He'd got hold of some leaflets from the intelligence chaps – in German – saying that the families at home in Germany were all starving, living on rats, children all had rickets, wives prostituting themselves for food, selling themselves to Israelite hucksters, Bolsheviks round every corner, you know the sort of bogeyman stories that a soldier would laugh at if they didn't scare him half to death. Someone was ordered to take out a party and sow the leaflets round the German trenches. Me.

'I decided not to come back that night. I decided to slip into the first Hun trench with my hands up and hope for the best. If they shot me, it couldn't be as bad as creeping round in the dark like a rat, every night. Only it wasn't as simple as that. A Verey light went up – phosphorescent white, turning the dead landscape to silver and our skin to the colour of corpses and our eyes to black holes – and the whole party was caught in its light. Sitting ducks. I hid behind a body and watched the others twist and spin in the hailstorm of Spandau fire. I heard the bullets whack into the corpse. They made a soggy plock, plock, plock. I was lucky, some would have said. They cut it to rags, but it saved me.

'And when it was over, I couldn't go forward and I couldn't go back. Roding was in a funk again. When the attack began the next morning, Edwin found me – fell headlong over me, actually. If it had been anyone but him...

'He tried to jolly me along with him. School prefect stuff, captain of cross-country and all that – you know. But I wouldn't move. Any minute now, a mortar shell would drop on my head and that would be that and good riddance. If I moved, it might miss me. I couldn't take the risk. The last thing I wanted to do was *survive*. Then he tried to persuade me to go back, say I'd been hurt – he couldn't go with me because he was supposed to be going forward. But I wouldn't do that either. I was waiting to die, the sooner the better.

'The attacking waves washed against us and split and passed on. Edwin should have left me. It would have been better.' He looked up briefly, as though only just realizing that I was there. It was a tormented glance.

'Then there was a fearful bang. The earth fountained up and splashed back down on us, scattering us with things ... things ... I was deafened by the crash and dazed by the impact and blinded by the grit blasted into my face. Edwin was blown on to his back. There was blood all over his face.

'When I could see again, I began to run – not forwards or backwards, but sideways, along the line of trenches, across the line of attack, scrambling across bodies, on my hands and knees half the time. And Edwin came after me.

473

He had always been faster at school, but he couldn't catch me that day. I didn't see him again until he was under arrest.

'I wandered in a circle and, at the end of the day, I was back where I had started. I dropped back into our front-line trench, all in one piece, not a mark on me. I had *wanted* to die, but I was not allowed to, yet there were thousands that day who died before they were ready. How do you explain that?

'I was the only one of the night party left alive. They congratulated me on making it back at all. Edwin came back later still, much, much later, long after the advance had wavered and died, and was arrested and charged with leaving the scene of the attack. I knew he'd been looking for me. He ought not to have done it, of course. He really ought to have left me. That was his first mistake. His second was to keep silent.

'That made sense to him, at the time, I suppose. He was an exemplary young officer, decorated, well thought of by his senior officers. I was nothing and no-one. With his record, he might get away with severe censure. I could only expect the worst. I never thought... I never believed...

'The CO was raging. The offensive had been a ghastly failure and had cost us the best part of a company. Someone was going to be forced to pay for it and Edwin was company commander. Edwin could have made up some cock-and-bull story about being knocked senseless, but that would have been beneath him. He faced his accusers in silence and he did it for me.'

Tom leaned forward and clasped his hands around the back of his neck. 'He died for me,' he whispered.

'But he didn't die, did he?'

'No.'

'And you knew that.'

'Yes.' His voice was lower with every answer. 'Not at first, I didn't know for a long time, but – yes, I knew in the end.'

'And you did nothing.'

'There's nothing you can do to me, Laura,' he answered with a sudden burst of spirit. 'Nothing you can say is worse than the things I have said to myself. You don't have to torment me. I do it every day. I look at Diana and know that I couldn't give her up. She mustn't know.' He grabbed at my arm. I flinched under the unexpected strength of his wiry, bony body. 'I'd do anything to shield Diana.'

'Even kill me.'

He nodded. 'You had a right to know. He was your father. But once you started looking, I couldn't let you go on. You do see that, don't you? And you are so determined – so like Edwin – you never give up. I'd do anything to save Diana from being hurt. I let my friend die so that I could have Diana. She mustn't be hurt any more.'

I looked at him and tried to whip up the anger and indignation that I knew I ought to feel. There was nothing. Disgust, resentment, all the importantly named feelings that the righteous have for the wrongdoers... they wouldn't come. I felt only pity. And love.

I put my hand on his head and he turned his face into my breast. I stroked his hair as he used to do mine, when I was little and miserable. He was still shuddering and I gathered him more closely to me.

'But Tom, it doesn't matter any more. It's all over. He's happy.'

'Diana must never know.'

'She won't know. He has a new life. He's happy. It's over.' I felt his body sag with relief and exhaustion and I let him go. 'Tom,' I urged softly. 'You're tired. Come home. Mother's waiting for you.'

'Yes. Yes, soon. You go. I've a bit to think about. I'll follow you soon.'

And in the morning, when he had not returned, I guessed. Maybe I knew all along. I daren't think about that.

I left Mother laying the table for breakfast and ran back to the walled garden. Then I had to run on to the village. Reg Shellard was already about, delivering the first post. He came back with me and helped cut Tom down from the walnut tree, before Mother saw him. Suicide —

Tom... oh, Tom. It wasn't meant to end like this...

It's getting cold, too cold and wet to sit any longer, without seeming noticeably eccentric. I shovel in the manure, just as I've seen it done before, and mix it with a spadeful of earth and a couple of handfuls of bone-meal.

'That's right. That's the proper way to do it,' he says, over my shoulder. I haven't heard him. His gumboots are silent through the sodden, fallen leaves. 'You learn quickly.'

'I've had good teachers,' I answer. 'Two of them.'

Like all the trees in Edwin's church, these two have names. One is for James and one is for Tom, who was as much a victim of the war as any other commemorated here. They look spindly, very frail, hardly capable of surviving the harsh weather that is still to come.

He seems to read my thoughts. 'They'll do,' he says.

And when we turn to leave, I see Martin crossing the bridge. From this distance, he looks no older than the boy I remember in Ansty Parva. But I know that when he is closer, I'll see the marks that war has left on him. As he will on me. We are both older, greyer, tougher, harder, but we have come through with our principles and beliefs intact.

And now I see, with sudden clarity, that our love has survived, too. I see it in his smile, in the quickening of his step as he notices me, in the diffident way he begins to wave to me and then stops, as he sees I'm not alone. Martin has come home.

'Hello, Martin,' I say and I'm shy and young again. 'I'd like you to meet a friend of mine.'

And Edwin Ansty holds out his hand to Martin.

The publishers hope that this book has given you enjoyable reading. Large Print Books are especially designed to be as easy to see and hold as possible. If you wish a complete list of our books please ask at your local library or write directly to:

Magna Large Print Books
Magna House, Long Preston,
Skipton, North Yorkshire.
BD23 4ND

This Large Print Book for the partially sighted, who cannot read normal print, is published under the auspices of

THE ULVERSCROFT FOUNDATION

THE ULVERSCROFT FOUNDATION

... we hope that you have enjoyed this Large Print Book. Please think for a moment about those people who have worse eyesight problems than you ... and are unable to even read or enjoy Large Print, without great difficulty.

You can help them by sending a donation, large or small to:

**The Ulverscroft Foundation,
1, The Green, Bradgate Road,
Anstey, Leicestershire, LE7 7FU,
England.**
or request a copy of our brochure for more details.

The Foundation will use all your help to assist those people who are handicapped by various sight problems and need special attention.

Thank you very much for your help.